George MacDonald

MICHAEL R. PHILLIPS, EDITOR

The Musician's Quest

D1009161

BETHANY HOUSE PUBLISHERS
MINNEAPOLIS, MINNESOTA 55438
A Division of Bethany Fellowship, Inc.

Originally published in 1868 under the title *Robert Falconer* by Hurst and Blackett, London.

Copyright © 1984
Michael R. Phillips
All Rights Reserved

Published by Bethany House Publishers
A Division of Bethany Fellowship, Inc.
6820 Auto Club Road, Minneapolis, MN 55438

Printed in the United States of America

Library of Congress Cataloging in Publication Data

MacDonald, George, 1824-1905.
    The musicians's quest.

    Shortened and updated ed. of: Robert Falconer. 1868.
    I. Phillips, Michael R., 1946-   . II. MacDonald, George, 1824-1905.
Robert Falconer.   III. Title.
PR4967.M8   1984   823'.8   84-18508
ISBN 0-87123-444-0

Other Scottish Romances by George MacDonald
retold for today's reader by Michael Phillips:

The two-volume story of Malcolm:
 The Fisherman's Lady
 The Marquis' Secret

Companion stories of Gibbie and his friend Donal:
 The Baronet's Song
 The Shepherd's Castle

Companion stories of Hugh Sutherland and Robert Falconer:
 The Tutor's First Love
 The Musician's Quest

Contents

Introduction_____

When more than a dozen years ago, I began my own search to unearth George MacDonald's ancient, out-of-print novels, I had scarcely an inkling where that investigation would lead. Rummaging through a huge bookstore of used books in Seattle, I uncovered on a dusty bottom shelf, obscured by other volumes stacked in front of it, the first original MacDonald I had ever seen. It carried the inauspicious title *Robert Falconer*. I bought it for a couple of dollars—knowing absolutely nothing about the contents.

Several days later an adventure had begun. What I had discovered was not simply the tale of some fictional hero; this was the portrayal of MacDonald's personal search for a faith of his own. Through MacDonald's title character, I discovered the essence of what the author considered that faith to be.

In the Introduction to *The Shepherd's Castle*, a previous book in this series, I briefly outlined the circumstances which led George MacDonald to become a novelist after feeling called to the ministry. Throughout his entire life, MacDonald found himself at odds with the strict Calvinism of the nineteenth century. It had begun in his boyhood relationship with his rigid, orthodox grandmother and continued through his dispute with the deacons of his church, who eventually removed him from the pastorate. His internal battle against the narrow viewpoints they represented invigorated the fertile soil of his creative mind. He could never satisfy himself with stale precepts and prejudicial outlooks; they were no substitute for the human warmth of the gospel. He was driven instead toward the original, unbiased truth and the God who established it.

Therefore, the characters in MacDonald's books often pose questions which typified his own growth. He found himself reasoning out the Christian faith afresh each time he set pen to paper. Creed-bound minds are afraid of large questions. MacDonald wasn't. In this story, the young boy Robert Falconer frames the question: ''If the devil was to repent, would God forgive him?''

It's a staggering notion . . . one for which we have no answer. MacDonald never postulated a firm answer either; we do not know whether he even reached the point of attempting one. But the guardians of the ecclesiastical gates of his day were aghast at his audacity even to inquire in that direction.

George MacDonald feared no query, even of such weighty theological magnitude. He was so confident of a great-hearted, loving, tenderly compassionate God that to him nothing was too large or too small to bring before him. MacDonald's straight-hewn mind remained always focused on the core of God's loving, just character.

In 1868 one of MacDonald's most oft-quoted and memorable novels was published—*Robert Falconer*, the story of a boy's growth into manhood, and one which poignantly portrays the solitary melancholy of childhood. Though not strictly autobiographical, one is immediately struck with many parallels between young Robert and MacDonald's memory of his own boyhood. The locale and scenery is similar. "Bleaching" had been a MacDonald family business. Robert's grandmother is a precise characterization of George's own; her views on music as well as her subversive relationship to Robert's violin are based entirely on fact, with the same end result. And from the opening pages we sense about Robert what MacDonald wrote of himself: "From my very childhood I rejoiced in being alone. The sense of room about me was one of my greatest delights . . . that desolate hill, the top of which was only a wide expanse of moorland, rugged with height and hollow . . . my refuge, my home within a home, my study . . . and my house of dreams."

And yet beyond such comparisons, in young Robert Falconer we see a very intimate search to come to terms with the truths of life. And in that struggle, recalling the spiritual trials of his own life, are we not looking through a window into the very soul of MacDonald himself?

Undoubtedly this is one of the reasons this novel seems to have been among the author's favorites—he named one of his sons Robert Falconer MacDonald and brought the fictional Falconer into other books as well. Robert Falconer represented both the young man MacDonald had been and, at the same time, the mature man he aspired to be. Robert Falconer seems to have become a role model to MacDonald himself, exemplifying the search for truth and, once found, the living of that truth. The book's narrator adds to the realism of Falconer in MacDonald's eyes, intruding himself into the story as one who had been profoundly affected by him. The narrator is clearly a fictional sketch of the author himself.

The story line of the novel merely recounts Robert's life. There is no electrifying "plot." There are no castles, no dungeons, no heroines in danger, no villains, no surprise twists.

Yet the sheer weight of Falconer's person sneaks up on you. He has forceful impact on those around him simply by virtue of the man he has become. You find yourself looking at people and situations differently, wondering what Falconer might do. When I finished my most recent reading of the book, quite unexpectedly I was overwhelmed and nearly burst into tears. MacDonald fashioned a character of strength and integrity which stood above and outlasted many others he would later write about—a man fortified through questioning, energized by sparring with the issues of life, and perfected through service to others and devotion to God.

The original *Robert Falconer* ran well over 500 pages long, and large portions were written in difficult-to-understand Scottish brogue. Though it was enormously popular between 1870 and 1890, serialized in magazines and published in many editions, it has now been out-of-print and unavailable for more than 60 years. This new edition, *The Musician's Quest*, published as the sixth book in the Bethany House series, has been shortened and edited so that MacDonald's Robert Falconer can make acquaintance with modern-day readers.

As the editor of George MacDonald's books, it is always my desire to give you, the reader, pleasure and satisfaction. I hope you enjoy this book as much as the others you have read. But something more is here, and I pray you'll discover that as well.

Michael R. Phillips
Eureka, California

1 / A Recollection ——————————————

Fourteen-year-old schoolboy Robert Falconer was a quiet child. There was little in his situation to offer excitement and still less about his environment to inspire boyish adventure. He lived with his grandmother and often retreated to a bare little attic room to be alone with his thoughts. In a recess behind the door stood an empty bedstead. This was the only piece of furniture in the room other than some shelves crowded with dusty papers tied up in bundles and a cupboard in the wall. There was no carpet on the floor and no windows in the walls. The only light came through the door and a small skylight in the sloping roof, which indicated it was a garret room.

Not much light came in from the open door, however, for there was no window on the walled stair to which it opened. Opposite the door, a few steps led up into another attic, larger but with a lower roof perforated with two or three panes of glass no larger than the small blue slates which covered the roof. From these panes a little dim brown light tumbled down the steps and into the room where the boy sat on the floor, with his head almost between his knees, thinking.

He did not remember his father distinctly. He sometimes wondered if he had ever seen him at all. Yet as he sat, the more assured he became that he had seen his father somewhere, maybe six years before. For there dawned upon his memory the vision of one Sunday afternoon. Betty had gone to church and he was alone with his grandmother, reading to her the *Pilgrim's Progress*, when a tap came on the street door and he went to open it. There he saw a tall, somewhat haggard-looking man in a shabby black coat, his hat pulled down to his eyebrows, and his shoes very dusty as if he had made a long journey on foot. It was a hot Sunday; he remembered that. The man looked at him very strangely, and without a word pushed him aside and went straight into his grandmother's parlor, shutting the door behind him. Robert followed, not doubting that the man must have a right to go there, but questioning very much his right to shut him out. When he reached the door, however, he found it bolted; and he had had to stay outside all alone, in the desolate remainder of the house, till Betty came home from church.

Now that he thought about it, he could recall how drearily the afternoon had passed. He had opened the street door again and looked out. There was nothing alive to be seen, except a sparrow picking up crumbs. The Royal Oak Inn down the street had not even a horse or cart standing before it. At the other end of the empty street, he looked toward the distant uplands with the fields of waving corn and grass; and beyond them rose one blue, truncated peak in the distance, all of them wearily at rest this dreary Sabbath day. However, in comparison there was one thing on which all this was an improvement, and that was being at church. To Robert, church was the very essence of dreariness.

He had closed the door and gone into the kitchen. That was nearly as bad as the empty street. The kettle was on the fire, to be sure, in anticipation of tea. But the coals under it were black on the top, and it made only faint efforts, after immeasurable intervals of silence, to break into a song—giving a hum like that of a distant bee and then relapsing into hopeless inactivity. Having just had his dinner, he was not hungry enough to find any resource in the drawer where the oatcakes lay. And, unfortunately, the old wooden clock in the corner was going, else there would have been some amusement in trying to torment it into demonstrations of life, as he had often done in less desperate circumstances than the present.

At last he had trudged upstairs to this very room, had sat down on the floor just as he was sitting now, and had taken refuge with his *Pilgrim's Progress* till Betty came home. When she had called him to tea he had expected to go down to join his grandmother and the stranger, but found instead that he was to have his tea with Betty in the kitchen; afterward he had again taken refuge with Bunyan in the garret. He had remained there till it grew dark, when Betty had come in search of him and put him to bed. In the morning every trace of the visitor had vanished, even the walking stick which he had placed behind the door as he entered.

As the reviving memory of that day melted into the present, he raised his head and looked about him. There was even less light than usual in the room now, though it was only half past four and the sun would not set for more than half an hour yet, for a thick covering of snow lay over the glass of the small skylight. A partial thaw, followed by a frost, had fixed it there. It was a cold place to sit, but the boy had some faculty for enduring cold when that was the price to be paid for solitude. And besides, when he fell into one of his thinking moods, he usually forgot cold and everything else but what he was thinking about.

If he had gone down the stair, which described half the turn of a screw in its descent, and had crossed the landing, he could have entered another bedroom, called the gable room, equally at his service for retirement. But though carpeted and comfortably furnished, and having two windows at right angles which commanded two streets (for it was a corner house), the boy preferred the garret room—he could not tell why. Possibly windows to the streets were not congenial to the meditations in which even now, as I have said, the boy indulged.

His mother had been dead for so many years that he had only the vaguest recollections of her tenderness, and none of her person. All he was told of his father was that he had gone abroad. His grandmother would never talk about him, although he was her own son. When the boy ventured to ask a question about where he was or when he would return, she always replied, ''Bairns suld haud their tongues.'' Nor would she give another answer to any question that seemed to her to approach that subject from the farthest distance. ''Bairns maun learn to haud their tongues'' was the sole variation she allowed. And the boy did learn to hold his tongue. Perhaps he would have thought less about his father if he had had brothers or sisters, or even if the nature of his grandmother had been such as to allow their relationship to draw closer—into personal confidence or at least some measure of companionship.

Robert rose to his feet and walked from the room. At the foot of the garret stair, between it and the door of the gable room, stood another door at right angles to both. He was scarcely aware of its existence, simply because he had not seen it all his life and had never seen it open. Turning his back on this last door, which he took for a blind one, he went down a short, broad stair, at the foot of which was a window. He then turned left into a long passage, passed the kitchen door on the one hand and the double-leaved street door on the other. But instead of going into the parlor, the door which closed off the passage, he stopped at the window on his right and stood there looking out.

What was to be seen from this window certainly could not be called pleasant. A broad street with low houses of cold, gray stone, as uninteresting a street as most any to be found in the world, was that upon which Robert looked. As previously described of another occasion, not a single member of the animal creation was to be seen in it. The sole motion was the occasional drift of a film of white powder which the wind would lift like dust from the snowy carpet that covered the street. Wafting it along for a few yards, it would drop again to its repose, foretelling the wind on the rise at sundown—a wind cold and bitter as death—which would rush over the street and raise a denser cloud of the white dust to sting the face of any improbable person who might meet it in its passage. What Robert saw to make him stand at the desolate window, I do not know. There he did stand, however, for the space of five minutes, gazing at a bald spot on the crown of the street where the wind had swept away the snow, leaving it brown and bare—a spot of March in the middle of January.

While he stood, a gentle tap came to the door, so gentle indeed that Betty in the kitchen did not hear it or she would have answered it before the long-legged dreamer reached the door, though he was not more than three yards from it. But having nothing better to do, Robert eventually answered the summons. As he opened the door, these words greeted him from a young fellow on the steps: "Is Robert at—eh! It's Bob himself! Bob, I'm exceedingly cold."

"Why don't you go home then?"

"What for wasna' ye at the school today?"

"I put one question to you and you answer me with another."

"Well, I hae nae home t' go t'."

"And I had a headache. But where's your home gone to, then?"

"The hoose is there a' right, but whaur my mither is I dinna know. The door's locked. I don't doubt but my mither's awa' upon the tramp again, an' what's t' come o' me, the Lord knows."

"What's all this?" interposed a severe voice, breaking up the conversation between the two boys. For the parlor door had opened without Robert's hearing it and Mrs. Falconer, his grandmother, had drawn near to the speakers.

"What's all this?" she asked again. "Who's that ye're conversin' wi' at the door, Robert? If it be a decent laddie, tell him t' come in and not stand i' the door on such a day as this."

As Robert hesitated with his reply, she looked round the open half of the door; but she no sooner saw with whom he was talking than her tone changed. But this time, Betty, wiping her hand in her apron, had completed the group by taking her stand in the kitchen door.

"No, no," said Mrs. Falconer, "we want none o' such here! What does he want wi' ye, Robert?—Give him a piece o' bread, Betty, an' let him go. Eh! the lad haen't even a stockin' foot on him—an' i' such weather!"

For before she had finished her brief speech, the visitor, as if in terror of her nearer approach, had turned away and literally showed her, if not a clean pair of heels, yet a pair of naked heels from between the soles and uppers of his shoes. If he had any socks at all, they ceased before they reached his ankles.

"What ails him at me?" continued Mrs. Falconer, "that he runs as if I were a boodie? But it's no wonder he can't abide the sight of a decent body, for he's not used t' it. What does he want wi' ye, Robert?"

But Robert had a reason for not telling his grandmother what the boy had told him; he thought the news about his mother would only make her disapprove of him the more. But he did not quite know his grandmother yet.

"He's in my class at the school," said Robert evasively.

"Him? What class?"

Robert hesitated one moment, but compelled to give some answer said with confidence, "The Bible class."

"I thought as much! What makes ye play cat-'n-mouse wi' me? Don't ye think I know well enough that there's no lad or lass at the school but's i' the Bible class? What did he want here?"

"You hardly gave him time to tell me, Grannie. You frightened him."

"Me frighten *him*? Why would I frighten him, laddie?"

The old lady turned with visible, though by no means profound, offense, and, walking back into her parlor where Robert could see the fire burning cheerily, shut the door and left him and Betty standing together in the hall. The latter returned to the kitchen to resume the washing of the dinner dishes; and the former to his vigil at the window.

By this time the twilight was falling; for though the sun had not yet set, miles of frozen vapor came between it and this part of the world, and its light was never very powerful so far north at this season of the year. Robert had not stood more than half a minute, thinking what was to be done with his schoolfellow deserted of his mother, when the sound of a coach horn drew his attention to the right down the street. A minute later the mail came in sight and disappeared, going up the hill toward the chief hostelry of the town as fast as four horses, tired with the bad footing, could draw it after them.

Robert turned into the kitchen and began to put on his shoes. He had made up his mind.

"Ye're not going out, Robert?" said Betty in a hoarse tone of expostulation.

" 'Deed I am, Betty. Why not?"

"Ye've been in all day with a headache. I'll just go and tell the mistress, and we'll see what she'll please t' do aboot it."

"You'll do nothing of the kind, Betty. Are you going to turn telltale at *your* age?"

"What do ye know aboot my age? There's not a man in town that knows a thing aboot my age."

"It's too much for anybody to remember, is it, Betty?"

"Don't be ill-tongued, Robert, or I'll just go t' the mistress."

"Betty, who began with being ill-tongued? Go and tell my grandmother that I went out, and I'll go to the schoolmaster of Muckledrum and get a look at the christening book. And if your name isn't there, I'll let it be known that our Betty was never christened. And you know what they'll think then!''

''Hoot! Was there ever such a laddie!'' said Betty, attempting to laugh it off. ''Be sure ye're back before tea time, 'cause your grannie'll be asking aboot ye, and ye wouldn't have me lie aboot ye?''

''I would have nobody lie about me. Just don't let on that you hear her. You can be deaf when it pleases you, Betty. But I'll be back before tea time.''

Betty was in far greater fear of her age being discovered than of being unchristianized in the search. But the fact was she knew nothing certain about the latter and had no desire to be enlightened, feeling as if she was thus left at liberty to hint at what she pleased. She never had any intention of ''going to the mistress,'' for the threat was merely the rod of terror which she thought convenient to hold over the boy, whom she always supposed to be in some mischief unless he were in her own presence and visibly reading a book. If he were reading aloud, so much the better.

Robert likewise kept a rod for his defense, and that was Betty's age, which he had discovered to be such a precious secret that one would have thought her virtue depended upon the concealment of it. And certainly nature favored Betty's weakness, casting a mist about the number of her years. Some said Betty was forty; others said she was sixty-five, and in fact, almost everybody who knew her had a different opinion on the matter.

By this time Robert had conquered the difficulty of pulling on boots as unyielding as a thorough wetting and thorough drying could make them, and now stood prepared to go. His object in setting out was to find the boy whom his grandmother had driven from the door with a hastier flight than she had in the least intended. If his grandmother should miss him, as Betty suggested, and inquire where he had been, he did not mind misleading her, but he had a great objection to telling her a lie. His grandmother herself delivered him from this difficulty.

''Robert, come here,'' she called from the parlor door. Robert obeyed.

''Is it snowing out?'' she asked.

''No, Grannie; it's only blowing about on the ground.''

''Well, just ye put on yer boots then an' run up t' Miss Napier's o' the Square an' tell her I would be obliged t' her if she would lend me that fine recipe o' hers for tea cakes.''

This commission fell in admirably with Robert's plans and he started at once.

2 / Shargar

Miss Napier was the eldest of three maiden sisters who kept the principal hostelry of Rothieden, called the Boar's Head. As Robert reached the square in the dusk, the mail coach was moving away from the entrance with a fresh quaternion of horses. He found a good many boxes on the pavement close by the archway that led to the inn yard, and around them had gathered a group of loungers, not too cold to be interested. They were looking toward the windows of the inn, where the owner of the boxes had evidently disappeared.

"Saw ye ever such a sight?" remarked Dooble Sanny, as people generally called him, using his nickname. His Christian name was Alexander Alexander, pronounced by those who chose to speak of him with more respect, "Sandy Elshender." Dooble Sanny was a shoemaker, remarkable for his love of sweet sounds and whiskey. He was also the town crier who went about with a drum at certain hours of the morning and evening, making various public announcements of sales, losses, etc.

"What's the sight, Sandy?" asked Robert, coming up with his hands in the pockets of his trousers.

"Such a sight as ye never saw, man," returned Sandy. "The bonniest young lady I've set eyes on. Not much older than ye yerself, Robert," he added, casting the boy a quick glance through eyes that twinkled.

"Hoot, Sandy!" said Robert. "You'd think she was lost and you were making the fact known throughout the town. Speak lower, man, or she'll hear you. Is she in the inn there?"

"Ay, she is," answered Sandy. "See all the boxes and chests she brought?" he continued, pointing toward the pile of luggage. "It just beats me to think what one person could do with all that. I can't make it out."

The boxes might well surprise Sandy if we may draw any conclusions from the fact that the sole implement of personal adornment which he possessed was two inches of a broken comb, for which, when he happened to want it, he had to search in the drawer of his workbench among awls, lumps of rosin for his violin, masses of the same substance wrought into shoemaker's wax, and packets of boar's bristles.

"Are they all hers?" asked Robert.

" 'Deed they are. I would hae thought she was going t' The Bothie; but if she had been that, there would hae been a carriage t' meet her. An' I judge she couldn't be a day more than seventeen, if that, which is still a mite on the yoong side even for the Baron. What she can be doin' here, an' travelin' alone an' so yoong, I canna' tell."

The Bothie was the name facetiously given by Baron Emerich Rothie, son of the Marquis of Boarshead, to a house he had built in the neighborhood, chiefly for the accommodation of his bachelor friends from London during the shooting season. It had housed a number of visiting ladies as well.

Robert turned and walked into the inn and delivered his message to Miss Napier, who sat in an armchair by the fire. She was an old lady—nearly as old as Mrs. Falconer—and wore glasses, but they could not conceal the kindness of her eyes. Probably from giving less heed to the systematic theology of the Book and more heed to the Person of the Book, she had nothing of that sternness which first struck a stranger on seeing Robert's grandmother. But then if she had been married and had had sons, perhaps a sternness not dissimilar might have shown itself in her nature.

After a few minutes, with his grandmother's request in hand, Robert went out again into the thin drift of snow. Crossing the wide, desolate-looking square, he turned down an entry leading to a kind of court which had once been inhabited by a well-to-do class of the townspeople but had now fallen upon hard times. Upon a stone at the door of what seemed an outhouse, he discovered the object of his search.

"What are you sitting there for, Shargar?* Did nobody offer to take you in?"

"No, none o' them. Most people must be in their beds by now. I'm most dreadful cold."

The fact was that Shargar's character, whether by imputation from his mother or derived from his own actions, was not considered the best. As a consequence, although probably none of the neighbors would have allowed him to sit in the snow all night, each was willing to wait yet a while in the hope that someone else's humanity would give in first, thus saving them the necessity of offering him a seat by the fireside and a share of the oatmeal porridge which would probably be scanty enough for their own households.

Shargar is a word of Gaelic origin applied with some sense of the ridiculous to a thin, wasted, dried-up creature. In the present case it was the nickname by which the boy was known at school and throughout the town.

"Get up them, Shargar, you lazy beggar. Or are you frozen to the door stone?"

"No, Bob, I'm not stuck. I'm only stiff with the cold; for, wow! but I *am* cold!" said Shargar, rising with difficulty. "Give me a hold o' yer hand, Bob."

Robert gave him his hand.

"Now come as fast and as quiet as you can."

"What are ye goin' t' do wi' me, Bob?"

"What's that to you, Shargar?"

"Nothin'. Only I would like t' know."

"Have patience and you will know. Only mind you do as I tell you and don't speak a word."

Shargar followed in silence.

On the way Robert stopped at the baker's shop.

"Wait here till I come out," said Robert and disappeared inside.

Shargar stood and shivered at the door, trying to keep warm by massaging himself furiously with his hands.

Coming out of the baker's with a penny loaf in one hand and a twopenny loaf in the other, Robert saw a man talking to Shargar. The moment his eyes fell upon the two, he was struck by the resemblance between them. When Robert approached, the man turned and walked down the street.

"Who's that?" asked Robert.

"I don't know," answered Shargar. "He spoke t' me before I even saw him standin' there."

"And what did he say to you?"

"He said it was the devil at my back that made me do nothin' but rub my hands t' bits on my shoulders."

"And what did you say to that?"

"I said I wished he was, for he'd no doubt hae some spare heat about him, and I haen't quite enough."

"Well done, Shargar! What did he say to that?"

"He laughed, but just then ye came out an' he went away."

"And you don't know who it was?"

"It was some like my brither, Lord Emerich, but I don't know," said Shargar. "But give me a bit o' the bread, Bob. I'm as hungry as I am cold."

"Just wait a while," returned Robert. "There's a time for all things and your time's not come to make your acquaintance with this loaf just yet. But doesn't it smell fine? It's fresh from the oven not ten minutes ago. I know by the feel of it."

"Let me feel," said Shargar, stretching out one hand.

"No, your hands can't be clean."

Shargar yielded and slunk behind while Robert again led the way till they came to his grandmother's door.

"Go to the end of the house there, Shargar, and just peek around the corner at me. And if I whistle to you, come up to the door as quietly as you can. If I don't, wait till I come to you."

Robert opened the door cautiously. It was never locked except at night or when Betty had gone on some errand or to the prayer meeting. He looked first to the right along the passage and saw that his grandmother's door was shut; then across the passage to the left and saw that the kitchen door was likewise shut because of the cold. Closing the door but keeping the handle in his hand and the bolt drawn back, he turned to the street and whistled soft and low. In a moment Shargar had dragged his heavy feet, ready to part company with their worn-out shoes at any instant, to Robert's side. He bent his ear to Robert's whisper.

"Go in there, and creep like a mouse to the foot of the stair. I must close the door behind us."

"I'm frightened, Robert."

"Don't be a fool. Grannie won't bite your head off. Go on in."

Shargar hesitated no longer. Taking about four steps a minute, he slunk past the kitchen like a thief—not so carefully, however, but that one of his soles, yet looser than the other, gave one clap upon the stone floor. Betty immediately stood in the kitchen door, a fierce picture in a wood frame. By this time Robert had closed the outer door and was following at Shargar's heels.

"What's this?" she cried, but not so loud as to reach the ears of Mrs. Falconer; for with true Scotch foresight she would not willingly call in another power before the situation clearly demanded it. "Where's Shargar going that way?"

"With me. Don't you see me with him? I'm no thief, neither is Shargar."

"There may be two opinions about that, Robert. I'll just be off to the mistress. I'll have no such doings in *my* house."

"It's not your house, Betty. Don't lie."

"Well, I'll have no such things going by my kitchen door. There, Robert! What'll ye make o' that?"

Meantime Shargar was standing on the stones, looking like a terrified white rabbit and shaking from head to foot with cold and fright combined.

"I'll take him out of your hallway and up the stair, Betty. And if you say anything about it, I swear to you as sure as death, I'll go down to Muckledrum on Saturday in the afternoon."

"Go away with your loaves. Only, if the mistress asks anything about it, what am I to say?"

"Wait till she asks. And, Betty, do you have a cold potato?"

"I'll look and see. Wouldn't ye like it heated up?"

"Oh, yes, if you won't be long about it."

Suddenly a bell rang, shrill and peremptory, right above Shargar's head, causing in him a responsive increase of trembling.

"Out of my way," said Betty, "there's the mistress's bell."

"Just wait till we're round the corner and onto the stair," said Robert, now leading the way.

Betty watched them safe around the corner before she made for the parlor, little thinking to what she had become an unwilling accomplice, for she never imagined that more than an evening's visit was intended by Shargar. And this in itself seemed to her improper enough, even for such an eccentric boy as Robert to encourage.

Shargar followed Robert in mortal terror. Once onto the stairs, two strides of three steps each took them to the top of the first landing, Shargar knocking his head in the darkness against the never-opened door. Again, three strides brought them to the top of the second flight; and turning once more, still to the right, Robert led Shargar up the few steps into the higher of the two garrets.

Here there was just glimmer enough from the sky to discover the hollow of an enclosed bedstead, built in under the sloping roof. Fortunately, though it had not been used for many years, it had an old mattress covering the boards with which it was bottomed.

"Go in there, Shargar. You'll be warmer there, anyway, than on the doorstep. Take off your shoes."

Shargar obeyed, full of delight at finding himself in such good quarters. Robert went to a forsaken closet in the room and brought out an ancient cloak of tartan, a blue dress coat with gilt buttons, and several other garments, among them a kilt, and heaped them over Shargar as he lay on the mattress. He then handed him the twopenny and the penny loaves, which were all his resources had reached to the purchase of, and left him, saying, "I must get down to my tea, Shargar. I'll fetch you a potato if Betty has any. Lie still, and whatever you do, don't come out."

This last injunction was entirely unnecessary.

"Eh, Bob, I'm just in heaven!" said the poor creature, for his skin began to feel the precious possibility of reviving warmth.

Now that he had gained a new burrow, the human animal soon recovered from his fears as well. It seemed to him, in the novelty of the place, that he had made so many doublings to reach it that there could be no danger of even the mistress of the house finding him out. For she could hardly be supposed to look after such a remote corner of her dominions. And then he was boxed in with the bed and covered with no end of warm garments, while the friendly darkness closed him and his shelter all around. Except for the faintest blue gleam from one of the panes in the roof there was no hint of light anywhere; and this was just sufficient to make the darkness visible and thus add artistic effect to the operation of it upon Shargar's imagination—a faculty certainly uneducated in Shargar, but far from being therefore nonexistent. As he lay and devoured the bakery bread, his satisfaction reached a pitch he had never conceived possible. The power of enjoying the present without anticipation of the future or regard of the past is the special privilege of the animal nature and the more simple of the human nature. Herein lies the happiness of cab horses and tramps: to them the gift of forgetfulness is of worth inestimable. Shargar's heaven was for the present gained.

3 / Mrs. Falconer

Meantime Robert was seated in the parlor at the small, dark mahogany table in which the lamp, shaded toward his grandmother's side, was brilliantly reflected. Her face being thus hidden both by the light and the shadow, he could not observe the keen look of stern benevolence with which she regarded him as he ate his thick oatcake of Betty's skillful manufacture, well loaded with the sweetest butter, and drank the tea she had poured out and sugared for him. It was a comfortable little room despite the fact that its inlaid mahogany chairs and ancient horsehair sofa had a certain look of hardness. A shepherdess and lamb, worked in silks whose brilliance had now faded halfway to neutrality, hung in a black frame with brass rosettes at the corners over the chimneypiece— the sole approach to art in the homely little place. Besides the muslin stretched across the lower part, the window was undefended by curtains. Mrs. Falconer sat in one of the armchairs, leaning back in contemplation of her grandson as she took her tea.

She was a handsome old lady—little, but she had once been taller, for she was more than seventy now. She wore a plain cap of muslin, lying close to her face and bordered a little way from the edge with a broad black ribbon, which went round her face and then, turning at right angles, went round the back of her neck. Her gray hair peeped a little way from under this cap. A clear but shortsighted eye of a light hazel shone under a smooth, thoughtful forehead; a straight and well-elevated, but rather short nose, which left the firm upper lip long and capable of expressing a world of dignified offense, rose over a well-formed mouth, revealing more moral than temperamental sweetness; while the chin took little share in indicating the remarkable character possessed by the old lady.

After gazing at Robert for some time, she took a piece of oatcake from a plate by her side—the only luxury in which she indulged, for it was made with cream instead of water; she ate very little of anything— and held it out to Robert in a hand white, soft, and smooth. "Have it, Robert," she said; and Robert received it with a "Thank you, Grannie"; but when he thought she did not see him, he slipped it under the table and into his pocket. She saw him well enough, however. Although she would not condescend to ask him why he put it away instead of eating it, the endeavor to discover what could have been his reason for doing so cost her two hours of sleep that night. She would always be at the bottom of a thing if reflection could reach it, but she generally declined taking the most ordinary measures to expedite the process.

When Robert had finished his tea, instead of rising to get his books for his lessons, in regard to which his grandmother seldom found any cause to complain—although she would have considered herself guilty of high treason against the boy's future if she allowed herself once to acknowledge as much—he drew his chair toward the fire and said, "Grandmama?"

He's going to tell me something, thought Mrs. Falconer to herself. *Will it be aboot the poor barefoot creature they call Shargar, or will it be aboot the piece he put into his pocket?*

"Well, laddie?" she said aloud, willing to encourage him.

"Is it true that my grandfather was the blind piper of Portcloddie?"

"Where'd ye hear that?"

"Some of the men at the inn were teasing me once and one of them said so. Is it true, Grannie?"

"Ay, laddie, true enough. Hoots, but nor yer grandfather, but yer father's grandfather, laddie—my husband's father."

"How did it come about?"

"Well, ye see, he was out i' the Forty-five. He wasn't wi' his own clan at the battle, for his father had brought him t' the lowlands when he was but a lad; but he played the pipes for a regiment raised by the Laird of Portcloddie. After the battle o' Culloden,* he had t' run for it. An' for weeks he had t' hide among the rocks. An' they took his property from him. It wasn't much—a few sheds, a cabbage patch or two, wi' a small farm on top o' a cold hill near the seashore. But it was enough, an' when they took it from him, he had nothing left i' the world but his sons.

"Yer grandfather was born the very day o' the battle; an' the very day that the news came, the mother died. But yer great-grandfather wasn't long before he married another wife. He was such a man as any woman would hae been proud t' marry. She was the daughter o' an Episcopalian minister an' she kept a school i' Portcloddie. I saw him first myself when I was aboot twenty—that was just the year before I married. He was a considerably old man then, but as straight as a tree an' powerful beyond belief. His wrist was as thick as both mine. An'

*See Appendices in *The Fisherman's Lady,* published by Bethany House, particularly Appendix 2 for further historical background concerning Culloden.

years an' years after that, when he took his son, my husband, an' his grandson, my Andrew . . .''

"What ails you, Grannie? Why don't you go on with the story?"

After a somewhat lengthened pause, Mrs. Falconer resumed as if she had not stopped at all.

". . . one i' each hand, just for the fun o' it, he knocked their heads together as if they had been two stalks o' rib grass. But maybe it was the laughing o' the two lads, for they thought it such fun. They almost died laughing. But the last time he did it the poor old man coughed so bad afterward that he had t' go an' lie down. He didn't live long after that. But it wasn't that that killed him, ye know."

"But how did he come to play the pipes?"

"He liked the pipes. And yer grandfather, he took t' the fiddle."

"But why did they call him the blind piper of Portcloddie."

"Because he turned blind long before his end came an' there was nothing else he could do. An' he would make an honest coin when he could, for money was very scarce at that time among the Falconers. So he went through the town at five o'clock every morning playing his pipes, t' let those who were up know they were up i' time, and them that wasn't that it was time t' rise. And then he played them again aboot eight o'clock at night, t' let them know it was time fer decent folk t' go t' their beds. Ye see, there weren't so many clocks an' watches then as there are now."

"Was he a good piper, Grannie?"

"Why do ye ask that?"

"Because Lumley cast up to me that my grandfather was nothing but a blind piper."

"An' what did ye say?"

"I dared him to say that he didn't pipe well."

"Well done, laddie! An' ye might say it wi' a good conscience, for he wouldn't hae been piper t' his regiment at the battle o' Culloden if he haen't piped well. Yonder's his kilt hanging i' the closet i' the attic. Ye'll hae t' grow, Robert, my man, before ye'll fill that."

"And whose was that blue coat with the pretty buttons on it?" asked Robert, who thought he had discovered a new approach to an impregnable hold, which he would gladly storm if he could.

"Let the coat sit. What has that t' do wi' the kilt? A blue coat an' a tartan kilt don't go well together."

"Except in an old press where nobody sees them. You wouldn't care, Grannie, would you, if I was to cut off the pretty buttons?"

"Don't lay a finger on them! Ye would be going playing at pitch an' toss or other such games wi' them. No, no, let them sit."

"I would only exchange them for marbles."

"I dare ye t' touch the coat or anything else that's i' that press!"

"Well, well, Grannie. I'll go and get my lessons ready for the morning."

"It's time, laddie. Ye hae been jabbering too much. Tell Betty t' come an' take away the tea things."

Robert went to the kitchen, got a couple of hot potatoes and a candle, and carried them upstairs to Shargar, who was fast asleep. The moment the light shone on his face he started up, with his eyes, if not his senses, wide awake.

"It wasn't me, Mither! I tell ye it wasn't me!" He covered his head with both arms, as if to defend it from a shower of blows.

"Hold your tongue, Shargar. It's me."

But before Shargar could come to his senses, the light of the candle falling upon the blue coat made the buttons flash confused suspicions into his mind.

"Mither," he said, "ye've gone too far this time. There's too many o' them. We'll both be hanged as sure as there's a devil in hell."

Robert caught him by the shoulders and shook him awake with gentle hands. He began to rub his eyes and mutter sleepily, "Is that ye, Bob? I've been dreaming."

"If you don't learn to dream quieter, you'll get you and me into more trouble than I dare to think about, you rascal. Hold your tongue if you want anything more, and eat this potato. And here's a piece of creamy cake too. You won't get this in every house in the town. It's my grannie's special."

Shargar was somewhat overpowered at this fresh proof of Robert's friendship.

"How did ye get it?" asked Shargar, evidently supposing he had stolen it.

"She gets me a bit now and then."

Robert took the blue coat carefully from the bed and hung it in its place again, satisfied now from the way his grannie had spoken, or rather declined to speak about it, that it had belonged to his father.

"Am I t' get up?" asked Shargar, not understanding the action.

"No, no, lie still. You'll be warm enough without this. I'll let you out in the morning after Grannie's up. We'll settle about it at school in the morning. Only we must be careful, you know."

"Ye couldn't lay yer hand on a drop o' whiskey, could ye, Bob?"

Robert stared in horror. A boy like that asking for whiskey! And in his grandmother's house too! "Shargar," he said, "there's not a drop of whiskey in this house. It's awful to hear you mention such a thing.

My grannie would smell the very name of it a mile away. I don't doubt that's her foot on the stair already.''

Robert crept to the door and Shargar sat staring with horror, his eyes looking from the gloom of the bed like those of a half-strangled dog. But it was a false alarm.

"If you ever so much as mention whiskey again, not to say drink a drop of it, you and me part company, Shargar," Robert said in an emphatic whisper.

"I'll never look at it; I'll never think even o' dreamin' o' it," answered Shargar coweringly. "If she puts it into my mouth, I'll spit it out. But if ye turn me away, Bob, I'll cut my throat—I weel. An' that'll be seen an' heard tell o'.''

All this time, save during the alarm of Mrs. Falconer's possible approach when he sat with a mouthful of hot potato unable to move his jaws for terror, Shargar had been devouring the provisions Robert had brought him, as if he had not seen food all that day. As soon as they were finished he begged for a drink of water, which Robert managed to procure for him. He then left for the night, for his longer absence might have brought his grandmother after him, who had perhaps only too good reason for being doubtful, if not suspicious, about boys in general, though certainly not about Robert in particular. He carried his books from the other garret room where he kept them, and sat down at the table by his grandmother, preparing his Latin and geography by her lamp, while she sat knitting a white stocking with fingers as rapid as thought. She never looked at her work but stared into the fire, seeing visions there which Robert would have given anything to see, and then would have given his life to blot out of the world if he had seen them. Quietly the evening passed, by the peaceful lamp and the cheerful fire, with the Latin on the one side of the table and the stocking on the other, as if ripe and purified old age and hopeful, unsustained youth had been the only extremes of humanity known to the world. But the bitter wind was howling by fits in the chimney and the offspring of a nobleman and a Gypsy lay asleep in the garret, covered with the tartan cloak of an old Highland rebel.

At nine o'clock, Mrs. Falconer rang the bell for Betty and they had worship. Robert read a chapter and his grandmother prayed an extemporary prayer in which they that looked at the wine when it is red in the cup and they that worshiped the human clothed in scarlet and seated upon the seven hills came in for a strange mixture, in which vengeance yielded only to pity.

"Lord, lead them t' see the error o' their ways!" she cried. "Let the rod o' thy wrath awake the worm o' their conscience that they may know verily that there is a God that ruleth i' the earth. Don't let them go t' hell, O Lord, we beseech thee.''

As soon as prayers were over, Robert had a tumbler of milk and some more oatcake and was sent to bed, after which it was impossible for him to hold any further communication with Shargar. For his grandmother, little as one might suspect it who entered the parlor in the daytime, always slept in the same room, in a bed closed in with doors like those of a large closet in the wall. Robert slept in a small room looking into the garden at the back of the house, the door of which opened from the parlor near the head of his grandmother's bed. It was just large enough to hold his bed, a chest of drawers, a bureau, a clock, and one chair. He was never allowed a candle at night, for light enough came through the parlor, his grandmother thought. So he was soon extended between the whitest of cold sheets, with his knees up to his chin, and his thoughts following his lost father over all the spaces of the earth with which his geography book had made him acquainted.

He was in the habit of leaving his room and creeping through his grandmother's parlor every morning before she was awake—or at least before she had given any signs that she was restored to consciousness and that the life of the house must proceed. He therefore found no difficulty in liberating Shargar from his prison, except the boy's own unwillingness to forsake his comfortable quarters for the fierce encounter of the January blast which awaited him. But Robert did not turn him out before the last possible moment of safety had arrived. By the aid of signs known only to him, he watched the progress of his grandmother's dressing until Betty was called in to give her careful assistance to the final disposition of the bed, and then Shargar's exit could be delayed no longer. He mounted to the foot of the second stair and called in a keen whisper, ''Now, Shargar, cut out for your life!''

And down came the poor fellow, with long, gliding steps, ragged and reluctant. Without a word or a look, he launched himself out into the cold and sped away he knew not whither. As he left the door the only suspicion of light was the dull and doubtful shimmer of snow that covered the street, keen particles of which were blown in his face by the wind which seemed delighted to find one unprotected human being whom it might badger at its own bitter will. Outcast Shargar! Where he spent the interval between Mrs. Falconer's door and that of the school, I do not know. There was a report among his schoolfellows that he had been found lying at full length upon the back of an old horse, which, either from compassion or indifference, had not cared to rise up under the burden. Questioned, Shargar's only defense was to say that the horse was warmer than the stones of the street and that he had done the horse no ill, had not even drawn a hair from his tail—which would have been a difficult feat, seeing the horse's tail was as bare as his hooves.

4 / School

The oddity of Shargar's personal appearance, his supposed imbecility, and the bad character borne by his mother placed him in a very unenviable position in relation to the more tyrannical of his schoolfellows. He was long and lean, with pale red hair, pinkish eyes, no visible eyebrows or eyelashes, and a very pale face—nearly an albino. His arms and legs seemed of equal length, both exceedingly long. The handsomeness of his mother and the well-bred birth of his father appeared only in the good shape of his nose and mouth and his small, delicate hands. His feet, however, were supposed to be enormous—an assumption made on the basis of the difficulty with which he dragged after him the huge floppy shoes in which they were generally encased during winter.

The imbecility, like the large feet, was only imputed. He certainly was not brilliant, but neither did he make a fool of himself in any of the few branches of learning available at the parish school. However, his nature was without so much as a particle of the aggressive. Had he been a dog he would never have thought of doing anything for his own protection. He was an absolute sepulchre in swallowing oppression and ill-usage without an echo of complaint, no murmur of resentment. The blows that fell upon him resounded not, and no one but God remembered them.

His mother made her living as she could, with occasional well-begrudged assistance from the parish. Her chief resource was no doubt begging from house to house for a handful of oatmeal, the recognized dole upon which every beggar had a claim. And if she inobstrusively picked up at the same time a chicken or a rabbit or any other stray luxury, she was only following the general rule of society that your first duty is to take care of yourself. She was generally regarded as a Gypsy, but I doubt if she had any Gypsy blood in her veins. She was simply a tramper, with occasional fits of localization. Her worst fault was the way she treated her son, whom she starved, apparently that she might continue able to beat him.

Shargar's one true friend, Robert, was himself at this time very tall and lanky, with especially long arms much like Shargar. He had large black eyes, deep sunk, and a Roman nose. He was dark-complexioned, with dark hair destined to grow darker still, and well-proportioned hands and feet. When his mind was not oppressed with the consideration of some important mental question, he learned his lessons well and got along at school without undue difficulty.

On a certain Saturday of brilliant but intermittent sunshine, swift, white clouds seen from the school windows indicated that fresh breezes friendly to kites were frolicking in the upper regions. Nearly a dozen boys were kept in for not being able to write down from memory the usual installment of Shorter Catechism due at the close of the week. Among these boys were Robert and Shargar. The windows and locked doors were too painful. As the feeling of having nothing to do increased, the more restless did the active element in the boys become, and the more ready to break into some abnormal manifestation. Sun, wind, and clouds were jointly calling them to come and join the fun, and activity which is both excited and restrained at the same time naturally turns to mischief. The eyes of three or four of the eldest fell simultaneously upon Shargar.

Robert was sitting plunged in one of his daydreams when his thoughts were arrested by a shout of laughter. The boys had tied Shargar's feet to the desk at which he sat—likewise his hands. And then, having attached about a dozen strings to as many locks of his pale red hair, which was hardly ever cut or trimmed, they had tied them to various pegs in the wall behind him so that the poor fellow could not stir. They were now crushing up pieces of waste paper, not a few pages of stray schoolbooks being regarded in that light, into bullets, dipping them in ink and aiming them at Shargar's white face.

For some time Shargar had not uttered a word, and Robert, although somewhat indignant at the treatment the victim was receiving, felt as yet no impulse to interfere, for success in that vein was doubtful. And, indeed, he was not very easily roused to action of any kind, for he was as yet mostly in the larva condition of character when everything is transacted inside. But the fun grew more furious and spot after spot of ink dotted Shargar's face. Robert did not seem to notice much until he saw the tears stealing down Shargar's patient cheeks, making channels through the ink which now nearly covered them. Then Robert could bear it no longer. He took out his knife, and, under pretense of joining in the sport, approached Shargar and rapidly cut the cords.

The boys of course turned on Robert. But just at that moment Mrs. Innes, the schoolmaster's wife, appeared at the door bearing in her hands a huge bowl of potato soup. She and her husband lived above the school and her motherly heart could not endure the thought of dinnerless boys.

Her husband would not have allowed it, for were they not kept in to be punished? But he being engaged at a parish meeting, she had her chance.

However, she had no more than set foot inside when Wattie Morrison took the bowl from her and, out of spite at Robert, emptied its contents on the head of Shargar with the words, "Shargar, I appoint thee king over us, and here is thy crown," giving the bowl, as he said so, a push onto his head, where it remained.

Shargar did not move and for one moment could not speak. The next he gave such a shriek that made Robert think he was scalded far worse than turned out to be the case. Robert in a rage darted to him, grabbed the bowl from his head and flung it with all his force at Morrison, knocking him to the floor. At the next moment the master entered by the street door. In the middle of the room the other boys surrounded the fallen tyrant while Robert looked on with the red face of wrath and Shargar with a complexion that was the mingled result of tears, ink, and potato soup—the latter clothing him from head to foot. I need not follow the story further than to say that both Robert and Morrison got a sound licking.

From that day Robert assumed the acknowledged position of Shargar's defender. And if there was pride and a sense of propriety mingled with his advocacy of Shargar's rights, it nevertheless had its share in the development of his higher nature. There may have been in it the exercise of some patronage; but at least it was a loving patronage and from it the good in Robert's nature, which was as yet only in a state of solution, began to crystallize into character.

The effect of the new relationship was far more remarkable on Shargar. As incapable of self-defense as ever, yet he was in a moment roused to fury by any attack on the person or dignity of Robert. From that day on Shargar was Robert's faithful and devoted slave. That very evening, when Betty went to take a parting peep outside before locking the door for the night, she found him sitting upon the doorstep only to send him off with a box on his ear. For the character of his mother was always associated with the unfortunate boy and avenged upon him. I must, however, allow that those delicate, dirty fingers of his could not be warranted against occasionally picking and stealing also.

5 / A Night Visitor ─────────────

Although Betty seemed to hold little communication with the outer world, she contrived somehow or another to bring home to the ears of her mistress, who had very few visitors, what gossip was going about the town. For while her neighbors held Mrs. Falconer in great respect, she was not the sort of person to sit down and share *news* with. There was a certain self-contained dignity about her which the common mind felt chilling and repellent.

On the evening following Shargar's introduction to Mrs. Falconer's house, Betty came home from the butcher's—for it was Saturday night and she had gone to fetch the beef for their Sunday soup—with the news that the people next door, round the corner on the next street, had a visitor. The house in question had been built by Robert's father, was larger than Mrs. Falconer's and very handsome. Robert had been born in it and had spent a few years of his life there, but could recall nothing of the facts of those early days. It had passed into other hands and was now quite strange to him. It had been bought by a retired naval officer who lived in it with his wife.

Robert was upstairs when Betty emptied her newsbag and so heard nothing of this bit of gossip. He had just assured Shargar that as soon as his grandmother was asleep, he would look about for what food he could find and bring it up to him in the garret. The household always retired early on Saturday in preparation for the Sabbath, and by ten o'clock Grannie and Betty were in bed. Robert was in his own bed too, but he had lain down in his clothes, waiting for the time when he could reasonably hope for his grandmother to be asleep. Several times, thinking of poor Shargar lying in hunger above him, he got up, resolved to make his attempt, but just as often his courage failed and he lay down again. When the clock beside him struck eleven, he could bear the tension of waiting no longer and finally rose.

Slowly and softly opening the door of his bedroom off the parlor, he crept on his hands and knees into the middle of it, feeling like a thief—indeed, in a measure, he was, though from a selfless motive. But just as he had accomplished half the distance to the opposite door he stopped, fixed with terror. A deep sigh came from Grannie's closet bed, followed by her voice in prayer. He thought at first she had heard him but soon found he was mistaken. Still the fear of discovery held him there on all fours, like a chained animal. A dull, red gleam from the embers of the fire was the sole light in the room. Everything so common to his eyes in the daylight seemed now strange and eerie in the dying coals at what to the boy was an unearthly hour of the night.

He felt he ought not listen to Grannie, but terror made him unable to move.

"Oh no! Oh no!" moaned Grannie from the bed. "I've a sore heart. I've a sore heart i' my breast, O Lord, thou knowest. My own Andrew! T' think o' my child that I carried an' who laughed i' my arms—t' think o' him being a reprobate! O Lord, couldn't he be elected yet? Is there no turning from thy decrees? No, no, that wouldn't do at all. But while there's life, there's hope. But who knows whether he be alive or not? Gladly would I look on his dead face if I could believe that his soul wasn't among the lost. But the torments o' that place! An' the stench that goes up forever. An' my Andrew down i' the heart o' it crying! An' me not able t' get t' him! O Lord! I *can't* say, 'Thy will be done.' But don't hold it against me. But if ye was a mother yerself ye wouldn't put him there. Forgive me, Lord, for I hardly know what I'm saying. He was my own baby, my own Andrew, an' ye gave him t' me yerself. An' now he's for the finger o' scorn t' point at—an outcast an' a wanderer from his own country who dares not even come within sight o' it for them that would take him t' the law. It's drink—drink an' ill company. He would hae done well enough if only they would hae let him be. Eh! if I were but as young as when he was born, I would be up an' away this very night t' look for him. But it's no use my trying it. O God! Once more I pray thee t' turn him from the error o' his ways. An' don't let Robert go after him, as he is likely enough t' do. Give me grace t' hold him tight, that he may be t' yer praise an' glory for ever an' ever. Amen."

Whether the weary woman fell asleep after this or was simply too exhausted to go on, Robert heard no more, though he remained there frozen for many minutes after his grandmother had ceased. *So this is the reason she will never speak to me about my father!* Robert's thoughts tumbled over each other. *She keeps all her thoughts about him for the lonely silence of the night and the God who never sleeps but watches the wicked all through the dark. And my father is one of the wicked! And God is against him! When he dies, he will go to hell!*

But he was not dead yet; Robert was sure of that. And when he grew to be a man he would go and seek him and beg him to repent and come back to God, who would forgive him and take him to heaven when he died. And there he would be good, and good people would love him.

Something like this conclusion passed through the boy's mind before he began to creep from the room. By now he had almost forgotten his mission, and had it not been that he had promised Shargar, he would now have crept back to his bed and left him to bear his hunger as best he could. But now, first his right hand, then his left knee, and on and on he crawled to the door. He rose only to his knees to open it, taking almost a whole minute for the operation, then dropped and crawled again till he was outside it. He turned and drew the door almost closed, leaving it slightly ajar, before it struck him that eventually the same terrible return passage must be gone through to return to his own room. But he rose to his feet, for he had no shoes on and since he knew the house so well there was little danger of making any noise, although it was pitch dark. With gathering courage he felt his way to the kitchen and there groped about. But he could find nothing beyond a few pieces of oatcake, which, with a mug of water, he proceeded to carry up to Shargar in the garret.

When he exited the kitchen door to begin his trek upward with the scanty provisions, he was struck with amazement and for a moment a fresh dose of fear. A light was shining into the hall from the stair. He knew it could not be Grannie since he had just left her safe in bed, and he heard Betty snoring in her own den which opened from the kitchen. He thought it must be Shargar, who had grown impatient, but how he had got hold of a light he could not think.

As soon as he turned the corner, however, the mystery grew still more profound. At the top of the broad, low stair stood the form of a woman with a candle in her hand, gazing about as if wondering which way to go. The light fell full upon her face, one of such beauty that, with her dress, which was white—being in fact a nightgown—and her hair, which was hanging loose about her shoulders and down to her waist, Robert at once concluded (his reasoning faculties already shaken by the events of the night) that she was an angel come down to comfort his grannie. He kneeled involuntarily at the foot of the stair, gazing up at her, with the cakes in one hand and the mug of water in the other, like an offering. Whether he had closed his eyes or bowed his head he could not say, but he suddenly became aware that the angel had vanished—he knew not how. This only confirmed his assurance that it was an angel.

Both elated and awed by the vision, he felt his way up the stair in the new darkness, as if walking in a holy dream on sacred ground as he crossed the landing where the angel had stood. Up and up he went and found Shargar wide awake with expectant hunger. He too had caught a glimmer of the light. But Robert did not tell him what he had seen. That was too sacred a subject to enter upon with Shargar, and he was intent enough upon his meager supper not to be inquisitive.

Robert left him and returned to cross his grandmother's room once more, half expecting to find the angel standing by her bedside. But it was all dark and still. Creeping back as he had come, he heard her quiet, deep breathing and his mind was at ease about her for the night. What if the angel had come only to appear to Grannie in her sleep? There were such stories in the Bible, and Grannie was certainly as good as some of the people in the Bible who saw angels. And if the angels came to see Grannie, why should they not have some care over his father as well?

As Robert settled at last into his bed, in the neighboring house lay another for whom also the moment for peaceful slumber had come. She was the owner of the boxes he had seen at the Boar's Head, come from England for an extended visit with the Captain and his wife, her aunt. In reality but sixteen, far younger than she had appeared to Robert's over-excited brain and Dooble Sanny's imaginative fancy, she had been looking around her room before going to bed. Seeing a trap in the floor near the wall, she had raised it and discovered a few steps of a stair leading down to a door. Curiosity naturally led her to examine it, and the key rested in the lock. It opened outward and there she found herself, to her surprise, in the heart of another, somewhat lower, house. She never saw Robert; for while he approached with shoeless feet, she had been glancing through the open door of the gable room; and when he knelt, the light which she held in her hand had hidden him from her. He, on his part, had not observed that the unopened door stood open for the first time in recent memory.

The house adjoining had been built by Robert's father. The young lady's room was that which he had occupied with his wife, and in it Robert had been born. The door, with its trap steps, was a natural invention for uniting the levels of the two houses and desirable in not a few of the forms which the weather assumed in that region. When the larger house had been sold it had never entered the mind of Robert's grandmother to build over the doorway between them, and by now she had all but forgotten that it even existed.

6 / A Magnificent Discovery————————

The friendship of Robert had gained Shargar the favorable notice of a few other of the boys at school, chiefly those from the country who were ready to follow the example set for them by a town boy. Once his homeless state was known, moved both by their compassion for him and their respect for Robert, they began to give him a portion of the lunches they had brought with them. Never in his life had Shargar fared so well as the first week after he had been cast out upon the mercy of the world. But in proportion as the novelty faded, so did their interest in him; eventually their appetites reasserted former claims, and Shargar once more began to feel the pangs of hunger. All that Robert could manage to procure for him, without attracting the attention he was so anxious to avoid, was little more than sufficient to keep Shargar's hunger alive; he was gifted with a great appetite and Robert had no allowance of pocket money from his grandmother. The threepence he had been able to spend on Shargar were what remained of a sixpence Mr. Innes had given him for an exercise which he wrote in blank verse instead of prose—an achievement of which the schoolmaster was proud.

So Robert went on pocketing instead of eating all that he dared, watching anxiously for opportunities to evade the eyes of his grandmother. On her dimness of sight, however, he depended too confidently. For either she was not so blind as he thought or she made up for the defect of her vision by the keenness of her observation. She saw enough to cause her considerable annoyance, though it suggested nothing further to her than that there was something underhanded going on. First, she tried to persuade herself that he wanted to take the provisions to school with him and eat them there. Next she concluded that he must have a pair of rabbits hidden away. And so conjecture followed conjecture for a whole week, one after the other of the suppositions being dismissed as improbable, during which time not even Betty knew that Shargar slept in the house. So careful and watchful were the two boys that although she could not help suspecting something from Robert's expression and behavior, what that something might be she could not imagine; nor had she and her mistress as yet exchanged confidences on the subject. Her observations coincided with that of her mistress as to the disappearance of odds and ends of eatables—potatoes, cold porridge, bits of oatcake, and on one occasion when Shargar happened to be especially ravenous, a half-dried haddock which the lad devoured raw. He went to school that morning smelling so strong they thought he must have spent the night in Mr. Scroggie's fish cart.

The housing of Shargar in the garret had made Robert familiar with all the ins and outs of the little room. There were several closets in it and a few chests, only two of which he had yet ventured to peep into. One evening when Betty was gone out, he had gotten hold of her candle and had gone up to keep Shargar company for a few minutes. A sudden impulse seized him to have a look into all the chests and corners of the place he had hitherto missed. Among many papers and old garments, he found nothing very interesting till he arrived at the bottom of an ancient-looking chest toward the very back of one of the more neglected corners. Out of it he drew a long, strangely shaped case into the flickering light of the candle.

"Look here, Shargar!" he said under his breath, for they never dared to speak aloud. "What can there be in this box?"

Having roamed the country a good deal more than Robert and having been present at some merry-makings with his mother, Shargar was for once better informed than his friend.

"Eh, Bob, don't ye know what that is? I thought ye knew everything. That's a fiddle."

"Stuff and nonsense, Shargar. Don't you think I know a fiddle when I see one?"

"Stuff and nonsense yerself!" cried Shargar in indignation. "Give it t' me."

Robert handed him the case. Shargar undid the hooks in a moment and revealed the magnificent creature lying silent in its shell.

"I told ye so!" he exclaimed triumphantly. "Maybe ye'll trust me next time."

"Losh!" His whisper was hoarse and full of awe. "It must be my grandfather's fiddle that I've heard about."

"Not t' know a fiddle case!" reflected Shargar with as much of contempt as it was possible for him to show.

"I tell you what, Shargar," returned Robert, "you may know the box of a fiddle better than I do, but the devil have me if I don't know the fiddle itself better than you do in two weeks' time! I'll take it to Dooble Sanny; he can play the fiddle fine. And I'll learn to play it too."

"Eh, man! that'll be grand!" cried Shargar, incapable of jealousy. "We can go t' all the markets together an' play for pennies."

To this Robert returned no reply, for hearing Betty come in downstairs he judged it time to restore the violin to its case and Betty's candle to the kitchen lest she should invade the upper regions in search of it. But that very evening he managed to have an interview with the venerable shoemaker, and it was arranged between them that Robert should bring his violin on the next evening.

When the time arrived, Robert no sooner heard the fiddle utter a few mournful sounds in the hands of the shoemaker, who was tolerably capable as a performer, than he longed to learn to make the strange instrument respond to his own touch as well. He wanted it to tell him the secrets of its queerly twisted skull, full of sweet sounds instead of brains. From that moment he determined that he would be a musician for music's own sake.

What added considerably to the excitement of his feelings was the expression of reverence and awe with which the shoemaker took the instrument from its case, and the tenderness with which he handled it. The fact was that he had not had a violin in his hands for nearly a year, having been compelled to pawn his own in order to alleviate the sickness brought on his wife by his ill-treatment of her once when he arrived home drunk. It was strange to think that such dirty hands should be able to bring such sounds out of the instrument the moment he got it safely positioned under his cheek. So dirty were they that it was said Dooble Sanny never required any rosin for a fiddle, his own fingers having always enough upon them for one bow at least. Yet those fingers never lost the delicacy of their touch. Some people thought this was in virtue of their being washed only once a week—a custom Alexander justified on the ground that, in a trade like his, it was of no use to wash oftener, for he would be just as dirty again before night.

The moment he began to play, the face of the shoemaker grew ecstatic. He stopped at the very first note, let his arms fall, one with the bow and the other with the violin, at his sides and exclaimed solemnly, "The creature must be a Straddle Various at least! Listen t' her! I hae never had such a combination o' wood an' catgut a'tween my fingers before."

As to its being a Stradivarius, the testimony of Dooble Sanny was not worth much. But the shoemaker's admiration roused in the boy's mind a reverence for the individual instrument which he never lost.

From that day on the two were fast friends.

Suddenly the shoemaker started playing at full speed in a strathspey, which was soon lost in the wail of a Highland psalmtune, giving place to "Such a wife as Willie had!" And on he went, without a pause, till Robert dared not stay any longer. The fiddle had bewitched the fiddler.

"Come as often as ye like, Robert, if ye bring this leddy wi' ye," said the shoemaker. And he stroked the back of the violin tenderly with his open palm.

"Would you have an objection to keeping it here and letting me come whenever I can?" Robert requested.

"Objection, laddie? I would as soon object t' letting my own wife lie beside me."

"Ay," said Robert slowly, seized with some anxiety about the violin as he remembered the fate of the wife.

Softened by the proximity of the violin and stung by the boy's look as his conscience had often stung him before, the tears rose in Elshender's eyes—for he loved his wife, save when the demon of drink possessed him.

"Take her away," he said in an unsteady voice, holding the violin out to Robert. "I don't deserve t' hae such a thing i' my house."

"No," returned Robert, "I must just trust you, Sandy. I can't stay longer tonight. But maybe you'll tell me how to hold her the next time I come—will you?"

"That I will, Robert; come when ye like. An' if ye're the one who can play this fiddle as she deserves t' be played, ye'll do me credit."

"You remember what that Lumley said to me the other day, Sandy, about my grandfather?"

"Ay, well enough. A dish o' drunken lies."

"It was true enough about my great-grandfather though."

"Was it really?"

"Ay. He was the best piper in his regiment of Culloden. If they had fought as he piped, there would have been another tale to tell. And he was the town piper after that, just like you, Sandy."

"Well, who would hae thought it? Faith! We must hae ye fiddlin' as well as yer lucky daddy piped."

As Robert departed he thought about *Alexander ab Alexandro*, as Mr. Innes facetiously styled him. He was in more ways than one worthy of the name *Dooble*. There seemed to be two natures in the man, which all his music had not yet been able to blend.

7 / Another Discovery in the Garret ⸺

Little did Robert dream of the reception that awaited him at home. Almost as soon as he had left the house, the following took place.

The mistress's bell rang and Betty went to see what was wanted. This conversation ensued.

"Who was that at the door, Betty?" asked Mrs. Falconer, for Robert had not shut the door so carefully as he ought, seeing that the deafness of his grandmother was of much the same faculty as her blindness.

Had Robert not had a hold of Betty by the forelock of her age, he would have been unable to steal any liberty at all. Still Betty had a conscience, and although she would not give Robert away if she could help it, yet she would not lie.

"Deed, mem, I can't just distinctly say that I heard the door," she answered.

"Where's Robert?" was her next question.

"He's generally up the stair aboot this hour, mem—that is, when he's not in the parlor at his lessons."

"What does he go up the stairs so much for, Betty, do ye know? It's something out o' the ordinary that's going on wi' him."

"Deed, I don't know, mem. I never took it into my head to consider it. He'll have some scheme of his own, no doubt. Laddies will be laddies, ye know, mem."

"I doubt, Betty, ye'll be aiding an' abetting. An' it doesn't become yer years, Betty."

"My years are not t' find fault wi', mem. They're well enough."

"That's nothing t' the point, Betty. What's the laddie up t'?"

"Do ye mean when he goes up the stair, mem?"

"Ay. Ye know well enough what I mean."

"Well, mem, I tell ye I don't know. And ye never heard me tell ye a lie since I was i' yer service, mem."

"No, not outright. Ye walk around an' aboot it, an' by the end ye come so near lying that if ye spoke another word ye would be at it, an' that frightens me from asking one question more o' ye. An' that's how ye win out. But now that it's aboot my own grandson, I'm not going t' lose him t' save a woman o' yer years, who ought t' know better. An'

44

so I'll ask it o' ye, though ye should be driven t' lie like Satan himself—
What's he aboot when he goes up the stair? Now!''

"Well, as sure as death, I don't know. Ye drive me t' swearing,
mem, and not t' lying.''

"Hae ye no idea aboot it, Betty?"

"Well, mem, I think sometimes he can't be well an' must have a
fox or something o' that nature in his stomach. For what he eats is awful.
An' I think he just goes up the stair t' eat by himself.''

"That's what I've noticed, Betty. Do ye think he might hae a rabbit
or maybe a pair o' them i' some box up i' the attic?''

"Or guinea pigs," suggested Betty.

"Well?"

"Or maybe a pup or two. I knew a laddie once that kept a whole
family o' kittens. Or maybe he might have a little lamb. There was an
uncle of my own—"

"Hold yer tongue, Betty. Ye hae too much t' say for all the sense
there is i' it.''

"Well, mem, ye asked the question o' me."

"Well, I've had enough o' yer answers, Betty. Go an' tell Robert
t' come here directly.''

Betty went, knowing perfectly well that Robert had gone out, and
returned with the information. Her mistress searched her face with a
keen eye.

"That must've been him a while ago when ye thought ye heard the
door,'' responded Betty helpfully.

"It's a strange thing that I should hear him clear i' here wi' my own
door shut, an' yer door open right close by an' ye not hear him, Betty.
An' me so deaf as well.''

"Deed, mem," retorted Betty, losing her temper a little. "I can be
as deaf as other folk myself once in a while.''

When Betty grew angry, Mrs. Falconer invariably grew calm, or at
least put her temper out of sight. She was silent now and continued silent
till Betty moved to return to her kitchen, when she said in a tone of one
who had just arrived at an important resolution, "Betty, we'll just go
up the stair an' hae a look.''

"Well, mem, I have no objections."

"No objections! Why should ye or anyone else hae any objections
t' me going where I like i' my own house? Umph!'' exclaimed Mrs.
Falconer, turning and facing her maid.

"Of course, mem. I only meant I had no objections t' go wi' ye.''

"And why should ye or any other woman that I paid two pounds

five for half a year dare t' hae objections t' going where I wanted ye t'
go i' my own house?''

"Hoot, mem! It was but a slip o' the tongue—nothing more.''

"Slip me no such slips, or ye'll come by a fall at last, I doubt,
Betty,'' concluded Mrs. Falconer in a mollified tone as she turned and
led the way from the room.

They got a candle in the kitchen and proceeded upstairs, Mrs. Falconer still leading and Betty following. They did not even look in the
first room, not doubting that the dignity of the best bedroom was in no
danger of being violated, even by Robert. They took their way upward
to the room in which he kept his schoolbooks—almost the only articles
of property which the boy possessed. They found nothing suspicious in
the room. All was in the best possible order—hardly unusual, seeing a
few books and a slate were the only things there besides the papers on
the shelves. They then continued still higher.

What the feelings of Shargar must have been when he heard the steps
and voices and saw the light approaching his place of refuge, we will
not change our point of view to inquire. He certainly was as little to be
envied at that moment as at any moment during the whole of his existence.

The first sense Mrs. Falconer made use of in the search after possible
animals lay in her nose. She kept sniffing constantly, but beyond the
usual musty smell of neglected rooms had as yet discovered nothing.
But the moment she entered the upper garret, ''There's an ill-fared smell
here, Betty,'' she said, believing that they had at last found the trail of
the mystery, ''but it's not the smell o' rabbits. Just look i' the corner
there behind the door.''

"There's nothing there,'' responded Betty.

"Round the end o' that chest there. I'll look i' the closet.''

As Betty rose from her search behind the chest and turned toward
her mistress, her eyes crossed the cavernous opening of the bed. There,
to her horror, she beheld a face like that of a galvanized corpse staring
at her from the darkness. Shargar was in a sitting posture, paralyzed
with terror, waiting like a fascinated bird till Mrs. Falconer and Betty
should make the final spring upon him and do whatever was the equivalent to devouring him on the spot. He had sat up to listen to the noise
of their ascending footsteps and fear had so overmastered him that he
either could not, or forgot that he could, lie down and cover his head
with some of the many garments scattered around him.

"I didn't say *whiskey*, did I?'' he kept repeating to himself in utter
imbecility of fear.

"The Lord preserve us!'' exclaimed Betty the moment she could speak; for during the first few seconds, having caught the infection of Shargar's expression, she stood equally paralyzed. "The Lord preserve us!" she repeated.

"Once is enough," said Mrs. Falconer sharply, turning round to see what the cause of Betty's ejaculation might be.

I have said that the grandmother was dim-sighted. The candle they had was little better than a penny dip. The bed was darker than the rest of the room. Shargar's face had none of the more distinctive characteristics of manhood upon it.

"God preserve us!" exclaimed Mrs. Falconer in her turn, "It's a wumman!"

Poor deluded Shargar, thinking himself safer under any form than that which he actually bore, attempted no protest against the mistake. But indeed he was incapable of speech. The two women flew upon him to drag him out of the bed. In that moment recovering his powers of motion, he sprang up in an agony of fear and darted out between them, overturning Betty in his course.

"Ye rouch limmer!" cried Betty from the floor. "Ye long-legged jade!" she added as she rose—and at the same moment Shargar banged the street door behind him in his flight.

With sunken head, poor Mrs. Falconer walked out of the garret in the silence of despair. She went slowly down the steep stair, supporting herself against the wall, her round-toed shoes creaking solemnly as she went. She took refuge in the master bedroom and burst into a violent fit of weeping. For such depravity she was not prepared. What a terrible curse hung over her family. Surely they were all reprobate from birth, not one elected for salvation from the guilt of Adam's fall, and therefore abandoned to Satan as his natural prey to be led captive of him at his will. She threw herself on her knees at the side of the bed and prayed brokenheartedly. Betty heard her as she limped past the door on her way back to her kitchen.

Meantime, Shargar had rushed across the next street on his bare feet into the Crookit Wynd. He never stopped until he reached his mother's deserted abode. There he ran to hide like a hunted fox. Rushing at the door, forgetful of everything but refuge, he found it unlocked, and, closing it behind him, stood panting like the hart that has found the waterbrooks. The owner had looked in one day to see whether the place was worth repairing, for it was a mere shack, and had forgotten to turn the key when he left it. Poor Shargar! Was it more or less of a refuge since the mother that bore him was not there either to curse or welcome his return? Still, she was his mother, and as he once said later in his life, "Ye see, a mither's a mither, be she the very devil."

Searching about in the dark, he found the one article unsold by the landlord—a stool with but two of its natural three legs. On this he balanced himself and waited—simply for what Robert would do. His faith in Robert was unbounded, and he had no other hope on earth. Shargar was not miserable. In that wretched hovel, his bare feet clasping the clay floor with pitch darkness around him and incapable of the simplest philosophical or religious reflection, he yet found life good. For it had *interest*. And more, it had hope.

While Shargar sat there, Robert, thinking him snug in the garret, was walking quietly home from the shoemaker's; and his first impulse on entering was to run up and recount the particulars of his interview with Alexander. Arriving in the dark garret, he called to Shargar, as usual in a whisper. There was no reply and Robert thought he was asleep. He called louder, for he had received a penny from his grandmother that day for bringing home two pails of water for Betty, and had just spent it on a loaf for him. Still no reply, He went to the bed to lay hold of him and shake him. But his searching hands found no Shargar. Alarmed, he ran downstairs to beg a candle from Betty.

When he reached the kitchen he found Betty's nose as much in the air as its construction would permit. For a hooknosed body she certainly was the most harmless and ovine creature in the world. But this was a case in which feminine modesty was both concerned and aggrieved. She showed her resentment no further, however, than by simply returning no answer in syllable or sound or motion to Robert's request. She was washing up the tea things, and went on with her work as if she had been in absolute solitude. Robert plainly saw, to his great concern, that his secret had been discovered and that Shargar had been expelled. But, with an instinct of facing the worst at once, which accompanied him through life, he went straight to his grandmother's parlor.

"Well, Grandmamma," he said, trying to speak as cheerfuly as he could.

Grannie's prayers had softened her a little, else she would have been as silent as Betty; for it was from her mistress that Betty had learned this mode of torturing a criminal. She was just able to return his greeting in the words, "Well, Robert!" pronounced with a finality of tone that indicated she had done her utmost and had nothing to add.

Here's a pickle! thought Robert to himself. Yet still believing that the best principle was to meet the first mischief he saw head-on, he addressed his grandmother at once. The effort necessary gave an unfortunate tone of defiance to his words.

"Why won't you speak to me, Grannie?" he said. "I'm not a heathen, not even a papist."

"Ye're worse than both i' one, Robert."

"Hoots! You don't mean that, Grannie," returned Robert, who even at the age of fourteen, when once compelled to assert himself, assumed a modest superiority.

"None o' such impudence!" retorted Mrs. Falconer. "I wonder where ye learned that. But it's no wonder. Evil communications corrupt good manners. Ye're a lost prodigal, Robert, like yer own father before ye. I've just been sitting here thinking t' myself whether it wouldn't be better for both o' us t' let ye go an' reap the fruit o' yer doings at once, for the hard way is the best road for transgressors. I'm not bound t' keep ye."

"Well, well, I'll be off to Shargar. He and me'll hold on together better than you and me, Grannie. He's a poor creature, but he can stick with you."

"What are ye running on about Shargar for, ye hypocrite simpleton? Ye'll not go t' Shargar, I'll warrant! Ye'll be after that vile limmer that's turned my honest house int' a sty this last fortnight."

"Grannie, I don't know what you mean."

"*She* knows, then. I sent her off like one o' Samson's foxes, wi' a firebrand at her tail. It's a pity it wasn't tied between the two o' ye."

"Preserve us, Grannie! Is it possible you've taken Shargar for one of the womankind?"

"I know nothing aboot Shargar, I tell ye. I know that Betty an' me found an ill-fared girl i' the bed i' the garret."

Could it be his mother? thought Robert in bewilderment; but he recovered himself in a moment and answered, "Shargar may be a princess after all, for anything I know to the contrary, but I took him for a simpleton. Faith, such a princess he'd make!"

And careless to resist the ludicrousness of the idea, he burst into a loud fit of laughter, which did more to reassure his grannie than any amount of protestation could have done. However, she pretended to take offense at his ill-timed merriment. Seeing his grandmother uncertain, Robert gathered courage to assume the offensive.

"But, Grannie! However Betty, not to say you, could have driven out a poor, half-starving creature like Shargar, even supposing he might have been wearing one of the old kilts from the closet instead of trousers—and his mother run away leaving him—it's more than I can understand. I don't doubt that maybe by now he's gone and drowned himself."

Robert knew well enough that Shargar would not drown himself without at least bidding him good-bye. But he knew too that his grandmother could be moved. Her conscience was more tender than her feelings. The first relation she bore to most that came near her was one of severity and rebuke. But underneath her cold outside lay a sensitive heart, to which conscience acted the part of a somewhat capricious stroker, now quenching its heat with the cold water of duty, now stirring it up with the poker of reproach. But her conscience was on the whole a more influential friend to her than her heart. I cannot help thinking that she not unfrequently took refuge in severity of tone and manner from the threatened breaking forth of feelings which she could not otherwise control and which she was ashamed to manifest.

At the words "drowned himself," Mrs. Falconer started.

"Run, laddie, run," she said, "an' fetch him back directly!—Betty, Betty, go wi' Robert an' help him look for Shargar! Ye old, blind body, can't ye tell a lad from a lass!"

"No, no, Grannie. I'm not going out with a dame like her trailing at my feet. She'd be nothing but a hindrance. If Shargar's to be gotten, I'll get him without Betty. And if you don't know him for the creature you found in the garret, he must be some changed since I left him there."

"Well, Robert, go yer way. But if ye be deceiving me, may the Lord forgive ye, Robert, for ye'll sore need it."

"No fear of that, Grannie," returned Robert from the street door, and vanished.

Mrs. Falconer stalked with a certain stately air back through the house to Betty. She felt strangly soft at the heart, Robert not being *yet* proved a reprobate; but she was not therefore prepared to drop one atom of the dignity of her relation to her servant.

"Betty," she said, "ye made a mistake."

"What's that, mem?" returned Betty.

"Ye said it was a lass up there; it was that creature Shargar."

"Ye said it was a lass yerself first, mem."

"Ye know well enough that I'm shortsighted, an' hae been from the day o' my birth."

"I'm not old enough t' know aboot that, mem," returned Betty in an undertone as if she did not intend her mistress to hear her. And although Mrs. Falconer heard well enough, her mistress adopted the subterfuge and did not respond. Betty continued, "But I'll swear the creature I saw was in petticoats."

"Don't swear at all, Betty. Ye hae made a mistake anyway."

"Who says that?"

"Robert."

"Well, if he be telling the truth—"

"Dare ye insinuate that a son o' mine would tell anything but the truth?"

"No, no, mem. But if that wasn't a leddy, ye can't deny but she looked a lot like one, and not a bashful one either."

"If he was a simpleton, he wouldn't look like a bashful lass anyway, Betty. An' there ye're wrong."

"Well, well, mem, have it yer own way," muttered Betty.

"I will hae it my own way," retorted her mistress, "because it's the right way, Betty. An' now, ye must go up the stair an' get the place cleaned out an' put i' order."

"I will do that, mem."

"Ay, ye will. An' look well aboot, Betty, ye that can see so well, i' case there should be anything foul aboot, for he's none o' the cleanest!"

"I will do that, mem."

"An' go directly, before he comes back."

"Who comes back?"

"Robert, o' course."

"Why do it before he comes back?"

" 'Cause he's coming wi' him."

"*Who's* coming wi' 'im?"

"Why, Shargar."

"Who says that?" exclaimed Betty, sniffing and starting at once.

"I say that. So ye go an' do what I tell ye, this minute!"

Betty obeyed instantly, for the tone in which the last words were spoken was one she was not accustomed to dispute. She only muttered as she went, "It'll all come upon me as usual."

Betty's job was long ended before Robert returned. Never dreaming that Shargar might have gone back to the old haunt, he had looked for him everywhere before that occurred to him as a last chance. Nor would he have found him even then, for he would not have thought of his being inside the deserted house had not Shargar heard his footsteps in the street.

He started up from his stool but was not sure enough to go to the door; he might be mistaken; it might be the landlord. He heard the feet stop and did not move; but when he heard them begin to go away again, he rushed to the door and called out, "Bob, Bob!"

"Eh, ye creature!" said Robert, "are you in there after all?"

"Eh, Bob!" exclaimed Shargar, and burst into tears. "I thought ye would come after me."

"Of course," answered Robert. "Come on home."

"Where t'?" asked Shargar in dismay.

"Home to your own bed at my grannie's."

"No, no," said Shargar hurriedly, retreating within the door of the hovel. "No, no, Bob. I'll not do that. She's an awful woman, that grannie o' yours. I can't think how ye can bide wi' her."

It required a good deal of persuasion, but at last Robert prevailed upon Shargar to return. At length they entered Mrs. Falconer's parlor, Robert dragging Shargar after him, having failed altogether in encouraging him to enter in a more dignified fashion.

No sooner had Mrs. Falconer cast her eyes upon him than she was utterly convinced of the truth of all Robert had told her.

"Here he is, Grannie, and if you aren't satisfied yet—"

"Hold yer tongue, laddie. Ye hae given me no cause t' doubt yer word."

Indeed, during Robert's absence, his grandmother had had leisure to perceive of what an absurd folly she had been guilty. She had also had time to make up her mind as to her duty with regard to Shargar. And the more she thought about it, the more she admired the conduct of her grandson. No doubt she was the more inclined toward benevolence since she had as it were received her grandson back from the jaws of death.

When the two lads entered, from her armchair Mrs. Falconer examined Shargar from head to foot with a countenance immovable in stern gentleness till Shargar would gladly have sunk into the shelter of the voluminous kilt from the garret closet he still had wrapped around his trousers.

At length she spoke. "Robert, take him away."

"Where'll I take him to, Grannie?"

"Take him up t' the garret. Betty'll hae taken a tub o' hot water up there by this time an' ye must see that he washes himself from head t' foot, or he won't stay i' my house. Go an' see t' it this minute."

She dismissed them, and Shargar, by and by, found himself in bed, clean, and for the first time in his life, between a pair of linen sheets—not a thing altogether to his satisfaction.

But greater trials awaited him. In the morning he was visited by Brodie the tailor and Elshender the shoemaker, both of whom he held in awe as his superiors in the social scale. By them he was handled and measured from head to foot; after which he had to lie in bed for three days till his clothes came. For Betty had carefully committed every article of his former dress to the kitchen fire, not without a sense of adding pollution to the bottom of her kettle. Thus grievous was Shargar's introduction to the comforts of respectability. Nor did he like it much better when he was dressed and able to go out. For not only was he uncomfortable in his new clothes, which after the very easy fit of the old ones felt like a suit of armor, but he was liable to be sent for at any

52

moment by the awful sovereignty in whose dominions he found himself.
Mrs. Falconer proceeded to instruct him not merely in his own religious
duties, but in the religious theories of his ancestors, if indeed Shargar's
ancestors ever had any. And now the Shorter Catechism seemed likely
to be changed into the Longer Catechism, for he had it on so many days
of the week, Mrs. Falconer apparently hoping to make up for lost time
in short order. Indeed, so dreary did Shargar find it all that his love for
Robert was never put to such a severe test. If it had not been for that,
he would have run for it. Twenty times a day he was so tempted.

At school, though it was better, yet it was bad. For he was ten times
as much laughed at for his new clothes, though they were of the plainest.
Still he bore all the pangs of an unwelcome advancement without a
grumble for the sake of his friend alone, whose faithful pet he remained
as much as ever. But his past life of cold and neglect, hunger and blows,
homelessness and rags began to glimmer as a distant vaporous sunset,
and the loveless freedom he had then enjoyed gave it a bloom as of
summer roses.

I wonder whether there may not have been in some unknown corner
of the old lady's mind this lingering remnant of paganism, that, in
reclaiming the outcast from the error of his ways, she was making an
offering acceptable to God whom her mere prayers could not move to
look with favor upon her own prodigal son, Andrew.

8 / The Violin ———————————————————

The winter passed slowly away. Robert and Shargar went to school together and studied their lessons in the evening at Mrs. Falconer's table. Shargar soon learned to behave with tolerable propriety; was obedient as far as eye-service went; looked as unusual as ever; did what he pleased—which was nothing very wicked—the moment he was out of the old lady's sight; was well fed and well cared for; and when he was asked how he was, gave the invariable answer, "Middlin'." The poor boy was not very happy.

Robert went time and again to Dooble Sanny for the fiddle as often as he dared. Though not too religious to get drunk occasionally, the shoemaker was a great deal too religious to play his fiddle on the Sabbath; he would not willingly anger the powers above. But it became a sore temptation after he got possession of old Mr. Falconer's wonderful instrument, which now became his delight as well as Robert's.

"Hoots, man!" he would say to Robert, "don't handle her as if she were an egg box. Take hold o' her as if she were a living creature. Just strike her carefully an' then lure the music out o' her. For she's like a woman. If ye be rough with her, ye won't get a word out o' her—come t' me, my bonny leddy. Ye'll tell me yer story, won't ye, my pet?"

And with every gesture, as if he were humoring a shy and invalid girl, he would wile the music out of her in sobs and wails till the instrument, gathering courage in his embrace, grew gently merry in its confidence and broke at last into airy laughter. He always spoke of, and apparently thought of, his violin as a woman, just as a sailor does of his craft. But apart from his love for music and its instruments, there was nothing about him to suggest other than a most uncivilized nature. To all appearances the animal in his nature held the upper hand over any spiritual influences. But upon occasion, when playing the violin, his heavenly companion succeeded in raising him a few feet above the mire and clay of his daily existence. Worthy Mr. Falconer would have been horrified to see his instrument in such society as that into which she was now introduced at times.

Nevertheless, the shoemaker was a good and patient teacher and Robert made steady progress. It could not be rapid, however, seeing that all he could give to the violin was an hour at a time, two evenings in the week. Even with this moderation, the risk of his absence exciting his grandmother's suspicion and inquiry was far from small.

And now many faded old memories of his grandfather and his merry kindness—all so different from the solemn benevolence of his grandmother—revived in his mind with the revival of the violin. The instrument surely had a story laid up in its hollow breast and was now beginning to tell out its dreams about the old times in the ear of the listening boy. It also began to assume something of that mystery and life which was having such a softening and elevating influence on his shoemaker teacher.

At length the love of the violin grew so upon Robert that he could think of nothing but how he might enjoy more of its company. It would not do, for many reasons, to go oftener to the shoemaker's, especially now that the days were getting longer. Nor was that what he wanted. He wanted opportunity for practice. He wanted to be alone with the creature, to see if she would not say something more to him than she had yet said. Wafts and odors of melodies began to steal upon him in the half lights between sleeping and waking before he was fully aware. If only he could entice them to creep out of the violin!

In Rothieden, there was a building so deserted that its very history seemed to have come to a standstill. It was the property of Mrs. Falconer, left by her husband. Trade had gradually ebbed away from the town till the thread factory stood unoccupied with all its machinery rusting, just as the workers had risen and left it one hot summer day when they were told their services were no longer required. Some of the thread even remained on the spools, and in the hollows of some of the sockets the oil had as yet dried only into a paste. But to Robert the desertion of the place appeared immemorial.

The factory stood a furlong's distance from the house, on the outskirts of the town. There was a large, neglected garden behind it, with some good fruit trees and plenty of the bushes which boys love for the sake of their berries. After Grannie's jam pots were properly filled, the remnant of these was at Robert's disposal. Haunting this garden the previous summer he had, for the first time, made acquaintance with the interior of the deserted building. He had discovered a back entrance less securely fastened than the front and with a strange mingling of fear and curiosity had from time to time extended his rambles over what seemed to him the huge desolation of the place. Half of it was well built of stone and lime, but the upper part was built of wood, which now showed considerable signs of decay. One room opened into another through the length of the place, revealing a vista of machines, standing with an air of the last folding of the wings of silence over them.

Their activity was not so far vanished but that by degrees Robert came to fancy he had some time or other seen a woman seated at each of those silent machines, whose single hand set the whole frame in motion, with its numberless spindles and spools rapidly revolving—a vague mystery of endless threads in orderly complication. Now all was still as the church on a weekday, still as the school on a Saturday afternoon. Nay, the silence seemed to have settled down like the dust and grown old and thick, so dead and old that the ghost of the ancient noise had risen to haunt the place.

It was there that Robert would carry his violin, and there he would woo her.

"I'm thinking I must take her with me tonight, Sandy," he said, holding the fiddle lovingly to his chest after he had finished his lesson.

The shoemaker looked blank.

"Ye're not goin' to desert me, are ye?"

"No, no, nothing like that," returned Robert. "But I want to try her at home. I must get used to her a little, you know, before I can do anything with her."

"I wish ye hadn't brought her here then. What am I to do wantin' her!"

"Why don't you get your own back?"

"I haven't the money, man. An', besides, I doubt I would be content with her now that I've had yers. I used to think my own grand. But that bonny leddy o' yers has taken her clean out o' me."

"But you can't have her, you know, Sandy. She's not mine. She's my grannie's, you know."

"What's the use o' her to _her_? She puts no value upon her. Eh, man, if she would give her to me, I would keep yer grannie in the best o' shoes the rest o' her days!"

"That wouldn't be much, Sandy, for she hasn't had a new pair since ever I can remember."

"But I would keep Betty in shoes as well."

"Betty pays for her own shoes, I reckon."

"Well, I would keep _ye_ in shoes, an' yer bairns and yer bairns' bairns!" cried the shoemaker with enthusiasm.

"Hoot, man! Long before that you'll be fiddling in the New Jerusalem."

"Eh, man," said Alexander looking up, "do ye think there'll be fiddles there? I thought there were all harps, a thing I never saw. But it can't be as pretty as a fiddle."

"I don't know," answered Robert. "But you should make a point of seeing for yourself."

"If I thought there would be fiddles there, faith, I would have it a try. It wouldn't be much o' a Jerusalem for me without my fiddle. But if there be fiddles, I dare say they would be grand ones. I dare say they would give me a new one—I mean one old as Noah's that he played in the ark when the devil came by to listen. I would fain have a try. Ye know all about it with that grannie o' yers; how's a body to begin?"

"By giving up the drink, man."

"Ay—ay—ay—I reckon yer right. Well . . . I'll think about it, once I'm through with this job. That'll be next week or thereabouts, or maybe two days after. I'll have some leisure then."

Before he had finished speaking, he had caught up his awl and begun to work vigorously on the shoe before him.

"Good night to you," said Robert, with the fiddle case under his arm.

The shoemaker looked up, with his hands bound in his threads.

"Ye're not goin' to take her from me tonight?"

"Ay, I am, but I'll bring her back again. I'm not going to Jericho with her."

"Go to Hecklebirnie with her, an' that's three miles beyond hell!"

"No, we've got to get farther than that. There can't be much fiddling there."

"Well, take her to the New Jerusalem then! I'm going down to Lucky Leary's an' fill myself roarin' full, and it'll all be yer fault!"

Dooble Sanny caught up a huge boot, the sole of which was filled with broadheaded nails as thick as they could be driven and, in a rage, threw it at Robert as he darted out. Through its clang against the door the shoemaker heard a cry from the instrument. He cast everything from him and sprang after Robert who was down the street like a long-legged greyhound. It was love and grief over what he had done, apprehension and remorse rather than vengeance that winged his heels.

"Robert! Robert!" he cried. "Stop, for God's sake! Is she hurt?"

Robert stopped at once and turned.

"No, Sandy," he said. "But you'll make a cripple of her yet, or worse, if you don't curb your anger," he added with indignation.

With a humble sigh and a "Praise be thanked," the shoemaker turned and went to his lonely stool and home "untreasured of his mistress." Robert went home too, and stole like a thief to his room.

The next day was a Saturday, half of which was the real Sabbath to the schoolboys of Rothieden. Even Robert's grannie was Hebrew enough, or rather Christian enough, to respect this remnant of the fourth commandment, and he had the half day to himself. So as soon as he had eaten his dinner, he managed to give Shargar the slip, leaving him to the inroads of desolate despondency, and stole away to the old factory garden. He had managed to purloin the gate key of the fence surrounding it from the kitchen where it hung, and there was little danger of its absence being discovered, seeing that in winter no one thought of the garden. The smuggling of the violin out of the house was the greatest danger. But by spying and speeding he managed it and soon found himself safe within the high walls of the garden.

It was early spring. There had been a heavy fall of sleet in the morning, and now the wind blew gustfully about the place. The neglected trees shook showers upon him as he passed under them, his boots trampling down the weedy growth of the walking paths. The long twigs of the wall-trees had been torn down by the snow and the blasts of winter. The gooseberry and currant bushes, bare and leafless, neither reminded him of the feasts of the past summer nor gave him any hope for the next. He strode carelessly through it all to gain the door of the building before him. It yielded to a push and he entered. He mounted a broad stair in the main part of the factory, passing the silent clock in one of its corners, a motionless reminder of the false accusations it had brought against the workers below.

Now that he was alone for the first time with the violin, he hoped that she would respond to his gentle touches and realize his dreams and give substance to the fluttering in his soul. It was no wonder that he felt an ethereal foretaste of the expectation that haunts the approach of two souls. The proceedings involved something of that awe and mystery with which an older youth approaches the maiden he loves.

But I am not going to describe his first tete-a-tete with his violin. Perhaps he returned from it somewhat disappointed. Probably he found her coy, unwilling to acknowledge his demands on her attention. But no less enthusiastically did he return again and again with her to the solitude of the ruinous factory. On every safe occasion, becoming more and more frequent as the days grew longer, he stole away from home; and every time he was a little more capable of drawing the coherence of melody from that matrix of sweet sounds.

At length the people about began to say that the factory was haunted, that the ghost of old Mr. Falconer, unable to repose in his grave while neglect was ruining the precious results of his industry, visited the place night after night and solaced himself with his favorite violin.

One gusty afternoon late in the spring, Robert went as usual to this secret haunt. He had played for some time and now, from a sudden impulse, had ceased and begun to look around him. The only light came from two long, pale cracks in the rain clouds of the west. The wind was blowing through the broken windows. A dreary, windy gloom pervaded the desolate place. An eerie sense of discomfort came over him as he gazed about, and he lifted his violin to dispel the strange, unpleasant feeling growing upon him.

But at the first long stroke across the strings, an awful sound arose in a farther room, a sound that made him all but drop the bow. It was the old, all but forgotten whirr of bobbins, mingled with the gentle groans of the revolving horizontal wheel, but magnified in the silence of the place and the echoing imagination of the boy into something preternaturally awful. Yielding for a moment to the growth of gooseskin and the insurrection of hair, he recovered himself by a violent effort and walked to the door of the room he was in.

The figure of an old woman sat solemnly turning and turning the handwheel. It was only a blind woman everybody knew—so old that she had become childish. But it was still many moments before Robert could tame his rapid pulse. The woman had heard the reports of the factory being haunted and, groping about with her half-withered brain also full of ghosts, had found the garden and the back door open and had climbed up to the second floor by a farther stair, well known to her when she used to work that very machine. She had seated herself instinctively and had set it in motion at once.

Yielding to an impulse of experiment, Robert began to play again. Thereupon her disordered ideas broke out in words, and Robert soon began to feel it could hardly be more ghastly to look upon a ghost than to be taken for one.

"Ay, sir," said the old woman, "I don't wonder that ye can't lie still. But what makes ye go wandering about this place? Ye should go home t' yer wife. She might say a word t' quiet yer old bones, for she's a wise woman—the mistress."

Then followed a pause. There was a horror about the woman's voice, already half dissolved by death, in this desolate place that almost took from Robert the power of motion. But his violin sent forth an accidental twang and that set her going again.

"Ye was a kind and honest gentleman yersel'. But I would hae thought that glory might hae held ye in. But yer son! Eh! It's a sad thing he was bound t' go the wrong way. I doobt it won't be t' ye he'll go at the last. There won't be room for him in Abraham's bosom. And then t' behave so ill t' that winsome wife o' his! I don't wonder that ye can't lie still. But, sir, since ye are up, I wish ye would speak t' John Thompson not t' take off the day that I was away last week, for I was very unwell, and had t' stay in bed."

Robert was beginning to feel uneasy as to how he should get rid of her, but just then she rose. Saying, "Ay, ay, I know it's six o'clock," she went out as she had come in. Robert followed and saw her safely out of the garden, but did not return to the factory.

Old Janet told a strange story the next day of how she had *seen* the ghost and had had a long talk with him and of what he had said and of how he groaned and played the fiddle between. And finding that the report had reached his gandmother's ears, Robert thought it prudent to discontinue his visits to the factory. Mrs. Falconer, of course, received the rumor with indignant scorn and peremptorily refused to allow any examination of the premises.

But to have the violin beside him and not hear her speak was a trial too great for Robert to bear. One evening the longing after her voice grew upon him till he could resist it no longer. He shut the door of his garret room and, with Shargar by him, took her out and began to play softly, gently—oh, so softly and gently! Shargar was enraptured. Robert went on playing.

Suddenly the door opened and his grannie stood awfully revealed before them. Betty had heard the violin and had flown to the parlor in the belief that, unable to get anyone to heed him at the factory, the ghost had taken old Janet's advice and come home.

But his wife smiled a smile of contempt, went with Betty to the kitchen—directly under Robert's room—heard the sounds, took off her creaking shoes, stole upstairs on her soft white lamb's-wool stockings, and caught the pair. The violin was seized, put in its case, and carried off; and Mrs. Falconer rejoiced to think she had broken a trap set by Satan for the unwary feet of her poor Robert. Little she knew the wonder of that violin—how it had kept the soul of her husband alive! Little she knew how dangerous it is to shut an open door, with ever so narrow a peep into the eternal, in the face of a son of Adam! And little she knew how determinedly and restlessly a nature like Robert's would search for another, to open one possibly ten times more dangerous in her mind than that which she had closed.

When Alexander heard of the affair, he was at first overwhelmed with the misfortune. But gathering little heart at last, he set to working "like a very devil," as he said himself. And as he was the best shoe-maker in the town, and for the time abstained completely from whiskey, he soon managed to save the money necessary to redeem his old fiddle. But even Robert's inexperienced ear could readily tell the difference. It was, however, all they had for the present, and they had to make do.

9 / Robert's Plan of Salvation —————————

For some time after the loss of his friend, Robert went loitering and mooning about, quite neglecting his lessons. Even when seated at his grannie's table, he could do no more than fix his eyes on his book. But his was a nature which, foiled in one direction, must immediately send out its searching roots in another. Of all forces, that of growth is the one irresistible, for it is the creating power of God, the law of life and being. Therefore no checks and forbiddings from all the good grannies in the world could have prevented Robert from striking root downward and bearing fruit upward, though, as in all higher natures, the fruit was a long way off yet.

His soul was sad and hungry. He was not unhappy, for he had been guilty of nothing that weighed on his conscience. He had been doing many things lately, it is true, without asking his grandmother's permission. But Robert felt nothing immoral in playing his grandfather's violin. Therefore he was not unhappy, only much disappointed, very empty, and somewhat gloomy. There was nothing to look forward to now, no secret full of riches and endless in hope—in short, no violin.

To feel the full force of his loss one must remember that around the childhood of Robert, which he was fast leaving behind him, there had gathered no tenderness—none at least recognizable as such to him. The only women he came in contact with were his grandmother and Betty. He had no recollection of having ever been kissed. From the embryo-darkness of that existence, his nature had been unconsciously striving to escape—struggling to get into the sunlit air, sighing after a freedom he could not have defined. Of the beauty of life, with its wonder and its deepness and unknown glory, his fiddle had been the type. And now that it was gone, his soul turned itself away from the sun.

Now arose within him the evil images of a theology which explained all God's doings from a low rather than a lofty base. In such a system, hell is invariably the deepest truth, and the love of God is not so deep as hell. Hence, as foundations must be laid in the deepest, the system is founded in hell and the first article in the creed that Robert Falconer learned was, "I believe in hell." As often as a thought of religious duty arose in his mind, it appeared in the form of escaping hell, of fleeing from the wrath to come.

He was told that God was just, awfully just, punishing those who did not go through a certain process of mind which it was impossible they should go through without help from him. This help he gave to some and withheld from others. And this God, they also added, was love. It was logically absurd, of course, yet they continued to say God was love and many of them succeeded in believing it. Still, the former article of God's harsh justice was the characteristic of his nature they taught chiefly to their children. No one dreamed of saying that nobody can do without the help of the Father any more than a newborn babe could of itself live and grow to be a man. No one said that out of the loving fatherhood of God the world was made, and that we were born into it, and that God lives and loves infinitely more than the most loving man or woman on earth.

Robert consequently began to make efforts toward the saving of his soul, a most rational and prudent exercise but hardly Christian in its nature. His imagination began to busy itself concerning the dire consequences of not entering into the refuge of faith. He made many frantic efforts to believe that he believed and took to keeping the Sabbath very carefully—that is, he went to church three times, never said a word on any subject unconnected with religion, read only religious books, never whistled, stopped thinking of his lost fiddle, and so on—all the time feeling that God was ready to pounce on him if he failed once.

But even through the horrible vapors of these vain endeavors, which denied God altogether as the maker of the world and denied Robert of his soul and heart and brain, there broke a little light from the dim windows of the few books that came his way. In one of these he read a story of a cherub who repents of making his choice with Satan, mourns over his apostasy, and haunts unseen the steps of our Savior. He would gladly return to his lost duties in heaven if only he might. The doubtful situation was left unsolved in the volume, and thus remained unsolved in Robert's mind as well. Would poor Abaddon be forgiven and taken home again?

By Robert's own instincts, he felt there could be no question of his being forgiven. But according to what he had been taught, there could be no question of his perdition. Having no one to talk to, he questioned with himself on the matter, usually siding with the instinctively correct half of himself which supported the merciful view of the case. For all his efforts at keeping the Sabbath had, in his own honest judgment, failed so entirely that he had now come to believe himself not one of those elected for salvation. Therefore, this situation with the fallen angel was no mere mental exercise; for all he knew he might find himself in such a position one day—out of the fold and wanting to get back in.

He made one attempt to open the subject with Shargar.

"Shargar, what do you think?" he said suddenly one day. "If a devil were to repent, would God forgive him?"

"There's no saying what folk would do till once they've tried," returned Shargar cautiously.

Robert did not care to resume the question with one who so circumspectly refused to take a view of the matter.

He made an attempt with his grandmother.

One Sunday, after trying for a time to revolve his thoughts in orbit around the mind of the Rev. Hugh MacCleary, as projected in a sermon which he had scraped up out of a commentary, Robert could contain them no longer. The preacher no doubt supposed St. Matthew, not St. Matthew Henry, accountable for the origin of his words. Nevertheless, Robert's thoughts flew off into what the aforementioned gentleman would have pronounced "very dangerous speculation."

After dinner, when the table had been cleared by Betty, they drew their chairs to the fire and Robert began reading, as was the custom, to his grandmother out of the family Bible while Shargar sat listening. Robert had not read long, however, before he looked up and asked, "Wasn't that a mean trick of Joseph, Grandmother, to put that cup, and a silver one too, into Benjamin's sack?"

"Why, laddie? He wanted t' make them come back again, ye know."

"But he needn't have done it in such a trick-like way. He didn't need to let them wait without telling them he was their brother."

"They had behaved very badly t' him."

"He used to tell tales to them, though."

"Laddie, take care what ye say aboot Joseph, for he was a type o' Christ."

"How was that, Grandmother?"

"They sold him t' the Ishmaelites for silver, as Judas did t' the Lord."

"Did he bear the sins of them that sold him?"

"Ye could say, i' a way, he did, for he was sore afflicted before he made it up t' be the king's right hand. And then he kept a whole heap o' punishment off his brothers."

"So, Grandmother, other folk than Christ might suffer for the sins of their neighbors?"

"Ay, laddie, many a one has t' do that. But not t' make atonement, ye know. Nothing but the suffering o' the spotless could do that. The Lord wouldn't be satisfied wi' less than that. It must be the innocent t' suffer for the guilty."

"I understand that," said Robert, who had heard it so often that he had not yet thought of trying to understand it. "But if we get to the good place, we'll all be innocent, won't we, Grannie?"

"Ay, we will—washed spotless an' pure an' clean an' dressed i' the wedding garment an' set down at the table wi' him an' wi' his Father. That's them that believes i' him, ye know."

"Of course, Grannie.—Well, you see, I have been thinking of a plan for almost emptying hell."

"What's i' the boy's head now? Truth, ye shouldn't be meddling wi' such subjects, laddie!"

"I don't want to say anything to vex you, Grannie. I'll go on with the chapter."

"Oh, go on wi' what ye were going t' say. Ye won't say much wrong before I'll cry *stop*," said Mrs. Falconer, curious to know what had been moving in the boy's mind, but watching him like a cat, ready to spring on the first visible hair of the old Adam.

Robert, for his part, recalling the outbreak of terrible grief which he had heard from his grandmother on that memorable night, truly thought that his project would bring comfort to a mind burdened with such care. Thus he went on with the explaining of his plan.

"All them that sits down to the supper of the Lamb will sit there because Christ suffered the punishment due to their sins—won't they, Grannie?"

"Doubtless, laddie."

"But it'll be weighing hard on their hearts to be sitting there eating and drinking and talking away and enjoying themselves when every now and then there'll come a sigh of wailing up from the bad place, and the smell of burning hard to stand."

"What put that int' yer head, laddie? There's no reason t' think that hell's so near heaven as that. The Lord forbid it."

"Well, but, Grannie, they'll know all the same, whether they smell it or not. And I can't help thinking that the farther away I thought they were, the worse it would be to think about them. Indeed, it would be worse."

"What are ye driving at, laddie? I can't understand ye," said Mrs. Falconer, feeling very uncomfortable and yet curious to hear what would come next. "I don't imagine we'd hae t' think much—"

But here I presume the thought of the added desolation of her Andrew if she too were to forget him, as well as his Father in heaven, stopped the flow of her words. She paused, and Robert took up his parable and went on, first with yet another question.

"Do you think, Grannie, that a body would be allowed to speak a word in public there—at the big, long table, I mean?"

"Why not, if it were done wi' modesty an' for a good reason. But really, laddie, I doubt ye're rambling altogether. Ye heard nothing like that today from Mr. MacCleary."

"No, no, he said nothing about it. But maybe I'll go and ask him though."

"What aboot?"

"What I'm going to tell you, Grannie."

"Well, tell away an' hae done wi' it. I'm growing tired o' it."

It was something else than tired she was growing.

"Well, I'm going to try as hard as I can to make it there."

"I hope ye will. Strive an' pray. Resist the devil. Walk i' the light. Trust not t' yerself, but trust i' Christ an' his salvation."

"Ay, ay, Grannie. Well—"

"Aren't ye done yet?"

"No. I'm but just beginning."

"Beginning, are ye? Humph!"

"Well, if I make it there, the very first night I sit down with the rest of them I'm going to stand up and say—that is if the Master at the head of the table doesn't tell me to sit down—'Brothers and sisters, listen to me for one minute, and—O Lord, if I say something wrong, just take the speech from me and I'll sit down dumb and rebuked.—We're all here by grace and not by merit, except his, as you all know better than me because you have been here longer than me. But it's just tugging at my heart to think of them that's down there. Now we have no merit, and they have no merit. So why are we here and them there? But now we're washed clean and innocent. So now, when there's no punishment left on us, it seems to me that we might bear some of the sins of them that has too many. I call upon each and every one of you that has a friend or neighbor down yonder to rise up and taste not a bite nor drink a drink till we go up together to the foot of the throne and pray the Lord to let us go and do as the Master did before us, and bear their griefs and carry their sorrows down in hell there. And if they repent it may be that they will get remission of their sins and come up here with us at last, and sit down with us at this table—all through the merits of our Savior Jesus Christ, at the head of the table there."

Half ashamed of his long speech, half overcome by the feelings fighting within him, and altogether bewildered, Robert burst out crying like a baby and ran out of the room—up to his own place of meditation, where he threw himself on the floor. Shargar, who had made neither head nor tail of it all, sat staring at Mrs. Falconer. She rose, and going into Robert's little bedroom, closed the door and prayed earnestly for his soul.

When she came out, she rang the bell for tea and sent Shargar to look for Robert. When he appeared she was so gentle to him that it woke quite a new sensation in him. But after tea was over, she said, "Noo, Robert, let's hae no more o' this. Ye know as well as I do that them that goes *there*, their doom is fixed an' nothing can alter it. An' we're not t' allow oor imaginations t' carry beyond the Scripture. We have oor own salvation t' work out wi' fear an' trembling. We hae nothing t' do wi' what's hidden. Only see that ye make it there yerself. That's enough for ye t' mind."

After tea, Mrs. Falconer sent Shargar to church with Betty. When Robert and she were alone together, "Laddie," she said, "ye must beware o' judging the Almighty. What looks t' ye like a wrong may be a right. We don't know all things. An' he's—he's not dead yet—I don't believe that he is—an' he may make it there yet."

Here her voice failed her. And Robert had nothing to say. He had had all his say before.

"Pray, Robert, pray for yer father, laddie," she resumed, "for we hae good reason t' be anxious aboot him. Pray while there's life an' hope. Give the Lord no rest. Pray t' him night an' day, as I do, that he would lead him t' see the error o' his ways an' turn t' the Lord who's ready t' pardon. If yer mother had lived, I would hae more hope, I confess, for she was a good lady an' pretty and sweet-tongued. But it was the care o' her heart aboot him that shortened her days. An' all that'll be laid upon him; he'll hae t' account for it. Eh, Robert, my man, be a good lad an' serve the Lord wi' all yer heart, an' soul, an' strength, an' mind. For if ye go wrong, yer own father will hae t' bear nobody knows how much punishment, for he's done nothing t' bring ye up i' the way ye should go. For the sake o' yer poor father, hold t' the right road. It may spare him a pang or two at the bad place. Eh, if the Lord would only take me an' let him go!"

Involuntarily and unconsciously the mother's love was adopting the hope which she had denounced in her grandson. Robert saw it, but was never one to push a victory. He said nothing. Only a tear or two at the memory of the wayward man he remembered rolled down his cheeks. His grandmother, herself weeping silently, took her neatly folded handkerchief from her pocket and wiped her grandson's fresh cheeks, then wiped her own withered face. And from that moment Robert knew that he loved her.

Then followed the Sabbath-evening prayer. They knelt down together and she uttered a long, extemporary prayer, full of Scripture phrases but not the less earnest and simple, for it flowed from a heart of goodness. Then Robert had to pray after her, loud in her ear, that she might hear him thoroughly, so that he often felt as if he were praying to her and not to God at all.

She had begun to teach him to pray so early in his life that the custom reached beyond the confines of his memory. At first he had had to repeat the words after her. Then she made him construct his own utterances, now and then giving him a suggestion when he fell silent, or putting a phrase into what she considered more suitable language.

On the present occasion, after she had ended her petitions with those for Jews and pagans and for the "Pope o' Rome," she turned to Robert with the usual, "Noo, Robert," and Robert began. But after he had gone on for some time with the ordinary phrases, he turned all at once into a new track. Instead of praying in general terms for "those that would not walk in the right way," he said, "O Lord! save my father," and there paused.

"If it be thy will," suggested his grandmother.

But Robert remained silent. His grandmother repeated the clause.

"I'm trying, Grandmother," said Robert, "but I can't say it. I dare not say an *if* about it. It would be like giving in to his damnation. We *must have* him saved, Grannie!"

"Laddie, laddie! hold yer tongue!" remonstrated Mrs. Falconer in a tone of distress. "O Lord, forgive him. He's young an' doesn't know better yet. He can't understand thy ways, nor for that matter can I pretend t' understand them myself. But thou art all light an' i' thee is no darkness at all. An' thy light comes int' oor blind eyes an' makes them blinder yet. But, O Lord, if it would please thee t' hear oor prayer—eh! how we would praise thee! An' my Andrew would praise thee more than ninety an' nine o' them that need no repentance."

A long pause followed. And then the only words that would come were, "For Christ's sake. Amen."

They rose from their knees and Mrs. Falconer sat down by her fire, with her feet on her little wooden stool, and began to quietly review her past life and follow her son through all conditions and circumstances to her imaginable. And when the world to come arose before her, clad in all the glories which her fancy, chilled by education and years, could supply, it was but to vanish in the gloom of the remembrance of poor Andrew with whom she dared not hope to share it.

She felt bound to go on believing as she had been taught, for sometimes the most original mind has the strongest sense of law upon it. Obedience was indeed an essential element of her creed. But she had not yet been sufficiently impressed with the truth that while obedience is the law of the kingdom, it is of considerable importance that that which is obeyed should in truth be the will of God. Mrs. Falconer's submission and obedience led her to accept as the will of God that which was anything but giving him honor to accept as such. Therefore, her love for God was too like the love of the slave or the dog, too little like the love of the child, whose obedience the Father cannot be satisfied with until he cares for His reason as the highest form of His will. True, the child who most faithfully desires to know the inward will or reason of the Father will be the most ready to obey without it. Only for obedience of this blind kind, it is essential that the apparent command at least be such as he can suppose attributable to the Father. Had Abraham doubted whether it was in any case right to slay his son, he would have been justified in doubting whether God really required it of him and would have been bound to delay action until the arrival of more light. The will of God can never be other than good; but I doubt if any man can ever be sure that a thing is the will of God except by seeing into its nature and character and beholding its goodness. Whatever God does must be right, but are we sure that we know what he does? That which men say he does may be very wrong indeed.

This burden she in her turn laid upon Robert. Her way with him was shaped after that which she recognized as God's way with her. "Ask no questions an' do as ye're told." And it was anything but a bad lesson for the boy. It was one of the best he could have had—that of authority. It is a grand thing to obey without asking any questions, so long as there is nothing evil in what is commanded. But though God makes no secrets, Grannie concealed her reasons without reason.

She sat with her feet on the little wooden stool, with Robert beside her staring into the fire, till they heard the outer door open. Shargar and Betty had come in from church.

10 / Robert's Mother _____

Early on the following morning, while Mrs. Falconer, Robert and Shargar were at breakfast, Mr. Lammie came to call. Older than Andrew, he had been a great friend of his father and likewise of some of Mrs. Falconer's own family. Therefore he was received with a kindly welcome. He had delayed coming with the intelligence he had received till he should be more certain of its truth. There was a cloud on his brow, which in a moment revealed that his errand was not a pleasant one.

"I haen't seen ye for a long time, Mr. Lammie.—It must be aboot school time for ye boys.—Sit down, Mr. Lammie, an' let's hear yer news."

"I came from Aberdeen last night, Mrs. Falconer," he began. "There's been some news."

"Humph!" returned the old lady. "Not aboot Andrew?"

" 'Deed it is, mem. And ill news, I'm sorry t' say."

"Is he taken?"

"Ay he is—by a jailor that won't lose the grip o' him."

"He's not dead, John Lammie? Don't say it."

"I must say it, Mrs. Falconer. I had it from Dr. Anderson, yer own cousin. I'm awfully sorry t' be the bearer o' such ill news, Mrs. Falconer, but I had no choice."

"Oh no! Oh no! The day o' grace is by at last. My poor Andrew!" exclaimed Mrs. Falconer and sat down in dumb silence.

Mr. Lammie tried to comfort her with some of the usual comfortless commonplaces. She neither wept nor replied; her face seemingly set in stone, she stared into her lap, till he finally rose and left her alone with her grief. A few minutes after he was gone, she rang the bell and told Betty to send Robert to her.

"He's gone t' the school, mem."

"Then run after him an' tell him t' come home."

When Robert appeared, wondering what his grandmother could want with him, she said, "Close the door, Robert. I can't let ye go t' school today. We must leave him out now."

"Leave what out, Grannie?"

"Him, *him*—Andrew. Yer father, laddie. I think my heart'll break."

"Leave him out of what, Grannie? I don't understand you."

"Leave him out o' oor prayers, laddie, an' I can't stand it."

"Why?"

"He's dead."

"Are you sure?" Robert's heart thudded in his chest.

"Ay, very sure—very sure, laddie."

"Well, I don't believe it."

"Why not?"

" 'Cause I won't believe it. I'm not bound to believe it, am I?"

"What's the good o' that? Why not believe it? Dr. Anderson's sent word o' it t' John Lammie. Oh no! Oh no!"

"I tell you, I won't believe it, Grannie, except God himself tells me. As long as I don't believe he's dead, I can keep him in my prayers. I'm not going to leave him out, I tell you, Grannie."

"Well, laddie, I can't argue wi' ye. I hae no heart t'. Come on."

She took him by the hand and rose, then let him go again, saying, "Shut the door, laddie."

Robert bolted the door and his grandmother, again taking his hand, led him to the usual corner. There they knelt down together and the old woman's prayer was one great and bitter cry for submission to the divine will. She rose a little strengthened, if not comforted, saying, "Ye must pray alone, laddie. But be a good lad, for ye're all that I hae left; an' if ye go wrong too, ye'll bring down my gray hairs wi' sorrow t' the grave. But if ye turn out well, I'll maybe hold my head up a bit yet. But oh, Andrew! my son! my son! Would t' God I had died for thee!"

The words opened the floodgates of her heart, and she wept in agony of heart. Robert left her weeping, and closed the door quietly as if his dead father had been lying in the room.

He went to his own garret, closed that door too, and sat down upon the floor with his back against the empty bedstead. There were no more castles to build now. It was all very well to say that he would not believe the news and would keep praying for his father. But he did believe it. His favorite pastime, seated there, had previously been to imagine how he would grow to become a great man and set out to seek his father, and would find him, and stand by him, and be his son and servant. Oh! to have the man stroke his head and pat his cheek and love him! One moment he imagined himself his defender, the next he would be climbing on his father's knee as if he were still a little child and laying his head on his shoulder. His heart yearned for a loving touch.

But all this was gone now. A dreary time lay before him, with nobody to please, nobody to serve, nobody to praise him. Grannie never praised him. She must have thought praise something wicked. And his father was in misery forever! Yet somehow that thought was not quite thinkable. It was more the vanishing of hope from his own life than a sense of his father's fate that oppressed him.

He cast his eyes, as in a hungry despair, around the empty room. It seemed as empty as life. There was nothing for his eyes to rest upon but those bundles and bundles of dust-browned papers on the shelves. What were they all about? He understood that they were his father's; now that he was dead, it would be no sacrilege to look at them. Nobody cared about them. He would at least see what they were.

Bills and receipts was all that met his view. Bundle after bundle he tried, with no better success toward anything of interest. But as he drew near the middle of the second shelf, on which they lay several rows deep, he saw something dark, hurriedly placed behind the packets. He reached out and withdrew a small workbox. His heart was beating like the prince in the fairy tale when he comes to the door of Sleeping Beauty.

He opened it with bated breath. The first thing he saw was a little gold thimble. Then his eyes met a lovely face, in miniature, with dark hair and what must have been deep blue eyes, looking earnestly upward at him from the box where she kept her few trifles. The picture was in an oval shape all set 'round with pearls. How Robert knew them to be pearls he could not tell, for he did not know that he had ever seen any pearls before; but he knew they were pearls and that pearls had something to do with the New Jerusalem. But the sadness of it all at length overpowered him and he burst out crying. It was awfully sad that his mother's portrait should be in her own box.

He took a bit of red yarn off a bundle of the papers, put it through the eye of the setting, and hung the tiny picture round his neck, inside his clothes, for Grannie must not see it. She would take that away as she had taken his fiddle. He had a nameless something now for which he had been longing for years.

Looking again in the box, he found a little bit of paper, discolored with age. Unfolding it he found written a well-known hymn, and at the bottom of the hymn, the words, "O Lord! my heart is very sore."

The treasure upon Robert's bosom was no longer the symbol of a mother's love, but of a woman's sadness, which he could not reach out to comfort. In that hour the boy made a great stride toward manhood. Doubtless his mother's grief had been the same as Grannie's—the fear that she would lose her husband forever. He looked no farther, but took the portrait from his neck and replaced it with the paper and put the box back, and walled it up in solitude once more with the dusty bundles. Then he went down to his grandmother, sadder and more desolate than ever.

He found her seated in his usual place. Her large print New Testament lay on the table beside her unopened; for where in its pages could she find comfort for a grief like hers? That it was the will of God might well comfort any suffering of her own, but would it comfort Andrew? And if there was no comfort for Andrew, how was Andrew's mother to be comforted?

Yet if God had given his firstborn son to save his brethren, how could he be pleased that she should dry her tears and be comforted? The awful questions with unknown answers plagued her unsettled mind. She could explain it to herself in some unknown force of necessity in God's economy of judgment and justice. But this did not make God more kind, for didn't he know the results every time he made a man? And would God have Andrew's very mother forget him, or worse still, remember him and try to be happy?

"Read a chapter t' me, laddie," she said.

Robert opened the book and read till he came to the words, " 'I pray not for the world.' "

"Andrew was o' the world," announced the old woman, "an' if Christ wouldn't pray for him, why should I?"

Already, so soon after her son's death, her theology had begun to harden her heart. The strife resulting from believing that the higher love demands the suppression of the lower is the most discordant example of the human house divided against itself; one moment all is given up for the will of God, the next the human tenderness rushes back in a flood. Mrs. Falconer burst into a very agony of weeping. From that day on, for many years, the name of her lost son Andrew never passed her lips in the hearing of her grandson.

But in a few weeks she was more cheerful. It is one of the mysteries of humanity how the infinite Love of the universe can support those in her circumstances, coming to them like sleep from the roots of their being at a level far beyond their opinions or beliefs. Not being able to trust the Father entirely, they yet say, "Who can tell what took place at the last moment? Who can tell whether God did not please to grant them saving faith at the eleventh hour?"—this God could do; this perhaps he might do for the son beloved of his mother!

O rebellious mother heart, so dear to God. If you would only read by your own large inner light instead of the glimmer from the phosphorescent brains of theologians, you might be able to understand the simple words of the Savior. Wishing his disciples to know of the regard he had for them, he said to his Father in their hearing, "I pray not for the world, but for them"—not for the world now, but for them, a meaningless statement if he never prayed for the world. It was a word of small

72

meaning if it was not his regular custom to pray for the world, for men as individuals whom he loved.

Lord Christ, not alone from the pains of hell or the darkness of self do we come to thee, but also to escape from the wretched words spoken in thy name. We seek thy feet to deliver us from the anger that arises within us at the degradation of thee and thy Father in the mouths of those that claim to have found thee. Pray for them also, Jesus, for they know not what they do.

11 / Mary St. John

After this, day followed day in calm, dull progress. Robert did not care for the games of his schoolfellows, so he passed his leisure time in the society of his grandmother and Shargar, except the few hours a week occupied by the lessons of the shoemaker. For he went ahead, though half-heartedly, with those lessons, given now upon Sandy's redeemed violin which he called his "auld wife," and made a little progress.

He took more and more to brooding in the garret. And as more questions presented themselves, he became more and more anxious to arrive at a solution, and more uneasy as he failed to satisfy himself that he had arrived at it. I believe that even the newborn infant is, in some of its moods, already grappling with the deepest metaphysical problems, in forms infinitely too rudimental for the understanding of the grown philosopher. If this be the case, it is no wonder that at Robert's age the deepest questions of his coming manhood should be in active operation, though still surrounded with the yoke of common belief. Thus, the embryo faith—which in minds like his always takes the form of doubt—could hardly yet be defined.

I have given a hint at the tendency of his mind already, in the fact that one of the most regular inquiries of his active brain was whether God would have mercy upon a repentant devil. He pondered many such weighty, if not impossible, dilemmas. He puzzled himself about perpetual motion; he wondered about the possibilities of somehow eluding the omniscience of God. While reading *Paradise Lost* he could not help sympathizing with Satan, and feeling that the Almighty seemed pompous, scarcely reasonable, and somewhat revengeful.

He was recognized among his schoolfellows as remarakable for his love of fair play; so much so that he was always their referee. Yet, notwithstanding his sympathy with Satan, he almost invariably sided with Mr. Innes against any seditious movement against the boys, even when unjustly punished himself as the result of an occasional appearance of seeming defiance. And even then he never showed any resentment.

He had long before this discovered who the "angel" was who had appeared to him at the top of the stair on that memorable night. One brief glimpse of her at the window as he passed in the street had told

73

him all he needed to know. But he had hardly seen her again. During the whole winter she scarcely left the house, partly from the negative influence on her health at the sudden change to a northern climate, and partly from the attention required by her aunt. It was to aid in nursing her that she had left the warmer South.

But long before the winter was over, Rothieden had discovered that the stranger, the English girl—most, however, called her the English "leddy," her looks making her appear several years older than she actually was—Mary St. John, had a musical gift altogether as new as her name. For not only was she an admirable performer on the piano, but when she sang as she played, it was not unusual for quite a small crowd to gather in the evening by the window of Mrs. Forsyth's drawing room to listen. More than once, when Robert had not found Sandy Elshender at home on the lesson night and had gone to seek him, he had discovered him leaning against the wall of the Captain's house, lying in wait like a fowler to catch the sweet sounds that flew from the cage of her instrument.

On the first such occasion, Robert stared at the shoemaker, doubting at first whether he had not been drinking. But the intoxication of music produced such a different expression from that of drink that Robert soon saw that if he had indeed been drinking, at least by now the music had gained the upper hand. As long as the playing went on, Elshender was not to be moved from the window. Robert, however, being as yet more capable of melody than harmony, grudged to lose a lesson on Sandy's "auld wife of a fiddle" for any moment of Miss St. John's playing.

One gusty evening—it was the last day of March—a bleak wind was driving up the long street of the town, and Robert was standing looking out one of the windows of his upstairs room. The late afternoon was closing into night. He hardly knew how he had come to be there; but when he thought about it, he remembered it was play-Wednesday and that he had been all the half-holiday trying in vain one thing after another to interest himself. He knew nothing about east winds; but nonetheless, this day's weary wind of the dreary March had cast a spirit of melancholy over his soul.

They had had tea early and his grandmother had taken to her bed, bitten to the very bones from the chill wind and slanting rain driving against the windowpanes. Betty busied herself in the kitchen when not attending to Mrs. Falconer's persistent sickbell. Shargar had by this time been given liberty throughout most of the house and now occupied himself in the parlor, where, I presume, the warmth of the fire rather than the duty of his lessons served as the primary attraction. Robert had been alone in the upper regions of the house for some time, and remained there, even after night had well-enclosed Rothieden.

How long he stood thus before the windows, which revealed nothing but wintry blackness, he could not have told. All at once he heard from behind him a noise.

Awaking from his reverie he glanced behind him, thinking it to be Shargar or Betty coming to look for him. But what the scraping sound could be, like that of a stubborn doorjamb, he was not able to imagine.

Turning, he approached the stair hallway. There were no footsteps advancing up the stairs, and indeed, no Shargar nor Betty. Instead his eyes became aware of a strange, faint flickering light. He peeped out and saw, to his amazement, that it originated from the handleless door at the landing, which stood open some eight to ten inches.

Robert stole closer, but as he reached it from the blind side, the door began silently to close, the uncertain hand on its other side apparently deciding further entry too perilous.

"Wait," he whispered as loudly as he dared, glancing back down the stairs to the occupied portion of the house.

The retreat of the door halted. Robert placed his hand on the door's edge and drew it slowly open toward him as he stepped around it and into the light of the candle, which now threw its wavering shadows into the darkened stairway of his once private haunt.

There stood, just as he had seen her before, Robert's one-time angel, candle in hand, exploring again the regions of her new abode.

"Excuse me," she said. "I'm sorry, I didn't mean to—"

Robert quickly silenced her with a finger on his lips.

"Not here," he whispered. "My grandmother, even in her bedroom, has uncanny hearing."

She remained motionless for an awkward moment of silence, eyes darting about the darkness, perhaps wondering from what corner ever-vigilant Mrs. Falconer might swoop down upon this unwelcome intruder into her home.

Seeing the fright on her face, and not knowing what to do, Robert hesitated, then said in a low voice, "Would you—would you like to see our garret room?"

She waivered, uncertain, glanced into the face of the boy gazing at her from out of the darkness, apparently judged herself in good hands, and finally nodded.

"Is it safe?" she whispered, stepping onto the landing.

Robert nodded, then led the way up to Shargar's room. She followed, candle in hand. Once inside Robert closed the door.

"This is the top of the house," he said, venturing to speak above a whisper. "The Captain's, where you are, is a floor taller."

"My room is on the second floor," she replied. "A little trapdoor opening into it is what led me to the door where you found me."

"My father built that house," said Robert. "I was born in it."

"How delightful!" she responded with a smile.

"I saw you here once before," said Robert, "but I don't think you saw me that night. I thought you were an angel."

She laughed a sweet, muscial laughter. "No angel. Only a curious neighbor. Are you Mrs. Falconer's grandson?"

"Yes, miss. My name's Robert Falconer."

"And mine's Mary St. John. I'm the Captain's niece."

"Everyone in town knows your name. I've watched you play your piano a time or two from the street."

Her blush was hidden in the obscure light. "Is this your room, Robert?" she asked.

"Oh, no. This is where Shargar stays. I sleep downstairs in a tiny room next to my grannie."

"Is he that tall odd-looking boy I've seen you walking to school with? Your brother, I suppose?"

Now it was Robert's turn to laugh.

"Not my brother. Just a homeless creature Grannie took in."

"From what I've heard of your grandmother, I didn't think she had room in her heart for outcasts."

"Grannie's heart's bigger than it looks, miss. But maybe you're right. I suppose it was me that befriended him, and then Grannie agreed to let him stay till his mother comes back to claim him."

"His mother left him?" asked Mary in alarm.

"Ay. She's a Gypsy, you know."

"That's so sad," she said with a sigh, then stopped.

Robert looked toward her and thought he detected a tear falling down her cheek.

"How could a mother do such a thing?" she asked at length.

"I don't know, miss. I never knew my mother."

"Oh, Robert! What a wonderful thing, then, for you to take Shargar in like you have. There must truly be love in your heart."

"I try to do what's right, that's all. There's no more in my heart than yours, miss. You should see the faces of the men listening to the music you make."

"Oh, that's easy. I love music. My love for playing and singing is something they feel, I guess. But to serve others like that!"

"Dooble Sanny says you're taking care of your invalid aunt."

"Dooble Sanny?"

"The village shoemaker. He's teaching me to play the violin."

"A musician too!"

"Only one who dreams to be, miss."

"Please, Robert. I'm not old enough to be a 'miss.' Call me Mary."

"If you please, miss—Mary. But I'm afraid we mustn't stay here longer. My grannie has already discovered more than one plot hatched in this room."

They rose to leave.

And just in time. For as they approached the door between the two houses, Robert could hear Shargar's clumping step passing the kitchen. With a parting look Robert shut the door softly behind her, heard the latch click on the other side, and was again left alone.

Turning away from the door, behind him he heard the words: "Eh, Bob."

12 / Dreams

This was not the last of such night meetings between the Scottish lad and English maiden. Mary soon contrived, by listening intently at the door, to determine whether Robert was alone or whether Shargar was also in the precincts of the garret. And Robert more than once took himself to experimenting with a gentle knocking on his side of the door, seeing if he might arouse the mysterious angel-lass to attempt a visit. And it must be admitted, notwithstanding his terror of discovery by his grandmother, that Robert sought the upper regions of the house more frequently in the constant hope of seeing the one whose candlelit face and radiant eyes he could not remove from his mind's eye.

What he felt was not yet love, not even puppy love, but indeed an infatuation of a different sort—far deeper and more lasting if nurtured properly. And the bond between the two young people, though slow to form, found nourishment. For it was a bond not only of secret friendship but of a mutual attraction born out of respect. From their first meeting each saw in the other a quality of life which, though at their ages they would not have stopped to define as such, a desire to serve others.

After several brief encounters in Shargar's garret, Robert ventured, upon Mary's request, into the Captain's house. Terror nearly froze his every footstep, however, and he only managed to stay some two or three minutes before the compulsion became overpowering to return to the security of Grannie's home, over which her watchful eye and listening ear reigned supreme.

That night he dreamed himself alone with Mary in her room, seated on her bed playing cards (a thing in reality he would never dare). As he sat there, suddenly the door burst open and in rushed the Captain to the center of the room in full military adornment. But as Robert looked up, behold it was Grannie's face, more awful in its wrath than he had yet imagined it. Not a word she spoke but extended her long arm in stern command pointing to the door with a long, bony finger, banishing Robert from her sight forever.

Outside he walked. Snow fell in a fury. He had neither cap nor coat and was clothed in rags. His feet were bare. Away from the house he slowly trudged, turning once to look back. Grannie stood at the door, stone-faced in her silent rebuke, still pointing him away—away. Down the street he walked toward what should have been Rothieden. But no houses, no shops, no town was there. Only desolation. In the distance he could see flames which grew larger with every step he took. He knew then that he had not merely been turned out of Grannie's house and cast adrift, but that he had been banished to hell and had already arrived at its outskirts.

On he walked. The freezing of his feet did not abate as he neared the towering fire which was now all about him. The flames licked his bare legs and burned his unprotected feet. Around him the flames swarmed, charring his skin black, searing his eyes to blindness. The pain grew agonizing; laughing voices tormented him. Still he walked, deeper into the fire. Flames were now all he could see—hot, burning flames. Still he walked, deeper into the abyss of eternal punishment.

In the distance the flames parted and he perceived a small hut, no more than a shack. It burned but was not consumed. Still the mocking voices urged him on, and he knew in his soul that this house symbolized the life he had made for himself by his wicked life, the house prepared for him in which to sit out his eternity in the fires of hell. Into the shack he walked. And behold, it was Shargar's old hovel with nothing inside but a two-legged stool. He sat down, alone, and began to weep. Suddenly he cried out, "But, Grannie, I didn't mean to do anything wrong! Please forgive me."

Instantly he awoke, sitting up in his own bed, drenched in a cold sweat. Anxiously he glanced toward Grannie's room, but she still slept soundly. Breathing deeply, with heart pounding, he eased himself back down under the blankets. But it was some time before he slept again that night.

It was two weeks before Robert saw Mary again. The dream had terrified him, and certain doubtful glances Grannie had cast his way caused him to dread what might be passing in her thoughts. She had unearthed Shargar in his hiding place; she had discovered the precious violin. Was she not certain to detect something in his countenance to reveal his clandestine meetings as well? Together late at night with a girl, and in her bedroom too—who could tell but that such might indeed be a sin punishable by several thousand years in the flames of hell. In any case, he dared not rouse his Grannie's innate curiosity any further than absolutely necessary.

On one of the first mornings in the beginning of summer, Robert awoke early and lay, as was his custom, thinking. Looking out the window at the brilliant morning light he saw a long streamer of honeysuckle, not yet in bloom but alive with the life of spring, blown by the gentle wind against his windowpane and making a gentle tapping, as if calling him to get up and look out.

He rose from the bed but was startled to see, within a few feet of his window, the lovely face he had never seen up close except by candlelight. And now that the sunlight fell full on it, he was certain of what before he had only suspected—that it was the most beautiful face he had ever seen. For the window looked directly into the garden of the next house; its honeysuckle tapped at his window; its sweetpeas grew against his windowsill. How different her face looked when illuminated by the morning sun—at one moment older and more ladylike; at the next more childlike and innocent. The first thought that came to him was the shoemaker's idea about his grandfather's violin being a woman. A vaguest dream-vision of her having escaped from his grandmother's closet to wander free amid the wind and among the flowers outside his window crossed his mind before he had recovered sufficiently from his surprise at seeing her.

For a few moments Robert sat on his bed gazing at her face which brooded over the bush she was attending to, falling back into the reverie she had interrupted. When he awoke to the present some moments later and was about to tap quietly on the glass, all at once she raised herself, turned, and vanished from the field of the window.

Even after this, when the evening grew dark, Robert would steal out of the house, leaving his book open by Grannie's lamp that it might seem to say, "He will come back presently," and dart round the corner with quick, quiet step, to hear if Mary was playing. If she was not, he would return to the Sabbath stillness of the parlor where his grandmother sat meditating or reading, and Shargar sat brooding over the freedom of the old days before Mrs. Falconer had begun to reclaim him. There he would set himself once more at his book, to rise again in another hour and listen again to see whether the stream might not be flowing now. If he found her at her piano, he would stand listening in delight until the fear of being missed drove him in. Thus strangely did his evening life oscillate between the somber silence of Grannie's parlor and the gladness of the Captain's window. And skillfully did he manage his retreats and returns, curtailing his absences with such moderation that, for a long time, they awoke no suspicion in the mind of his grandmother.

I suspect that the old lady thought he had gone to his prayers in the garret, having no idea that the garret now represented equal enchantment to her grandson for the possibilities it bore. I believe she thought he was praying for his dead father, a Catholic observance she could hardly sanction. But neither would she interfere, for she knew Robert would defend himself with the simple assertion that he did not believe his father was dead. Shargar would glance up at him with a questioning look as he came in from these excursions, drop his head over his task again, look busy and miserable, and all would glide on as before.

13 / Mr. Lammie's Farm _____

When the first real summer weather came, Mr. Lammie paid Mrs. Falconer another visit. He had not been able to get over the memory of the desolation in which he had left her and wanted to do something for her. He was accompanied by his daughter, a woman approaching the further verge of youth, bulky and florid, and as full of tenderness as her large frame could hold. The purpose of his call was to try to persuade Mrs. Falconer to pay them a visit for a couple of weeks at their home, some three miles from Rothieden. After much, and for a long time apparently useless persuasion, they at last believed they had prevailed upon her to accept their invitation. But then she retreated within another of her defenses.

"I can't leave the two laddies alone. They would be up t' no end o' mischief."

"There's Betty to look after them," suggested Miss Lammie.

"Betty!" returned Mrs. Falconer with scorn. "Betty's nothing but a bairn herself!"

"But why shouldn't ye bring the lads with ye?" suggested Mr. Lammie.

"I've no right t' burden ye wi' them."

"Well, I've often wondered what made ye burden yerself with that Shargar, as I understand they call him," said Miss Lammie.

"Just a bit o' greed," returned the old lady, with the nearest approach to a smile that had shown itself upon her face in weeks.

"I don't understand ye, Mistress Falconer."

"I'm sure o' having it back, ye know—wi' interest," she returned.

"How's that? His father won't send ye any thanks for keeping him alive."

"He that giveth t' the poor lendeth t' the Lord, ye know."

"Well, if ye like to trust to that bank, no doubt one way or another it'll go to yer account," said Miss Lammie.

"It would ill become us, anyway, not t' give him shelter for yer sake, Mrs. Falconer, since it's yer will t' make the poor lad one o' the family. They say his own mother's run away and left 'im."

" 'Deed, she's done that."

"Can ye make anything o' 'im?"

"He's quiet enough. An' Robert says he does not so bad at the school."

"Well, just bring him with ye. We'll have some place or other t' put him."

"No, no, there's the schooling. What's t' be done wi' that?"

"They can go in the morning, and get their dinner with Betty here at the house, and then come to our home to their four o'clock tea when school's over in the afternoon. 'Deed, mem, ye must just come for the sake o' the old friendship a'tween the families."

"Well, if it must be so, it must be so," yielded Mrs. Falconer with a sigh.

She had not left her house for a single night for ten years. Nor is it likely she would have now given in, for immovableness was one of the most marked of her characteristics, had she not been so broken by mental suffering that she did not care much about anything.

Innumerable were the instructions in propriety of behavior which she gave the boys. The probability being that they would behave just as well as at home, these instructions were altogether unnecessary. Scarcely less unnecessary were the directions she gave Betty for her absence, who received them all in erect submission, with her hands under her apron.

"Now, Betty, ye must be quiet. An' don't stand at the door i' the evening. An' don't stand clacking an' jawing wi' the other lasses when ye go t' the well for water. And when ye go int' a shop, don't hae them saying behind yer back as soon as ye're out again, 'She's her own mistress now,' or such like. An' mind ye hae worship wi' yerself when I'm not here t' hae it wi' ye. Ye can come int' the parlor if ye like. An' don't give the lads everything they want. Give them plenty t' eat, but not too much. Folk should quit wi' still a little appetite."

Mr. Lammie brought his gig at last and took Grannie away to Bodyfauld. When the boys returned from school at the dinner hour, it was to exult in a freedom which Robert had never before imagined. But even he could not know what a relief it was to Shargar to eat without the eyes of Mrs. Falconer watching, as it seemed to him, the progress of every mouthful down his throat. The old lady would have been shocked to learn how the imagination of the ill-mothered lad interpreted her care over him. But she would not have been surprised to know that the two were merry in her absence. She knew that, in some of her moods, it would be a relief to think that the awful eye of God was not upon her. But she little thought that, even in the lawless proceedings about to follow, her Robert, who now felt such a relief in her absence, would in actuality be walking straight on toward his own sunrise of faith.

Merriment, however, was not in Robert's thoughts, and still less was mischief. For the latter, whatever his grandmother might think, he had no capacity. The world was already too serious for mischief. But from the moment he heard of his grandmother's intended visit, one wild hope had arisen within him.

When Betty came to the parlor door to set the table for their midday dinner that first day, she found it locked.

"Open the door!" she cried, but in vain. She grew impatient, then passionate. But still there came no response from within. For the two boys, this was an opportunity not to be lost by any means. Dull Betty never suspected what they were about. They were ranging about the place, looking high and low and in every corner for the dead old gentleman's violin. How eagerly they sought it! Sometimes Robert would stop, stand still in the middle of the room, cast a mathematical glance about, surveying its cubic contents, and then dart off in whatever direction suggested further search. Shargar, on the other hand, appeared to rummage blindly, without seeming to cast as much as a single thought upon his endeavors. Yet to him in the end fell the success. When hope was growing dim, after a long period of vain looking in every conceivable recess, a sudden scream heralded the resurrection of "the leddy." He had found the instrument in Mrs. Falconer's bed, at the foot between the feathers and mattress. For one happy moment Shargar was the benefactor and Robert the grateful recipient. Nor do I believe that this thread of the thickening cable that bound them was ever forgotten; broken it could not be.

Robert drew the recovered treasure from its hiding place and opened the case with trembling eagerness. He drew it out by the neck, grasped the bow in his other hand, and for a moment seemed ready to dare confront even the silence of the parlor with music.

"Betty'll hear ye," said Shargar, perceiving his intent.

"What do I care? She won't dare tell. I know how to manage her."

"But wouldn't it be better she didn't know?"

"She's sure to find out when she makes the bed. She turns it over and over, just like a dog playing with a rat."

"If we do it right, she'll be none the wiser. Ye don't play tunes on the box, man," was Shargar's perceptive response.

Robert caught the idea at last. He lifted the "bonny leddy" from her coffin, and while he was absorbed in contemplating her beauty, Shargar picked up a huge devotional book, the torment of his life on the Sunday evenings when it was his turn to spend it alone with Mrs. Falconer, and threw it into the case, which he then buried carefully in the bed. He took care Robert should not know of the substitution of the book for the fiddle, because he knew Robert could not tell a lie and when it turned up missing, he was certain Mrs. Falconer would question them intently about it.

Robert now had to hide the violin better than his grannie had done. And at the same time he had to be far more delicate, seeing it had lost its shell and he did not want to put her in the hands of the shoemaker again. It took a good deal of thought to decide on the place that would be the least unsuitable. First he put it in the well of the clock case, but then thoughts of the awful consequences if one of the weights should fall from the gradual decay of its cord. He had heard of such a thing happening. Then he thought he would put it in the room of his dreams and meditations. But what if Betty should take a fancy to change her bedroom or some friend of Grannie's come to spend the night? If he put her under the bed, the mice would get at her strings—or perhaps gnaw a hole right through her beautiful body. At length he decided to wrap her in a piece of paper and place her on the top of the chintz tester of his bed, where there was just room between it and the ceiling. That would serve till he could find some better sanctuary. In the meantime she was safe, and the boy was the blessedest boy in creation.

These things done, they were just in the humor to have a lark with Betty. So they unbolted the parlor door, rang the bell, and when Betty appeared, red-faced and wrathful, they asked her very seriously and politely whether they were not going to have something to eat before they went back to school; they now had only twenty minutes left. Betty was so dumbfounded with their impudence that she could hardly say a word, and revealed her indignation only in her manner of hastily casting the things on the table.

That afternoon, after school was out, what a delightful walk of three miles the boys had to Mr. Lammie's farm—over hill and dale and moor and farm. That first summer walk, with a goal before them, in all the freshness of the recent spring, was to Robert something to remember in after years with nothing short of ecstasy. The westering sun threw long shadows before them as they trudged away eastward, lightly laden with the books they needed for tomorrow's lessons. Once beyond the immediate environs of the town and the various places of land occupied by its inhabitants, they crossed a small river and entered a region of little hills, some covered with trees, others cultivated, and some bearing only heather, now nursing in secret its purple flame for the outburst of the autumn. The road wound between, now swampy and worn into deep ruts, now sandy and broken with large stones. Here and there green fields, fenced with stones overgrown with moss, would stretch away on both sides, sprinkled with busily feeding cattle. They passed through an occasional farmstead, perfumed with the breath of cows and the odor of burning peat. The scent of the oaks and larches would steal from the hill, or the wind would waft the odor of the white clover to Robert's nostrils, and he would turn aside to pull his grandmother a handful. Then they climbed a high ridge, on the top of which spread a moorland, dreary and desolate. This crossed, they descended between young plantations of firs and rowan trees and birches till they reached a warm house on the side of the slope, with farm buildings and ricks of corn and hay all about it, the front overgrown with roses and honeysuckle. From the open kitchen door came the smell of something good. But beyond all was the welcome of Miss Lammie, whose small, pudgy hand closed upon his like a very love pudding, after partaking of which even his grandmother's stately reception, followed immediately by the words, "Now be quiet," could not chill the warmth in his heart.

What a wonderful time were those next few days at Bodyfauld. To a boy like Robert, the daily changes from country to town with the bright morning, from town to country with the sober evening, were a source of boundless delight. Instead of houses he saw the horizon; instead of streets or walled gardens he roamed over the fields, bathed in sunlight and wind. Here it was especially good to get up before the sun, for then he could see the sun get up. And of all things, those evening shadows, lengthening out over the grassy wildernesses, were a deepening marvel.

14 / The Factory_____

Grannie's first action every evening, the moment the boys entered the room, was to glance up at the clock that she might see whether they had arrived in reasonable time. This was not pleasant because it reminded Robert how impossible it was for him to have a lesson on his own violin so long as the visit to Bodyfauld lasted. If they had only been allowed to sleep at Rothieden, what a universe of freedom would have been theirs! As it was, he had but two hours to himself in the middle of the day. Dooble Sanny might have given him a lesson at that time, but he did not dare carry his instrument through the streets of the town, for the proceeding would be certain to come to his grandmother's ears. Several days passed before he made up his mind as to how he was to reap any immediate benefit from the recovery of the violin. And even after he had decided to run the risk of midday solos in the old factory, he was not prepared to carry the instrument through the streets, or be seen entering the place with it.

But the factory lay at the opposite corner of a quadrangle of gardens, the largest of which was its own. And the corner of this garden touched the corner of Captain Forsyth's, which had formerly belonged to Andrew Falconer. Robert's father had had a door made in the walls at this point of junction so that he could go from his house to his business. If this door were not locked and Robert could pass without offense, what a "northwest passage" it would be for him! The little garden belonging to his grandmother's house had only a slight wooden fence to divide it from the other, in the middle of which was a little gate. The blessed thought came to him as he lay in bed at Bodyfauld: he would attempt the passage the very next day, through his grandmother's yard, across the Captain's garden to the garden of the factory, and into the building— unseen by anyone.

That following afternoon with his violin in its paper under his arm, he sped like a hare from the gate to the door between the two gardens, found it not even latched, only pushed shut and rusted so badly that it was dangerous to the hinges to disturb it. He opened it carefully, however, without any accident, and went through. Then closing it behind him, he continued on more leisurely through the tangled grass of his grandmother's property. When he reached the factory he thought it prudent to look for a more secret nook, one more full of silence—that is, where the sounds would be less likely to reach the ears of the passersby. Finally he came upon a small room, near the top, which had been the manager's bedroom and which no one had apparently entered for years. It seemed the safest place in the world.

He undid his instrument carefully, tuned its strings tenderly, and soon found that his former facility, such as it was, had not left him beyond recovery. Hastening back as he had come, he was just in time for his dinner and narrowly escaped encountering Betty in the hall. He had been tempted to leave the instrument in the factory, but who could tell what might happen?

He did the same for several days without interrupton; not, however, without observation. Returning from his fourth visit, when he opened the door between the gardens, he started back in dismay, for there stood his friend of the night.

Robert hesitated for a moment between whether to fly or speak. The previous familiarity which had arisen between them somehow vanished in the surprise of seeing her unexpectedly, bathed in sunlight, standing right before him. He froze there with the secret violin under his arm.

"I beg your pardon, miss. I thought nobody would see me."

"I've been watching you from the house these last two days," said Mary, "and wondering what you were up to."

"I haven't done ill to the Captain's garden."

"I had not the least suspicion of it," laughed Mary. "But I do suspect that some music is not far off."

"You won't tell anybody, will you, Mary?"

"Not if you play me a melody, Robert."

"Oh, I dare not, miss. You see, I found my grandfather's fiddle, but my grandmother thinks the fiddle is evil. So she took it and hid it. But I found it again. And I dare not play it in the house, though my grannie's in the country, for Betty would hear me and tell her. And so I go to the old factory there. It belongs to my grannie and so does the garden. And this house and yard was once my father's and so he had that door put there, they tell me. And I thought if it should be open it would be a fine way for me to come and go without people seeing me. Please, you won't tell the Captain or his wife, will you, else word'll get out one way or another to my grannie?"

She nodded with a smile that reminded Robert not of an angel but of a princess. He took off his cap, thanked her with much heartiness, if not with much polish, and ran back to his grandmother's through the gate.

She restrained her musical hopes that day, but when she saw Robert pass the next afternoon, young Mary St. John put on her bonnet and, after allowing him time to reach his den, followed him in the hope of finding out for herself how well he could play. For by now her interest in Robert was equally the equivalent of his in her.

She felt a little eerie as she entered the factory, wasted and silent with its motionless machines all about. Hearing no violin, she waited for a while on the ground floor of the building, but still hearing nothing she finally made her way up to the second floor. But here likewise all was silence. She hesitated, but at length gathered what remained of her courage and ventured up the next stair, beginning, however, to feel not only eerie but troubled as well—the silence was so obstinately persistent. It wasn't possible, was it, that there was no violin in the brown paper and that the boy was a liar?

Passing shelves piled up with stores of old thread, still she went on, led by a curiosity stronger than her gathering fear. At last she came to a little room, the door of which was open. And there, to her horror, she saw Robert lying on the floor with his head in a small pool of blood.

Now, Mary St. John was both brave and kind. Though clearly she too was in danger where violence had so soon before been used on Robert, she set about assisting him at once. His face was deathlike, but she did not think he was dead. She tried to drag him out into the passage, but though she was a year or two older, Robert's frame was considerably larger than her own, and she had a difficult time moving him. She did what she could to revive him, but it was some time before he began to breathe more easily. At last his lips moved and he murmured, "Sandy, Sandy, you've broken my bonny leddy."

Then he opened his eyes, and seeing a face to dream about bending over him, closed them again with a smile and a sigh, as if to prolong his dream.

The blood now returned quickly to his pale cheeks and began to ooze from the wound in his head. Mary took out her handkerchief and bound it up. He tried to rise, though with difficulty, and stared wildly about him, saying with blurred articulation, "Father, father!" Then he looked at the girl stooped over him with a kind of dazed questioning in his eyes, tried several times to speak, but could not.

"Can you walk at all?" she asked, supporting him, for she was anxious to leave the place.

"Yes, miss, well enough," he answered.

"Come along, then."

"But, Mary!" he said suddenly in alarm, as if just recognizing her, "How do you come to be here?"

"Never mind that, Robert. You're hurt. Come. I will help you home."

"No, no," he said, as if he had just recalled something. "Don't mind me. Run home, Mary, or he'll see you."

"Who will see me?"

Robert stared about more wildly, put his hand to his head, and made no reply. She half led, half supported him down the stair as far as the first landing, where he cried out in a tone of anguish: "My bonny leddy!"

"What is it, Robert?" she asked, thinking he meant her.

"My fiddle! my fiddle! She'll be all in bits," he answered, and turned to go up again.

"Sit down here," she said, "and I'll fetch it."

Though not without considerable fear, she hurried back up to the room. She then turned faint for the first time, but determinedly supporting herself, she looked about the room. Seeing a brown-paper parcel on a shelf revived her enough for her to lay her hands on the prized instrument and leave the room with a shudder.

Robert stood leaning against the wall. He stretched out his hands eagerly.

"Give me her. Give me her."

"You had better let me carry it, Robert."

"No, no, miss. You don't know how easy she is to hurt."

"Oh, yes, I do, Robert," returned Mary smiling, and Robert could not withstand the smile.

"Well, take care of her as you would your own self, Mary," he said, yielding.

He was now much better, and before he had been in the open air two minutes, insisted that he was quite well. When they reached Captain Forsyth's garden, he again held out his hands for his violin.

"No, no," said his friend. "You wouldn't have Betty see you like that, would you?"

"No, miss, but I'll put the fiddle at my own window and she won't see it," answered Robert, not understanding her. Though he felt a good deal of pain, he had no idea how dreadful he looked.

"Don't you know that you have a wound on your head?" she asked.

"No! have I?" said Robert, putting up his hand. "But I must go—there's nothing I can do about it. If I could only get to my room without Betty seeing me. Eh, miss, I have spoiled your dress."

"Don't mind that, Robert, It's no matter. But you must come with me. I must see what I can do for your head."

"You are kind. You must be like my mamma was."

The word *mamma* was the only remnant of her that lingered in his speech. They were now walking toward the house.

"Is she dead?"

"For a long time. And, so they tell me, is yours."

"Yes, and my father too. Your father is alive, I hope?"

Robert made no answer. A strange look came over his face and he seemed to struggle with something in his throat. She thought he was going to faint again and hurried him into the drawing room. It was unoccupied; her uncle was out and her aunt was in her own room.

"Sit down," she said, and Robert sat on the edge of a chair. Then she left the room and presently returned with a little brandy. "There," she said, offering the glass. "This will do you good."

"What is it?"

"Brandy. Mixed with water of course."

"I daren't touch it. Grannie couldn't stand me to touch it."

So determined was he that the girl was forced to yield. She wondered that the boy who would deceive his grandmother about a violin should be so immovable with regard to a drink of brandy for medicinal purposes.

"Eh, miss! If you would play something on *her*," Robert resumed, pointing to the piano. "It would do me more good than a whole bottle of brandy, or whiskey either."

"How do *you* know that?" Mary asked, proceeding to sponge his wound lightly.

" 'Cause many's the time I've stood out on the street listening. Dooble Sanny says that you play just as if you were my grandfather's fiddle herself, turned into the bonniest creature ever God made."

Mary blushed imperceptibly and turned away briefly, then quickly changed the subject. "How did you get such a terrible cut?"

Robert was silent. Mary glanced into his face, but he was staring as if he had heard nothing.

"Did you fall? Or how else did you cut your head, Robert?"

"Yes, yes, miss, I fell," he answered hastily, with an air of relief, and with what seemed a tone of gratitude for the suggestion of a true answer.

"What made you fall?"

Silence was his only reply once more. Thereafter she too was silent, and Robert thought she was offended. Possibly he felt a change in the touch of her fingers, cool and soft, on his forehead where she was still ministering gently to the cut in question.

"Miss—Mary. I would like to tell you," he said, "but I daren't."

"That's all right; never mind," she returned kindly.

"Would you promise not to tell anybody?"

"I don't want to know," she answered. "It would be best for you not to tell me."

An uncomfortable silence followed.

"You had better go," said Mary at length, "or Betty will miss you."

"Could you not just play me something, anything, before I do?"

She smiled, then nodded and walked to the piano. When she had finished a lovely little air, which sounded to Robert like the touch of her hands and the warmth of her breath on his forehead, he sat in rapt silence for a few moments, then rose to take his leave. He thanked her, made a bow in which awkwardness and grace were curiously mingled, took up his precious parcel, and slowly left the house.

Not even to Shargar did he communicate his adventure. And he did not return to the deserted factory to play there. Fate had again interposed between him and his bonny leddy.

When he reached Bodyfauld that evening, he fancied his grandmother's eyes more watchful of him than usual. But he managed to keep his wound a secret by keeping his hair combed down over it.

When he woke the next morning, it was with the consciousness of having seen something strange, and only when he came to himself and realized he was not in his own room at home was he convinced that it must have been a dream. For in the night he had awakened, or so he thought, to see the moon shining onto the face of the clock whose hands stood at midnight. Close by the clock stood the bureau, with its end against the partition forming the head of his grannie's bed.

All at once he saw a tall man in a blue coat and bright buttons about to open the lid of the bureau. The same moment he saw a little elderly man in a brown coat and a brown wig, standing by his side, who sought to remove his hand from the lock. Next appeared a huge stalwart figure, in shabby old tartans, who laid his hand on the head of each of the other two. The wonder widened, for then came a stately Highlander, with his broadsword by his side and an eagle's feather in his hat, who laid his hand on the other Highlander's arm.

When Robert looked in the direction where all this had taken place, the head of his grannie's bed had vanished and a wild hillside, covered with stones and heather, sloped away in the distance. Over it passed man after man, each with an ancestral air, while on the gray sea to the left, galleys covered with Norsemen tore up the white foam. How long he gazed he did not know, but when he withdrew his eyes from the scene, there stood the figure of his father, still trying to open the lid of the bureau, his grandfather resisting him, the blind piper with his hand on the head of both, and the stately chief with his hand on the piper's arm. Then a mist gathered over the whole, till at last he awoke and found himself in the little wooden room at Bodyfauld. Doubtless his loss of blood the day before had something to do with the dream. He rose and after a good breakfast, found himself very little the worse, and forgot all about the dream till something happened not long afterward which recalled it vividly to mind.

The enchantment of Bodyfauld soon wore off. The boys had no time to enter into the full enjoyment of country ways because of the weary lessons over which Mrs. Falconer kept as strict a watch as ever. To Robert, having to leave his violin and Miss St. John to make the afternoon walk to the country caused it to become almost a drudgery. After two weeks, the return to home in town was almost as happy an event to him as the first going had been. And now he could resume his music lessons with the shoemaker!

15 / Nature's Claim on Robert ⎯⎯⎯⎯⎯⎯

Before the day of return arrived, Robert had taken care to remove the violin from his bedroom and take it once more to its old retreat in Shargar's garret. The very first evening that Grannie again spent in her own armchair, he left the house as soon as it grew dusk and made his way with his brown-paper parcel to Sandy Elshender's.

Entering the narrow passage from which his shop door opened and hearing him hammering away at a sole, Robert stood and unfolded his treasure. Then he drew a low sigh from her with his bow and awaited the result. He heard the lapstone fall thundering on the floor and in an instant Dooble Sanny appeared in the door with his leather in one hand and the hammer in the other.

"Lordsake, man! Have ye gotten her back again? Give me a hold o' her!" he cried, dropping leather and hammer.

"No, no," returned Robert, retreating toward the outer door. "You must swear upon her that when I want her, I'll have her without argument, or I won't let you lay a bow upon her."

"I swear't, Robert; I swear't upon *her*," said the shoemaker hurriedly, stretching out both his hands as if to receive some human being into his embrace.

Robert placed the violin into the grimy hands. A look of heavenly delight dawned over the hairy and dirt-smeared face, which drooped into tenderness as he drew the bow across the instrument and wiled from her a thin wail as a sorrow at their long separation. He then retreated into his den and was soon sunk into a trance, deaf to everything but the violin. None of Robert's entreaties, who longed for a lesson, could rouse him, and he eventually had to go home unrewarded for the risk he had run in venturing the stolen visit.

Next time, however, he fared better, and he contrived so well that from the middle of June to the end of August he had two lessons a week, mostly on the afternoons of holidays, and he made great progress.

The linen manufacturing trade of Robert's grandfather had by this time ceased, although the family still retained the bleachery belonging to it, commonly called the bleachfield, devoting it now mostly to the whitening of such yarn as the country housewives still spun at home and what they got from private looms. When the pile of linen which the week had accumulated at the office was on Saturday heaped high on the base of a broad-wheeled cart, it was a wondrous pleasure to Robert and Shargar to get up on it and be carried to the bleachfield which lay along the bank of the river. Sitting high on the pile of softness, gazing into the blue sky, they traversed the streets in a holiday triumph. And although once they had arrived, the manager did not fail to get some labor out of them, yet the store of amusement was endless.

The grassy bank of the gently flowing river was one of Robert's favorite haunts, and one Saturday afternoon in the end of July, when the westering sun was hotter than at midday, he went down to the lower end of a favorite field where the river was confined by a dam and plunged from the bank into the deep water. After a swim of half an hour, he ascended the higher part of the field and lay down to bask in the sun. In his ears was the hush rather than the rush of the water over the dam and the occasional murmur of a belt of trees that skirted the border of the field.

He lay gazing up into the depth of the sky, rendered deeper and bluer by the masses of white cloud that hung almost motionless below it. A gentle wind, laden with pine odors from the sun-heated trees behind him, flapped its light wing in his face. And all at once the humanity of the world smote his heart. The great sky towered up over him, and its divinity entered his soul; a strange longing after something "he knew not nor could name" awoke within him, followed by the pang of a sudden fear that there was no such thing as that which he sought.

Suddenly the voice of Shargar broke the spell, calling to him from afar to come and see a great salmon that lay by a stone in the water. But once aroused, the feeling that had come over him was never stilled; the desire never left him, sometimes growing to a passion that was relieved only by a flood of tears.

Strange as it may sound to those who have never thought of such things except in connection with Sundays and Bibles and churches and sermons, that which was now working in Falconer's mind was the first dull and faint movement of the greatest need that the human heart possesses—the need of God. There must be truth in the scent of that pine-wood; someone must mean it. There must be a glory in those heavens that depends not upon our imagination; some power greater than they must dwell in them. Some spirit must move in that wind that haunts us with a kind of human sorrow; some soul must look up to us from the eye of that starry flower.

Little did Robert think that such was his need—that his soul was searching after One whose form was constantly presented to him, but as constantly obscured by the words without knowledge spoken in the religious assemblies of the land. Little did he realize that he was longing without knowing it on Saturday for that from which on the Sunday he would be repelled, again without knowing it.

For weeks the mood broken by the voice of his companion did not return, though the forms of nature were after that full of a pleasure he had never known before. He loved the grass; the water was more gracious to him; he would leave his bed early that he might gaze on the clouds of the east with their borders gold-blasted with sunrise; he would linger in the fields, that the amber and purple and green and red of the sunset might not escape after the sun unseen. And as long as he felt the mystery, the revelation of the mystery lay before and not behind him.

And Shargar—had he any soul for such things? Doubtless, but how could it but be far different than with Robert? For the latter had ancestors—that is, he came of a people with a mental and spiritual history, while the former had been born the birth of an animal—of a noble sire whose family had for generations filled the earth with fire, famine, slaughter, and licentiousness, and of a wandering, outcast mother, who blindly loved the fields and woods, but retained her affection for her offspring scarcely beyond the period while she suckled them. The love of freedom and of wild animals that she had given him, however, was far more precious than any share his male ancestor had borne in his mental constitution. After his fashion he as well as Robert enjoyed the sun and the wind and the water and the sky. And he had sympathies with the salmon and the rooks and the wild rabbits even stronger than those of Robert.

16 / A Daring Rescue

The period of harvest holiday drew near, and over the north of Scotland thousands of half-grown hearts were beating with glad anticipation. Most found a way to cheat themselves into the half-belief of expediting a blessed approach by marking its rate on a calendar or even carving notches on a stick. There was one particular amusement into which Robert entered with the whole of his energy during this time of year, and that was kite flying. The moment the harvest drew near, Robert proceeded to make his kite, or dragon, as he called it.

Of how many pleasures does pocket money deprive the unfortunate possessor!

What is going into a shop and buying what you want compared with the gentle delight of hours and days filled with gaining effort toward the attainment of your end? No boy that bought his kite could have half the enjoyment of Robert from the moment he went to the cooper's to ask for an old hoop to the moment when he said, "Now, Shargar!" and the kite rose slowly from the ground.

To begin with, the hoop was carefully examined, the best portion cut away from it, that pared to a light strength, its ends confined to the proper curve by a string, and then away went Robert to the wright's shop. There a slip of wood, of proper length and thickness, was readily granted to his request, free as the daisies of the field. In Robert's kite the only thing that cost money was the string to fly it with, and that the grandmother willingly provided, for not even her ingenuity could discover any evil, direct or implicit, in kite flying. Indeed, I believe the old lady felt not a little sympathy with the exultation of the boy when he saw his kite far aloft, diminished to a speck in the vast blue, a sympathy, it may be, rooted in the religious aspirations which she did so much to rouse and at the same time to suppress in the heart of her grandson.

But I have said nothing of the kite's tail. As soon as the body of the dragon was completed, Robert attached to its spine the string and at a proper distance from the body joined to the string the first of the crosspieces of folded paper which in this animal represented the continued vertebral processes. Every morning, the moment he left his room, he proceeded to the garret where the monster lay to add yet another joint to his tail. At length the day should arrive when, the lessons over for a blessed eternity of five or six weeks, he would send it aloft. This was Robert's way of numbering the countdown till harvest time.

Upon this occasion the dragon was an enormous one. With a little help from Shargar, he had laid a skeleton of a six-foot specimen, and had carried the body to satisfactory completion. The tail was still growing, having as yet only sixteen joints, when Mr. Lammie had called with an invitation for the boys to spend their harvest holidays with him. It was fortunate for Robert that he was in the room when Mr. Lammie presented his petition, otherwise he would never have heard of it till the day of departure arrived and would thus have lost all the delights of anticipation. In frantic effort to control his ecstasy, he sped to the garret, and with trembling hands tied the second joint of the day to the tail of the dragon. It was the first time he had ever broken the one-joint-per-day law of its growth. Once broken, however, that law soon became nothing but an object of scorn and the tail grew with frightful rapidity.

It was indeed a great dragon. And none of the paltry fields about Rothieden should be honored with its first flight, but from Bodyfauld should the majestic child of earth ascend into the regions of upper air.

Even though Robert had previously been only too glad to return to Rothieden from his former visit in the country, now his anticipation for the harvest knew no bounds—for the circumstances would indeed be different. This time there would be neither Grannie nor school to interfere with the delights of Bodyfauld!

As the blessed day approached, Robert and Shargar held many consultations about how best they might contrive to get Robert's violin also to Bodyfauld. The difficulty was how to get her from the shoemaker's and free of Rothieden in broad daylight.

The holiday commenced on a Saturday, but not till the Monday were they to be set at liberty. Wearily the hours of mental labor called the Sabbath passed away and at length the millennial morning dawned. Robert and Shargar were up before the sun. But strenuous were the efforts they made to suppress all indications of excitement, lest Grannie, fearing the immoral influence of gladness itself, should give orders to delay their departure for an awfully infinite period, which might be an hour, a day, or even a week. Their behavior was so decorous that not even a hinted threat escaped the lips of Mrs. Falconer.

They set out three hours before noon, carrying the great kite and Robert's schoolbag full of sundries; a cart was to fetch their luggage later in the day. As soon as they were clear of the houses, Shargar lay down behind a dyke with the kite and Robert set off at full speed for

Dooble Sanny's shop, making a half-circuit of the town in order to avoid the chance of being seen by Grannie or Betty. Having already given the shoemaker due warning that his violin would be wanted, he found the brown-paper parcel ready for him, and he carried it off in fearful triumph without even glancing inside. He joined Shargar in safety, and they set out on their journey as rich and happy as a pair of tramps as ever walked the fields, having six weeks of their own in their pockets to spend and not spare.

A hearty welcome awaited them, and they were soon reveling in the glories of the place, the first installment of which was in the shape of curds and cream, with oatcake and butter—as much as they liked. After this they were anxious to try their kite, for the wind had been blowing bravely all morning. Out to the pasture they went with it.

Slowly the great-headed creature arose from the hands of Shargar and ascended about twenty feet when, as if seized with a sudden fit of fierce indignation, it turned right round and dashed itself with headlong fury to the earth, as if sooner than submit to such influences a moment longer, it would beat out its brains at once.

"It hasn't enough tail!" cried Robert. "It's a queer thing that things won't go up without being held down. Grab a handful of grass, Shargar, and tie it on the end."

Upon the next attempt the kite rose triumphantly. But just as it reached the length of string it shot into a faster current of air and Robert found himself first dragged along in spite of his efforts to hold it back, and then nearly lifted from his feet. After carrying him a few yards, the dragon broke the string, dropped him into a ditch, and drifted away fluttering and waggling downwards in the distance.

"Look where she goes, Shargar!" cried Robert.

Experience coming to his aid, Shargar watched and hastened after it and before long they found it with its tail entangled in the topmost branches of a hawthorn tree and its head beating the ground at its foot. It was agreed at once that they would not fly it again till they got some stronger string.

Having heard the adventure, Mr. Lammie produced a shilling from the pocket of his corduroys and gave it to Robert to spend on the needful string; he, in turn, resolved to go to the town the next morning and make his grand purchase. During the afternoon he roamed about the farm with his hands in his pockets while Shargar followed like a pup at the heels of Miss Lammie, to whom, during his previous visit, he had become greatly attached.

In the evening, resolved to make a confidante of Miss Lammie, and indeed cast himself upon the kindness of the whole household, Robert went to his room to release his violin from its prison of brown paper. What was his dismay to find—not his bonny leddy, but her poor cousin, the shoemaker's auld wife! *Dooble* Sanny indeed!

He first stared, then went into a rage, and then came out of it with a resolution. He replaced the unwelcome fiddle in the parcel and came downstairs gloomy and still wrathful, but silent. The evening passed and the inhabitants of the farmhouse went to bed early. Robert tossed about on his. He had not undressed.

About eleven o'clock, after all had been still for more than an hour, he took his shoes in one hand and the brown parcel in the other, descended the stairs like a thief, undid the quiet wooded bar that secured the door, and let himself out. All was darkness, for the moon was not yet up. He had never been out so late before.

It was a cloudy and still night. Nothing was to be heard but his own footsteps. The cattle in the fields were all asleep. The larch and spruce trees on the top of the hill were as still as the clouds. A star or two sparkled where the clouds broke, though there was little light. But he never thought of turning back, eerie as it was. The way grew so dark at one point as the road wound through a corner of a pine wood that he had to feel the edge of the road with his foot to make sure he was still upon it. Then he passed a farm and the motions of horses came through the dark and a doubtful crow from a young, inexperienced chicken who did not yet know the moon from the sun. Then a sleepy lowing in his ear startled him and made him quicken his pace involuntarily.

By the time he reached Rothieden all the lights were out, which was just what he wanted.

The outer door of Dooble Sanny's house was always unlocked because several families lived in the building; the shoemaker's workshop opened from the passage near this door, therefore its door was locked. But the key hung on a nail just inside the shoemaker's bedroom. All this Robert knew quite well.

Arrived at the house, he lifted the latch, closed the door behind him, took off his shoes like a housebreaker, as indeed he was, and felt his way up the stair to the bedroom. There was a sound of snoring within. The door was a little ajar. He reached the key and descended, his heart beating more and more wildly as he approached the realization of his hopes. Gently as he could, he turned it in the lock. In a moment more he had his hands on the spot where the shoemaker always laid his violin.

But his heart sank within him; there was no violin there!

Blank dismay held him motionless and thoughtless for a few brief seconds. Suddenly he heard footsteps, which he knew well, approaching in the street. He slunk at once into a corner. Elshender entered, feeling his way carefully, and muttering at his wife. He was tipsy, most likely, but that had never interfered with the safety of his fiddle. Robert heard its faint echo as he laid it gently down. But he was not too tipsy to lock the door behind him with the key Robert had left in the lock, leaving Robert incarcerated among the old boots and leather and rosin.

For one moment the boy's heart failed him. The next he was in action. Hastily he undid his parcel and carefully enveloped his own violin in the paper. Then he took the auld wife of the shoemaker and proceeded to perform upon her a trick which, in a merry moment, his master had taught him.

The shoemaker's room was overhead. Before Dooble Sanny was even half gone beside his sleeping wife, he heard a frightful sound from below. He sprang from his bed and hastened in dismay back down the stairs to his workshop.

The moment Robert heard his movements he put the old violin in its place and took his place poised by the door. The shoemaker came tumbling down the stair and rushed at the door but found he had to go back for the key. When he at last, with unsteady hand, had opened it, he went straight to the nest of his treasure while Robert slipped out noiselessly. He was in the middle of the street before Dooble Sanny, having found the fiddle uninjured and, not discovering the substitution in the dark, concluded that the whiskey and his imagination had played him a very discourteous trick.

It was not until Robert had cut his foot quite badly on a piece of glass that he discovered he had left his shoes behind him. He tied the foot up with his handkerchief and limped home the three miles, too happy to think of the consequences. Before he had gone far the moon floated up on the horizon, large and shaped like the broad side of a barrel. She stared at him in amazement to see him out at such a time of the night. But he grasped his violin and went on. He had no fear now, even when he passed again over the desolate moor, although he saw the stagnant pools glimmering about him in the moonlight. He reached home in safety, found the door as he had left it, and ascended to his bed, triumphant in his fiddle. Ever after this he had a fancy for roaming at night.

In the morning, bloody prints were discovered on the stair and traced to the door of his room. Miss Lammie entered in some alarm and found him fast asleep on his bed, still dressed, with a brown-paper parcel in his arms and one of his feet evidently the source of the frightful stain. Inquiry, however, was postponed till they met at breakfast.

"Robert, my lad," asked Mr. Lammie kindly, "how did ye come by that bloody foot?"

Robert began the story and, guided by a few questions from his host, at length told the tale of the violin from beginning to end. Many a guffaw from Mr. Lammie greeted its progress, and Miss Lammie laughed till the tears rolled down her cheeks, especially when Shargar imparted his private share in the comedy. The whole business advanced the boys in favor at Bodyfauld, for the Lammies were not the kind to be censorious upon such exploits; and the urgent requests of Robert that nothing should reach his grandmother's ears were entirely unnecessary.

After breakfast Miss Lammie dressed the wounded foot. But what was to be done for shoes? Ordinarily it would have been no great hardship to go barefoot for the rest of the autumn; but the cut was a rather serious one. Thus his feet came to be cased in a pair of Mr. Lammie's Sunday boots. Their size made it so difficult for him to get along that he did not go far from the house that day but revelled in the company of his violin in the cornyard among last year's ricks, in the new barn, and in the hayloft, playing all the tunes he knew and trying over one or two more from a very dirty old book of Scotch airs which his teacher had lent him.

In the evening, as they sat together after supper, Mr. Lammie said, "Well, Robert, how's the fiddle?"

"Fine, thank you," answered Robert.

"Let's hear what ye can do with it."

Robert fetched the instrument and complied.

"That's good," remarked the farmer. "But, eh! Ye should have heard yer grandfather handle the bow. That *was* something to hear. Ye would have just thought the strings had been drawn from his own inside, he knew them so well with his fingers. Eh! T' hear him play the 'Flowers o' the Forest' would have just made ye cry."

"Could my father play?" asked Robert.

"Ay, well enough for him. He could do anything he liked. I never saw such a man. He played on the bagpipes and the flute and the bugle and I don't know what all. But altogether they didn't come within sight o' his father on the fiddle. Let's have a look at her."

He took the instrument in his hands reverently, turned it over and over, and said, "Ay, Ay. This small creature's now worth a hundred pounds, I warrant." He then restored it carefully into Robert's hands, to whom it was honey and spice to hear his bonny leddy paid her due honors. "Can ye play 'Flowers o' the Forest'?" he added.

"Ay, can I," answered Robert with some pride, and laid the bow on the violin and played the air through without missing a single note.

"Well, that's very good," said Mr. Lammie, "but Robert, my man, ye must put more soul int' yer fiddlin'. Ye can't play the fiddle till ye can make it cry. . . . My father played the fiddle, but not like yer grandfather.''

Robert was silent. He spent the whole of the next morning in reiterated attempts to alter his style of playing the air in question, but in vain. He laid the instrument down in despair and sat for an hour disconsolate upon the bedside. His visit had not as yet been at all so fertile in pleasure as he had anticipated. He could not fly his kite; he could not walk; he had lost his shoes; Mr. Lammie had not approved of his playing; and, although he had his will of the fiddle, he could not get his will out of it. Nothing but manly pride kept him from crying. He was sorely disappointed and dissatisfied, and the world seemed dreary, even at Bodyfauld.

17 / The Dragon Kite

The wound on Robert's foot festered and had not yet healed when the sickle was first put to the barley. He hobbled out, however, to the reapers, for he could not bear to be left alone with his violin, so dreadfully oppressive was the knowledge that he could not use it after its nature. He began to wonder whether his incapacity might not be a judgment upon him for taking it away from the shoemaker, who could do so much more with it. The pain in his foot, likewise, had been very depressing.

Shargar, on the other hand, was happier than he had ever been in his life. His white face hung about Miss Lammie and haunted her steps from storeroom to milkhouse.

Late one evening Robert was out in the fields. The sky was partly clouded and the air cold and as he limped slowly homeward, his soul was laden with mournfulness. As he reached the middle of a newly cut field, the wind suddenly arose from out of the northwest. The heads of barley in the sheaves leaned away from it with a soft rustling. Then the wind swept away to the pine-covered hill and raised a rushing and wailing among its thin-clad branches, and to the ear of Robert the trees were singing. The meaning, the music of the night awoke in his soul. He forgot his lame foot and the weight of Mr. Lammie's great boots, and ran home and up the stair to his own room, seized his violin with eager haste and did not lay it down again until he could draw from it the sound like the moaning of the wind over the stubble field. Then he knew he could play "Flowers of the Forest."

He tried the air once over in the dark, and then carried his violin down to the room where Mr. and Miss Lammie sat.

"I think I can play it now, Mr. Lammie," blurted Robert.

"Play what?" asked his host.

" 'Flowers of the Forest.' "

"Play away then."

And Robert played—not so well as he had hoped. I dare say it was a humble enough performance. But he gave something at least of the expression Mr. Lammie desired, for the moment the tune was over, he exclaimed, "Well done, Robert man! Ye'll be a fiddler someday yet!"

And Robert was well satisfied with the praise.

"I wish yer mother was alive," the farmer went on. "She would have been real proud t' hear ye play like that. Eh, she liked the fiddle. And she could play on the piano herself. It was something t' hear the two o' them playing together, him on the fiddle—that very fiddle o' his father's that ye have in yer hand—and her on the piano. Eh! She was as pretty a woman as I ever saw!"

"What was my mother like, Mr. Lammie?" asked Robert.

"Eh, my man! Ye should have seen her on that bonny bay mare that yer father gave her. Faith! She sat so straight, with just the slightest hang o' her head, like the head on a stalk o' wild oats."

I need hardly say that from that night Robert was more diligent than ever with his violin.

The next day his foot was so much better that he sent Shargar to Rothieden to buy the string, taking with him Robert's schoolbag in which to carry off his Sunday shoes from the house. As to those left at Dooble Sanny's, they judged it unsafe to go in quest of them; the shoemaker could hardly be in a humor fit to be intruded upon.

Having procured the string, Shargar went to Mrs. Falconer's. Anxious not to encounter her but, if possible to bag the boots quietly, he opened the door, peeped in, and seeing no one, made his way toward the kitchen. As he crossed the passage he was arrested by the voice of Mrs. Falconer calling, "Who's that?" There she was at the parlor door.

It paralyzed him. His first impulse was to make a rush and escape. But the boots—he could not go without at least an attempt upon them. So he turned and faced her with inward trembling.

"Who's that?" repeated the old lady, regarding him fixedly. "Oh, it's ye. What do *you* want? Ye can't hae come t' see me, I'm thinking. What hae ye i' that bag?"

"I came t' buy twine fer the dragon," answered Shargar.

"Ye had twine enough before."

"It broke. It wasn't strong enough."

"Where did ye get the money t' buy more. Let's see it."

Shargar took the string from the bag.

"Such a sight o' twine! What did ye pay for it?"

"A shillin'."

"Where'd ye get the shilling?"

"Mr. Lammie gave't t' Robert.

"I won't be haeing ye taking money from nobody. It's ill manners. Here!" said the old lady, putting her hand in her pocket and taking out a shilling. "Give Mr. Lammie back his shilling an' tell him that I wouldn't hae ye learn such bad customs as t' take money. Are they well?''

"Ay, very well," answered Shargar, putting the shilling in his pocket.

In another moment Shargar had, without a word of adieu, embezzled the shoes and escaped the house without seeing Betty. He went straight to the shop he had just left and bought another shilling's worth of string.

When he got home he concealed nothing from Robert, whom he found seated in the barn with his fiddle.

Robert started to his feet. He could appropriate his grandfather's violin, to which, possibly, he might have shown as good a right as his grandmother. But her money was sacred.

"Shargar!" he cried. "You fetch that shilling back. Take the twine and make them give you back the shilling."

"They won't break a purchase!" cried Shargar, beginning almost to whimper, for a savory smell of dinner was coming across the yard.

"Tell them it's stolen money, and they'll be in hot water about it if they don't give it back."

"I must have my dinner first," remonstrated Shargar.

But the spirit of his grandmother was strong in Robert, and in a matter of rectitude there must be no temporizing. Therein he could be as tyrannical as the old lady herself.

"You'll not have a bite or a sup down your throat till I see that shilling."

There was no help for it. Six hungry miles must be trudged by Shargar before he got a morsel to eat. Two hours and a half passed before he reappeared. But he brought the shilling. As to how he recovered it, Robert questioned him in vain. Shargar, in his turn, was obstinate.

"She's some unmanageable a wife, that grannie o' yer's," said Mr. Lammie when Robert returned the shilling with Mrs. Falconer's message. "But I reckon I must put it in my pocket, for she will have her own way and I don't want t' cross her. But if any o' ye be in want o' a shilling one day, lads, as long as I'm about—this one'll have grown two or maybe more by that time."

So saying, the farmer put the shilling into his pocket.

The dragon flew splendidly now, and its strength was mighty. It was Robert's custom to drive a stake into the ground, slanting it against the wind, and thereby tether the animal, as if it were up there grazing in its own natural region. Then he would lie down by the stake and read *The Arabian Nights*, which he had discovered at the farm, every now and then casting a glance upward at the creature alone in the waste air, yet all in his power by the string at his side. Somehow the high-flying dragon was a bond between him and the blue; he seemed nearer to the sky while it flew, or at least the heaven seemed less inaccessible.

While he lay there gazing, all at once he would find that his soul was up with the dragon, feeling as it felt, tossing about with it in the torrents of the air. Sometimes, to aid his aspiration, he would take a bit of paper, make a hole in it, pass the end of the string through the hole, and send the messenger scuddling along the line, carried by the wind. If it stuck along the way, he would get a telescope of Mr. Lammie's and watch the paper's struggles till it broke loose, and then follow it careening up to the kite. Away with each successive paper his imagination would fly and a sense of air and height and freedom settled from his play into his very soul, a germ to sprout hereafter and enrich the forms of his aspirations.

Sometimes he would throw down his book and, sitting up with his back against the stake, lift his bonny leddy from his side and play as he had never played in Rothieden, playing to the dragon aloft, to keep him strong in his soaring and fierce in his battling with the winds of heaven. Then he fancied that the monster swooped and swept in arcs, and swayed curving to and fro, in rhythmic response to the music floating up through the wind.

What a full symbolism lay around the heart of the boy during those days—in his book, his violin, and his kite!

One afternoon as they were sitting at their tea, a footstep in the garden approached the house and then a figure passed the window. Mr. Lammie started to his feet.

"Bless my soul, it's Anderson!" he cried, and hurried to the door.

His daughter followed. The boys kept their seats. A loud and hearty salutation reached their ears, but the voice of the farmer was all they heard. Presently he returned bringing with him the tallest and slenderest man Robert had ever seen. He was considerably over six feet with a gentle look in his blue eyes and a slow, clear voice which sounded as if it were thinking about every word it uttered. The hot sun of India seemed to have burned out everything self-assertive, leaving him quietly comtemplative.

"Come in, come in," repeated Mr. Lammie, overflowing with glad welcome. "And here's a lad o' yer own kin," he continued, pointing to Robert, "and a fine boy." Then lowering his voice he added, "A son o' poor Andrew's, ye know, Doctor."

The boys rose and Dr. Anderson, stretching his long arms across the table, shook hands kindly with Robert and Shargar. Then he sat down and began to help himself to the oatcakes. Miss Lammie presently came in with the teapot and some additional dainties, and the boys took the opportunity of beginning their tea again.

Dr. Anderson remained for a few days at Bodyfauld. During this time Mr. Lammie was much occupied with his farm affairs, anxious to get his harvest in as quickly as possible, because a change of weather was to be dreaded. The doctor, therefore, wandered about a good deal and did not object to the companionship which Robert implicitly offered him. Before many hours were over the two were friends.

Various things attracted Robert to the doctor. First, he was a relation of his own, and though the relationship was not an immediate one, it was the first such Robert had known. Secondly, he was a *gentleman*. And third, the doctor was kind and gentle, and above all, respectful to him; to be respected was a new sensation to Robert altogether. But lastly, he could tell stories of elephants and tiger hunts and all "The Arabian Nights" of India.

And equally, something in the boy attracted the man to him as well. For the brief length of Dr. Anderson's visit, kite and violin were all forgotten and Robert followed him like a puppy. To have such a gentleman for a relation was grand indeed. But all the time Robert could not get him to speak about his father. He studiously avoided the subject.

When he went away, the two boys walked with him to the Boar's Head. They caught a glimpse of his Hindu attendant, and much to their wonderment, received from the doctor a sovereign apiece and a kind good-bye, and returned to Bodyfauld.

Dr. Anderson remained a few days longer at Rothieden, and among others visited Mrs. Falconer, who was his first cousin. What passed between them Robert never heard, nor did his grandmother even allude to the visit. The doctor then left by the mail coach from Rothieden to Aberdeen, and whether he should ever see him again Robert did not know.

He flew his kite no more for a while, but took himself to the work of the harvest field, in which he was now able to do his share. But his violin was no longer neglected.

Day after day passed in the delights of labor, broken for Robert by *The Arabian Nights* and the violin, and for Shargar by attendance upon Miss Lammie, till the fields lay bare of their harvest and the nightwind of autumn moaned everywhere over the vanished glory of the country, and it was time to go back to school.

18 / Catastrophe! _____

The morning at length arrived when Robert and Shargar must return to Rothieden. A keen autumnal wind was blowing far-off feathery clouds across a sky of pale blue. The cold freshened the spirits of the boys and tightened their nerves and muscles till they were like bow strings. No doubt the winter was coming, but the sun, although his day's work was short and slack, was still as clear as ever. So gladsome was the world that the boys received the day as a fresh holiday, and strenuously forgot tomorrow. The wind blew straight from Rothieden, and between sun and wind, a bright thought awoke in Robert. The dragon should not be carried—he should fly home.

After they had said farewell—in which Shargar seemed to suffer more than Robert—and had turned the corner of the stables, they heard the good farmer shouting after them, ''There'll be another harvest next year, boys,'' which wonderfully restored their spirits.

When they reached the open road, Robert laid his violin carefully into a broom bush. Then the kite's tail was unrolled, and the dragon ascended steady as an angel whose work is done. Shargar took the stick at the end of the string and Robert resumed his violin. The creature was hard to lead in such a wind, so they made a loop on the string and passed it around Shargar's chest. Robert longed to take his share in the struggle, but he could not trust his violin to Shargar and so had to ingloriously walk along beside him.

On the way they laid their plans for the accommodation of the dragon. But the violin was the greater difficulty. Robert would not hear of the factory, for reasons best known to himself, and there were several objections to taking it to Dooble Sanny. It was resolved that the only way was to seize the right moment and creep upstairs with it before presenting themselves to Mrs. Falconer. Their intended maneuvers with the kite would favor the concealment of this stroke.

Before they entered the town they drew in the kite a little way and cut off a dozen yards of string, which Robert put in his pocket with a stone tied to the end. When they reached the house, Shargar went into the little garden and tied the string of the kite to the paling between that and Captain Forsyth's. Robert opened the street door and, having turned his head on all sides like a thief, darted with his violin up the stairs. Having laid his treasure in one of the presses in Shargar's garret, he went to his own room and from the skylight threw the stone down into the Captain's garden, fastening the other end of the string to the bedstead.

Escaping as cautiously as he had entered, he passed hurriedly into their neighbor's garden, found the stone, and joined Shargar. The ends were soon united and the kite let go. It sunk for a moment, then, arrested by the bedstead, towered again to its former height, sailing over Rothieden, grand and unconcerned, in the expanse of the air.

But the end of the tether was in Robert's garret. And that to him a sense of power, a thought of glad mystery. There was henceforth, while the dragon flew, a relation between the desolate little chamber in that lowly house buried among so many more aspiring abodes, and the unmeasured depths and spaces, the stars, and the unknown heavens. And in the next room lay the fiddle, free once more, yet another magical power whereby Robert's spirit could leave the earth and mount heavenward.

All that night, all the next day, and all the next night the dragon flew.

Not one smile broke over the face of the old lady as she received them. Was it because she did not know what acts of disobedience, what breaches of the moral law, the two children of possible perdition might have committed while they were beyond her care, and she must not run the risk of smiling upon inquiry? I think it was rather that there was no smile in her religion. How could she smile? Did not the world lie under the wrath and curse of God? Was not her son in hell forever? Had not the blood of the Son of God been shed for him in vain?

"Noo, be quiet," she said, the moment she had shaken hands with them, with her cold hands, so clean and soft and smooth. With a volcanic heart of love, her outside remained still and cold. Ah, if she had only known intimately the God who claimed her submission. But there is time enough for every heart to know him.

"Noo, be quiet," she repeated, "an' sit doon, an' tell me aboot the folk at Bodyfauld. I hope ye thank't them before ye left, for their kindness t' ye."

The boys were silent.

"Didn't ye thank them?"

"No, Grannie, I don't think we did," Robert finally responded.

"Well, that was ill-mannered o' ye. Eh, but the heart is deceitful above all things an' desperately wicked. Who can know it? Come on, Robert, close the door."

And she led them to the corner for prayer, and poured forth a confession of sin for them and for herself such as left little that could have been added by her own profligate son had he joined in the prayer. But the horrible words did little harm, for Robert's mind was full of the kite and the violin and was probably nearer God than if he had been trying to feel as wicked as his grandmother told God that he was. Shargar was even more divinely employed at the time than either; for though he had not had the manners to thank his benefactor, his heart had all the way home been full of tender thoughts of Miss Lammie's kindness. And now, instead of confessing sins that were not his, he was loving her over and over and wishing to be back with her instead of with this woman in whose presence there was no peace, for all the atmosphere of silence and calm in which she sat.

Confession over and the boys at liberty again, a new anxiety seized them. Grannie would find out that Robert's shoes were missing, and what account was to be given of the misfortune, for Robert would not, could not, lie? In the midst of their discussion, a bright idea flashed upon Shargar which, however, he kept to himself; he would steal them and bring them home in triumph, emulating thus Robert's exploit in delivering his bonny leddy.

The shoemaker often sat behind his door to be out of the draft. Shargar would be able to see a great part of the workshop without being seen himself, and he could pick out Robert's shoes from among a hundred. Probably they lay just where Robert had laid them, for Dooble Sanny paid attention to any job only in proportion to the persecution accompanying it.

So the next day Shargar contrived to slip out of school just as the writing lesson began, for he had great skill in conveying himself unseen, and with his book bag, slunk barefooted into the shoemaker's entry.

The shop door was just a little way open and the reddish eyes of Shargar had only the corner next to it into which to peer. But there he saw the shoes. He got down on his hands and knees and crept nearer. Yes, they were, beyond a doubt, Robert's shoes.

Like a beast of prey, his long arm reached out and seized them; losing his presence of mind upon possession, he drew them too hastily toward him. The shoemaker saw them as they vanished through the door and darted after them.

Shargar was off at full speed and Sandy followed him with a great hue and cry. Every idle person in the street joined in the pursuit, and all who were too busy or too respectable to run crowded to doors and windows to watch. Shargar made instinctively for his mother's old lair, but then, thinking better of it and knowing nowhere else to go, fled in terror to Mrs. Falconer's, still, however, holding fast to the shoes, for they were Robert's.

As Robert came home from school a short time later, wondering what could have become of his companion, he saw a crowd about his grandmother's door. Pushing through it in some dismay, he found Dooble Sanny and Shargar confronting each other before the stern justice of Mrs. Falconer.

"Ye're a liar!" the shoemaker was panting out. "I haven't had a pair o' Robert's shoes in my hands for three months. Those shoes—let me see them—they're— Here's Robert himself. Are these shoes yers, noo, Robert?"

"Ay, they are. You made them yourself."

"How did they come to be in my shop, then?"

"Ask no more questions than's worth answering," said Robert, casting a look at him meant to be significant. "They're my shoes and I'll keep them. You don't seem to know what shoes you have or when they came to you."

"Why didn't Shargar come an' ask for them, then, instead o' making a thief out o' himself that way?"

"You may hold your tongue," returned Robert, with yet more significance.

"I was an idiot," said Shargar in apologetic reflection, looking awfully white and afraid to lift an eye to Mrs. Falconer, yet reassured a little by Robert's presence.

Some glimmering seemed now to have dawned upon the shoemaker, for he began to prepare a retreat. Meantime Mrs. Falconer stood silent, allowing no word that passed to escape her. She wanted to be at the bottom of the mysterious affair and therefore held her peace.

"Well, I'm sure, Robert, ye never told me about the shoes," returned Elshender. "I'll just take them back wi' me an' do what's wanted t' 'em. An' I'm sorry that I have given ye this trouble, Mistress Falconer. But it was all that fool's fault there. I didn't even know it was him till we were almost at the house."

"Let me see the shoes," said Mrs. Falconer, speaking for the first time. "What's the matter wi' them?"

Examining the shoes, she saw they were in a perfectly sound state and this confirmed her suspicion that there was more in the affair than had yet come out. Had she taken the straightforward measure of examining Robert, she would have arrived at the truth. But she had such a dread of causing a lie to be told that she would adopt any roundabout way rather than ask a plain question of a suspected culprit. So she laid the shoes down beside her, saying to the shoemaker: "There's nothing amiss wi' the shoes. Ye can leave them.''

Thereupon Sandy went away and Robert and Shargar would have given more than their dinner to follow him. Grannie asked neither any questions, however, nor made a single remark on what had passed. Dinner was served and eaten, and the boys returned to their afternoon school.

No sooner was she certain that they were safe under the schoolmaster's eye than the old lady put on her black silk bonnet and her black woolen shawl, took her green cotton umbrella, which served her for a staff, and refusing Betty's proffered assistance, set out for Dooble Sanny's shop.

As she drew near she heard the sounds of his violin. When she entered he laid his auld wife carefully aside and stood in an expectant attitude.

''Mr. Elshender, I want t' be at the bottom o' this,'' said Mrs. Falconer.

''Well, mem, go to the bottom o' it,'' returned Dooble Sanny; he dropped on his stool and taking his stone upon his lap began stroking it. Full of rough but real politeness to women when in good humor, he lost all manners along with his temper upon the slightest provocation, and her tone irritated him.

''How did Robert's shoes come t' be i' yer shop?''

''Somebody was bound t' have brought them t' me, mem. In all my experience, an' that's not small, I never knew o' a pair o' shoes walkin' without a pair o' feet in the womb o' them.''

''Hoots! what kind o' way is that t' speak t' a body! Who's feet was i' the shoes?''

''Devil have me if I know, mem.''

''Don't swear, whatever ye do.''

''The devil but I will swear, mem, an' if ye anger me, I'll swear somethin' awful.''

''I'm sure I hae no wish t' anger ye, man. Can't ye just help me get t' the bottom o' this thing without getting angry an' swearing?''

''Well, I don't know who brought me the shoes, as I told ye already.''

''But they didn't need mending.''

''I might have mended them an' forgotten it, mem.''

''Now ye're lying.''

''If ye go on like that, mem, I won't speak a word o' truth from this moment on.''

''Just tell me what ye know aboot the shoes, an' I'll not say another word.''

"Well, mem, I'll tell ye the truth. The devil brought them in one day an' he says, 'Elshender, mend these shoes fer poor Robby Falconer, an' double-sole them fer the life o' his'll soon have him down here our way, an' the ground's hot; an' I don't want to be too hard on him, for he's a fine child, an'll make a fine fiddler if he lives long enough.'"

Mrs. Falconer left the shop without another word, but with an awful suspicion, which the last heedless words of the shoemaker had aroused in her mind. She left him bursting with laughter over his lapstone. He caught up his fiddle and played "The Devil's in the Woman," lustily and with expression. But he little thought what he had done.

As soon as she reached her own room, she went straight to her bed and disinterred the bonny leddy's coffin. She opened the case and discovered the violin was gone! And in her place—horror of horrors!—lay the prized book, that body of divinity, she had been missing all this time.

Vexation, anger, disappointment, and grief possessed themselves of the old woman's mind. She ranged the house like a wild beast with its wildness pent up inside for a season, calm on the exterior but with a look of horrible determination raging in the depth of her eyes. But she failed to find the violin before the return of the boys. Not a word did she say all evening and their oppressed hearts foreboded ill. They could feel the gathering storm in the air, the sleeping thunder in the clouds. But how or when it would break they had no idea.

Robert came home to dinner the next day a few minutes before Shargar. As he entered his grandmother's parlor, a strange odor greeted his nose. A moment more and he stood rooted with horror and his hair began to rise on his head. His violin lay on its back on the fire, and a yellow tongue of flame was licking the red lips of a hole in its belly. All its strings were shriveled up save one, which burst as he gazed.

And beside the fireplace, stern as a Druidess, sat his grandmother in her chair, feeding her eyes with grim satisfaction on the detestable sacrifice. At length the rigidity of Robert's whole being ejected an involuntary howl like that of a wild beast. He turned and rushed from the house in a helpless agony of horror. Where he was going he knew not; only a blind instinct of modesty drove him to hide his passion from the eyes of men.

From her window Miss St. John saw him tearing, like one demented, toward the factory. He came back far sooner than she expected. For before he arrived at the factory, Robert began to hear strange sounds in the desolate place. When he reached the upper floor he found men with axes and hammers destroying the old woodwork, breaking the old jennies, pitching the balls of lead into baskets, and throwing the spools into crates.

Was there nothing but destruction in the world? Most horrible, his bonny leddy lay dying of flames, and the temple of his refuge torn to pieces by unhallowed hands! What could it mean? Was his grandmother's vengeance here too?

But he did not care. He only felt like the dove sent from the ark, that there was no rest for the sole of his foot; that there was no place to hide his head in his agony; that he was naked to the universe; and, like a heartless, wild thing, he turned and rushed back. At one end was the burning idol, at the other the desecrated temple.

No sooner had he entered the Captain's garden than Miss St. John met him.

"What is the matter with you, Robert?" she asked.

"Oh, Mary!" gasped Robert, and burst into a storm of weeping.

It was long before he could speak. Then he was embarrassed to raise his head. And at that moment the new fear struck him. What if his grandmother was gazing upon him from some window at this moment, or even from the blue vault above? There was no escaping her. She was the all-seeing eye personified—the eye of God of the theologians of his country, always searching out the evil and refusing to acknowledge the good. Yet so gentle and faithful was the heart of Robert that he never thought of her as cruel. He took it for granted that somehow or other she must be right. Only what a terrible thing such righteousness was!

Mary's heart was sore for her friend. At last, sorely interrupted by sobs, he managed to let her know the fate of his "bonny leddy." But when he came to the word, "She's burning in there on Grannie's fire," he broke out once more with the wild howl of despair, and then, ashamed of himself, ceased weeping altogether, though he could not help the intrusion of certain chokes and sobs to his normal breathing and speech.

When he had finished, in a gush of motherly indignation she kissed Robert on the forehead.

From that ordination of love and friendship, he arose a king.

He dried his eyes; not another sob broke from him. He gave her a look of gratitude, bade her good-bye, and walked composedly into his grandmother's parlor where the neck of the violin yet lay upon the fire only half consumed. The rest had utterly vanished.

"What are they doing at the factory, Grannie?" he asked.

"What's who doing, laddie?" returned his grandmother.

"They're taking it down."

"They're taking it down?" she returned with raised voice.

"Taking down the factory."

The old woman rose.

"Robert, ye may hae spite i' yer heart for what I've done this morning, but I could do no other. An' it's an ill thing t' take such amends on me as if I had done wrong, by making me think that yer grandfather's property was t' go the way o' an old, useless, ill-mannered scratch o' a fiddle."

"She was the bonniest fiddle in the countryside, Grannie. And she never got a scratch in her life except when she was handled in an unbecoming manner. But we'll say no more about her, for she's gone and not by a fair death either. She had no blood to cry for vengeance. But the snapping of her strings and the crackling of her bones may have made a cry to go far enough notwithstanding."

The old woman seemed for one moment rebuked under her grandson's eloquence. He had made a great stride toward manhood since the morning.

"The fiddle's my own," she said in a defensive tone. "An' so is the factory," she added, as if she had not quite reassured herself concerning it.

"The fiddle's yours no more, Grannie. And for the factory—you won't believe me; go and see yourself."

Therewith Robert retreated to his garret.

When he opened the door of it, the first thing he saw was the string of his kite, which strange to tell, so steady had been the wind, was still up in the air—still tugging the bedpost. Whether it was from the stinging thought that the true sky-soarer, the violin, had been devoured by the jaws of the fire-devil or from a dim feeling that the time of kites was gone by and manhood on the threshold, I cannot tell. But there was no longer any significance in the outward and visible sign of the dragon. He drew his knife from his pocket and with one downward stroke cut the string in twain. Away went the dragon, free, like a prodigal, to his ruin.

And with the dragon afar, into the past flew the childhood of Robert Falconer. He made one remorseless dart after the string as it swept out of the skylight, but it was gone. And never more, save in twilight dreams, did he lay hold on his childhood again.

19 / A Glorious Offer

As Robert's kite sank in the distance, Mrs. Falconer issued from the house and went down the street toward the factory. Before she came back, the cloth was laid for dinner and Robert and Shargar were both in the parlor awaiting her return. She entered, heated and dismayed, went into Robert's bedroom and shut the door hastily. They heard her open the old bureau. In a moment after, she came out with a more luminous expression upon her face than Robert had ever seen it bear. It was still as ever, but there was a strange light in her eyes which was not confined to her eyes but shone in a measure from her colorless forehead and cheeks as well. It was long before Robert was able to interpret that change in her look and that increase of kindness toward himself and Shargar, apparently such a contrast with the holocaust of the morning. Had they both been Benjamins they could not have had more abundant platefuls than she gave them that day. And when they left her to return to school, instead of the usual, "Noo, be quiet," she said, in gentle, almost loving tones, "Noo, be good lads, both o' ye."

The conclusion at which Robert arrived was that his grandmother had hurried home to see whether the title deeds of the factory were still in her possession, and had found that they were gone—taken, doubtless, by her son Andrew. At whatever period he had appropriated them, he must have parted with them only recently. And the hope rose like an uncaged bird that her son had not yet passed into that awful region of death.

The old factory was in part pulled down and out of its remains a granary constructed. Nor did the old lady interpose a word to arrest the alienation of her property. For some days Robert worked hard at his lessons, for he had nothing else to do. Life was very gloomy now. If only he could go to sea or away to keep sheep on the stormy mountains! If only there were some war going on in which he might enlist. Any fighting with the elements or with the oppressors of the nations would make life worth having, a man worth being. But seemingly God did not heed. To Robert's understanding, he leaned over the world, an immovable fate, bearing down with the weight of his presence all aspiration, all budding delights of children and young persons. All must crouch

117

before him and uphold his glory with the sacrificial death of every impulse, every admiration, every lightness of heart, every bubble of laughter.

But this gloom did not last long. When souls like Robert's have been ill-taught about God, the true God will not let them gaze too long upon the Moloch which men have set up to represent him. He will turn away their minds from that which men call him and fill them with some of his own lovely thoughts or works, such as may by degrees prepare the way for the vision of the true Father.

One afternoon Robert was passing the shoemaker's shop. He had never gone near him since his return. But now, almost mechanically, he went in at the open door.

"Weel, Robert, ye are a stranger. But what's the matter with ye? Faith, that was a mean thing to break into my shop an' steal the bonny leddy."

"Sandy," said Robert solemnly, "you don't know what you have done by that trick you played me. Don't ever mention her in my hearing again."

"The old witch hasn't gotten hold o' her again?" cried the shoe-maker, starting up in alarm. "She came in here askin' about the shoes. But I reckon I sorted her out!"

"I won't ask what you said," returned Robert. "It doesn't matter now." Tears rose to his eyes. His bonny leddy!

"The Lord guide us!" exclaimed the shoemaker. "What is the matter with the bonny leddy?"

"There's no more bonny leddy. I saw her burned to death before my very eyes."

The shoemaker sprang to his feet.

"For God's sake, say that ye're lying!" he cried.

"I wish I were lying," returned Robert.

The shoemaker uttered a terrible oath. "I'll murder the old—" The epithet he ended with is too ugly to write.

"Dare to say such a word in one breath with my grannie," cried Robert, "and I'll brain you in your own shop!"

Sandy burst into tears, which, before they were half down his face, turned into tar with the blackness of the same.

"I'm an awful sinner," he said, "an' vengeance has overtaken me. Go out o' my shop. I wasn't worthy o' her. Go, I say."

Robert went. In the street he met Mary. He pulled off his cap, and in his present frame of mind would have passed on by. But she stopped him.

"I am going for a walk a little way," she said. "Will you go with me?"

She had come out in the hope of finding him, for she had seen him go up the street.

"That I will," returned Robert, and they walked on together.

When they were beyond the last house, Mary said: "Would you like to play on the piano, Robert?"

"Eh, mem!" said Robert, longing in his voice. Then after a pause, "But do you think I could?"

"There's no fear of that. Not after how quickly you learned to play the violin. But do you think your grandmother would let you?"

"She must know nothing about it, mem. She would never allow it. She thinks music is from the devil. She would cry and pray and even lock me up before she'd let me play."

"Well, do you think you could come to me every day for half an hour and I will give you a lesson on my piano? Of course you would never learn only from that, so I'll tell you what you must do. I have a small piano in my own room. You know, the door between our houses leads straight to it. You can practice there. I will be downstairs with my aunt. Perhaps I could come up now and then to see how you are getting on. I will leave the door unlocked so that you can come in whenever you like. If I don't want you, I will lock the door."

"That sounds wonderful, mem. It's been so gloomy with no music. But I would be afraid to lay a hand on the piano. For it's little enough I could do with my fiddle. And for the piano! That's harder yet. I'm afraid I'd disgust you."

"If you really want to learn, there will be no fear of that," returned Mary with a laugh. "I don't think we'd be doing anything wrong," she added, half to herself, in a somewhat doubtful tone.

"Indeed, no, mem. You're just an angel unawares. For I sometimes think my grannie'll drive me mad. For there's nothing to read but devotional books, and nothing to sing but the psalms. And there's no fun about the house but Betty. And poor Shargar's nearly demented with it. And we have to pray with her whether we want to or not. And there's no comfort in the place, but plenty to eat, and that can't be good for anybody. She likes flowers, though, and would like me to make them grow. But I don't care about it; they take such a time before they come to anything."

Then Mary asked about Shargar, toward whom her heart had been tender since Robert first told her of him. After their walk and the offer of Mary's piano, Robert went home considerably more lighthearted than he had been for some time.

The next Sunday, the first time for many years, Dooble Sanny was at church with his wife, though how much good he got by going would be a serious question to discuss.

20 / The Gates of Paradise_____

Robert had his first lesson the next Saturday afternoon. Eager and undismayed by the presence of Mrs. Forsyth, he listened to every word Mary said, tried to combat every fault and awkwardness with patience, and made a tolerable beginning. Even Mrs. Forsyth, as he was leaving, stretched out her arm in modest congratulation, giving him two of her soft fingertips to do something or other with—Robert did not know what, and let them go.

About eight o'clock that same evening, his heart beating like a captured bird's, he crept from Grannie's parlor, past the kitchen, and up the low stair to the mysterious door. He had been trying for an hour to summon up courage to rise, feeling as if his grandmother must suspect where he was going.

Arriving at the barrier, twice his courage failed him; twice he turned and sped back to the parlor. A third time he made the essay, a third time he stood at the wondrous door. He laid his hand on the knob, withdrew it, thought he heard someone in the hallway, rushed up the garret stair and stood listening. He hastened down again, and with a sudden influx of determination, opened the door, saw that the trapdoor was raised, closed the door behind him, and, standing with his head on the level of the floor, gazed into the paradise of Mary St. John's room.

To have one peep into such a room was a kind of salvation to the half-starved nature of the boy. All before him was elegance, richness, mystery. Womanhood radiated from everything. A fire blazed in the chimney. A rug of long white wool lay before it. A little way off stood the piano. Ornaments sparkled and shone upon the dressing table. The door of a wardrobe had swung a little open and revealed the somber shimmer of a black silk dress. He dared not gaze any longer. He had already been guilty of immodesty. He hastened to climb the stairs and seated himself at the piano.

"Just think," Robert said to himself, "me in such a place! It's a palace. It's a fairy palace. And that angel of a lady lives here and sleeps over there! I wonder if she ever dreams about anything as pretty as herself!"

Had Robert been a year or two older or a year or two more experi-

121

enced in the ways of the world, he would no doubt at this moment have been in mortal danger of falling hopelessly in love, not only with Mary St. John but with the ideal of womanhood conjured up by his imagination at his mere presence in her bedroom. As it was, he merely sat as one amazed, as if a participant in his own dream.

Then his thoughts took another turn.

"I wonder if the room was anything like this when my mamma slept in it? I could never have been born in such a grand place! But my mamma might well have lain here."

The face of the miniature he had seen came back upon him and he bowed his head upon his hands. He was sitting thus when Mary came behind him and heard him murmur the one word "Mamma."

He started when he heard her. "I beg your pardon. I have no business to be here, except to play. But I couldn't help thinking about my mother, for I was born in this room. Should I go?"

He rose and turned toward the door.

"No, no," said Mary. "I only came to see if you were here. I can't stay now. But tomorrow you must tell me about your mother. Sit down and practice. If you stay too long, your grandmother will miss you."

"There's just one thing that vexes me, and I don't know what to think about it," said Robert.

"What is it?"

"I'm sure that when I leave the parlor, Grannie'll think that I'm going to my prayers. And I can't abide having her think better of me than I deserve."

"Don't mind what your grannie may think," she said, "so long as you aren't trying to make her think it. Good night."

Had she been indeed an angel from heaven, Robert could not have adored her more.

Mary St. John was the orphan daughter of an English clergyman. He had left her money enough to make her at least independent, though most of it was to be held in trust for her by the estate until she should come of age, living in the meantime with various relatives. Mrs. Forsyth, hearing that her niece was left alone in the world, and in ill-health herself, concluded that her society would be a pleasure to herself and a relief to the housekeeping.

Even before her father's death, Mary had been filled with two passions—one for justice, the other for music. And now out of her grief had come a strong desire to minister life and hope to others, and she had been looking about for some way of doing good. She had found little comfort in the society of her aunt and had, indeed, felt strongly tempted to return again to England. But she had gradually become thoroughly interested in the strange boy next door whose growing musical pinions were ever being clipped by the shears of unsympathetic age and crabbed religion.

Robert practiced the scales till his unaccustomed fingers were stiff, then shut the piano with reverence and departed, carefully peeping into the disenchanted region to see that no enemy lay in wait for him as he passed. He closed the door gently, and in one moment the rich, lovely room and the beautiful lady were behind him, and before him the bare stair between two whitewashed walls that led to his silent grandmother seated in her arm chair, gazing into the red coals, with her round-toed shoes pointed at them from the top of her little wooden stool.

He walked down the stairs, entered the parlor, and sat down to his open book as though nothing had happened. But his grandmother saw the light in his face and did indeed think he had just come from his prayers. And she blessed God that he had put it into her heart to burn the fiddle.

The next night Robert took with him the miniature of his mother and showed it to Mary who saw at once that, whatever might be his present surroundings, his mother must have been a lady. Then Robert took from his pocket the gold thimble, and said, "This thimble was my mamma's. Will you take it, for you know it's no use to me.

Mary hesitated for a moment.

"I will keep it for you if you like," she said, for she could not bear to refuse it, so much did Robert appear to want her to have it.

"No, Mary, I want you to keep it for yourself. I'm sure my mamma would have liked you to have it better than anyone else."

She reached out slowly and grasped one of Robert's hands. "Robert," she began, "you are a special boy."

Embarrassed by her words, Robert's cheeks turned crimson as he looked toward the floor. "What—whatever do you mean, mem?" he stammered.

"You're always thinking of others," she answered gently. "Me . . . your mother . . . that boy Shargar."

"Not always, Mary," he replied, regaining a portion of his composure. "It was for myself and my own loss that I wept when I saw you in the garden after Grannie burned my fiddle."

"Ah, Robert. But nevertheless, God is inside you. How else could you be the kind of person you are? I've watched you and Shargar. You are unique in the way you treat him, different in the way you treat everyone."

In reality, what Mary saw in Robert's daily kindness to his friend likely stemmed from the compassion blossoming in her ready and receptive heart. Robert was doing no more than what came naturally to him. And true enough, what came naturally to him was thinking of others. But not having considered his motives and actions in depth, Mary's assertion appeared larger than he deemed appropriate.

"I don't know how different I am," said Robert, "although the others at school do make fun of Shargar something awful sometimes. But I do find myself wanting to be good to people, to be kind, to help them."

"Oh, so do I!" exclaimed Mary. "So do I, Robert," she repeated. "What greater life could there be but a life of service?"

"Grannie says I am wicked, though," said Robert.

"She doesn't!"

"Oh, yes. In her prayers, almost every night she prays for her 'wayward grandson' to mend his ways."

"Shame on her! She is wicked for thinking such a thing!" cried Mary in an outburst of righteous indignation.

"The Lord forgive you for saying such a thing about my grannie," said Robert. "My grannie couldn't be wicked. She loves God too much."

"Well, maybe not," replied Mary, softening her tone, "but you are not at all wicked, Robert. Not at all. You are a good and kind boy, the kind of person God must want young boys to be like."

Robert said nothing.

"That's what I want to be, Robert," she resumed. "The kind of person God wants me to be. A servant of others. A compassionate and kind person. Don't you, Robert?"

"Yes, of course. But Grannie says—"

"Never mind what your grannie says, Robert," interrupted Mary. "Robert, I have an idea," she went on. "Let's you and I, right now, agree with each other to always want that, to always serve others."

"You mean sort of make a vow together?"

"Yes," she answered excitedly, "let's dedicate ourselves, as friends, to serve and to help one another if need be."

"All right," said Robert with mounting enthusiasm, for he had never had a friend with whom he could talk about such things, "I agree."

"And we'll never leave off being friends, and caring about each other, and caring about others," said Mary.

"Agreed," repeated Robert. "And now, Mary, will you take the thimble?" he asked.

"Well, I will take it and use it sometimes for your sake. As a token of this pledge we have made together. It will remind me of this night. But mind, Robert, I will not take it from you; I will only keep it for you."

"Well, if you will keep it till I should ask for it back, that'll do well enough for me," answered Robert with a smile.

She gave his hand a tight squeeze, then let it go. "But I must go downstairs to my aunt, and you must be about your practicing." She rose, went to the door, then turned back, smiled, and said, "Good night, my *new* friend."

Robert sighed deeply, a satisfied sigh from a heart of love, then opened the piano and began what at first seemed a tedious lesson. Little did the two youths realize what would come of the vow they had so spontaneously made to one another. Had they foreseen the consequences of the words they had uttered and the ideals to which they had committed themselves, they would no doubt have given deeper thought to their promises. As it was, it remained for the passage of time and the dawning of maturity to reveal what would come to them. For the present they remained content in the saying and in the secret sharing of the bond of their friendship.

Robert labored diligently at the piano and his progress corresponded to his labor. It was more than intellect that guided him; his heart was full of music.

Meantime, the love he bore his teacher and the influence of her refinement began to work subtle changes about him. He grew gradually more polished in his speech and dress. He became even more obedient to his grandmother and more diligent at school, and was gradually developing, without knowing it, into a true rustic gentleman.

The piano did not absorb all his faculties. Every divine influence tends to round out into perfection the whole. His love of nature grew more rapidly. Up till then it had been only in summer that he had felt the presence of a power in and above nature. In winter, now the sky was to him true and deep though the world was waste and sad. The tones of the wind that roared at night about the goddess-haunted house and moaned in the chimneys of the lowly dwelling that nestled against it woke harmonies within him. He tried to put expressions of his own into the simple things Mary gave him to play and even dreamed a little at his own will when alone with the passive instrument. Little did Mrs. Falconer think into what a seventh heaven of accursed music she had driven her boy. Music was in him. If it was not able to come out through his fingertips on a violin, then a piano would do equally well. And if that were to be taken away, what could still the music beating in his soul?

But not yet did he tell his friend, much as he loved and much as he trusted her, the little he knew of his mother's sorrows and his father's sins, or whose was the hand that struck him when she found him lying in the factory.

For a time, almost all his trouble about God went from him. I do not think that this was only because he rarely thought of him, but because God was now giving of himself in Mary St. John.

One evening Robert rose from the table, not unwatched of his grandmother, and sped swiftly and silently through the dark, as was his custom, to enter the chamber of enchantment. Never before had his hand failed to alight, sure as a lark on its nest, upon the brass handle of the door that admitted him to his paradise. It missed it now, and fell on something damp, and rough and repellent instead.

Horrible, but true suspicion!

While he was at school that day, his grandmother, moved by what doubt or by what certainty she never revealed, had had the doorway walled up. He felt the place all over. It was to his hands the living tomb of his mother's vicar on earth.

He returned to his book, pale as death, but said never a word. The next day the stones were plastered over.

Thus the door of bliss vanished from the earth. And neither the boy nor his grandmother ever said that it had been.

21 / Winter of Discontent_____

The remainder of that winter was dreary indeed. Every time Robert went up the stair, he passed the door of a tomb. With that gray mortar Mary St. John was walled up forever. He might have rung the bell at the street door and been admitted into the temple of his goddess; but a certain vague terror of his grannie, combined with equally vague qualms of conscience for having deceived her, and the approach in the far distance of a ghastly suspicion that violins, pianos, moonlight, and lovely girls were distasteful to the overruling Fate, drove him from it.

But though the loss of seeing Mary and playing upon her piano was the last blow, his sorrow did not rest there, but returned to brood over his bonny leddy. She was scattered to the winds. Would any of her ashes ever rise in the corn and moan in the ripening wind of autumn? Might not some atoms of the bonny leddy creep into the pines on the hill whose soft and soul-like sounds had taught him to play "Flowers of the Forest"? Or might not some particle find its way by winds and waters to a sycamore forest of Italy, there to creep up through the channels of its life to some finely rounded curve of noble tree, on the side that ever looks sunward, and be chosen once again by the violin-hunger to be wrought into a new and perhaps even more beautiful instrument?

Could it be that his bonny leddy had learned her wondrous music in those forests, from the shine of the sun and the sighing of the winds through the sycamores and pines? For Robert knew that the broad-leafed sycamore and the sharp needle-adorned pine each had its share in the violin. But even so, the glorious mystery of his bonny leddy was gone forever—and alas! she had no soul. He could never meet her again. His affections, which must live forever, were set upon that which had passed away. But the child that weeps because a mutilated doll will not rise from the dead shall yet find relief from sorrow. The child shall know that that which in the doll made that one love the doll has not passed away. And Robert must yet be comforted for the loss of his bonny leddy. If she had had a soul, nothing but her own self could ever satisfy him. As it was, that which in him had loved her would rise from the ashes of her death and love again.

But the time for that was not yet come.

In the meantime, the shears of Fate having cut the string of the sky-soaring kite of his imagination had left him with the stick in his hand. And thus the rest of that winter was dreary. The glow was out of his heart; the glow was out of the world. The bleak, kindless wind was hissing through those pines that clothed the hill above Bodyfauld and over the dead garden, where in the summertime the rose had looked down so lovingly. All he felt was a keen sense of personal misery and hopeless cold. Was the summer a lie?

Not so. The winter restrains that the summer may have the needful time to do its work well, for the winter is but the sleep of summer.

Now in the season of his discontent, and in nature finding no help, Robert was driven inwards—into his garret, into his soul. The door of his paradise being walled up, he began vaguely, blindly, to knock against other doors—sometimes against stone walls and rocks, taking them for doors. A door, out or in, he must find, or perish.

It happened too that Mary went to visit some friends who lived in a coast town some twenty miles off. A season of heavy snow followed and she was gone for six weeks. During this time, without a single care to trouble him from without, Robert was in the very desert of desolation. His spirits sank fearfully. He would pass his old music master in the street with scarce a recognition, as if the bond of their relation had been utterly broken, had vanished in the smoke of the martyred violin and all their affection had gone into the dustheap of the past.

Dooble Sanny's character did not improve. He took more and more whiskey, his bouts of drinking alternating as before with fits of hopeless repentance. His work was more neglected than ever and his wife, having no money to spend even upon necessities, applied in desperation also to her husband's bottle for comfort. Little did the whiskey-hating old Mrs. Falconer know to what god she had really offered up that violin.

But now began to appear in Robert the first signs of a practical outcome of such truths as his grandmother had taught him. She had taught him to look up—that there was a God. He would put it to the test. Not that he doubted it yet; he only doubted whether there was a hearing God. But was not that worse? For it is of far more consequence what kind of a God than whether a God or not. But, indeed, whether better or worse is no great matter, so long as he would see it or what there was. Robert had no comfort, and without reasoning about it, he felt that life ought to have comfort—from which he began to conclude that the only thing left was to try whether the God in whom his grandmother believed might not help him. If God would but hear him! For now that would be enough. If he spoke to Robert one kind word, it would be the very soul of comfort, for he could no more be lonely.

A fountain of glad imaginations gushed up in his heart at the very thought. What if, from the cold winter of his life, he had but to open the door of his garret room and, kneeling by the bare bedstead, enter into the summer of God's presence! What if God spoke to him face to face? He had so spoken to Moses. He sought him from no fear of the future, but from present desolation. And if God came near to him, it would not be with storm and tempest, but with the voice of a friend. And surely, if there was a God at all, he must hear the voice of the creature whom he had made, a voice that came crying out of the very need which he had created.

Hence, Robert continued to disappear from his grandmother's parlor at much the same hour as before. In the cold, desolate garret he knelt and cried out into that which lay beyond thought, the unknowable infinite, after the God that may be known as surely as a little child knows his mysterious mother. And from behind him, the pale blue, star-crowded sky shone upon his head through the window that looked upwards only.

Mrs. Falconer saw that he still went away as he had done, and instituted observations, the result of which was the knowledge that he went to his own room. Her heart smote her and she saw that the boy looked sad and troubled. There was scarcely room in her heart for increase of love, but much for increase of kindness, and she did increase it. And in truth, Robert needed but the smallest crumb of comfort.

Night after night he returned to the parlor cold to the very heart. God was not to be found, he said then. Later he said that even though God was with him, he knew it not.

The very first night he knelt and cried, "O Father in heaven, hear me, and let thy face shine upon me." But like a flash of burning fire the words shot from the door of his heart, "I don't care about him loving me if he doesn't love everybody," and he could not pray another word that night, although he knelt for an hour of agony in the freezing dark.

Loyal to what he had been taught, he struggled hard to reduce his rebellious will to what he supposed to be the will of God. It was all in vain. Ever a voice within him cast up questions he had been taught it was wicked to ask. He could not help feeling he would be a traitor to his face if he accepted a love, even from God, given him as an exception from his own kind. He did not care to have such a love. It was not what his heart yearned for. It was not *love*. He could not love such a love. Yet he strove against these feelings within himself—fighting for the religion of his grandmother against the love which his heart longed for. Night after night he returned to the battle, but with no permanent success. Night after night he came pale and worn from the conflict, found his grandmother and Shargar composed, and in the quietness of despair, sat down beside them to his Latin.

He little thought that every night, at the moment when he stirred to leave the upper room, a pale-faced, red-eyed figure rose from its seat on the top of the stair by the door, and sped with long-legged noise-lessness to resume its seat by the grandmother before he should enter. Shargar saw that Robert was unhappy, and the nearest he could come to the sharing of his unhappiness was to take his place outside the door within which he had retreated. Little, too, did Shargar, on his part, think that Robert, without knowing it, was pleading for him inside—pleading for him and for all his race in the weeping that would not be comforted.

Robert had not the vaguest fancy that God was with him—the Spirit of the Father groaning with the spirit of the boy. But God *was* with him, and was indeed victorious in the boy when he rose from his knees—for the last time, as he thought—saying, "I cannot yield. I cannot pray for special favor from God. I cannot pray for the assurance that God is my private friend while he capriciously turns his back on others and dooms them to an eternity in hell. I will pray no more."

With a burst of bitter tears he sat down on the bedside till the loudest of the storm was over. Then he dried his dull eyes, in which the old outlook had withered away, and walked unknowingly in the silent foot-steps of Shargar, who was ever one corner in advance of him, down to the dreary lessons and unheeded prayers.

My reader must not mistake my use of the words *special* and *private* by supposing that I do not believe in an individual relation between every man and God—yes, a *peculiar* relation. It was not this individu-ality which was repugnant to Robert, but the notion that God chooses certain people with whom to establish this sort of relation while arbi-trarily turning his back on others, and that no amount of goodness or repentance could ever alter the predestined divine decree.

Mrs. Falconer, before she went to sleep, gave thanks that the boys had been at their prayers together. And so, in a very deep sense, they had.

The next evening, having given up (as he supposed) his praying, Robert went out into the street. Nothing was to be seen there but faint blue air full of moonlight, solid houses, and shining snow. Bareheaded he wandered round the corner to the window where first he had heard the sweet sounds of the piano. The fire within lighted up the crimson curtains, but no voice of music came forth.

Not a form was in the street. The eyes of the houses gleamed here and there upon the snow. All at once a wailful sound arose in his head. He did not think for some time whether it was born in his brain or came from without. At length he recognized the "Flowers of the Forest" played as only the shoemaker could play it. But alas! the cry responsive to his bow came only from the auld fiddle—no more from his bonny leddy. The shoemaker, halfway to his goal of drunkenness, had begun to repent for the fiftieth time that year. With his repentance he had mingled the memory of the bonny leddy ruthlessly tormented to death for his wrong, and had glided into the tune almost without knowing it. The lament interpreted itself to his disconsolate pupil as he had never understood it before; it now spoke his own feelings of waste, misery, forsaken loneliness. Indeed, Robert learned more of music in those few minutes of the foggy winter night and open street than he could ever have from many many lessons, even from Mary St. John. He was cold to the heart, yet went in a little comforted.

Things had gone ill with him. Outside of Paradise, deserted of his angel, in the frost and snow, the voice of the despised violin once more the source of a sad comfort. But there is no better discipline than an occasional descent from what we count well-being, to a former despised or less happy condition. One of the results of this in Robert was that, when he was in bed that night his heart began to turn gently toward his old master. How much did he not owe him after all! Had he not acted ill and ungrateful in deserting him? With his own vessel filled to the brim with grief, had he not let the waters of its bitterness overflow into the heart of the shoemaker? The wail of that violin echoed now in Robert's heart. Comrades in misery, why should they part? What right had he to forsake an old friend and benefactor because he himself was unhappy? He would go and see him the very next night. And he would make friends once more with the suffering instrument he had so wrongfully despised.

22 / The Stroke

The following night Robert left his books on the table and sped to Dooble Sanny's shop, lifted the latch, and entered.

By the light of a single candle he saw the shoemaker seated on his stool, one hand lying on the lap of his leather apron, the other hanging down by his side, and the fiddle on the ground at his feet. His wife stood behind him, wiping her eyes with her blue apron. Through all its accumulated dirt, the face of the shoemaker looked ghastly, and they were eyes of despair that he lifted to the face of the youth who stood holding the latch in his hand.

"What on earth's the matter with you, Sandy?" said Robert.

"Eh, Robert!" returned the shoemaker in a mournful tone, "eh, the Almighty will have his own way, an' I'm in his grip now."

"He's had a stroke," said his wife, without removing her apron from her eyes.

"I've gotten my blows," resumed the shoemaker in a despairing voice. "I have gotten my blows for cryin' down my own 'auld wife' to set up yer bonny leddy. The one's gone to ashes an' dust, an' from the other"—he went on, looking down on the violin at his feet as if it had been something dead in its youth—"an' from the other I can't draw a sound, for my right hand has forgotten her cunning. Man, Robert, I can't lift it from my side."

"You must go to your bed," remonstrated Robert, greatly concerned.

"Ow, aye, I must go t' my bed an' then t' the churchyard, an' then t' hell—I know that well enough. Robert, I leave my fiddle t' ye. Be good t' the auld wife, man—better than I have been. An auld wife's better than no fiddle."

He stooped, lifted the violin with his left hand, gave it to Robert, rose, and made for the door. They helped him up the creaking stair, got him half undressed, and laid him in his bed. Robert put the violin on the top of a press within his sight, left him groaning, and ran for the doctor. Having seen him set out for the patient's dwelling, he ran home to his grandmother.

Now while Robert was absent, occasion to look for him arose when

132

the schoolmaster, Mr. Innes, had called. Shargar had been sent from the parlor and had seated himself outside Robert's room, never doubting that Robert was inside. Presently he heard the bell ring and then Betty came up the stair and said Robert was wanted. Shargar knocked at the door and, hearing nothing, opened it to discover that he had been watching an empty room. However, he made no haste to communicate this fact. Robert might return in a moment and his absence from the house not be discovered. He sat down on the bedstead and waited. But Betty came up again, and before Shargar could prevent her, walked into the room with her candle in her hand. In vain did Shargar beg her to go and say that Robert was coming. But Betty would not risk the danger of being discovered in connivance, and descended to break open all over again the fountain of the old lady's anxiety.

Mrs. Falconer had asked the schoolmaster to visit her to consult about Robert's future. Mr. Innes expressed a high opinion of the boy's faculties and strongly urged that he should be sent to college. Mrs. Falconer inwardly shuddered at the temptations to which this would expose him, but he was at the age when he must either leave home or be apprenticed to some trade. While the schoolmaster was presenting the argument that Robert was pretty sure to gain a good *bursary,* and his grandmother would thus be relieved for four years—probably forever—from further expense on his account, Robert entered.

"Where hae ye been, Robert?" asked Mrs. Falconer.

"At Dooble Sanny's," answered the boy.

"What were ye at there?"

"Helping him to his bed."

"What's come over him?"

"A stroke."

"That's what comes o' playing the fiddle."

"I never heard of a stroke coming from a fiddle, Grannie. It comes out of a cloud sometimes. If he had been holding to his fiddle, he would have been playing her tonight instead of his arm lying at his side like a shoemaker's thread."

"Hmm!" said his grandmother, concealing her indignation at this freedom of speech. "Ye don't believe i' God's judgments?"

"Not upon fiddles," returned Robert.

Mr. Innes sat and said nothing, with difficulty concealing his amusement at this passage between them.

It was only within the last few days that Robert had become capable of speaking freely like this. His nature had at length arrived at the point of casting off the incubus of his grandmother's authority to the point where he could assert some measure of freedom and act openly. His very hopelessness of a hearing in heaven had made him indifferent to things on earth, and therefore bolder. But it was not despair alone that gave him strength. On his way home from the shoemaker's, he had been thinking what he could do for him; and he had resolved, come of it what might, that he would visit him every evening and see if he might be able to comfort him a little by playing on his violin. Therefore, it was lovingkindness toward man, as well as despair toward his grannie's God, that gave him strength to resolve that between him and she all should from this point on be above board.

"Not upon fiddles," Robert had said.

"But upon them that plays them," returned his grandmother.

"No, nor upon them that burns them," retorted Robert—impudently, it must be confessed.

But Mrs. Falconer had too much regard for her own dignity to give way to her feelings, especially in front of Mr. Innes. Possibly, too, her sense of justice as well as some movement of her conscience interfered. In any case, she was silent, and Robert rushed into the breach which his last discharge had effected.

"And I want to tell you, Grannie, that I mean to go and play the fiddle to poor Sandy every night for the best part of an hour, and except you lock the door and hide the key, I *will* go. The poor sinner shall not be deserted by God and man both."

He scarcely knew what he was saying before it was out of his mouth; and as if to cover it up he hurried on: "And there's more. Dr. Anderson gave Shargar and me a sovereign apiece. And Dooble Sanny shall have them, to keep him from dying of hunger and cold."

"Why didn't ye tell me that Dr. Anderson had given ye such a heap o' money? It was wrong o' ye—an' him as well!"

" 'Cause you would have sent it back to him, and Shargar and me thought we would rather keep it."

"Considering that I'm at so much expense wi' ye both, it wouldn't hae been ill-contrived t' hae brought the money t' me, an' letten me do wi' it as I thought fit—Don't go away, laddie," she added as she saw Robert about to leave the room.

"I'll be back in a minute, Grannie," returned Robert.

"He's a fine lad!" said Mr. Innes, "and good'll come of him."

"If he had but the grace o' God, there wouldn't be much t' complain o'," acquiesced his grandmother.

Robert returned before Mr. Innes had made up his mind as to whether the old lady intended to continue or expected a comment from him.

"Here, Grannie," Robert said, going up to her and putting the two sovereigns in her white hand. He had found some difficulty in making

Shargar give up his, else he would have returned sooner.

"What's this, laddie?" said Mrs. Falconer. "Hoots! I'm not going t' take yer money. Let the poor shoemaker hae it. But don't give them more than a shilling or two at once—just t' keep them i' life. They deserve no more. But they mustn't starve. An' just tell them, laddie, that if they spend sixpence o' it upon whiskey they'll get no more."

"Ay, ay, Grannie," responded Robert with a glimmer of gladness in his heart. "And what about the fiddling, Grannie?" he added, half playfully, hoping for some kind concession therein as well.

But he had gone too far.

She gave no reply and her face grew stern with offense. It was one thing to give bread to eat, another to give music and gladness. No music but that which sprang from the perseverance of the saints could be lawful in a world that was under the wrath and curse of God. Robert waited in vain for a reply.

"Go yer way," she said at length. "Mr. Innes and me has some business t' make an end, an' we want no assistance."

Robert joined Shargar, who was still bemoaning the loss of his sovereign. His face brightened when he saw its well-known yellow shine once more, but darkened again as soon as Robert told him to what service it was now devoted.

"It's my own," he grumbled.

Robert threw the coin on the floor. "Take your filthy lucre!" he exclaimed and turned to leave Shargar alone in the garret with his sovereign.

"Bob!" Shargar almost screamed, "Take it or I'll cut my throat." This was his constant threat when he was thoroughly in earnest.

"Cut it and have done with it," said Robert cruelly.

Shargar burst out crying.

"Lend me your knife then, Bob," he sobbed, holding out his hand.

Robert burst into a roar of laughter, caught up the sovereign from the floor, sped with it to the baker's, who refused to change it because he had no knowledge of anything representing the sum of twenty shillings except a pound note. Robert succeeded in getting silver for it at the bank, and then ran to the shoemaker's.

After he had left the parlor, the discussion of his fate was resumed and finally settled between his grandmother and the schoolmaster. The former, in regard of the boy's determination to befriend the shoemaker in the matter of music as well as of money, would now have sent him at once to the grammar school in Old Aberdeen to prepare for the testing competition in the month of November. But the latter persuaded her that if the boy gave his whole attention to Latin till the next summer, and then went to the grammar school for three months or so, he would have an excellent chance of success. As to the violin, the schoolmaster said, wisely enough: "He that *will* do a thing *must* do it. If you interfere with him on the shore road, he'll take to the hill road. And I'll warrant a determined lad like Robert'll find many a one in Aberdeen that'll be ready enough to give him a lift with the fiddle, and maybe take him into worse company than the poor bedridden shoemaker."

"Hmm!" was the old lady's comprehensive response.

It was further arranged that Robert should be informed of their conclusion and so roused to effort in anticipation to study strenuously for the schooling upon which his course in life must depend.

Nothing could have been better for Robert than the prospect of a college education. And so practical and thorough was he in all his proposals and means that before half an hour was gone, he had taken to his studies more diligently than ever. He gained permission from his grandmother to bed down in his own garret. There, from the bedstead at which he no longer kneeled, he would often rise at four in the morning, even when the snow lay a foot thick on the skylight, kindle his lamp by means of a tinder box and a splinter of wood dipped in sulphur, and sitting down in the keen cold translate half a page of Addison or something else into as near perfect Latin as he could. He read Caesar, Virgil, or Tacitus every day as well, sometimes at the same hour. After an hour and a half or two hours he would tumble again into bed, blue and stiff, and sleep till it was time to get up and go to the morning school before breakfast. His health was excellent, else it could never have stood such treatment.

23 / Dooble Sanny

Robert's sole relaxation almost lay in the visit he paid every evening to the shoemaker and his wife. Their home was a wretched place. But notwithstanding the utmost poverty in which they were now sunk, Robert soon began to see a change, like the dawning of light, in the appearance of something white here and there about the room. Robert's visits had set the poor woman trying to make the place look decent. It soon became clean at least, and there is a very real sense in which cleanliness truly is next to godliness. If the people who want to do good among the poor would stop patronizing them and trying to convert them, and instead simply visit them as those who have just as good a right to be here as they have, it would be all the better for both.

For the first week or so, Alexander, unable either to work or play and deprived of his usual consolation of drink, was very testy and unmanageable. But almost immediately after he had made any outburst, invariably the shoemaker would ask forgiveness. Holding out his left hand, from which nothing could efface the stains of rosin and lampblack and heel-ball, except the sweet cleansing of mother earth, he would say, "Robert, ye'll just have to forgive the swearin' with all the rest. I'm an ill-tongued wretch, an' I'm beginnin' to see it. But, man, ye're just behavin' to me as kindly as God himself."

And every evening, as Robert was leaving, he asked with some anxiety, "Ye will be here tomorrow night—won't ye?"

"Of course I will," Robert would answer.

"Good night, then, good night. I'll try an' get a hold o' my sins once more," he added one evening. "If only I could be a little sorrier for them, I reckon he would forgive me. Don't ye think he would, Robert?"

"No doubt, no doubt," answered Robert, hurriedly. "They say that if a man repents the right way, he'll forgive him."

He could not say more than "they say," for his own horizon was still all dark, and even in saying this much he felt like a hypocrite. A terrible waste, heaped thick with the potsherds of hope, lay outside that door of prayer which he had, as he thought, nailed up forever.

"An' what is the right way?" asked the shoemaker.

"Indeed, that's more than I know, Sandy," answered Robert in a sad tone.

"Well, if *ye* don't know, what's to come o' *me*?" asked Alexander seriously.

"You must ask him yourself," returned Robert, "and just tell him that you don't know, but you'll do anything he likes."

With these words he quickly took his leave, somewhat amazed to find that he had given the shoemaker the strange advice to try just what he had tried so unavailingly himself. And, stranger still, he found himself, before he reached home, praying once more in his heart—both for Dooble Sanny and for himself. From that hour a faint hope was within him that someday he might try again, though he dared not embark upon such effort and agony.

All this time he had never doubted that there was a God, nor had he ventured to say within himself that perhaps God was not good. He had simply come to the conclusion that for him there was no approach to the fountain of his being.

In the course of two weeks or so, when Elshender's system had covered over its craving after whiskey, the irritability of the shoemaker almost vanished. It might have been feared that his conscience would likewise relax its activity, but it was not so. It grew yet more tender. He now began to give Robert some praise and make allowances for his faults, and Robert thus dared more and played with more spirit.

The time came at length when Miss St. John returned from her visit. It chanced that he was standing gazing out the windowpane next to the front door when the carriage bearing his friend turned noisily into the street, its thin wooden wheels crunching the frosty snow under them. Caring no longer what his grannie saw or what she might think, he burst through the door and ran to meet her.

"Robert, where are ye going!" Mrs. Falconer called after him.

But there was no answer save the slamming of the door after him. She hastened from the parlor to watch, in amazement and consternation, the proceedings which followed her. Her Robert was indeed a young man and not a boy any longer!

Robert dashed from the house and toward the street where stood two pawing and frothy horses, their mighty white breaths pulsating from flaming nostrils into the crisp, keen air. Robert ran up just as they had come to a halt.

With mingled boyish timidity and manly boldness, he stepped forward and reached for the door, opening it slowly outward. Inside, even prettier than he remembered her, sat his one-time angel. Neither spoke a word. Their eyes met; Mary dropped hers almost immediately, with the slightest hint of crimson rising from her neck into her cheeks, then took Robert's offered hand and stepped out of the carriage. Robert, tingling with the first real surge of joy he had felt in weeks, assisted her until her foot touched the ground, gently let go of the warm hand, and—still without having spoken a word—went around to the back of the carriage to help her with her bags. No words seemed necessary. In the meeting of their eyes, they each understood.

One evening a few days later, when Robert was again visiting Dooble Sanny, Mr. MacCleary walked in. Robert ceased his playing. The minister gave him one searching glance and then sat down by the bedside. Robert made a move to leave the room, but was interrupted by his friend.

"Don't go, Robert," implored Sandy.

The clergyman began by talking in the vaguest of terms to the shoemaker. He was one of those prudent men who are afraid of dealing out the truth freely lest it should fall on thorns or stony places. Hence, the good ground came in for a scanty share too. Believing that a certain repentant condition of mind was necessary for its proper reception, he endeavored to bring about that condition first. He did not know that the truth makes its own nest in the ready heart and that the heart may be ready for it before the priest can perceive the fact. He therefore dwelt upon the sins of the shoemaker, magnifying them in the imagination of poor Dooble Sanny, while of the special tenderness of God to the sinner he said not a word. Robert was offended, he scarcely knew why, with the minister's mode of treating his friend, and after Mr. MacCleary had taken his leave of them, Robert sat still and oppressed.

"It's all true," mourned the shoemaker, "but, man, Robert, don't ye think the minister was too sore on me?"

"I do think so," answered Robert.

"Somethin' in me tells me that he wouldn't be so hard on me himself. There's somethin' in the New Testament, some thought that's puttin' itself into my head; though, faith, I don't know where to look for it. Can ye help me out with it?"

Robert could think of nothing but the parable of the prodigal son. Sandy's wife got him the New Testament and he read the parable. She sat at the foot of the bed listening.

"There!" cried the shoemaker triumphantly. "I told ye so! Not a word about the poor lad's sins! It was all just a hurry an' a scurry to get the new shoes on him so he could get to the fiddlin' an' the dancin'. O Lord," he broke out, "I'm comin' home as fast as I can, but my sins are just like some old shoes holdin' my feet down an' they won't let me be. I expect no ring an' no robe, but how I would like a fiddle in my hands when the next prodigal comes home! O Lord, if I ever get up again an' back to work, I swear I'll put in every stitch as if the shoes were for the feet o' the prodigal himself. It shall be good work, O Lord. An' I'll never let the taste o' whiskey into my mouth—nor the smell o' it into my nose—if I can help it. I swear it, O Lord. An' if I be not raised up again—''

Here his voice trembled and ceased, and silence ensued for a short minute. Then he called his wife.

"Come here, Bell. Give me a kiss, my bonny lass. I've been an ill man to ye.''

"No, no, Sandy. Ye have aye been good t' me—better'n I deserved. Ye have been nobody's enemy but yer own.''

"Hold yer tongue. Ye'll be speakin' more nonsense than the minister. I tell ye I've been a scoundrel to ye. Ah, but ye were a bonny lass when I married ye. I have spoiled ye altogether. But if I were up, see if I wouldn't give ye a new gown, and that would make ye like yerself again. I'm affronted with myself that I've been such a brute. But ye must forgive me, for I do believe in my heart that the Lord's forgiven me. Give me another kiss, lass. God be praised, an' many thanks to *you*! Ye might have run away from me a long time ago.—Robert, play a tune.''

Robert struck up with an air. When he had played it over two or three times, he laid the fiddle in its place and departed—just able to see, by the light of the neglected candle, that Bell sat by the bedside stroking the rosiny hand of her husband, the rhinoceros hide of which was yet delicate enough to let the love through to his heart.

After this the shoemaker never called his fiddle his auld wife.

Henceforth Robert had more to do in reading the New Testament than in playing the fiddle to the shoemaker, though they never parted without a musical air or two. Sandy continued hopeful and generally cheerful, with alterations which the reading generally fixed on the right side for the night. Robert never attempted any comments, but left him to take from the Word what nourishment he could. There was no return of strength to the helpless arm, and his constitution was gradually yielding.

The rumor got out that he was a "changed character"—how was not far to seek, for Mr. MacCleary fancied himself the honored instrument of his conversion, whereas paralysis and the New Testament were the chief agents, and even the violin had more share in it than the minister. For the Spirit of God lies all about the spirit of man like a mighty sea, ready to rush in at the smallest chink in the walls that shut him out from his own—walls which even the tone of a violin or the smell of a rose is sometimes enough to rend.

And now till the day of his death, the shoemaker had need of nothing. Food, wine, and delicacies were sent him by many, who, while they considered him outside the kingdom, would have troubled themselves in no way about him. What with visits of condolence and flattery, inquiries into his experience, and long prayers by his bedside, they now did their best to send him back among the wine. The shoemaker's humor, however, aided by his violin, was a strong antidote against these dark influences.

"I don't doubt but I'm going to die, Robert," he said at length one evening as the lad sat by his bedside.

"Well, that won't do you no harm," answered Robert.

"I don't care about the dyin'. But I just want to live long enough to let the Lord know I'm in downright earnest about it. I have no chance o' drinkin' so long as I'm lyin' here."

"Don't fret your head about that. You can trust that to him, for it's his own business. He'll see that you're all right. Don't think that he'll let you off."

"The Lord forbid," responded the shoemaker earnestly. "It must be put right. I wouldn't have him content with cobbler's work." After a few minutes' pause, he resumed, "The Lord's easy to please, but hard to satisfy. I'm so pleased with yer playin', Robert, but it's nothin' like the right thing yet. It does me good to hear ye, though for all that."

The very next night Robert found him evidently sinking fast. He took the violin and was about to play, but the shoemaker stretched out his left hand and took it from him, laid it across his chest and his arm over it for a few moments, as if he were bidding it farewell, then held it out to Robert, saying, "Here, Robert. She's yers. Death's a painful divorce. Maybe they'll have an extra fiddle where I'm goin', though. Think o' a Rothieden shoemaker playin' before his Grace!"

Robert saw that his mind was wandering. He began to play. For a little while Sandy seemed to follow and comprehend the tones, but by slow degrees the light departed from his face. At length his jaw fell and with a sigh the body parted from Dooble Sanny, and he went to God.

His wife closed mouth and eyes without a word, laid the two arms, equally powerless now, straight by his sides, then, seating herself on the edge of the bed, said, "Don't stay, Robert. It's over now. He's gone home. . . . If only I were with him, wherever he is!"

She burst into tears, but dried her eyes a moment after and, seeing that Robert still lingered, said, "Go, Robert, and send Mistress Downie to me. Don't grieve—there's a good lad. But take yer fiddle and go. Ye can be no more use."

Robert obeyed. With his violin in his hand, he went home and, with his violin still in his hand, walked into his grandmother's parlor.

"How dare ye bring such a thing int' my house?" she said, roused by the apparent defiance of her grandson. "How dare ye after what's come an' gone?"

" 'Cause Dooble Sanny's come and gone, Grannie, and left nothing but this behind him. And this one's now mine, whose ever the other might have been. His wife's left without a penny, and I'll warrant the good fold of Rothieden won't go out of their way to help her. So I must make the best that I can of the fiddle for her. And you mustn't touch this one, Grannie, for though you may think it right to burn fiddles, other folk don't. And this has to do with other folk, Grannie; it's not between you and me, you know"— Robert went on, fearful lest she might consider herself divinely commissioned to extirpate the whole race of stringed instruments —"for I must sell it for her."

"Take it out o' my sight," said Mrs. Falconer, and said no more.

He carried the instrument up to his room, laid it on his bed, locked his door, put the key in his pocket, and descended to the parlor.

"He's dead, is he?" said his grandmother, as he reentered.

"Ay, he is, Grannie," answered Robert. "He died a repentant man."

"An' a believin' one?" asked Mrs. Falconer.

"Well, Grannie, I can't say that he believed all things that ever was, for a body might not know everything."

"Toots, laddie! Was it savin' faith?"

"I don't rightly know what you mean by that, but I'm thinkin' it was much the same kind of faith that the prodigal had, for they both turned and went toward home."

"Indeed, maybe ye're right, laddie," returned Mrs. Falconer after a moment's thought. "We'll hope the best."

All the remainder of the evening she sat motionless, with her eyes fixed on the rug before her, thinking no doubt of the repentance and salvation of the fiddler, and what hope there might yet be for her own lost son.

The next day being Saturday, Robert set out for Bodyfauld, taking the violin with him. He went alone, for he was in no mood for Shargar's company. It was a fine spring day, the woods were budding and the fragrances of the larches floated across his way. There was a lovely sadness in the sky and in the motions of the clouds and in the scent of the earth. And Robert wondered how it was that everything should look so different. Even Bodyfauld seemed to have lost its enchantment, though his friends were as kind as ever.

Mr. Lammie went into a rage at the story of the lost violin, and Miss

Lammie cried from sympathy with Robert's distress at the fate of his bonny leddy. Then Robert came to the reason for his visit, which was to beg Mr. Lammie, when he went to Aberdeen next, to take the shoemaker's fiddle and get what he could for it, to help Sandy's widow.

"Poor Sandy!" said Robert, "it never came into his head to sell her."

Mr. Lammie undertook the commission and the next time he saw Robert, handed him ten pounds as the result of the negotiation. It was all Robert could do, however, to get the poor woman to take the money. But eventually Robert succeeded in overcoming her scruples and she did take it; with it she provided a store of *sweeties*, and reels of cotton, and tobacco, for sale in Sandy's workshop. She certainly did not make money by her merchandise, for her anxiety to be honest rose to the absurd. But she contrived to live without being reduced to prey upon her own gingerbread and rock candy.

24 / To Aberdeen

Since her return, having heard how much Robert was taken up with his dying friend, Mary judged it better to leave alone for the present her intended proposal of renewing the music lessons. Meeting him, however, soon after Alexander's death, she introduced the subject, and Robert was enraptured at the prospect of the reopening of the gates of his paradise. If he did not inform his grandmother of the fact, neither did he attempt to conceal it, but she took no notice, probably thinking that the whole affair would be effectually disposed of by his departure for college. Till that time arrived he had a lesson almost every evening, and Mary was almost as surprised as his grannie to find out how the boy had grown since the door had been built up.

Robert's grandmother had arranged that he should accompany Mr. Lammie to Aberdeen, business drawing him there about the same time as Robert's school was to begin. The evening before his departure for Bodyfauld, as he was having his last lesson, Mrs. Forsyth left the room. Robert, who had been dejected all day at the thought of the separation from Mary, found his heart beating so violently that he could hardly breathe. Probably she saw his emotion, for she put her hand on the keys, as if to cover it by showing him how some movement was to be made. He seized her hand and lifted it to his lips. But when he found that, instead of snatching it away, she yielded it and even gently pressed it to his face, he dropped on his knees.

"Hush, Robert! Don't be foolish," she said, quietly and tenderly. "Here is my aunt coming."

The same moment he was at the piano again playing so well as to admonish both Mary and himself as well. Then he rose, bade a hasty good night, and hurried away.

A strange conflict arose in his mind at the prospect of leaving the old place, on every house of whose streets, on every swell of whose surrounding hills he left the clinging shadows of thought and feeling. A faintly purpled mist arose and enwrapped all the past, changing even his gayest troubles into tales of fairyland and his deepest griefs into songs of a sad music. Then he thought of Shargar, and what was to become of him after he was gone. The lad was paler and his eyes were

144

redder than ever, for he had been weeping in secret. Robert went to his grandmother and begged that Shargar might accompany him to Body-fauld.

"He must stay at home an' mind his books," she answered, "for he won't hae them much longer. He must be doing something for him-self."

So the next morning the boys parted—Shargar to school and Robert to Bodyfauld—Shargar left behind with his desolation, his sun gone down in a west that was not even stormy, only gray and hopeless, and Robert moving toward an east which reflected, like a faint prophecy, the west behind him tinged with love, death, and music, but mingled the colors with its own hint of coming dawn.

When he reached Bodyfauld he marveled to find that all its glory had returned. He found Miss Lammie busy among the rich yellow pools in her dairy, and went out into the garden, now in the height of summer. Great cabbage roses hung heavy-laden; tall white lilies mingled with the blossoms of currant bushes, and at their feet the narcissi pressed their warmhearted paleness into the thicket of the many-striped gardener's garters. Robert's whole mind was flooded with a sense of sunny wealth. The farmer's neglected garden blossomed into higher glory in his soul. Oh, how much would he have liked to gather a posy to offer Mary St. John! But, alas! he was no poet, or rather he had but the half of the poet's inheritance—he could see, but he could not say.

The next morning he awoke at early dawn, hearing the birds at his window. He rose and went out. The air was clear and fresh. Clouds were bent across the eastern quarter of the sky. Everything was waiting to conduct him across the far horizon to the south, where lay the stored-up wonder of his coming life. The lark sang of something greater than he could tell; the wind got up, whispered at it, and lay down to sleep again. The sun was at hand to bathe the world in the light and gladness that alone typified the radiance of Robert's thoughts.

Just as the sun rushed across the horizon, he heard the tramp of a heavy horse in the yard, passing from the stable to the cart that was to carry his trunk to the turnpike road, three miles off, where the coach would pass. Then Miss Lammie came and called him to breakfast, and there sat the farmer in his Sunday suit of black, already busy. Robert was almost too excited to eat. He had not swallowed two mouthfuls before the sun rose unheeded, the lark sang out loudly, and the roses sparkled with the dew. By the time they had finished, Mr. Lammie's gig was at the door and they mounted and followed the cart.

Not even the recurring doubt and fear that hollowness was at the heart of it all, that God could not be meaning such sunny gladness, could prevent the truth of the present joy from sinking deep into the lad's heart. In his mind he saw a boat moored to a rock, with no one on board, heaving on the waters of a rising tide and waiting to bear him out on the seas of the unknown.

The gig and the cart reached the road together. One of the men who had accompanied the cart took the gig, and they were left on the roadside with Robert's trunk and box—the latter a present from Miss Lammie.

Their places had been secured and the guard knew where he had to pick them up. Long before the coach appeared, the notes of his horn came echoing from the side of the heathery, stony hill under which they stood. She pulled up gallantly; the wheelers lay on their hindquarters, and the leaders parted theirs from the pole. The boxes were hoisted up; Mr. Lammie climbed up and Robert scrambled to his seat; the horn blew; the coachman spoke oracularly; the horses obeyed; and away careered the gorgeous symbol of sovereignty. Robert's delight did not stop during the entire journey, certainly not when he first saw the blue line of the sea in the distance.

Mrs. Falconer had consulted the Misses Napier from the Boar's Head, who had many acquaintances in Aberdeen, as to a place proper for Robert and suitable to her means. Upon these points Miss Letty had been able to satisfy her. In a small house of two floors and a garret, in the old town, Mr. Lammie left Robert.

It was from a garret window still, but a storm window now, that Robert looked, eastward across fields and sand hills to the blue expanse of waters—not blue like southern seas, but slaty blue, like the eyes of northmen. It was rather dreary; the sun was shining from overhead now, casting short shadows and much heat. He was alone; the end of his journey was come and was not anything very remarkable. His landlady interrupted his gaze to ask what he would like for dinner, but he merely replied that anything would be fine. When she left the room he did not return to the window but sat down upon his trunk. His eye fell upon the other, a big wooden box, given him by Miss Lammie. Of its contents he knew nothing.

He would investigate. It was nailed up. He borrowed a screwdriver and opened it. At the top lay a linen bag full of oatmeal. Underneath that was a thick layer of oatcake, underneath that two cheeses, a pound of butter, and six pots of jam, and various other delights from the young woman's kitchen. At the very bottom lay a black case which strangely recalled Shargar's garret and one of its closets. With beating heart he opened it and lo, to his marvel, there was the violin which Dooble Sanny had left him!

In a flutter of delight he sat down on his trunk again and played the most mournful of tunes. Two white pigeons that had been talking to each other in the heat of the roof came and peeped into the room. He forgot all about school and college and went on playing till his landlady brought up his dinner, which he swallowed hastily that he might return to the spells of his old friend!

25 / Dr. Anderson

If Robert's schoolwork was dry, at least it was thorough. Robert leaned to the collar and labored steadily, not greatly moved by ambition but much by the hope of the bursary and the college life in the near distance. Slowly the hours went and yet the dreaded, hoped-for day came quickly. October faded softly by and November came, chill and drear. And at length Robert found himself taking his place with the rest of the assembly before the bench of the incorruptible. They were given a portion of Robertson's "History of Scotland" to turn into Latin; and soon there was nothing to be heard in the great hall but the turning of the leaves of dictionaries and the scratching of pens constructing the first rough copy of the Latinized theme.

Finally it was done. Four weary hours, nearly five—one or two of which passed like minutes, the others as if each minute had been an hour—went by, and Robert, in a kind of desperation, after a final reading of the Latin, handed in his paper and left the room. When he got home he asked his landlady if he might have some tea. Till it was ready he would take his violin. But even the violin had grown dull and would not speak freely.

He returned to the torture—took out his first copy, and went over it once more. Horror of horrors! Mary Queen of Scots had been left so far behind in the beginning of the paper that she forgot the rights of her sex in the middle, and in the accusative of a future participle passive had submitted to be *dum*, and her rightful *dam* was henceforth and forever debarred. It was a *maximus error*!

He rushed out of the house, down through the garden, across two fields and a wide road, and so to the moaning of the sea, where he paced up and down—for how long only God, who was watching him, knew.

The next day he had to translate a passage from "Tacitus." After executing it somewhat heartlessly, he did not open a Latin book for a whole week. The very sight of one was disgusting to him. He wandered about the new town, along Union Street, up and down the stairs that led to the lower parts, haunted the quay, watched the vessels, and made friends with a certain Dutch captain whom he heard playing the violin in his cabin.

The day of decision at length arrived. Again the black-robed powers assembled and again the hoping, fearing young men gathered to hear their fate. Name after name was called out—a twenty-pound bursary to the first, one of seventeen to the next, three of fifteen, and so on, for about twenty, and still no Robert Falconer. At last, lagging wearily in the rear, he heard his name, went up listlessly, and was awarded five pounds. He crept home, wrote to his grandmother, and awaited her reply. It was not long in coming. It was to the effect that his grandmother was sorry that he had not been more successful, but that Mr. Innes thought it would be quite worthwhile to try again, and he must therefore come home for another year.

This was mortifying enough, though not so bad as it might have been. Robert began to pack his box. But before he had finished it he shut the lid and sat upon it. To meet Mary thus disgraced was more than he could bear. If he remained, he had a chance of winning prizes at the end of the session, and that would more than repair his honor. The five-pound bursars were privileged in paying half-fees, and if he could only get some modest job, he could manage. But who would recommend him? The thought of Dr. Anderson flashed into his mind, and he rushed from the house without even knowing where he lived.

At the post office, however, he obtained the desired information at once. Dr. Anderson lived on Union Street, toward the west end of it. Away went Robert to find the house.

That was easy. What a grand house of smooth granite and wide approach it was! The great door was opened by a manservant, who looked at the country boy from head to foot.

"Is the doctor in?" asked Robert.

"Yes."

"I would like to see him."

"Whom shall I say wants him?"

"Say the laddie he saw at Bodyfauld."

The man left Robert in the hall. Returning presently he led him through noiseless swinging doors into a large library. Never had Robert conceived such luxury.

"Sit down there," said the servant, "and the doctor'll be with you in one minute."

He was hardly out of the room before a door opened in the middle of the shelves of books and the doctor appeared. He looked inquiringly at Robert for one moment, then made two long strides toward him, holding out his hand.

"I'm Robert Falconer," said Robert. "Maybe you'll remember, you were very kind to me once, and told me lots of stories—at Bodyfauld."

"I'm glad to see you, Robert," said Dr. Anderson. "Of course I remember you perfectly! But my servant did not bring your name and I did not know whether it might be the other boy—I forget his name."

"You mean Shargar, sir. It's not him."

"I can see that," said the doctor, laughing, "although you are changed. You have grown into quite a man. I am very glad to see you," he repeated, shaking hands with him again. "When did you come to town?"

"I have been at the grammar school in the old town for the last three months," said Robert.

"Three months!" exclaimed Dr. Anderson. "And never came to see me till now!"

"Well, sir, I didn't know better. And I had a heap to do, and all for nothing after it's all over. But if I had known you would have liked to see me, I would have liked to come sooner."

"I have been away most of the summer," said the doctor, "but I have been at home for the last month. You haven't had your dinner, have you?"

"No, not exactly," said Robert. "I was planning to leave town."

"Well, you must stay long enough to dine with me. Come into my room till dinnertime," he said, leading Robert through the door by which he had entered.

To Robert's astonishment he found himself in a room bare as that of the poorest cottage. A small square window looked out upon a neatly kept garden. The walls were white, the ceiling was of bare boards, and the floor was sprinkled with a little white sand. The table and chairs were of common deal, white and clean, except that the former was spotted with ink. A greater contrast to the soft, large, richly colored room they had left could hardly be imagined. A few bookshelves on the wall were filled with old books. A fire blazed cheerily in the little grate.

"This is the nicest room in the house, Robert," said the doctor. "When I was a student like you—"

"I'm no student yet," said Robert shaking his head, but the doctor went on.

"—I had the end of my father's cottage to study in, for he treated me like a stranger-gentleman when I came home from college. The father respected the son, for whose advantage he was working like a slave from morning till night. My heart is sometimes sore with the gratitude I feel to him. Though he has been dead for thirty years—would you believe it, Robert?—Well, I can't talk more about him now. I made this room as like my father's as I could, and I am happier here than anywhere in the world."

By this time Robert was perfectly at home. Before the dinner was ready he had not only told Dr. Anderson his present difficulty but his whole story as far back as he could remember. The good man listened eagerly, gazed at the boy with more and more interest, which deepened till his eyes glistened as he gazed, and when a ludicrous passage chanced to be said, welcomed the laughter as an excuse for wiping them. When dinner was announced, he rose without a word and led the way to the dining room. Robert followed and they sat down to a meal simple enough for such a house, but which to Robert seemed a feast. After they had done eating, they retired to his room again, and Robert found the table covered with a snowy cloth with wine and fruits arranged upon it.

It was far into the night before he rose to go home. It was raining and he was wet to the skin long before he reached his lodgings in the old town; but, notwithstanding, his heart was as warm as the under side of a bird's wing. After drying himself he immediately sat down to write to his grandmother, informing her that Dr. Anderson had employed him to copy for the printers a book of his on the "Medical Boards of India." As he was going to pay him for that and for other work at a rate which would earn him ten shillings a week, it would be a pity to lose a year, merely for the chance of getting a bursary next winter.

The doctor did want the manuscript copied, and he knew that the only chance of getting Mrs. Falconer's consent to Robert's receiving any assistance from him was to make some business arrangement of the sort. He also wrote to her the same night and, after mentioning the unexpected pleasure of Robert's visit, not only explained the advantage to himself of the arrangement he had proposed, but set forth the greater advantage to Robert. He judged that, although Mrs. Falconer had no great opinion of his religion, she would yet consider his influence rather on the side of good than otherwise in the case of a boy else abandoned to his own resources.

The end of it all was that his grandmother yielded and Robert was immediately both a student and employed as a copier.

A week later, after three difficult days clothed in the red gown of the Aberdeen student attending the Humanity and Greek classes, he was seated at his table preparing his "Virgil" for the next day. He found himself growing very weary, and no wonder, for except for the walk of a few hundred yards to and from the college, he had had no open air for those three dyas. It had been raining in a persistent November fashion and he thought of the sea tossing uneasily way off in the night.

His eye fell on his violin. He had been so full of his new position and its requirements that he had not touched it since the session opened. Now it was just what he wanted. He caught it up eagerly, hastened from his room into the open air, half ran toward the open fields, and began to play. The power of the music seized him and he went on playing, forgetful of everything else, for more than an hour. When at length he ascended the stairs to his room once more, a great relaxedness of mind had settled upon him and he felt once more capable of study. Opening the door he heard the words, at once so familiar and yet so foreign to his ear: "Eh, Bob!"

"Shargar!" he exclaimed. "How do you come to be here?"

"Weel, I'm not up t' the lyin' as I used t' be. A lie comes too rough through my windpipe now. Faith! I could have lied once as weel as anybody, barrin' the devil. But I won't lie. The fact's just this: I couldn't bide behind ye any longer."

"But what in heaven's name am I to do with you!" returned Robert, in real perplexity, though only pretending displeasure and in fact only too delighted to see his friend.

"Give me somethin' t' eat, an' I'll tell ye what t' do with me," answered Shargar. "I don't care what it is."

Robert had some porridge sent up and then sat listening to Shargar's story. He had heard a rumor that Grannie was about to apprentice him to a tailor and that very night had dropped from the gable window to the ground and with three halfpence in his pocket had wandered and begged his way to Aberdeen, arriving with one halfpenny left.

"But what am I to do with you?" said Robert once more, in as much perplexity as ever.

"Wait till I have told ye," answered Shargar. "Don't think ye that I'm the careless an' helpless creature I used t' be. I have been in Aberdeen three days! Ay, an' I have seen ye every day in yer red gown. But look ye here!"

He put his hand in his pocket and pulled out what amounted to two or three shillings, chiefly in coppers, which he exposed with triumph on the table.

"Where did you get all that money, man?" asked Robert.

"Here an' there. I don't know where—runnin' here an' runnin' there, carryin' boxes t' an' from the ships, an' doin' whatever anyone asked me t' do, an' more besides. Yesterday mornin' I got three pence by hangin' about the Royal before coaches started. I looked up an' down the street till I saw somebody comin' along with a suitcase. I ran up t' him an' he was an old man, an' almost at his last gasp from the weight o' it, I picked it up an' helped him by carryin' it. An' who else do ye think gave me a shillin' the very first night?—Who but my brither Emerich?"

"Lord Rothie?"

"Ay, faith. I knew him weel enough, but little he knew me. There he was upon Black Geordie. What on earth makes him go around on that devil o' a horse, I don't know. An' Black Geordie's turnin' old now. An' the older the worse inclined. An' so it is, I'm thinkin', with his master too."

"Did you ever see your father, Shargar?"

"No. Nor do I want t'. I'm on my mither's side. But that's nothin' t' the point. All that I want o' you, Bob, is t' let me come home here at night an' lie on the floor. I swear I'll lie in the street if ye don't let me. I'll sleep as sound as Peter MacInnes when MacCleary's preachin'. An' I won't eat much. And all the coppers I get I'll fetch home t' ye, for ye t' do with what ye like."

Robert was astonished at the change that had passed upon Shargar. His departure had cast him upon his own resources and allowed the individuality repressed by every event of his history to begin to develop itself. Miserable for a few weeks, he had revived in the fancy that to work hard at school would give him some chance of rejoining Robert. Thence, too, he had watched to please Mrs. Falconer, and had indeed begun to buy golden opinions from all sorts of people. But into the midst fell the whisper of the apprenticeship like a thunderbolt out of a clear sky. He fled at once.

"Well, you can stay here tonight," agreed Robert.

Shargar finished his porridge and, each on one side of the fire, they conversed about all the old times—for the youngest life has its old times, its golden age, and its nostalgic adventures. Shargar was at length deposited upon the little bit of hearthrug which adorned rather than enriched the room, with Robert's plaid of shepherd tartan around him and an Ainsworth's dictionary under his head for a pillow.

"Man, I'm just like a happy sheep dog," said Shargar. "When I close my eyes I'll not be sure that I'm not inside yer own daddy's kilt in the garret back home. The Lord preserve me from ever such a fright again as yer grannie an' Betty gave me that night they found me in't! I don't think it's natural t' have such a fright twice in one lifetime. So I'll fall asleep at once an' say no more—except as much o' my prayers as I can remember now that Grannie's not at my ear."

"Hold your impudence, and your tongue altogether," reproved Robert. "Mind that my grannie's been the best friend you ever had."

" 'Cept my own mither," returned Shargar, with a sleepy doggedness in his tone.

As soon as Shargar was disposed of, Robert walked to the window and stood looking out. Some upper wind had swept the clouds from the sky and the whole world of stars was radiant over the earth and its griefs.

"O God, where are you?" he said in his heart, then turned and followed Shargar into the dreamy world of sleep.

26 / A Conversation _____

When Robert awoke he found to his surprise that Shargar was gone, and for a moment he doubted whether he had not been dreaming about all that had passed between them the night before. His plaid was folded up and laid upon a chair, as if it had been there all night, and his Ainsworth was on the table. But beside it was the money Shargar had drawn from his pockets.

While he was still pondering the fate of his friend, he heard a knock on the door and there stood Dr. Anderson.

"I thought I would call to see how you were getting on," he said as Robert opened the door. Perceiving the lingering look of perplexity on Robert's face, he asked about it.

Therewith Robert explained that the night before he had had a visit from a friend from Rothieden.

"The boy with the odd name?" asked the doctor. "I seem to have already forgotten it again."

"Yes, Shargar," said Robert. "But that's only his nickname. His real name, they say his mother says, is George Moray. Do you see, sir?" concluded Robert with a look of significance.

"No, I'm afraid I don't," answered the doctor.

"They say he's the son of the old marquis. His mother's a Gypsy that wanders about the country. There's no doubt about *her*. And by all accounts the father's likely enough."

"And how on earth did you come to have such a questionable companion?" asked the doctor as he sat down, while Robert attempted to coax the fire back to life.

"Shargar's as fine a creature as ever God made," returned Robert. "You'll allow that God made him, doctor, although his father and mother didn't think much about him. And Shargar couldn't help it. It might have been you or me, for that matter."

"I beg your pardon, Robert," said Dr. Anderson, delighted with the fervor of his young kinsman. "I only wanted to know how he came to be your companion."

"It was my grannie's doing, God bless her!—for well he may, and much she needs it."

"Oh, yes. Now I remember all your grandmother's part in the story," returned the doctor. "But how did he come to be here?"

"She was going to make a tailor of him. So he just ran away and came to me."

"It was too bad of him, after all she had done for him."

"Oh, no, doctor. Even when you bought a man and paid for him, according to the Jewish law, you couldn't make a slave of him. But, eh, if only she could get my father home!" sighed Robert, after a pause.

"Why should she want him home?" asked Dr. Anderson.

"I didn't mean home to Rothieden. I believe she could stand to never see him again if only he wasn't in the bad place. She has awful notions about God letting certain people burn forever and ever. Doctor, I do believe she would go and be burned herself with great thanksgiving if it would let any poor creature out of it—not to say my father. And I doubt that many of them that put it into her head would do as much."

They talked further, and when Dr. Anderson finally went home, he had much to cogitate on. This boy, this cousin of his, seemed quite an independent thinker who made a vortex of good about him into which whoever came near was drawn. He seemed at the same time quite unaware of anything worthy in his conduct. The good he did sprang from inward necessity rather than from any conscious exercise of religious motive. Yet in another way, religion had everything to do with it. Robert had not yet found in God a reason for being true to his fellows. But if God was leading him to be the man he would become, how could any good results of this be anything other than God-inspired?

All good is of God. Robert began where he could. The first plateau was too high for him; thus he began with the second. If a man loves his brother whom he has seen, the love of God whom he has not seen is not very far off. These results in Robert were the first outcome of divine influences; they were the buds of the fruit hereafter to be gathered in greater devotion. But little would Robert acknowledge all this, simply on the basis of his friendship to Shargar and his kindness toward everyone he met. Though God was at work in him, he continued unaware of his conscious presence.

To return to Dr. Anderson, he had labored most of his life in India. He returned from it halfway down the hill of life, sad, gentle, kind and rich. Whence his sadness came, we need not inquire. To return home without a wife to accompany him or child to meet him; to sit by his riches like a man over a fire of straw in a Siberian frost; to know that old faces were gone and old hearts changed and that the chill evenings of autumn were settling down into longer and longer nights, and that no hope lay anymore beyond the mountains—surely this was enough to make a gentle-minded man sad.

It was natural that he should be interested in the fine promise of Robert, in whom he saw the hopes of his own youth revived, but in a nature at once more robust and more ideal. Where the doctor was refined, Robert was strong; where the doctor was firm with a firmness he had cultivated, Robert was imperious in a manner which time would mellow; where the doctor was generous and careful at the same time, Robert gave his offering and forgot it. Robert was rugged in the simplicity of his truthfulness. All that would fall away as the spiky shell from the polished chestnut and be reabsorbed in the growth of the grand cone-flowering tree. It is no wonder that the doctor loved the boy and longed to do what lay in his power to further his plans. But he was too wise to overwhelm him all at once and, instead, blessed him with the merciful slow-building dew of progress.

"The fellow will bring me in for no end of expense," the doctor said, smiling to himself as he drove home in his gig, "especially if he takes a habit of helping every down-and-out man or woman he sees—which, judging from his attitudes, wouldn't surprise me. I must do something for that strange protegé of his too—that Shargar. The fellow is as good as a dog, and that's saying not a little in his favor. I wonder if he can learn."

He threw himself back in his seat and laughed with a delight he rarely felt. He was a providence watching over the boys, who expected nothing of him.

Robert wrote to his grandmother to tell her that Shargar was with him, working hard. Her reply was somewhat cold and offended, but was enclosed in a parcel containing all Shargar's garments, and ended with the assurance that as long as he did well, she was ready to do what she could.

27 / Shargar's Accident

Not many weeks passed before Shargar knew Aberdeen better than most Aberdonians. From the Pier-head to the Rubislaw Road he knew, if not every court, at least every street and shortcut. And Aberdeen began to know him. He was soon recognized as trustworthy and had pretty nearly as much to do as he could manage. He was all over the various parts of the city on most days and could have told at almost any hour where Dr. Anderson was to be found—generally in the lower parts of it, for the good man visited much among the poor. Shargar delighted in keeping an eye upon the doctor, carefully avoiding being seen himself.

One day as he was hurrying through the Green on a mission from the Rothieden mail carrier, he came upon the doctor's carriage standing in one of the narrowest streets, and, as usual, paused to look at it and get a peep of the owner. The morning was very sharp. There was no snow, but a cold fog, like vaporized hoarfrost, filled the air. His horses apparently liked the cold as little as the doctor. They had been moving about restlessly for some time before he made his appearance. The moment he got in and shut the door, one of them reared while the other began to haul on his reins, eager for a gallop. Something about the chain gave way, and the pole swerved round under the rearing horse. Great confusion and danger would have resulted had not Shargar rushed from his vantage point, sprung at the bit of the rearing horse and dragged him off the pole, over which he was just casting his near leg. As soon as his feet touched the ground he too pulled forward, and away went the buggy and down went Shargar. But in a moment more several men had laid hold of the horses' heads and stopped them.

"O Lord!" cried Shargar, as he rose with his arm dangling by his side. "I'm like t' faint. Stay away from that basket, ye gallow birds!" he cried, darting toward the hamper he had left in the entry of a court, round which a few ragged urchins had gathered. But just as he reached it he staggered and fell.

As soon as the coachman had got his harness put to rights, the doctor had driven back to see how Shargar had fared, for he had felt the carriage go over something. They found him lying beside his hamper and lifted Shargar into the carriage, senseless, and were now proceeding to deliver his parcel.

158

Gradually Shargar came to himself.

"Where am I? Where the devil am I?" he cried, jumping up, then falling back again.

"Don't you know me, Moray?" said the doctor.

"No, I don't know ye. Let me out—I beg yer pardon, doctor," he said, with an altered tone. "I thought ye was one o' those gallow birds runnin' away with my basket. Eh me! Such a pain in my arm. But nobody calls me Moray. They all call me Shargar. What right have I t' be called a Moray?"

"The coachman will deliver your parcel, Moray," said the doctor, this time repeating the name with emphasis.

"He dares not leave his seat with those devils o' horses!" cried Shargar. "What makes ye keep such horses, doctor? They'll play some bad mischief someday."

"Indeed, they've played enough already, my poor boy. They've broken your arm."

"Never mind that. That's not much. Ye're welcome, doctor, t' my two arms for what ye've done for Robert. But if ye could just pay him what I can't make for a day or two—it wouldn't be that much t' ye, doctor," added Shargar with a beseeching tone.

"Trust me for that, Moray," returned Dr. Anderson. "I owe you a good deal more than that. My brains might have been dashed out had it not been for you."

"The Lord be praised!" said Shargar, making his first profession of Christianity. "Robert'll think somethin' o' me now!"

All at once Shargar seemed to realize where they were.

"Thank ye fer the ride, doctor. Here we are at the very door. Good day t' ye," he said, and rose to leave, "an' I'm much obliged t' ye."

"My poor boy! You don't think I'm going to leave you here, do you?" said the doctor, proceeding to open the carriage door.

"But where's the hamper?" said Shargar, looking about him in dismay.

"The coachman has got it up on the box," answered the doctor.

"Eh, that'll never do. If the rampagin' brutes was t' start up again, what would come o' my basket? I must get it down directly."

"Sit still. I will get it down and deliver it myself." As he spoke the doctor got out.

"Take care o' it, sir; take care o' it. Mr. Walker said there was a jar o' honey in the basket; an' the children would miss it sorely if it was spilt."

"I will take good care of it," responded the doctor. He delivered the basket, returned to the carriage, and told the coachman to drive home.

"Where are ye takin' me?" exclaimed Shargar. "Willie hasn't paid me for the parcel."

"Never mind Willie. I'll pay you," said the doctor.

"But Robert wouldn't like me t' take money where I did no work for it," objected Shargar. "He's some precise—Robert is. But I'll just say ye made me, doctor. Maybe that'll satisfy him. An' faith! I'm right on t' worry about my left arm here."

"We'll soon set it all right," said the doctor.

When they reached his house he led the way to his surgery, and there put the broken limb in splints. He told Johnston to help the patient to bed.

"I must go home," objected Shargar. "What would Robert think?"

"I will tell him all about it," said the doctor.

"Yerself, sir?" stipulated Shargar.

"Yes, myself."

"Before night?"

"Directly," answered the doctor, and Shargar yielded.

"But what will Robert say?" were his last words, as he fell asleep, appreciating no doubt, the superiority of the bed to his usual lair upon the hearthrug.

Robert was delighted to hear how well Shargar had acquitted himself. There followed a small consultation about him, for the accident had ripened the doctor's intentions concerning the outcast.

"As soon as his arm is sound again, he shall go to the grammar school," he said.

"And the college?" asked Robert.

"I hope so," answered the doctor. "Do you think he could do well? He has plenty of courage, at all events, and that is a fine thing."

"Aye," answered Robert, "he's not short of spirit; that is, if it be for someone else. He would never lift a hand for himself, and that's what made me take to him so much. He's a fine creature."

"What do you think him fit for, then?"

Now Robert had been building castles for Shargar out of the hopes which the doctor's friendliness had given him. Therefore he was ready with his answer.

"If you could make sure he'd never be made a general, he would make a grand soldier. Set his face toward something and say 'quick march,' and he'd be off like a shot. But he'd never be able to stand if he was given a position of consequence."

Dr. Anderson laughed, but thought about it nonetheless, and went home to see how his patient was getting on.

Dr. Anderson kept George Moray, alias "Shargar," in bed for a few days, after which he went about for a while with his arm in a sling. But the season of bearing material burdens was over for him now. Dr. Anderson had an interview with the master of the grammar school. A class was assigned to Shargar, and with a delight, chiefly resulting from the resultant social approximation to Robert—which in one week elevated the whole character of his person, countenance, and bearing— George Moray bent himself to the task of mental growth. Having good helpers in Robert and Dr. Anderson, and his late-developed energy turning itself entirely into this new channel, he got on admirably. As there was no other room to be had in Mrs. Fyvie's house, he continued for the rest of the session to sleep on the rug, for he would not hear of going to another house. The doctor had advised to drop the nickname as much as possible; but the first time he called him Moray, Shargar threatened to cut his throat, and so between the two the name remained.

I presume that by this time Dr. Anderson had made up his mind to leave his money to Robert, but thought it better to say nothing about it and let the boy mature into independence on his own. He had him often to his house. Shargar frequently accompanied him and soon began, in his new circumstances, to develop something of the manners of a gentleman. Many talks did the elderly man hold with the two youths and his experience of life taught them much. Shargar was chiefly interested in his tales of adventure when in the service of the Indian army. His Gypsy blood and lawless childhood made him more responsive to these stories than Robert and his sparkling eye and pertinent remarks raised in the doctor's mind the question whether a commission in India might not give him his best start in life.

28 / The Heart of the King_____

Robert worked hard at his studies that prizes might be a witness of his success to his grandmother and Mary St. John, wiping out the blot, as he considered it, of his failure in gaining a significant bursary at the beginning of the term.

The end of the session drew near. Robert's work paid off and he gained the first Greek and the third Latin prize. The evening of the last day arrived, and on the morrow the students would be gone—some to their homes of idleness, others to hard labor in the fields; some to steady reading in preparation for the next session, and others to be tutors all the summer months. Shargar was to remain at the grammar school.

That last evening Robert sat with Shargar in his room. It was a cold night, and a bitter wind blew about the house. They talked, but in general the mood was sober.

"I wonder what Grannie'll say to me," said Robert at length.

"She'll be glad t' see ye, no doubt," said Shargar. "An' though I'll miss ye sore, Bob, I'm glad not t' be going back under that lady's roof."

"She's a good woman, Shargar. Like I told you, she was a good friend to you when you had but few."

The next morning Shargar intended to rouse Robert early, but Robert was awake long before his friend. The all but soulless light of the dreary season awoke him and he rose and looked out. Gathering his things, which he had made ready the night before, he left Shargar still asleep and descended the stairs, thinking to leave the house undisturbed. But Mrs. Fyvie was watching for him and insisted on his taking the breakfast she had prepared. He then set out on his journey of forty miles, with half a loaf of bread in his pockets, and money enough to get bread and cheese and a bottle of the cheapest ale at the far-parted roadside inns along the way.

When Shargar awoke, he wept in desolation, then crept into Robert's bed and fell fast asleep again.

When Robert opened the door of his grandmother's parlor three days later, he found the old lady seated at breakfast. She rose, pushed back her chair, met him in the middle of the room, put her old arms around

162

him, offered her smooth white cheek to him, and wept. Robert wondered that she did not look older; for the time that he had been away seemed an age, although in truth only eight months.

"How are ye, laddie?" she said. "I'm right glad, for I hae been long wantin' t' see ye. Sit ye doon."

Betty rushed in, drying her hands on her apron. She had not heard him enter.

"Eh, losh!" she cried, and put her wet apron to her eyes. "Such a man ye've grown t' be, Robert! A poor body like me mustn't be speaking t' ye now."

"There's no change in me, Betty," returned Robert.

" 'Deed but there is. Ye're six feet tall and maybe more, I'll warrant."

"I said there was no change *in* me, Betty," persisted Robert, laughing.

"I don't know what may be *in* ye," retorted Betty, "but there's plenty o' changes upon ye."

"Hold yer tongue, Betty," said her mistress. "Ye ought t' know better than t' stand there jawin' wi' young men. Fetch more o' the creamy cakes."

"Maybe Robert would like a drop o' porridge."

"Anything, Betty," said Robert. "I'm at death's door with hunger."

"Run, Betty, for the cakes. And fetch a loaf o' white bread; we can't wait for the porridge."

Robert fell to his breakfast, and while he ate—somewhat ravenously—he told his grandmother the adventures of his walk home and about school.

"Well, well, laddie. Eh! I'm glad t' see ye. Hae ye gotten any prizes noo?"

"Ay, have I. I'm sorry they're not both of them first. But I have the first in one and the third in the other."

"I am pleased at that, Robert. Ye'll be a man someday if ye hold away from drink an' from—from lying."

"I never told a lie in my life, Grannie."

"No. I didn't think ye ever did—an' what's that creature Shargar aboot?"

"Oh, he's going to be a crown of glory to you, Grannie. He worked like a horse till Dr. Anderson took him by the hand and sent him to the school. He's a fine creature, Shargar."

"He took a moonlight flittin' from here," rejoined the old lady in a tone of offense. "He might at least hae said good-bye t' me, I think."

"He was afraid of you, Grannie."

"Afraid o' *me*, laddie! Who ever was afraid o' me? I never scared anybody i' my life."

So little did the dear old lady know that she was a terror to the neighborhood!

Mrs. Falconer's courtesy did not fail her. Her grandson had ceased to be a child; her responsibility had insofar ceased; her conscience was relieved at being rid of it, and the humanity of her great heart came out to greet the youth.

When Robert went forth into the streets, he was surprised to find how friendly everyone was. Even old William MacGregor shook him kindly by the hand, inquired after his health, told him not to study too hard, informed him that he had a copy of a strange old book that he would like to see, etc., etc. Upon reflection Robert discovered the cause. Although he had scarcely gained a bursary, he *had* gained prizes; and in a little place like Rothieden—long may there be such places!—everybody with any brains at all took a share in the distinction he had merited.

One of the first things Robert did was to arrange to see Mary, that he might play his violin for her and, if possible, play beside her and her piano, uniting his humble music with her own.

When he told his grandmother of the appointment he had made, she only remarked, in a tone of some satisfaction, "Well, she's a fine lass, Miss St. John, an' if ye take t' one another, ye couldn't do better."

But Robert's thoughts were so different from Mrs. Falconer's that he did not even suspect what she meant. He no more dreamed of marrying Mary St. John than of marrying his grandmother. Yet she was no less at this period the ruling influence of his life; and if it had not been for her presence, this part of his history would have been torn by inward troubles. It is not good that a man should batter day and night at the gate of heaven; the very noise of the siege will sometimes drown the still, small voice that calls from the open postern. There is a door open in the wall, not far from any one of us, even when he least can find it.

Notwithstanding the pedestal upon which Mary stood in his worshiping regard, Robert began to be aware that his feeling toward her was losing something of the placid flow of its former innocence. And I imagine that she now and then saw on his face a look which made her tremble a little and doubt whether she stood on safe ground with a youth just waking into manhood. Her fear would have found itself more than justified if she had walked into the room and surprised him kissing her glove, and then replacing it where he had found it, with the air of one consciously guilty of presumption.

Perhaps Miss St. John may have had to confess to herself that, though she was two years his senior, she found no little attraction in the noble bearing and handsome face of young Falconer. His features had grown into complete harmony; his eyes glowed and gleamed with humanity, and his whole countenance bore self-evident witness of being a true face and no mere mask. As it was, she admired and loved him. After all, had they not already shared youthful secrets, and even a certain intimacy, together? Whether she was in danger of falling in love with him, even she could not for the moment tell.

Meantime, the violin of the dead shoemaker blended its wails with the rich harmonies of Mary St. John's piano, and the soul of Robert went forth upon the level of the sound and hovered about the beauty of his friend.

But the heart of the king is in the hands of the Lord.

29 / A Grave from the Past

Robert was happier than he ever could have expected to be in his grandmother's house. She treated him like an honored guest, let him do as he would and go where he pleased. Betty kept the gable room in the best of order for him and, pattern of housemaids, dusted his table without disturbing his papers. For he began to have papers; nor were they occupied only with the mathematics to which he was now giving his chief attention, preparing, with the occasional help of Mr. Innes, for his second session.

He had fits of wandering; visited all the old places, spent a week or two more than once at Bodyfauld; rode Mr. Lammie's half-broken filly; and reveled in the glories of the summer once more. He went out to tea occasionally with the schoolmaster, and, except going to church on Sunday, which was a weariness to every inch of flesh upon his bones, enjoyed everything.

One thing, however, that troubled Robert on this his first return home was the discovery that the surroundings of his childhood had deserted him. There they were as before, but they seemed to have nothing to say to him—no remembrance of him. It was that everything seemed to be conscious only of the past and cared nothing for him now. The very chairs, with their inlaid backs, had an embalmed look, and stood as in a dream. He could even pass the walled-up door without emotion, for all the feeling that had been gathered about the knob that admitted him to Mary had transferred itself to the brass bellpull at her street door.

But one day, after standing for a while at the window, looking down on the quiet street—which seemed so awfully still after the roar of Aberdeen, a passing cart seeming to shudder at the loneliness of the noise it made—a certain old mood began to revive in him. He had been working at quadratic equations all morning. It was one of those dreary, rainy mornings—dull, depressing, persistent. His thoughts turned to the place where he had suffered the most—his old room in the garret. Up till now he had shrunk from visiting it; but now he turned from the window, went up the steep stairs, with their one sharp corkscrew curve, pushed the door, which clung unwillingly to the floor, and entered. It was a nothing of a place. There was the window that looked up toward

166

heaven. There was the empty bedstead against the wall, where he had so often kneeled, sending forth vain prayers to a deaf heaven! Had they indeed been vain prayers, and to a deaf heaven? or had they been prayers which a hearing God must answer, not according to the haste of the praying child, but according to the ealm course of his own infinite law of love?

Here, somehow or other, the things about him did not seem so much absorbed in the past, despite those untroubled rows of papers bundled in red tape. True, they looked almost awful in their lack of interest and their nonhumanity, but his mother's workbox lay behind them. And, strange to say, the side of that bed drew him to kneel down; he did not yet believe that prayer was in vain. If God had not answered him before, that gave no certainty that he would not answer him now. It was, he found, still as rational as it had ever been to hope that God would answer the man that cried to him. This came, I think, from the fact that God had been answering him all the time, although he had not recognized his gifts as answers.

Surely such doubts as Robert held—true and good and reverent doubts, springing from devoutness and aspiration—are far more precious in the sight of God than many so-called beliefs!

Robert kneeled and sent forth one cry after the Father, arose, and turned upwards toward the shelves, removed some of the bundles of letters, and drew out his mother's little box.

There lay the miniature, still and open-eyed as he had left it. There too lay the bit of paper, brown and dry, with the hymn and the few words of sorrow written on it. He looked at the portrait but did not open the folded paper. For the first time he thought whether there might not be something more in the box; what he had taken for the bottom seemed to be a tray. He lifted it by two little ears of ribbon, and there, underneath, lay a letter addressed to his father, in the same old-fashioned handwriting as the hymn. It was sealed with brown wax, full of spangles, impressed with a bush of something—he could not tell whether rushes or reeds or flags. Of course he dared not open it. His holy mother's words to his erring father must be sacred even from the eye of their son. But what other or fitter messenger than himself could bear it to its destination? It was for this that he had been guided to it.

For years he had regarded the finding of his father as the first duty of his manhood. It was as if his mother had now given her sanction to the quest, with this letter to carry to the husband, who, however he might have erred, was yet dear to her. He replaced it in the box, but did not put the box again on the forsaken shelf with its dreary barricade of soulless records. He carried it with him, and laid it in the bottom of his own box, which henceforth he kept carefully locked; there lay as it were the pledge of his father's salvation and his mother's redemption from an eternal grief.

He returned to his equation and found that the problem had cleared itself up; he worked it out in five minutes. Betty came to tell him that the dinner was ready, and he went down, peaceful and hopeful, to his grandmother.

While at home he never worked in the evenings; it was bad enough to have to do so at college. Hence nature had a chance with him again. Blessings on the wintry blasts that broke into the first youth of summer! They made him feel what summer was! Blessings on the cheerless days of rain and even sleet and hail that would shove the reluctant year back into January! Even the snow occasionally came in utter defiance of the calendar.

In general, after his lessons with Mary were over, he would go for a solitary walk. There was no one at Rothieden to whom his heart and intellect both were sufficiently drawn to make a close friendship. And with Mary, for the present, it seemed enough to share their music. On his way home he would often go into one of the shops where the neighbors congregated in the evenings and hold a little conversation with them. But with Mary filling his heart, ideas from the books he was reading filling his imagination, and geometry and algebra his intellect, great was the contrast between his own inner mood and the words by which he kept up human relations with his townsfolk. Yet in after years he counted it one of the greatest blessings of a lowly birth and education that he knew hearts and feelings which to understand one must have been young among them. He would not have had a chance of knowing such as these if he had been the son of Dr. Anderson and born in Aberdeen.

One lovely evening in midsummer he wandered out for a walk. After a round of a couple of miles he returned by way of a fir wood, through which went a pathway. In the heart of the trees it was growing very dusky; but he came to a spot where the trees stood away from each other and the blue sky looked in from above, with one cloud floating in it from which the rose of the sunset was fading. He seated himself on a little mound of moss that had gathered over an ancient stump by the footpath, and drew out several papers on which were written the verses of a poem he had been working on. Absorbed in his reading, he was not aware of an approach till the rustle of silk startled him. He lifted his eyes and saw Mary a few yards from him on the path. He rose.

"It's almost too dark to read now, isn't it, Robert?" she said.

"Yes, I suppose it is," he said, attempting a hasty retreat of the papers into his pocket. "But what are you doing so far from town?"

"I come here often," she replied. "It is one of my favorite spots. There is nothing like the smell of a fir wood on a warm day. But what is that you're working on?" she asked.

"Oh, nothing . . . just some work for school I was trying to finish up."

"Come now, Robert. I know you better than that. You're trying to keep something from me. Let me see those papers," she said playfully, approaching him slowly.

"Please, Mary. You don't want to see them. They're only some dry old poems."

"Of yours? How delightful!"

"No, please. They're not even worth your attention."

"Robert," she said insistently and reached out her hand toward him. "I must see them. I am, after all, your teacher now, you know."

"Only in music."

"Well then, we'll have to set your verses to song. Come now. Let me see them."

"If you must, at least let me read them to you," said Robert reluctantly, but with pounding chest, notwithstanding—for *she* wanted to see *his* poem! *That way they'll maybe sound as I meant them*, he thought.

Robert laid himself on the grass at her feet, and read:

> When the storm was proudest,
> And the wind was loudest,
> I heard the hollow caverns drinking down below.
>
> When the stars were bright,
> And the ground was white,
> I heard the grasses springing underneath the snow.
>
> Many voices spake—
> The river to the lake,
> The iron-ribbed sky was talking to the sea;
> And every starry spark
> Made music with the dark,
> And said how bright and beautiful everything must be.
>
> When the sun was setting,
> All the clouds were getting
> Beautiful and silvery in the rising moon;
> Beneath the leafless trees
> Wrangling in the breeze,
> I could hardly see them for the leaves of June.

When the day had ended,
And the night descended,
I heard the sound of streams that I heard not through the day,
And every peak afar,
Was ready for a star,
And they climbed and rolled around until the morning gray.

Then slumber, soft and holy,
Came down upon me slowly;
And I went I know not whither, and I lived I know not how;
My glory had been banished,
For when I woke it vanished;
But I waited on its coming, and I am waiting now.

An awkward silence followed.

"Robert," said Mary at length, "that was beautiful. You will let me try to set it to music, won't you?"

"If you would like to," he answered.

"I would," she said, reaching out again for the papers. This time Robert yielded them. "I shall take good care of it. But it's quite time I was going home."

They rose and walked again through the little wood toward the town. When they reached its outskirts, calling to mind the natural propensity to gossip of the shopkeepers and their friends—their labors over and now standing about in a speculative mood—Mary felt shy of showing herself on the square with Robert, and, saying that she had a little shopping to do, parted from him. Too simple still to suspect the real reason, but with a heart that delighted in obedience, Robert bade her good night at once and took another way.

As he passed the door of Merson, the haberdasher's shop, there stood William MacGregor, the weaver, looking at nothing and doing nothing. He was a remarkable compound of good nature and bad temper. People were generally afraid of him because he had a biting satire at his command, amounting even to wit, which found vent in verse. The only person he, on his part, was afraid of was his own wife. From lack of apprehension, his keenest irony fell upon her, as he said, "like water off a duck's back." In respect of her he had, therefore, no weapon of offense to strike terror with. Her dullness was her defense. He liked Robert. When he saw him he wakened up, laid hold of him by the button and drew him in.

"Come in, lad," he said, "and take a pinch. I'm waiting for Merson. How's the mathematics, Robert?"

"Thrivin'," answered Robert, falling into his good humor.

"Weel, that's very weel. Do ye remember, Robert, how when ye was about eight year old, ye came to me once in my shop about somethin' yer grandmother, honest woman, wanted? An' I by the way o' takin' my fun o' ye, said to ye, 'Robert, ye have grown desperate. Here yer a man already an' yer still runnin' errands fer yer grandmother.' And ye says to me, 'Ay, Mr. MacGregor, I want nothin' now but a watch an' a wife.' "

"I don't doubt I've forgotten about it, Mr. MacGregor," answered Robert. "But I've made some progress according to your story; for Dr. Anderson, before I came home, gave me a watch. And a fine creature it is, for it does its best, and so I excuse its shortcomings."

"Let the watch sit," returned the manufacturer, "where's the wife? Ye can't be a man yet, wantin' the wife—by yer own statement."

"The watch came unsought, Mr. MacGregor, and I'm thinking so must the wife," answered Robert, laughing, then turning resumed his walk down the street toward home. "Good night to you, Mr. Mac-Gregor!"

"Preserve me from a wife that comes unsought!" shouted the weaver after him.

30 / Shargar Aspires to Breeding

Two weeks later, Mary was accompanying Robert one evening on the piano, he again with his violin. But the music would not go right. They stopped as by common consent, and a moment's silence followed. All at once Mary broke out with something Robert had never heard before. Through a troubled harmony ran a silver thread of melody from far away. It was the caverns drinking from the tempest overhead, the grasses growing under the snow, the stars making music with the dark, the streams filling the night with the sounds the day had quenched, the whispering call of the dreams left behind in the fields of sleep. At length her voice took up the theme and suddenly Robert recognized the words of his poem. The silvery thread became song, and through all the opposing, supporting harmonies she led it to the solution of a final close.

She looked up and saw Robert kneeling at her side. As she turned from the piano his head dropped over her knee. She laid her hand on his clustering curls, stood, and left the room. Robert wandered out as in a dream. At midnight he found himself on a solitary hilltop, seated in the heather, with a few tiny fir trees about him and the sounds of a slight wind flowing through their branches. He heard the sound of it, but it did not touch him.

Where was God? In his mind, that was the only question.

The summer was coming to a close and the new session drawing nigh. Robert's heart was dreary when he climbed on the box seat of the mail coach at Rothieden; yet it was drearier when he got down at the Royal Hotel in the street of Bon Accord. Shargar met him at the coach, but Robert had scarcely a word to say as they walked to Mrs. Fyvie's.

"How are you getting on at the school?" Robert asked at length.

"Not that bad," answered Shargar. "I was at the head of my class yesterday for five minutes."

"And how did you like it?"

"Man, it was fine. I thought I was a gentleman all at once."

"Keep at it, man," said Robert, as if from the height of age and experience, "and maybe you will be a gentleman someday."

"Is't possible, Bob? A creature like me grow int' a gentleman?" said Shargar with wide eyes.

"Why not?"

"Eh, man!" He stood up excitedly, then sat down again, and was silent.

"For one thing," resumed Robert after a pause, during which he had been pondering the possibilities of Shargar's future, "for one thing, I doubt that Dr. Anderson would have taken such trouble with you if he hadn't thought you had the makings of a gentleman in you."

"Eh, man!" said Shargar again.

Next day Robert went to see Dr. Anderson and renewed their friendship. "You will have more to do than you had last year," the doctor told him. "You must mind your work; as often as you get tired of your books, shut them up and come to me. You may bring Shargar with you sometimes, but we must take care and not make too much of him all at once."

"Ay, doctor. But he's a fine creature, Shargar. What do you think he's turning over in that red head of his now?"

"I can't tell that. But there's something to come out of the red head, I do believe. What is he thinking of?"

"Whether it be possible for him ever to be a gentleman. I take that for a good sign in the likes of him."

"No doubt of it. What did you say to him?"

"I told him you wouldn't take such trouble with him if you hadn't some hopes of the kind for him."

"You said well. Tell him from me that I expect him to be a gentleman."

After a little further light conversation, Robert bade the doctor good evening and returned to his room.

Robert found Shargar busy over his Latin. With a "Weel, Shargar," he took his books and sat down. A few minutes later, Shargar lifted his head, stared a while at Robert, and then said: "Do ye really think it, Bob?"

"Think what? What are you yammering about, you gowk?"

"Do ye think that I ever *could* grow int' a gentleman?"

"Dr. Anderson says he expects it of you."

"Eh, man!"

A long pause followed, and Shargar spoke again. "How am I to begin, Robert?"

"Begin what?"

"To be a gentleman."

Robert scratched his head, and at length became oracular. "Speak the truth," he said.

"I'll do that. But what about my—my father?"

"Nobody'll cast your *father* up to you. You need have no fear of that."

"My mother then?" suggested Shargar, with hesitation.

"You must face up to the fact squarely."

"But if they say anything, ye know—about *her*?"

"If any man says a word against your mother, you must just knock him down on the spot."

"But I might not be able to."

"You could try anyway."

"He might knock *me* down, ye know."

"Well, go down then."

"Ay."

This was all the instruction Robert ever gave Shargar in the duties of a gentleman. And I doubt whether Shargar sought further enlightenment from anyone. He worked harder than ever, grew cleanly in his person, even to fastidiousness, and tried to speak better English. A wonderful change gradually, but rapidly, passed over his outer man. He grew taller and stronger, and as he grew stronger, his legs grew straighter, till the defect of his knocking knees all but vanished. His hair became darker, and the albino look less noticeable, though still he would remind one of a vegetable grown in a cellar. Dr. Anderson thought it well that he should have another year at the grammar school before going to college. The room across the hall from Robert's having become vacant, each youth now occupied one of his own.

One evening Shargar was later than usual in coming home from the walk, or rather ramble, without which he never could settle down to his work. He knocked at Robert's door.

"Where do ye think I've been, Robert?"

"How should I know, Shargar?" he answered, puzzling over a problem.

"I've been having a glass with Jock Mitchell."

"Who's Jock Mitchell?"

"My brother Emerich's groom, as I told ye before."

"You don't think I can remember everything you tell me. And where was the coming gentleman when you went to drink with a man like that, who, if my memory serves me, you told me yourself was in the midst of all his master's devilry?"

"Yer memory serves ye weel enough."

"Then what made you go with him at all? He isn't fit company for a gentleman."

"There may be reasons, ye know. An' ye needn't do as they do. Jock Mitchell was airing Red Rorie an' Black Geordie. An' I says—for

I wanted to know whether I was such a broom-bush as I used to be—
says I, 'How are ye, Jock Mitchell?' An' says Jock, 'Brawly. Who the
devil are ye?' An' says I, 'No more o' a devil than yerself, Jock Mitchell,
or Baron Rothie either—though maybe that's not such a little one.'
'Preserve me!' cried Jock. 'It's Shargar.' 'No more o' that, Jock,' says
I. 'If I'm not a gentleman yet, then I soon will be'—an' there I stopped,
for I saw I would be a fool to let anything more out to Jock. An' Jock
broke out with a great guffaw, an' then I joined in the laugh as if nothing
was really further from my thoughts than ever bein' a gentleman. 'Where
do ye put up, Jock?' I said. 'Oot by here,' he said; 'at Luckie Maitlan's.'
'That's a queer place for a baron t' put up, Jock,' says I. 'There's
reasons,' says he, an' he lays his forefinger on the side o' his nose. An'
I can hardly tell ye, Robert, what made me ask, but I just wanted to
know what that gentleman-brother o' mine was about. 'Take the horses
home,' says I, 'I'll just jump on Black Geordie, an' then we'll have a
glass together. I'll stand treat.' So he gave me the bridle an' I jumped
on. The devil tried to get a mouthful o' my hip, but, faith! I was too
quick for him; and away we rode.''

''I didn't know you could ride, Shargar.''

''Hoots! I couldn't help it. I was always takin' the horse to the water
at the Boar's Head or the Royal Oak or Lucky Happit's. That's how I
came to know Jock so well. We were good friends when I didn't care
about lying or swearin' or the like.''

''And what on earth did you want with him now?''

''I told ye, I wanted to know what that ne'er-do-well brother o' mine
was about. I had seen the horses standin' about two or three times in
the evening; an' knew Emerich must be about something ill if he was
about anything at all.''

''What can it matter to you, Shargar, what a man like him is about?''

''Well, ye see, Robert, my mother aye brought me up to know all
that folk was about, for she said ye could never tell when it might turn
out to the welfare o' yer advantage. But she was a terrible woman, my
mother, an' knew a heap o' things, more than it was good to know,
maybe. She went about the country so much, an' they say the Gypsies
she went among were a dreadful old people, an' had the wisdom o' the
Egyptians that Moses would have nothing to do with.''

''Where is she now?''

''I don't know. She may turn up one day.''

''There's one thing, though, Shargar; if you want to be a gentleman,
you mustn't go getting into other folk's affairs that way.''

''Then I won't say a word o' what Jock Mitchell told me about Lord
Emerich.''

"Ow, say away."

"No, no; ye wouldn't like to hear about other folk's affairs. My mother told me he did very ill to a stranger lass at Brussels. But that's neither here nor there."

"What is Lord Emerich after? What did the rascal tell you? Why do you make such a mystery of it?"

" 'Deed, I could make nothin' o' him. He winked an' he hinted an' he gave me to understand that the devil was after some lass or other, but about who—Jock was as dumb as the graveyard. An' the more he drank the less he would say. An' so I left him."

"Well, take care what you're about, Shargar. I don't think Dr. Anderson would like you to be in such company," said Robert; and Shargar departed to his own room and his studies.

31 / In the Desert

The session progressed slowly. Robert found his studies increasingly tedious. There was this time far less motivation to excel, having already done well—redeeming himself in his grandmother's and Mary St. John's eyes. Robert struggled to work hard, but gradually all the old questions came back to haunt him. The death of a close friend dealt his mental state a severe blow, and it was all he could do to complete the session. Increasingly he drew inward and less communicative with both Shargar and Dr. Anderson. After the distribution of the prizes, of which he gained three, Robert went the same evening to visit Dr. Anderson. The next morning he took the coach home, looking forward to a rest, and to playing his violin with Mary's piano. Though he did not know it at the time, a life lay behind young Robert Falconer, and a life lay before him. He stood on a shoal between.

The life before him was not yet born. And for the moment, what should issue from that dull, ghastly fog on the horizon he did not care. The tide setting eastward would carry him, and his future must be born. All he found he could care about was to leave the empty garments of the past. Travel, motion—ever on, ever away—was the sole impulse in his heart.

When he discovered that Mary had left Rothieden for a time, his desolation increased. Nor could he even think of remaining alone with Betty and his grandmother. No answers to the searching of his heart were to be found in the silent rooms of the house in which he had grown—only questions, doubts, emptiness.

The day after his arrival he told his grandmother that he was going back to Aberdeen. She looked in his face with surprise, but seeing trouble there, asked no questions. As if walking in a dream, he found himself at Dr. Anderson's door several days hence.

"Why, Robert," said the good man, "what has brought you back? I see anxiety on your face. What can I do for you?"

"I can't go on with my studies now, sir," answered Robert. "I have taken a great longing for travel. Will you give me a little money and let me go?"

"To be sure I will. Where do you want to go?"

177

"I don't know. Perhaps as I go I shall find myself wanting to go somewhere in particular. You're not afraid to trust me, are you?"

"Not in the least, Robert. You are a man now. I trust you perfectly. You shall do just as you please. Have you any idea how much money you will need?"

"No. Give me what you are willing I should spend; I will go by that."

"Come with me to the bank then. I will give you enough to start with. Write at once when you want more. Don't be too skimping with it. Enjoy yourself as well as you can. I shall not grudge it."

Robert smiled a wan smile at the idea of enjoying himself. His friend saw it and let it pass. There was no good in persuading a man, whose grief was all he had left, that he must before long part with that too. But Robert would never have believed that possible. He might rise above his grief; he might learn to contain his grief; but lose it, forget it? Never!

He went to bid Shargar farewell. As soon as he had a glimpse of what his friend meant, he burst out in an agony of pleading.

"Take me with ye, Robert!" he cried. "Ye're a gentleman now. I'll be yer servant. I'll put on a livery coat and go with ye. I'll go to Dr. Anderson. He's sure to let me go."

"No, Shargar," said Robert. "I can't have you with me. My heart is troubled, Shargar, and I must fight it out alone. I hope you can understand. You're a good friend, one of the best and truest friends a man could have. But I have to win through this by myself."

"Ay. I've seen it in yer face."

"But please, I can't talk about it just now. Besides, I've said more to you about the things that trouble me than to anyone."

"That is good o' ye, Robert. But am I never to see ye again? Are ye leavin' forever?"

"I don't know. I am sure we will meet again."

"That sounds none too certain, Robert."

"It's as much as can be said about everything, Shargar," returned Robert sadly.

"Weel, I must just take it as it comes," said Shargar, with a despairing philosophy derived from the days when his mother thrashed him.

They walked to Dr. Anderson's together, and spent the night there. In the morning Robert got on the coach for Edinburgh.

I cannot, if I would, follow him on all his travels. When later I knew him, the times were very rare indeed when he let fall even a few words that would cause the clouds that enveloped this period of his history to part even for a moment. I suspect that much of it left upon his mind no precise impressions, looking to himself only like a painful dream in retrospect. What the exact nature of his misery was I shall not even attempt to conjecture. That would be to intrude within the holy place of the human heart.

I do not even know in what direction he went first, but that he had seen many cities and many countries was apparent. Generally a silent man in company, he did talk freely when the time for speech arrived. Seldom, however, did he narrate any incidents from his travels except in connection with some truth of human nature. I do know that the first thing he always did on reaching any new place was to visit the church with the loftiest spire, but he never looked into the church itself until he had climbed as far up toward the steeple as that church's structure would allow. Breathing the air high above the church and the city, he found himself vaguely strengthened, yes, comforted. He said the wind up there on the heights of human aspiration always made him long and pray. Asking him one day something about his going to church so seldom, he answered thus:

"It does me ten times more good to get outside the spire than to go inside the church. God comes to me there—although I hardly knew it back in those days—far more intimately than through the so-called worship services inside, led by priests whose creed I sometimes think is: The knowledge of God is good, but the church is better!"

I never knew another man whose ordinary habits were so symbolic of his spiritual depth, or whose enjoyment of the sights of his eyes and the hearing of his ears was so much informed by his highest feelings. He looked upon all human affairs from the vantagepoint of the spiritual, as from their church spires he looked down on the red roofs of Antwerp, on the black roofs of Cologne, on the gray roofs of Strasburg, on the brown roofs of Basel.

He was taken ill at Valance and lay there for two weeks, oppressed with some kind of low fever. One night he awoke from a refreshing sleep, but he could not sleep again. It seemed to him afterward as if he had been lying waiting for something. A faint musical rain had gradually invaded his hearing, yet the night was clear and the moon was shining on his window. The sound came nearer and soon revealed itself as, instead of rain, a delicate tinkling of bells. It drew nearer still and nearer till at length a slow torrent of tinklings went past his window in the street below. A great multitude of sheep was being moved to new quarters in the night. But to his heart they were the messengers of the Most High. For into that heart, soothed by their thin harmony, at that moment came the words, unlooked for, "My peace I give unto you." The sounds died slowly away in the distance, fainting out of the air, even as they had grown upon it, but the words remained.

In a few moments he was fast asleep, comforted into repose. His dreams were of gentle, self-consoling griefs; and when he awoke in the morning, "My peace I give unto you" was the first thought of which he was conscious. It may be that the sound of the sheep bells made him think of the shepherds that watched their flocks by night, and they of the multitude of the heavenly host, and they of the song, "On earth peace . . ."—I do not know. The important point is not how the words came, but that the words remained—remained until he understood them, and they became to him spirit and life.

He soon recovered strength sufficiently to set out again on his travels, a great part of which he performed on foot. In this way he reached Avignon. Passing from one of its narrow streets into an open place, all at once he beheld towering above him, on a height that overlooked the whole city and surrounding country, a great crucifix. He bowed his head involuntarily. No matter that when he drew nearer the power of it vanished. The memory of it remained, with its first impression, and it had a share in what followed.

He made his way eastward toward the Alps. As he walked one day about noon over a desolate, heath-covered height, reminding him of the country of his childhood, the silence seized upon him. In the midst of the silence arose the crucifix and once more the words which had often returned upon him sounded in the ears of his inner hearing, "My peace I give unto you." They were words he had known from the earliest memory. He had heard them in infancy, in childhood, in boyhood, in youth. Now in manhood, it flashed upon him for the first time that the Lord did really mean that the peace of his soul should be the peace of the disciples' souls; that the peace at the very heart of the universe was henceforth theirs—open to them, to all the world, to enter and be still. He fell on his knees, bowed down in the birth of a great hope, held up his hands toward heaven, and cried, "Lord, give me your peace."

He said no more, but rose, caught up his stick, and strode forward, thinking.

He had learned what the sentence meant, but the peace he had not yet felt. Yet suddenly he was aware that the earth had begun to live again. The hum of insects arose from the heath around him; the odor of its flowers entered his dulled senses; the wind kissed him on the forehead; the sky domed up over his head; and the clouds veiled the distant mountaintops like the smoke of incense. All nature began to minister to one who had begun to lift his head from the baptism of fire.

I do not think this mood could have lasted over many miles of his journey. But such delicate inward revelations are nonetheless precious that they are evanescent. Many feelings are simply too good to last—using the phrase not in the unbelieving sense in which it is generally used, but to express the fact that intensity and endurance cannot coexist in the human frame. But the virtue of a mood depends by no means on its immediate presence. Like any other experience, it may be believed in, and, in its absence which leaves the mind free to contemplate it, works even more good than in its presence.

At length he came in sight of the Alpine regions. Far off, the heads of the great mountains rose into the upper countries of clouds where the snows settled on their stony heads. He came among the valleys at their feet, with their blue-green waters hurrying seawards; then to their sides of rock rising in gigantic terraces up to the heavens, with their scaling pines, erect and slight, ambitious to clothe the bare mass with green, till, failing at length in their upward efforts, the savage rock shot away and beyond and above them, the white and blue glaciers clinging cold and cruel to their ragged sides.

He drew near to the lower glaciers. He rejoiced over the velvety fields dotted with the toy-like houses of the mountaineers; he sat for hours listening by the sides of their streams. He grew weary, felt oppressed, longed for a wider view, and began to climb toward a mountain village, of which he had heard from a traveler. He hoped to find solitude and freedom in an air as lofty as if he climbed twelve of his beloved cathedral spires piled one on top of another.

After ascending for hours in zigzags through pine woods, where the only sound was of the little streams trotting down to the valley below, or the distant hush of some thin waterfall, he reached a level and came out of the woods. The path now led along the edge of a precipice descending sheer to the valley he had left, which was itself but a cleft in the mass of the mountain. The lovely heavens were over his head and the green grass under his feet. The grasshoppers chirped about him and the gorgeous butterflies flew. From regions beyond came the bells of goats. He reached a little inn and there took up his quarters.

I am able to be a little precise in my description because I have since visited the place myself. Great heights rise around it on all sides. It stands as between heaven and hell, suspended between peaks and gulfs. The wind must roar awfully there in the winter, but the mountains stand away with their avalanches, and all the summer long keep the cold off the grassy fields.

The same evening he was already weary. The next morning it rained—rained fiercely all day. He would leave the place on the morrow. In the evening it began to clear up. He walked out. The sun was setting. The snowy peaks were faintly tinged with rose and the masses of vapor that hung over the valleys were partially dyed a sulky orange-red. Then all faded into gray. But as the sunlight had vanished, a veil sank from the face of the moon, already halfway to the zenith, and she gathered courage and shone, till the mountain looked lovely as a ghost in the gleam of its snow and the glimmer of its glaciers.

The next morning rose brilliant—an ideal summer day. He would not go yet; he would spend one day more in the place. He opened his valise to get some lighter clothes. His eyes fell on a New Testament. Dr. Anderson had put it there. He had never opened it yet, and now he let it lie. Its time had not yet come. He went out.

Walking up the edge of the valley he came upon a little stream whose talk he had heard for some hundred yards. It flowed through a grassy hollow, with steeply sloping sides. Water is the same all the world over; but there was more than water here to bring his childhood back to Falconer. For at the spot where the path led him down to the burn, a little crag stood out from the bank—a gray stone, like many he knew on the stream that watered the valley of Rothieden. On the top of the stone grew a little heather; and beside it, bending toward the water, was a silver birch. He sat down on the foot of the rock, shut in by the high, grassy banks from the gaze of the mighty mountains. The sole unrest was the run of the water beside him, and it sounded so homey that he began to jabber in Scotch to it. With his country's birch tree beside him and the rock crowned with its turf of heather over his head, once more the words arose in his mind, "My peace I give unto you."

Now he fell to thinking what this peace could be. And it came into his mind, as he thought, that Jesus had spoken in another place about giving rest to those that came to him, while here he spoke about "*my* peace." Could this *my* mean a certain *kind* of peace that the Lord himself possessed? He then remembered the New Testament back in his room, and, resolving to try whether he could not make something more out of it, went back to the inn quieter in heart than since he left his home. In the evening he returned to the brook, and fell to searching the story, seeking after the peace of Jesus.

He did not leave the place for six weeks. Every day he went to the burn, as he called the stream, with his New Testament; every day tried yet again to make something more of what the Savior meant. By the end of the month it had dawned on him that the peace of Jesus must have been a peace that came from doing the will of his Father. From the account he gave of the discoveries he then made, I will venture to represent them here. They were these Jesus taught:

First—That a man's business is to do the will of God.

Second—That God will care for the man.

Third—That a man, therefore, must not be afraid but be at peace; and so,

Fourth—be left free to love God with all his heart, and his neighbor as himself.

But then a new question suddenly arose, "How am I to tell for certain that there ever was such a man as this one whose words I am reading?"

All this wilderness time he did nothing but read the four gospels and ponder over them. Therefore it is not surprising that he should already have become so familiar with the gospel story that the moment this question appeared, the following words should dart to the forefront of his mind:

"If any man chooses to do his will, he shall know whether my teaching comes from God or whether I speak of myself."

Here was a word from Jesus himself, giving the surest means of arriving at a conclusion of the truth or falsehood of all that he said, namely, by doing the will of God.

The next question naturally was, "What is this will of God?"

Here he found himself in difficulty. The theology of his grandmother rushed in upon him, threatening to overwhelm him with demands. They were repulsive to him. They appeared unreal and contradictory to the nature around him. Yet that alone could be no *proof* that they were not of God. Still, they demanded what *seemed* to him unjust; these demands were founded on what *seemed* to him untruth attributed to God, on ways of thinking and feeling which were degrading in a man. Thus he realized, as long as they appeared to be such to him, that to acknowledge these demands as truth, even if it turned out later that he misunderstood them, would be to wrong God.

For two more weeks he brooded and pondered over the question, as he wandered up and down that burnside or sat at the foot of the heather-crowned stone and the silver-barked birch, until the light began to dawn upon him.

It grew plain to him that what Jesus came to do was just lead his life, rather than adhering to the list of doctrinal demands he had himself been wrestling with. That he should do the work, and much besides, that the Father had given him to do—that was the will of God concerning him. With this perception arose the conviction that to *every* man and woman God has given a work to do. Each had to lead the life God meant him to lead. The will of God was thus to be found and done in the world, not solely in theology or doctrine or demands of the church. In seeking a true relation to the world, then, he would come to find his relation to God.

The time for action was come. The will of God could only be known by doing. He rose up from the stone of his meditation, took his staff in his hand, and went down the mountain, not knowing where he went. As he descended the mountain, the one question was—what was he now to *do*? If he had had the faintest track to follow he would have concluded that his business was to set out at once and find his father. But since the day when the hand of that father smote him and Mary St. John found him bleeding on the factory floor, he had not heard one word or conjecture about him. If he were to set out to find him now, it would be to search the earth for one who might have vanished from it years ago. When the time came for him to find his father, some sign would be given him—that is, some hint which he could follow with action. Until then there was no course of action open to him. As he continued to think and think, it became gradually plainer that he must begin his obedience by getting ready for anything that God might require of him. Therefore he must go on learning till the call came.

But he shivered at the thought of returning to Aberdeen. Might he not continue his studies in Germany? Would that not be as good—possibly better? But how was it to be decided? By submitting the matter to the friend who made either possible. Dr. Anderson had been to him as a father; he would be guided by him.

He wrote, therefore, to Dr. Anderson, saying that he would return at once if he wished, but that he should greatly prefer going to a German university for two years. The doctor replied that of course he would rather have him at home, but that he was confident Robert knew what was best for himself. Therefore he had only to settle where he thought was proper, and the next summer he would come and see the young man, for he was not tied to Aberdeen any more than Robert.

32 / Home Again

Four years passed before Falconer returned to his native country, during which period Dr. Anderson visited him twice and had found himself well satisfied with Robert's condition and pursuits. The doctor had likewise visited Rothieden and had comforted the heart of the grandmother with regard to her grandson.

Robert had not settled at any particular university, but had moved from one to the other as he saw fit, seeking the men who spoke with authority. The time of doubt and questioning was far from over, but the time was past when he could be driven about by the wind. However his intellect might be tossed on the waves of speculation, he found that the word the Lord had spoken to him remained steadfast. For in doing right and walking humbly, the conviction increased in him that Jesus knew the very secret of life. Now and then some great vision gleamed across his soul of the working of all things toward a far-off goal of simple obedience to a law of life, which God knew, and which his Son had justified through sorrow and pain. Ever and again some one of the dark perplexities of humanity began to glimmer with light.

Looking back to the time when it seemed that he cried and was not heard, he saw that God had been hearing, had been answering all the time, had been making him capable of receiving the gift for which he prayed.

At the close of these four years, with his spirit calm and hopeful, truth his passion, and music, which again he had resumed and diligently cultivated, his pleasure, Falconer returned to Aberdeen. He was received by Dr. Anderson as if he had in truth been his own son. In the room stood a tall figure, with his back toward them, pocketing a handkerchief. The next moment the figure turned, and—could it be?—yes, it was Shargar.

Doubt lingered only until he opened his mouth and said, "Eh, Bob!" with which exclamation he threw himself upon him, and after a very undignified fashion began crying heartily. Tall as he was, Robert's great black head towered above him, and his shoulders were like a rock against which Shargar's slight figure leaned. His eyes shimmered with feeling, but Robert's tears were kept for very solemn occasions.

"Shargar!" pronounced in a tone full of a thousand memories, was all the greeting he returned; but his great, manly hand pressed Shargar's delicate, long-fingered one with a grasp which must have satisfied his friend that everything was as it had been between them, and that their friendship from henceforth would take a new start. For with all that Robert had seen, thought, and heard, the old times and the old friends were now dearer than ever. Therefore he could not now rest until he had gone to see his grandmother.

"Will you come to Rothieden with me, Shargar? I beg your pardon—I oughtn't to keep up an old nickname," said Robert as they sat that evening with the doctor over a tumbler of toddy.

"If you call me anything else, I'll cut my throat, Robert, as I told you before. If anyone *else* does," he added, laughing, "I'll cut his throat."

"Can he go with me, doctor?" asked Robert, turning to their host.

"Certainly. He has not been to Rothieden since he took his degree. He's a Master of Arts now, and has distinguished himself besides. You'll see him in his uniform soon, I hope. Let's drink his health, Robert. Fill your glass."

The doctor filled his glass slowly and solemnly. He seldom drank even wine, but this was a rare occasion. He then rose, and with equal slowness and a tremor in his voice, said, "Robert, my son, let's drink the health of George Moray, Gentleman. Stand up."

Robert rose and, in his confusion, Shargar rose too and sat down again, blushing till his red hair looked yellow beside his cheeks. The men repeated the words, "George Moray, Gentleman," emptied their glasses, and resumed their seats. Shargar rose trembling, and tried in vain to speak. The reason in part was that he sought to utter himself in English.

"Hoots! This tongue o' mine won't min' me!" he broke out at last. "If I be a gentleman, Dr. Anderson an' Robert Falconer, it's ye two 'ats made me ane, an' God bless ye an' I'm yer hoomble servant to a' etairnity."

So saying, Shargar resumed his seat, filled his glass with a trembling hand, and emptied it in one gulp.

The next morning Robert and Shargar got on the coach and went to Rothieden. Robert knew that Mary had left some three years earlier; whether he was sorry or glad that he should not see her, he could not tell. He feared Rothieden would look like desolate Pompeii; but when the coach drove into the long, straggling street, he found the old love revive, and although the blood rushed back to his heart when Captain Forsyth's house came into view, he did not turn away, but made his eyes and his heart familiar with its desolation. He got down at the corner, and leaving Shargar to go on to the Boar's Head and look after the luggage, walked into his grandmother's house and straight into her little parlor.

She rose with her old stateliness when she saw the stranger enter the room and stood waiting his address.

"Well, Grannie," said Robert, and took her in his arms.

"The Lord's name be praised!" she faltered. "He's over good t' the likes o' me."

She had been informed of his coming, but she had not expected him till the evening. He was much altered, but old age is slow.

He had hardly placed her in her chair when Betty came in. If she had shown him respect before, it was reverence now.

"Eh, sir!" she said. "I didn't know it was ye or I wouldn't have come into the room without knocking at the door. I'll get back t' my kitchen."

So saying she turned to leave the room.

"Hoots! Betty," cried Robert. "Don't be a gowk. Give me a grip of your hand."

Betty stood staring and irresolute, overcome at the mere sight of the manly bulk before her.

"If you don't behave yourself, Betty, I'll just go over to Muckle-drum and have a look through the record book."

Betty laughed for the first time at the awful threat, and, the ice once broken, things returned somewhat to their old footing.

The next morning Robert paid a visit to Bodyfauld and found that time had there flowed so gently it had left but few wrinkles and few gray hairs. The fields too had little change to show, and the hill was all the same, except that the pines had grown.

Walking home in the evening he threaded the little forest of pines, climbing the hill till he came out on its bare crown, where nothing grew but heather and blueberries. There he threw himself down and gazed into the heavens. The sun was below the horizon; all the dazzle was gone out of the gold, and the roses were fast fading. The downy blue of the sky was trembling into stars over his head; the brown dusk was gathering in the air, and a wind full of gentleness and peace came to him from the west. He let his thoughts go where they would, and they went up into the abyss over his head.

"Lord . . . come to me," he cried in his heart. "I am yours. I abandon myself to you. Fill me with yourself. When I am full of you, my griefs themselves will grow golden in your sunlight. Lord, let me help those who are wretched because they do not know you. Let me tell them that they may partake of your great peace. Let me be broken if need be that your light may shine upon the lies which men tell in your name, and which eat away their hearts. Send me where you want me to go, and to the people you have for me to meet.''

Having persuaded Shargar to remain with Mrs. Falconer for a few days, and thus remove the feeling of offense she still held because of his "moonlight flittin'," Robert returned to Dr. Anderson, who now unfolded his plans for him. These were that he should attend the medical classes of the university, and at the same time accompany him in his visits to the poor. He was confident that a knowledge of medicine would be invaluable to him in whatever direction the course of his future life took. I think the good doctor must have foreseen the kind of life which Falconer would at length choose to lead, and with wisdom sought to prepare him for it. However this may be, Robert entertained the proposal gladly, went into the scheme with his whole heart, and began to widen his knowledge of the poor and sympathy with their plight.

In these studies and labors he again spent about four years, during which time he gathered much knowledge of human nature, great instincts for medicine, and far reaching compassion for those in need. He learned especially that he who cannot feel the humanity of his neighbor because he may be different in education, habits, opinion, morals, or circumstances is unfit to offer him aid.

Within this period Shargar had gone to India, where he had once or twice distinguished himself. Toward the close of the four years he had leave of absence and was on his way home. About the same time Robert was in much need of a rest, and Dr. Anderson proposed that he should meet Moray at Southampton.

Shargar had no expectation of seeing him and his delight broke out wildly. No thinnest film had grown over his heart, though in all else he was considerably changed. The army had done everything that was wanted for his outward show of man. He had a firm step and soldierly stride; his bearing was free, yet dignified; his high descent came out in the ease of his carriage and manners; there could be no doubt that at last Shargar was a gentleman. His hair had changed to a kind of red chestnut. His complexion was much darkened with the Indian sun. His eyes too were darker and no longer rolled slowly from one object to another, but instead indicated a mind ready to snap into action. His whole appearance was striking.

Robert was delighted with the improvement in him, and even more when he found that his mind's growth had kept pace with the body's change. The young men went to London together, to a hotel near St.

Paul's Church, and great was the pleasure they had. They both had much to tell; Shargar was proud of being able to communicate with Robert from an equal level, realizing that he now knew many things that Robert could not know.

33 / A Mere Glimpse _____

At the close of two weeks, Falconer thought it time to return to his duties in Aberdeen. The day before the steamer sailed, they found themselves in Grace-church Street about six o'clock. It was a fine summer evening. The street was less crowded than earlier in the afternoon, although there was a continuous stream of wagons and cabs in both directions. They stood on the curbstone, waiting to cross. In the middle of their conversation, Shargar suddenly became silent.

Robert glanced round at him. Shargar was staring with wide eyes into the crowd of vehicles that filled the street. His face was pale and strangely like the Shargar of old days.

"What's the matter with you?" Robert asked, in some bewilderment.

Receiving no answer, he followed Shargar's gaze into the middle of the crowded street where came a line of three donkey carts, heaped high with bundles and articles of Gypsy gear. The foremost was conducted by a middle-aged woman, of tall, commanding aspect, and expression both cunning and fierce. She walked by the donkey's head carrying a short stick, with which she struck him now and then, but which she oftener waved over his head like the truncheon of an excited marshal on the battlefield.

Robert took all this in in a moment. The same moment Shargar's spell was broken.

"Lord, it *is* my mother!" he cried, and darted under a horse's neck into the middle of the street.

He needled his way through till he reached the woman. She was swearing at a cabman whose wheel had caught the point of her donkey's shaft, and was hauling him round. Heedless of everything, Shargar threw his arms about her, crying: "Mother, Mother!"

"None o' yer blasted humbug!" she exclaimed as she vigorously freed herself from his embrace and pushed him away.

The moment she had him at arm's length, however, her hand closed upon his arm and her other hand went up to her brow. Her eyes shot up and down him from head to foot, and he could feel her hand beginning to relax its grip. He stood motionless, waiting the result of her scrutiny, unconscious that every vehicle within sight of the pair had stopped. A strange silence fell upon the street.

Suddenly a rough voice broke the spell. It was that of the cabman who had been in altercation with the woman. Bursting into an insulting laugh, he used words with regard to her which it is better to leave unrecorded. The same instant Shargar freed himself from her grasp and stood by the forewheel of the cab.

"Get down!" he said in a voice low and hoarse, yet determined.

The fellow whipped his horse but at the same instant Shargar sprang up on the box and dragged him, all but headlong, down from his seat.

"Now," he said, "beg my mother's pardon."

"Be hanged if I do!" said the cabman.

"Then defend yourself," said Shargar.

"Come on, you no good lout!" cried the cabman, plucking up heart and putting himself in fighting shape. But the next moment he lay between his horse's feet.

Shargar turned again toward the woman. The cabman, bleeding, rose, and, desiring no more of the same, climbed on his box and went off, belaboring his horse and pursued by a roar from the street, for the spectators were delighted at his punishment.

"Now, Mother," said Shargar, panting with excitement.

"What call they ye?" she asked, still doubtful, but as proud of being defended as if the coarse words of her assailant had had no truth in them. "Ye can't be my long-legged Geordie?"

"What for no?"

"Ye're a gentleman, faith."

"An' what for no again?" returned Shargar, beginning to smile.

"Weel, yer father was one, anyway—if so ye be as ye say ye are."

Shargar put his head close to hers and whispered some words that nobody heard but herself.

"It's too long past to mind that," she said in reply. "Weel, ye can be nobody but my Geordie. Haith, man!" she went on, regarding him once more from head to foot, "but ye're a credit to me, I must allow. Weel, give me a sovereign and I'll never come near ye."

Poor Shargar in his despair turned toward Robert.

"Come up the road here, to our public house, and take a glass with us, woman," said Falconer.

The temptation of a glass of something strong, and the hope of getting money out of them caused an instant agreement. She said a few words to a young woman accompanying her, who proceeded at once to tie her donkey's head to the tail of the other cart.

"Show the way, then," she said, turning toward Falconer.

Shargar and he led the way and the woman followed faithfully. The waiter stared when they entered.

"Bring a glass of wine," said Falconer. When it arrived she tossed it down and looked as if she would like another glass.

"Yer father'll have taken ye up, I'm thinkin', laddie?" she said, turning to her son.

"No," answered Shargar. "There's the man that took me up."

"An' who may ye be?" she asked, turning to Falconer.

"Mr. Falconer," said Shargar.

"Not a son o' Andrew Falconer?" she asked again, with evident interest.

"The same," answered Robert.

"Weel, Geordie," she said, turning once more to her son, "it's like mother, like father to the two o' ye."

"Did you know my father?" asked Robert eagerly.

Instead of answering him she made another remark to her son.

"He needn't be ashamed o' your company anyway, queer kind o' mother that I am."

"He never was ashamed of my company," said Shargar.

"Ay, I knew yer father weel enough," she said, now answering Robert, "more by token when I saw him last night. He was lookin' ill."

Robert sprang from his seat and caught her by the arm.

"Ow! Ye needn't go into such a flurry. He'll no come near ye, I'll warrant."

"Tell me where he is," implored Robert. "Where did you see him? I'll give you all that I have if you'll take me to him."

"Hooly! hooly! Who's to go lookin' for a needle in a haystack," she returned cooly. "I only said 'at I saw him."

"But are you sure it was him?"

"Ay, sure enough," she answered.

"What makes you so sure?"

" 'Cause I never was wrong yet. Set a man once between my two eyes and that'll be two that knows him even when his own mother's forgotten him."

"Did you speak to him?"

"Maybe ay, maybe no. I didn't come here to be hecklet before a jury."

"Tell me what he's like," said Robert, agitated with eager hope.

"If ye don't know what he's like, why should ye take the trouble to ask? But 'deed, ye'll know what he's like when ye fall in wi' him," she added, with a vindictive laugh—vindictive because he had given her only one glass.

With the laugh she rose and made for the door. They rose at the same moment to detain her. Like one who knew at once to fight and flee, she turned and stunned them as with a verbal blow—more powerful than a physical one: ''She's a fine yoong thing, yon sister o' yours, Geordie. She'll be worth a heap o' money by the time she's had a while at the school.''

The men looked at each other aghast. When they turned their eyes she had vanished. They rushed to the door, and, parting, searched in both directions. But it was of no use. She had probably found a back way into Peternoster Row, whence the outlets are numerous.

Now that Falconer had a ground, though a shadowy one, for hoping that his father might be in London, he could not return to Aberdeen. Shargar, who had no heart to hunt for his mother, left the next day by steamer. Falconer took to wandering about the labyrinthine city, and in a couple of months knew more about the metropolis than most people who had lived their whole lives in it. Day and night he wandered into all sorts of places; the worse they looked the more attractive he found them. He could not pass a dirty court or low-browed archway: He *might* be there. Or he might have been there. Or it was such a place as he would choose for shelter.

At first he was attracted only by tall, elderly men. Such a man he would sometimes follow till his following made him turn and demand what he wanted. If there was no suspicion of Scotch in his tone, Falconer easily apologized. If there was, he made such replies as might lead to some betrayal. He could not defend the course of action he was adopting; it had not the shadow of probability on its side. Still, the greatest successes the world has ever beheld had been at one time the greatest improbabilities. He could do nothing but go on, for as yet he could think of nothing else to try.

Neither could a man like Falconer long confine his interest to this immediate object. While he still made it his main purpose to find his father, that object became a center from which radiated a thousand influences upon those in the back alleys and poor sections of London who were like sheep without a shepherd. He fell back into his old ways at Aberdeen, only with a boundless sphere to work in, and with the hope of finding his father to hearten him. He haunted the streets at night, went into all sorts of places, and made his way into the lowest forms of life without introduction or protection.

There was a certain air of the hills about him which was often mistaken for country inexperience, and men thought they could make gain or game of him. But such found their mistake, and if not soon, then the more completely. Far from provoking or even meeting hostility, he soon satisfied those that persisted that he was a dangerous man to toy with. In two years he became well known to the poor of a large district, especially on both sides of Shoreditch, for whose sakes he made the exercise of his medical profession readily available.

He lived in lodgings in John Street—the same in which I found him when I came to know him. He made few acquaintances. He always carried a book in his pocket, but did not have much time to read. On Sundays he generally went to some of the many lonely parks or meadows of Surrey with his New Testament. When weary in London he would go to the reading room of the British Museum for an hour or two. He kept up a regular correspondence with Dr. Anderson.

At length he received a letter from him which occasioned his immediate departure for Aberdeen. Until now, his friend, who was entirely satisfied with his mode of life and supplied him freely with money, had not even expressed a wish to recall him, though he had often spoken of visiting him in London. It now appeared that, unwilling to cause him any needless anxiety, the doctor had abstained from mentioning the fact that his health had been declining. He had gotten suddenly worse, and Falconer hastened to obey the summons he had sent him.

With a heavy heart he walked up to the hospitable door, recalling, as he ascended the steps, how he had stood there a helpless youth, in want of a few pounds to save his hopes, when this friend received him and bid him Godspeed on the path he desired to follow. In a moment more he was shown into the study and was passing through it when Johnston laid his hand on his arm.

"The master's not up yet, sir," he said, with a very solemn look. "He's been desperate after seein' ye, and I must go and let him know ye're here at last, for fear it should be too much for him, seein' ye all at once. But eh, sir!" he added, the tears gathering in his eyes, "ye'll hardly know him. He's that changed!"

Johnston left the study by the door to the cottage room, and returned a moment later and invited Falconer to enter. In the bed lay the form of his friend. Falconer hastened to the bedside, kneeled down, and took his hand. The doctor was silent but a smile overspread his countenance and revealed an inward satisfaction. Robert's heart was full, and he could only gaze on the worn face. At length Robert was able to speak.

"Why didn't you send for me?" he said. "You never told me you were ailing."

"Because you were doing good, Robert, my boy, and I who had done so little had no right to interrupt what you were doing. I wonder if God will give me another chance. I would like to do better. I don't think I could sit singing psalms to all eternity," he added with a smile.

"Whatever good I may do before my time comes, I have you to thank for it. Eh, doctor! if it hadn't been for you!"

Robert's feelings overcame him. He resumed brokenly: "You gave me a man to believe in, when my own father had forsaken me. You have made me, doctor. With meat and drink and learning and money, and all things together, you have made me."

"Eh, Robert!" said the dying man, half rising on his elbow, "to think what God makes us to one another. My father did ten times for me what I have done for you. As I lie here thinking I may see him before the week's over, I'm just a child again."

As he spoke the polish of his speech was gone and the social refinement of his demeanor with it. The faces of his ancestors—noble, sensitive, earnest, but rugged, and weather-beaten, through centuries of windy ploughing, hail-stormed sheep-tending, long-paced seed-sowing, and labor—surely were not less honorable in the sight of God than the fighting of the noble. All this came back in the face of the dying physician.

Toward the close of the week he grew much more feeble. Falconer scarcely left his room. He awoke one midnight and murmured in the Scottish dialect of his youth, with many pauses: "Robert, my time's near, I'm thinkin'. For sometimes I almost feel that my father has a grip o' my hand. A minute ago I was walking through a terrible drift o' snow—eh, how it whistled and sang! And the cold of it was stingin', but my father had a hold o' me, and I didn't mind the snow and was just stampin' down on't with my wee feet, for I was like seven year old or thereabouts. An' then I heard my mother singin' and knew it was a dream. Eh! I wonder what the final waking'll be like."

After a pause he resumed: "Robert, my boy, ye're in the right way. Hold on and let nothing turn ye aside. Man, it's a great comfort to me to think that ye're my own flesh and blood and not that far off. My father an' yer great-grandfather, on the grandmother's side, were brothers. Ye're the only one on my father's side, ye and yer father, if he be alive. My will's in the bottom drawer on the left hand o' my writing table in the library; I have left ye everything I possess. Only there's one thing I want ye to do. First, ye must go on as yer doin' in London for ten years more. If dying men has any o' the foresight that's attributed to them, it's borne in on me that ye will see yer father again. At any event, ye'll be helping some ill-fared souls in the meantime. But if ye don't fall in with yer father within ten years, ye must just pack up yer box and go away over the sea to Calcutta and do what I have told ye to do in that will. I bind ye by no promise, Robert, and I won't have none. Things might happen to put ye in a terrible difficulty with a promise. I'm only telling ye what I would like. Especially if ye have found yer father, ye must go by yer own judgment about it, for there will be a lot to do with him once ye've found him. But now I must lay still and maybe sleep again, for I have spoken too much.''

Hoping that he would sleep and wake yet again, Robert sat still. After an hour he looked and saw that he was now breathing like a child. His countenance was peaceful as if he had already entered into his rest. Robert sat as a bird brooding over the breaking shell of the dying man.

On either hand we behold a birth, of which, as of the moon, we see but half. To the region where he goes, the man enters newly born. We forget that it is a birth and call it death. The body he leaves behind is but the placenta by which he drew his nourishment from his mother Earth. And as the childbed is watched on earth with anxious expectancy, so the couch of the dying, as we call it, may be surrounded by the birth-watchers of the other world, waiting like anxious servants to open the door to which this world is but the windblown porch.

Extremes meet. As a man draws nigh to his second birth, his heart looks back to his childhood. As Falconer sat thinking, the doctor spoke. They were low, faint sounds, for the lips were nearly at rest. Wanted no more for utterance, they were on their way back to the holy dust, which is yet God's.

''Father, Father!'' he cried quickly in the tone and speech of a Scotch laddie. ''I'm going down. Hold a grip o' my hand.''

When Robert hurried to the bedside, he found that the last breath had gone in the words. The thin right hand lay partly closed, as if it had been grasping a larger hand. On the face lay confidence just ruffled with apprehension; the latter melted away, and nothing remained but that awful and beautiful peace which is the farewell of the soul to its servant.

Robert knelt and thanked God for the noble man.

35 / A Talk with Grannie_____

As soon as, in the beautiful phrase of the Old Testament, John Anderson was gathered to his fathers, Robert went to pay a visit to his grandmother.

Dressed to every detail in the same manner in which he had known her from childhood, he found her little altered in appearance. She was one of those who, instead of stooping with age, settle downward. Her step was feebler, and when she prayed her voice quavered more. On her face sat the same settled, almost hard repose, as ever, but her behavior was still more gentle than when he had seen her last. However, even though she looked virtually the same, Robert felt that the mist of separation between her world and his was gathering. Her face was gradually turning from him toward the land of light.

"I have buried my best friend but yourself, Grannie," he said as he took a chair close by her side.

"I trust he's happy. He was a quiet an' well-behaved man, an' ye hae reason t' respect his memory. Did he die the death o' the righteous, do ye think, laddie?"

"I do not think, Grannie, I know it. He loved God, without a doubt."

"The Lord be praised!" said Mrs. Falconer. "An' folk say he's made a rich man o' ye, Robert."

"He left me everything, except something to his servant—who well deserved it."

"Eh, Robert! but it's a terrible snare. Money's an awful thing. My poor Andrew never began t' go the ill way till he began t' hae too much money."

"But it's not a bad thing itself, Grannie; for God made money as well as other things."

"He doesn't think much o' it, though, or he would give more o' it t' some folk. But as ye say, it's his, an' if ye hae grace t' use it right, it may be made a great blessing t' yerself an' other folk. But take care, for it's an awful thing t' be drowned i' riches. But t' be plain wi' ye, I haen't much fear, for I've heard the kind o' life that ye've been leadin'. God's hearkened t' my prayers for ye. Go on, my dear lad; go on holdin' out a helpin' hand t' anyone who'll take a grip o' it. Be a burnin' an'

198

shinin' light that men may praise yer Father i' heaven. Take the drunkard from his whiskey, the swearer from his oaths, the liar from his lies; an' don't give any o' them too much money at once. That's my advice t' ye, Robert.''

''But who told you what I was about in London?''

''Dr. Anderson himself. I had letter after letter from him about ye an' what ye were doin'. He kept me well acquainted wi' ye.''

This fresh proof of his friend's affection touched Robert deeply. He had himself written often to his grandmother, but had never given her any details of his doings, although the thought of her was ever beside the thought of his father.

''Do you know, Grannie, what's at the heart of my hopes in the misery and degradation I see from morning to night in the great city?''

''I trust it's the glory o' God, laddie.''

''I hope that's not lacking either. For I love God with all my heart. But it's oftener the saving of my earthly father than the glory of my heavenly one that I'm thinking about.''

Mrs. Falconer heaved a deep sigh.

''God grant ye success, Robert,'' she said. ''But that can't be right.''

''What can't be right?''

''Not t' put the glory o' God first an' foremost.''

''But you know there's no glory to God like the repenting of a sinner. What greater glory can God have than that?''

''It's true, what ye say. But still, if God cares for that same glory, ye ought t' think o' that first, even before the salvation o' yer father.''

''Maybe you're right, Grannie. And if it be as you say—he's promised to lead us into all truth, and he'll lead me into that truth. But I'm thinking it's more for our sakes than his own that he cares about his glory. I don't believe that he thinks about his glory except for the sake of truth and men's hearts dying for the lack of it.''

Mrs. Falconer thought for a moment. ''It may be that ye're right, laddie, but ye hae a way o' saying things that is some fearsome.''

''God's not like a proud man to take offense, Grannie. There's nothing that pleases him like the truth, and there's nothing that displeases him like lying, particularly when it's pretended praise. He wants no false praising. Now, *you* say things about him sometimes that sound fearsome to me.''

''What kind o' things, laddie?'' asked the old lady, with offense glooming in the background.

''Like when you speak of him as if he was a poor, proud man, full of his own importance and ready to be down on anybody that didn't call him by the name of his office—always thinking about his own glory, instead of the quiet, mighty, grand, self-forgetting, all-creating, loving being that he is. Eh, Grannie! Think of the face of that man of sorrows, that never said a hard word to a sinful woman or a despised publican. Was he thinking about his own glory, do you think? And whatever isn't like Christ isn't like God."

"But laddie, he came t' satisfy God's justice by sufferin' the punishment due t' oor sins, t' turn aside his wrath an' curse. So Jesus couldn't be *altogether* God."

"Oh, but he is, Grannie. He came to satisfy God's justice by giving him back his children, by making them see that God was just, by sending them back home to fall at his feet. He came to lift the weight of the sins off the shoulders of them that did them by making them turn against the sin and before God. And there isn't a word of reconciling God to us in the Testament, for there was no need of that; it was *us* that needed to be reconciled to him. And so he bore our sins and carried our sorrows, for those sins caused him no end of grief of mind and pain in his body. It wasn't his own sins or God's wrath that caused him suffering, but our own sins. And he took them away. He took our sins upon him, for he came into the middle of them and took them up—by no sleight of hand, by no quibbling of the preachers about imputing his righteousness to us and such like. But he took them and took them away, and here am I, Grannie, growing out of my sins in consequence, and there are you, growing out of yours in consequences, too."

"I wish that may be true, laddie. But I don't care how ye put it," returned his grandmother, bewildered no doubt, "just so long as ye put him first an' say wi' all yer heart, 'His will be done!'"

"His will be done, Grannie," responded Robert readily.

"Amen, amen! An' now, laddie, do ye think there's any likelihood that yer father's still i' the body? I dream aboot him sometimes so lifelike that I can't believe him dead. But that's superstitious."

"Would you know him if you saw him?" asked Robert.

"Know him!" she cried. "I would know him if he had been forty day i' the grave! How could ye ask such a question, laddie?"

"He may be changed, Grannie. He might be turning old by this time."

"Old! Like yerself, laddie. Hoots, hoots! Ye're right. I am forgetting. But nonetheless would I know him."

"I wish I knew what he was like. I saw him once—hardly twice, but all that I remember would hardly help me on the streets of London."

"I don't doubt that," returned Mrs. Falconer. "But I can let ye see a picture o' him, though I doubt it will show much t' ye as t' me. He had it painted t' give yer mother on their wedding day. Och hone! She did the same for him, but what came o' that little picture o' her, I don't know.''

Mrs. Falconer went into the little closet to the old bureau and, bringing out the miniature, gave it to Robert. It was a portrait of a young man, in an old blue coat and white waistcoat, looking innocent, and it must be confessed, dull and uninteresting. It had been painted by a traveling artist. It brought to Robert's mind no faintest shadow of recollection and gave him not the slightest hope that it could assist him in finding him of whom it had once been a shadowy resemblance.

"Is it like him, Grannie?" he asked.

As if to satisfy herself once more, she took the miniature and gazed at it for some time. Then, with a deep, hopeless sigh, she answered, "Ay, it's like him. But it's not him. Eh, the smiling eyes—smiling on everyone, an' on her most o' all, till he took t' the drink. It was money an' company—company that couldn't be merry without drinking.''

"Will you let me take this with me, Grannie?" said Robert, for though the portrait was useless for identification, it might serve a further purpose.

"Ow, ay, take it. I don't want it. I can see him well enough without it. But I hae no hope left that ye'll ever fall in wi' him.''

"God has a way of doing unlikely things, Grannie," said Robert.

"He's done all that he can do for him, I don't doubt, already.''

"Do you think that God couldn't save a man if he wanted to, then, Grannie?"

"God can do anything. There's no doubt but by the gift o' his Spirit he could save anyone.''

"And you think he's not merciful enough to do it?"

"It wouldn't do t' meddle wi' folks' free will. T' make people be good would be no goodness at all.''

"But if God could actually create the free will, don't you think he could help it to go right, without any makin'? We know so little about it, Grannie! How does his Spirit help anybody? Does he *make* them that accepts the offer of salvation?"

"No, I can't think that. But he shows them the truth i' such a way that they just can't help from turnin' t' him for peace an' rest.''

"Well, I believe that too. And until I'm sure that a man has had the truth shown him in such a way as that, then I can't allow myself to think that, however he may have sinned, he has finally rejected the truth. If I knew that a man had seen the truth as I have seen it sometimes, and had deliberately turned his back upon it, then maybe I'd be compelled to say there was no more salvation for him. But I don't believe that ever a man did so. But even then, I don't know.''

202

"I did all I could for him that I knew how t' do," said Mrs. Falconer with reflection. "Night an' mornin' an' midday prayin' for him an' wi' him."

"Maybe you turned him away from it, Grannie."

She gave a stifled cry of despair. "Don't say that, laddie, or ye'll drive me out o' my mind. God forgive me if that be true! I deserve hell more than my Andrew."

"But you see, Grannie, supposing it was true, that wouldn't be held against you, seeing you did the best you knew. And just think, if it be fair for one human being to influence another all that they can—and that's not interfering with their free will—it's impossible to measure what God could do with his Spirit coming at them from all sides, and able to put such thoughts and such pictures into them as we can't even imagine. It would be all true what he told them, and truth can never be meddling with the free will."

Mrs. Falconer made no reply, but evidently went on thinking.

"At any rate, Grannie," resumed her grandson, "*I* haven't done for him all I can yet. God'll give me my father sometime, Grannie, for what can a man do without a father? Human beings can't know all the ins and outs and sides of love except they have a father to love. I have had none, Grannie, and God knows that."

She made him no answer. She dared not say that he expected too much from God. Is it likely that Jesus will say so of any man or woman when he looks for faith in the earth?

Robert went out to see some of his old friends, and when he returned it was time for supper and worship. These were the same as of old: a plate of porridge and a wooden bowl of milk for it, a chapter and a hymn, both read, a prayer from Grannie, and then from Robert. And so they went to bed.

But Robert could not sleep. He rose, dressed himself, and went up to the empty garret, looking at the stars through the skylight; then knelt and prayed to the Father of all for his father and for all men. Then he softly descended the stairs and went out into the street.

36 / Shargar's Mother

It was a warm, still night in July; moonless, but not dark. There is no night there in the summer—only a long, ethereal twilight. He walked through the sleeping town so full of memories, all quiet in his mind now—quiet that ever broods over the house where a friend has dwelt. He left the town behind and walked—through the odors of grass and clover and of the yellow flowers on the old earth walls that divided the fields—sweet scents to which the darkness is friendly—down to the brink of the river that flowed scarcely murmuring through the night. He crossed the footbridge and turned into the bleach-field. Its houses were desolate, for that trade too had died away. The machinery stood rotting and rusting. The wheel gave no answering motion to the flow of the water that glided away beneath it. The water went slipping and sliding through the deserted places of the mill, a power whose use had departed. The canal, the delight of his childhood, was nearly choked with weeds. He climbed to the place where he had once lain and listened to the sounds of the belt of fir trees behind him. All the old things, the old ways, the old glories of childhood—were they gone? No, for to the God of the human heart nothing that has ever been a joy, a grief, or a passing interest can ever be forgotten. There is no fading at the breath of time, no dimming of old memories in the heart of him who has created us.

While he lay, the waning, fading moon had risen, weak and bleared and dull. She brightened and brightened until at last she lighted up the night. He rose and crossed the earthen dyke into the field beyond. He walked on; he had no inclination to go home. The solitariness of the night prevents most people from wandering far in it. But Robert had learned long ago to love the night and feel at home with every aspect of God's world. How this peace contrasted with the nights in the London streets!

His thoughts turned to Shargar's mother. If he could but find her! Being a wanderer far and wide, was it not possible that she might return to Rothieden? Such people have a love for their old haunts, stronger than that of orderly members of society for their old homes. He turned back and walked toward the town. He walked through the sleeping streets, straight to the back alley where he had once found Shargar sitting

203

on the doorstep. Could he believe his eyes? A feeble light was burning
in the shed. Some other poverty-stricken bird of the night, however,
might be there. He drew near and peeped in at the broken window. A
heap of something lay in a corner, watched only by a long-snuffed
candle.

The heap moved and a voice called out in a complaining tone, "Is
that you, Shargar, ye devil?"

Falconer's heart leaped. He hesitated no longer but lifted the latch
and entered. He took up the candle and approached the woman. When
the light fell on her face she sat up, staring wildly.

"Who are ye that won't let me die in peace and quiet?"

"I'm Robert Falconer."

"Come to ask after ye ne'er-do-weel o' a father, I reckon," she
said.

"Yes," he answered.

"Who's that behind ye?"

"Nobody's behind me."

"Don't lie. Who's that behind the door?"

"Nobody. I never tell lies."

"Where's Shargar? Why doesn't he come to his mother?"

"He's gone away over the seas—a captain of soldiers."

"It's a lie. He's an ill-fared scoundrel not to come to his mother an'
bid her good-bye, an' her goin' to hell."

"If you ask, Christ'll take you out of the very mouth of hell, woman."

"Christ! who's that? Ow, ay. It's him 'at they preach about in the
churches. No, no. There's no good o' that. There's no time to repent
now. I doubt such repentance as mine would count for much with the
likes o' him."

"He didn't come to save people like himself. He came to save the
likes of you and me."

" 'The likes o' you an' me!' said ye, laddie? There's no like a'tween
ye an' me. He'll have nothing to say to me but 'Go to hell with ye.' "

"He never said such a word in his life. He would say, 'Poor thing,
she was ill-used. You mustn't sin anymore. Come, and I'll help you.'
He would say something like that."

"An' I have given my bonny bairn to the devil with my own hands!
She'll come to hell after me to grin at me an' set them on me with their
red hot tongs, an' curse me. Och hone! Och hone!"

"Listen to me," said Falconer with as much authority as he could
assume. But she rolled herself over again in the corner and lay groaning.

"Tell me where she is," said Falconer, "and I'll get her away from
them, whoever they may be."

She sat up again and stared at him for a few moments without speaking.

"I left her with a woman worse than myself," she said at length. "God forgive me!"

"He will forgive you if you tell me where she is."

"Do ye think he will? Eh, Mister Falconer! The woman lives in a court off Clare Market. I don't remember the name o' it, though I could go to it with my eyes closed. Her name's Widow Walker—an old rowdie—curse her soul!"

"No, no, you mustn't say that if you want to be forgiven yourself. I'll find her. And I'm thinking it won't take me long. I'm going back to London in two or three days."

"Don't go till I'm dead. Stay an' keep the devil off me. He has a grip o' my heart now, scratchin' at me with his long nails—as long as bird's claws."

"I'll stay with you till we see what can be done for you. What's the matter with you? I'm a doctor now."

There was not a chair or box or stool on which to sit down. He therefore kneeled beside her. He felt her pulse, questioned her, and learned that she had long been suffering from an internal complaint, which had within the last week grown rapidly worse. He saw that there was no hope of her recovery, but while she lived he gave himself to her service as much as he would have to any living soul capable of love. The night was more than warm, but she had fits of shivering. He wrapped his coat round her and wiped the damp perspiration of suffering from the poor, degraded face. The woman was still alive, for she took the hand that ministered to her and kissed it with a moan.

When the morning came she fell asleep. He crept out and went to his grandmother's, where he roused Betty and asked her to get him some peat and coals. Finding his grandmother awake, he told her all, and taking the coals and the peat, carried them to the hut where he managed to light a fire on the hearth. After a while Betty appeared with two men carrying a mattress and some bedding. The noise they made awoke her.

"Don't take me!" she cried. "I won't do it again, an' I'm dyin', I tell ye, I'm dyin', an' that'll clear all the scores—on this side anyway," she added.

They lifted her onto the mattress and made her more comfortable than perhaps she had ever been in her life. But it was only her illness that made her capable of prizing such comfort. In health, the heather on a hillside was far more to her taste than bed and blankets. She had a wild, roving, savage nature, and the wind was dearer to her than house walls. But she, too, was eternal and surely was not to be fixed forever in a bewilderment of sin and ignorance, a wild-eyed soul staring about in hellfire for want of something it could not understand and had never beheld.

She was in less pain than during the night and lay quietly gazing at the fire. Things awful to another would no doubt cross her memory without any accompanying sense of dismay; tender things would return without moving her heart, but Falconer had a grip on her now. Nothing could be done for her body except to render its death as easy as might be, but something might be done for herself. He made no attempt to produce this or that condition of mind in the poor creature. He never made such attempts. "How can I tell the next lesson a soul is capable of learning?" he would say. "The Spirit of God is the teacher. My part is to tell the good news."

In the lulls of her pain he told her about the man Jesus—what he did for the poor creatures who came to him, how kindly he spoke to them, how he cured them. He told her how gentle he was with the sinning women, how he forgave them and told them to do so no more. He left the story without comment to work that faith which alone can redeem from selfishness. She gave him but little encouragement; he did not need it, for he believed in the Life.

He had no difficulty now in getting from her what information she could give him about his father. It seemed to him of the greatest importance, although it only amounted to this: when he was in London he used to lodge at the house of an old Scotch woman of the name of Macallister, who lived in Paradise Gardens, somewhere between Bethnal Green and Spitalfields. Whether he had been in London lately, she did not know. But if anybody could tell him where he was, it would be Mrs. Macallister.

His heart filled with gratitude and hope and the surging desire for the renewal of his London labors. But he could not leave the dying woman till she was beyond the reach of his comfort; he was her keeper now. And "he that believes shall not make haste." Labor without perturbation, readiness without hurry, no haste, and no hesitation, was the divine law of his activity.

Shargar's mother breathed her last holding his hand. They were alone. He kneeled by the bed and prayed: "Father, this woman is in your hands. Take care of her. Let your light rise up in her soul that she may love and trust you. I thank you that you have blessed me with this ministration. Now lead me to my father. Amen."

He rose and went to his grandmother and told her all. She put her arms around his neck and kissed him and said, "God bless ye, my bonny lad! An' he will bless ye. He will; he will. Noo go yer way an' do the work he gives ye t' do. Only remember, it's not ye; it's him.''

Next morning, with the sweet winds of his childhood wooing him to remain yet another day among their fields, he sat on the top of the Aberdeen coach, on his way back to London.

37 / The Silk Weaver

When Robert arrived he made it his first business to find Widow Walker. She was evidently one of the worst of her class. Could the girl's freedom have been accomplished without scandal and without disturbing the quietness upon which the success of his labors depended, he would have had no scruples against simply carrying off the child. As it was, however, he contrived to see her and the affair ended in his paying the woman a hundred and fifty pounds to give up the girl. He took little Nancy home with him and gave her into the charge of his housekeeper. Nancy cried a good deal and wanted to go back to Mother Walker, but he had no trouble with her after a time. She began to take a share in the housework, and at length to wait on him. But he soon realized that there was little more he himself could do for her. From this perplexity he was delivered in a wonderful way.

One afternoon he was prowling about Spitalfields where he had made many acquaintances among the silk weavers and their families. He climbed a dilapidated flight of stairs to call on a man by the name of De Fleuri. The poor man had lost his wife and three of his children. Only a daughter remained now and she lay sick from slow, consuming hunger. The man did not believe there was a God that ruled in the earth. But he supported his unbelief by no other argument than a hopeless, bitter glance at his long-empty loom.

"How is your daughter today, Mr. De Fleuri?" asked Falconer as he stepped inside the room.

"Very poorly, sir. She's going after the rest. Will you go and see my poor Katey, sir?"

"Would she like to see me?"

"It does her good to see you. I want her to die in peace. It is all I can do for her."

"Do you still persist in refusing help—for your daughter—I don't mean for yourself."

"I do. I won't kill her, and I won't kill myself. But I am not bound to accept charity. It's all right. I only want to leave the whole affair behind, and I sincerely hope there's nothing to come after this. If I were God, I should be ashamed of such a mess of a world."

Not believing in God, De Fleuri would not seek assistance from his fellowman. Falconer had never met with a similar instance in anyone.

"Well, no doubt you would have made something more to your liking. But I didn't come here to bore you. I'm going to see Katey."

Katey lay in a room overhead. Though he lacked food, this man contrived to pay for a separate room for his daughter, whom he treated with far more respect than many gentlemen treat their wives. Falconer found her lying on a wretched bed. Still, it was a bed; many in the same house had no bed to lie on. He had earlier visited a widow with four children. All of them lay on a floor where at night, awful rats came by many holes. The children could not sleep for horror. They did not mind the little ones, they said, but when the big ones came they were awake all night.

"Well, Katey, how are you?"

"No better," she answered.

She spoke as her father had taught her. Her face was worn and thin, but hardly deathlike. The extremes of hopelessness and quiet comfort met in it. Her hopelessness affected him more than her father's. But there was nothing he could do for her.

Then came a tap at the door.

"Come in," said Falconer involuntarily.

A lady in the dress of a Sister of Mercy entered with a large basket on her arm. She started, and hesitated for a moment when she saw him. He rose, thinking it better to go. She advanced to the bedside. As he turned at the door, he saw the lady kiss the girl on the forehead.

"I won't say good-bye yet, Katey," said Falconer, "for I'm going to have a chat with your father, and if you will let me, I will look in again."

At the sound of his voice, the lady started again, left the bedside and came toward him. Whether he knew her by her face or her voice first, he could not tell.

"Robert?" she said, holding out her hand.

It was Mary St. John.

Their hands joined fast and lingered as they each gazed in the other's face. It was nearly fourteen years since they had parted. The freshness of youth was gone from her cheek and the signs of approaching age were present on her forehead. But she was statelier, nobler, and gentler than ever. Falconer looked at her calmly, with only a small swelling at the heart, as if they had met on the threshold of heaven. All the selfishness of passion was gone and the earlier adoration had returned. She did not shrink from his gaze; she did not withdraw her hand from his clasp.

"I am so glad, Robert!" was all she said.

"So am I," he answered quietly. "The Lord must have known our hearts far better than we when we made that youthful vow so long ago; here we both are fulfilling it."

She smiled.

"Do you suppose we may meet sometimes?" he asked.

"Yes," Mary answered, "I would like that. Perhaps we can help each other."

"You can help me," said Falconer. "I have a girl I don't know what to do with."

"Send her to me. I will take care of her."

"I will bring her. But I must come and see you first."

She handed him a card. "This will tell you where I live. Good-bye."

"Till tomorrow," said Robert, and went back to Katey's father.

"I am going to take a liberty with you, Mr. De Fleuri," he said.

"As you please, Mr. Falconer."

"I want to tell you of a fault you need to correct."

"Yes."

"You don't do anything for the other people in the house. Whether you believe in God or not or will take any charity or not, you still ought to do what you can for your neighbor."

De Fleuri laughed bitterly. "And with what?"

"There are things better than money. Sympathy, for instance. You could talk to them a little. There's that widow with her four children in the garret. The poor little things are tormented by rats; couldn't you nail bits of wood over their holes?"

De Fleuri laughed again. "And where am I to get the wood and the nails?"

"Couldn't you ask some carpenter?"

"I won't ask a favor."

"*I* shouldn't mind asking."

"That's because you don't know the bitterness of needing."

"But you have no right to refuse for another what you wouldn't accept for yourself. Of course I could send in a man to do it, but if you would do it, that would do her heart good. That's what most wants doing good to—isn't it now?"

"I believe you're right there, sir. If it wasn't for the misery of it, I shouldn't mind the hunger."

"I should like to tell you how I came to go poking my nose into other people's affairs. Would you like to hear my story now?"

A little pallid curiosity seemed to rouse itself in the heart of the hopeless man. So Falconer began at once to tell him how he had been brought up and about his childhood adventures with Shargar. Then all at once, pulling out his watch, he said, "But it's time I had my tea and I haven't half done yet. I am not fond of being hungry like you, Mr. De Fleuri."

The poor fellow could manage only a very dubious smile.

"Tell you what," said Falconer, as if the thought had only just struck him, "come home with me and I'll tell you the rest at my own place."

"You must excuse me, but I can't leave Katey," answered the weaver with hesitation.

"Miss St. John is still here. I will ask her to stay till you come back."

Without waiting for an answer, he ran up the stairs and had speedily arranged it with Mary. Then he hurried De Fleuri away with him before he had the chance to complain further. Then, over their tea, he told him about his grandmother and about Dr. Anderson and how he came to give himself to the work he was at, partly for its own sake, partly in the hope of finding his father. He told him his only clue to finding him, and that he had called on Mrs. Macallister twice every week for two years, but had heard nothing of him. De Fleuri listened with what eventually rose to great interest before the story was finished. One of Falconer's ends at least was gained: the weaver by now felt at home with him.

"Do you want it kept a secret, sir?" he asked.

"I don't want it made a matter of gossip. But I do not mind how many respectable people like yourself know of it."

Before they had parted, De Fleuri had consented not only to repair Mrs. Chisholm's garret floor, but to take in hand the expenditure of a certain sum weekly, as he should judge expedient, for the people who lived in that and the neighboring houses. Thus did Falconer appoint a sorrow-made infidel to be the disperser of a portion of his Christian charity.

It was after this that my own acquaintance with Falconer began. I had just come out of one of the theaters in the neighborhood of the Strand. Turning northward I was walking along when my attention was attracted to a woman who came out of a gin shop, carrying a baby. She was obviously sick with the poisonous stuff she had been drinking. Yet while the poor woman stood there, the white, wasted baby was looking over her shoulder with the smile of an angel, perfectly unconscious of the hell around her.

"Children will see things as God sees them," said a voice beside me.

I turned and saw a tall man standing almost at my elbow, with his eyes fixed on the woman and the child and a strange smile of tenderness on his mouth, as if he were blessing the little creature in his heart. Aware from his tone that he was a fellow Scotsman, I responded and we struck up a conversation as I continued on my way. By the time we had parted, he had invited me to dinner on the following evening. I saw him go into the low public house, and I went on home.

At the time appointed the next day, I rang the bell and was led by an elderly woman up the stair and shown into a large room on the second floor—poorly furnished and with many signs of bachelor carelessness. Mr. Falconer rose from an old sofa to meet me as I entered.

He was considerably above six feet, square shouldered, long in the arms, and his hands were uncommonly large and powerful. His head was large and covered with dark, wavy hair, lightly streaked with gray. His broad forehead projected over deep sunken eyes that shone like black fire. His features, especially his Roman nose, were large and finely, though not delicately modeled. The expression of his mouth was of tender power, crossed with humor. He kept his lips a little compressed, which gave a certain sternness to his countenance; but when this sternness dissolved in a smile, it was something enchanting. He was plainly, rather shabbily, clothed. No one could have guessed at his profession or social position. He came forward and received me cordially. After a little inconsequential talk, he asked me if I had any other engagements for the evening.

"I never have engagements," I answered, "at least of a social kind. I am a bird alone; I know next to nobody."

"Then perhaps you would not mind going out with me for a stroll?"

"I shall be most happy to," I answered, having no idea how that night with him would change me.

There was something about the man I found exceedingly attractive, even compelling. I would wonder about this less and less the more I got to know him.

"We'll have our supper first," said Mr. Falconer, and he rang the bell.

While we ate our chops, I asked, "What design do you have on me this evening?"

"That will appear in due course," my host answered. "Now take a glass of wine and we'll set out."

We soon found ourselves in Holborn and my companion led the way toward the poorer section of the city. The evening was sultry.

"Nothing excites me more," said Mr. Falconer, "than a walk in the twilight through a crowded street. Do you find it affects you so?"

"I cannot say it with as much certainty as you do," I replied. "But I perfectly understand what you mean. Why is it, do you think?"

"Partly, I fancy, because of the tumult of possibilities. The germs of infinite adventure are floating around you like a snowstorm. You do not know what may arise in a moment and color all your future."

The streets swarmed with human faces. There stood a man who had lost one arm, earnestly pumping bilge-music out of an accordion with the other, holding it to his body with the stump. A row of little children, from two to five years of age, were seated upon the curbstone, chattering fast and apparently carrying on some game, happy as if they had been in the fields. There was a woman, pale with hunger and drink, three matchboxes in one extended hand and the other holding a baby to her breast. As we looked, the poor baby let go its hold, turned its little head, and smiled a wan, shriveled smile in our faces.

"Another happy baby," said Falconer. "A child fresh from God finds its heaven where no one else would."

"What can be done for all these people?" I said, half to myself.

"Yes," Falconer replied, "their lives and surroundings are often pitiable. But poverty will always be with us, and to even hope to put an end to it is nothing but a dream."

"But don't you care for their sufferings?"

"Certainly. But they are of secondary importance. If you had been among them as much as I, perhaps you would share my opinion that the poor do not feel so wretched as they seem to us. They live in a situation which is their own and they grow to find it not altogether unfriendly. Poverty can even be a blessing when it makes a man look up.''

"You sound almost, well, almost—indifferent to it.''

"Am I indifferent? But you do not know me yet. Even if I am I would have no less labor spent upon them. But there can be no true labor done except in as far as we are fellow-laborers with God.''

"What, then, is a man to do for the poor? How is he to work with God?'' I asked.

"He must be a man among them. Whatever you try to do for them, let your own being be the background, so that you provide a link between them and God. But I beg your pardon, I did not mean to preach at you.''

Of some of the places into which Falconer led me that night I will attempt no description. As we came into a very narrow, dirty street, a slatternly woman advanced from an open door and said, "Mr. Falconer.''

He looked at her for a moment.

"There's a poor creature a'dyin' upstairs,'' she said hurriedly, without waiting for a word from my companion. "I'm afear'd it'll go hard with her, for she throwed a Bible out o' a window this mornin', sir.''

"Would she like to see me?''

"She's got someone up there with her now reading that same Bible to her.''

"There can be no harm in my just looking in,'' he said, then cast a glance my way.

"I'll follow you wherever you like,'' I said.

"She's awful ill, sir; fever or summat,'' said the woman, as she led the way up the creaking stair.

We entered the room softly. Two or three women sat by the chimney and another by a low bed, covered with a torn patchwork. She was reading the story of David and Bathsheba. Moans came from the bed. We stood still and did not interrupt the reading.

"Ha! ha!'' laughed a coarse voice at length, "the saint was no better than the rest of us!''

"I think a good deal worse, just then,'' said Falconer, stepping forward.

"Gracious! here's Mr. Falconer,'' said another woman, rising.

"Then there's a chance for the likes of me yet,'' remarked the sick woman with voice of mingled sadness and bitterness. "King David was a saint, wasn't he? Ha! ha!''

"Yes, and you might be one too if you were as sorry for your faults as he was for his.''

"Sorry, indeed! I'll be hanged if I be sorry. What have I to be sorry for? I have took no man's wife nor murdered himself neither. There's yer saints! He was a rum un!''

Falconer approached her, then bent down and whispered something no one could hear but herself. She gave a smothered cry, and was silent.

"Give me the book," he said. "I'll read you something better than that. I'll read about someone that never did anything wrong."

Falconer sat down on the side of the bed and read the story of Simon the Pharisee, and the woman that was a sinner. When he ceased, the silence that followed was broken by a sob from somewhere in the room.

The sob came again. It was from a young, slender girl with a face disfigured by smallpox. Falconer said something gentle to her.

"I wish my hair were long enough to wash his feet," she said through her tears.

"Do you know what he would say to you, my girl?" Falconer asked.

"No. Do you really think he would speak to me?"

"He would say, 'Your sins are forgiven.' ''

"Would he?" she cried, starting up. "Take me to him—take me to him. Oh! I forget. He's dead. But he will come again, won't he? Would they crucify him again, sir?"

"No, they wouldn't crucify him now. They would only laugh at him, shake their heads at what he told them, and sneer at him and mock him in the newspapers."

Falconer took the girl's hand. "What is your name?" he said.

"Nell."

"That's all?"

"Nothing more."

"Well, Nelly," said Falconer.

"How kind of you to call me Nelly!" interrupted the poor girl. "They always just call me Nell."

"Nelly," repeated Falconer, "I will send a lady here tomorrow to take you away with her, if you like, and tell you more about how to find Jesus. People always find him when they want to."

"Don't go putting humbug into my child's head now, Mr. Falconer. Everybody knows my Nell's been an idiot since the day she was born. Poor child!''

"I ain't your child!" cried the girl with passion. "I ain't nobody's child.''

"You are God's child," said Falconer, who stood looking on with his eyes shining, but otherwise in a state of absolute composure.

"Am I? Am I really? You won't forget to send for me, sir?"

"That I won't," he answered. He turned, spoke some words I did not hear to the woman who was apparently Nell's guardian, then bade a general good night. When we reached the street, Falconer said: "It always comes back to me that women like some of these were of the first to understand our Lord."

We continued on. Through the city—though it was only when we crossed one of the main thoroughfares that I had any notion of where we were—we came into the region of Bethnal Green. From house to house, till it grew very late, Falconer went, and I went with him. Where I saw only dreadful darkness, Falconer would always perceive some glimmer of light. All the people into whose houses we went knew him. They were all in the depths of poverty. Many of them were respectable. With some he had long talks in private while I waited near. At length he said, "I think we had better be going home. You must be tired."

"I am, rather," I answered. "But it doesn't matter."

"We shall get a cab," he said.

"Not for me. I am not so tired but that I would rather walk," I said.

"Very well," he returned. "Where do you live?"

I told him.

"I will take you the nearest way."

"You know London marvelously."

"Pretty well now," he answered. "I have been doing this for some years."

We were somewhere near Leather Lane about one o'clock. Suddenly we came upon two tiny children, standing on the pavement, one on each side of the door of a public house. They could not have been more than two and three. They were sobbing a little—not much.

The house was closed, but there was light above the door. We went up to the children and spoke to them but could get nothing out of them. Falconer knocked at the door. A good-natured woman opened it a little way and peeped out.

"Here are two children crying at your door, ma'am," he said.

"Och, the darlin's! They want their mother."

"Do you know her, then?"

"Yes. No doubt she's out drinkin' and the poor creatures have waked up and run out lookin' for her. When that lady smells the drop o' gin, her head's gone entirely."

Falconer stood a moment as if thinking what would be best when suddenly the shriek of a woman rang through the night.

"There she is!" said the woman standing in the door. "For God's sake don't let her get hold o' the little darlin's. She's ravin' mad. I seen her try to kill them once."

The shrieks came nearer and nearer, and after a few moments the woman appeared in the moonlight, tossing her arms over her head and screaming in despair. Her hair was flying in tangles, her sleeves were torn. Whether it was only the drink or whether something awful had befallen her, it was impossible to tell; but before either of us could interfere she ran like a fury, still screaming, and dashed her head against the wall of the public house. She dropped on the pavement and lay still.

Springing into action, Falconer quickly directed me to take the children away while he ran to the wall where the woman lay. She was dead.

"Do you know where she lived?" he asked the woman who was standing nearby.

"No, sir. Somewhere not far off, though."

He hesitated for a few moments, then said to her, "I will inform the authorities about the woman." He took out one of his cards and handed it to her. "In the meantime, if any inquiry is made about the children, there is my address."

He hastened to where I stood, caught up the larger of the two children. "Will you take the other?" he said to me, and I immediately complied and followed him.

We walked a few streets, found a cab, and drove to Queen Square, Bloomsbury.

Falconer got out at the door of a large house and rang the bell, then got the children out and dismissed the cab. There we stood, in the middle of the night, in a silent, empty square, each with a child in his arms. In a few minutes we heard the bolts being withdrawn. The door opened and a tall, graceful form, wrapped in a dressing gown, appeared.

"I have brought you two babies, Mary," said Falconer. "Can you take them?"

"To be sure," she answered. "Bring them in."

We followed her into a little back room. She put down her candle and went straight to the cupboard. She brought out a sponge cake from which she cut a large piece for each of the children.

"What a mercy they are, Robert! I will wake my maid and we'll get them washed and put to bed at once."

We turned to leave.

"Oh, Mary," said Falconer, "I was forgetting. Could you go down to number thirteen in Soap Lane—you know it, don't you?"

"Yes. Quite well."

"Ask for a girl called Nell—a plain, pock-marked young girl—and take her away with you."

"When shall I go?"

"Tomorrow morning. But I shall be by. Don't go till you see me. Good night."

We took our leave.

"What a ladylike woman to be the matron of an asylum!" I said.
Falconer laughed.

"That is no asylum. It is a private house."

"And the lady?" I asked.

"Is a lady of private means," he answered, "who prefers Blooms-bury to some of the more luxurious sections of the city, because it is easier to do noble work in it. Her heaven is on the confines of hell."

"What will she do with those children?"

"Kiss them and wash them and put them to bed."

"And after that?"

"Give them bread and milk in the morning."

"And after that?"

"Oh, there's time enough. We'll see. There's only one thing she won't do."

"What is that?"

"Turn them out again."

A pause followed. I was thinking.

"Are you a society, then?" I asked at length.

"No. At least we don't use the word. And certainly no other society would acknowledge us."

"What are you, then?"

"Why should we be anything, so long as we do our work?"

"Do you lay claim to no designation of any sort?"

"We are a church if you like. There!"

"Who is your clergyman?"

"Nobody."

"Where do you meet?"

"Nowhere."

"What are your rules, then?"

"We have none."

"What makes you a church?"

"Divine service."

"What do you mean by that?"

"The sort of thing you have seen tonight."

"What is your creed?"

"Jesus Christ."

"But what do you believe about him?"

"We believe *in* him. We consider any belief *in* him—however small—far better than any amount of belief about him."

"But you must have some rules," I insisted.

"None whatever. They would only cause us trouble and take us from our work. We only do as he has instructed and as he has shown us through his life.''

"But who are the *we*?''

"Why, you—if you will do anything—and I and Miss St. John, and twenty others—and a great many more I don't know. It is our work that binds us together.'' ·

"But if there's nothing bigger, then when you stop, your ministry stops.''

"Ah, but there is something bigger—much bigger! We are not the life of the world. God is. And when we are gone he will send out more and better laborers into the harvest fields.''

"But surely the church must be constituted by more than this.''

"My dear sir, you forget; I said we were *a* church, not *the* church.''

"Do you belong to the Church of England?''

"Yes, some of us. She has preserved records and traditions and we owe her a great deal. And to leave her would inevitably start a quarrel, for which life is too serious in my eyes. I have no time for that.''

"Then you count the Church of England *the* Church?''

"Of the universe, no; that is constituted just like ours, with the living, working Lord for the heart of it.''

"Will you take me for a member?''

"No.''

"Will you not, if—?''

"You may make yourself one if you will. I will not speak a word to gain you. I have shown you work. Do something, and you are of Christ's Church.''

We were almost at the door of my lodging, and I was getting very weary in body, and indeed in mind, though I hope not in heart. Before we separated, I ventured to say, "Will you tell me why you invited me to come to see your work?''

He laughed gently, and answered, "The moment I saw you I knew you had to hear me. I knew I had to tell you my tale. And that was best accomplished in having you share it with me.''

Without another word, he shook hands with me and left me. Weary as I was, I stood in the street until I could hear his footsteps no longer.

39 / The Brothers

One day as Falconer sat at a late breakfast, Shargar burst into his room. Falconer had not even known that he was coming home, for he had outstripped the letter he had sent. He had his arm in a sling, which accounted for his leave.

"Shargar!" cried Falconer, starting up in delight.

"Major Shargar, if you please. Give me all my honors, Robert," he said, presenting his left hand.

"I congratulate you, my friend. Well, this is delightful! But you are wounded."

"It's nearly right again. I'll tell you about it by and by. I am too full of something else to talk about trifles like bullets and broken arms. I want you to help me."

He then rushed into the announcement that he had fallen desperately in love with a lady who had come on board with her maid at Malta, where she had been spending the winter. She was about his own age, and enchantingly beautiful. How she could have remained so long unmarried he could not imagine. She must have had many offers, for she was an heiress too. But Shargar felt that to be a disadvantage for him. All the progress he could yet boast of was that his attentions had not been, so far as he could judge, disagreeable to her. What was more to the point, she had given him her address in London and he was going to call upon her the next day. She was on a visit to Lady Janet Gordon, an elderly spinster, who lived in Park Street.

"Have you told her all about yourself?"

"No!" answered Shargar, growing suddenly pale. "I never thought about that."

"Well, I reckon your wounds and your medals ought to weigh well against that. And there's this comfort, that if she's not worthy of you, old friend, she won't take you."

Shargar did not seem to see the comfort of it. He was depressed for the remainder of the day. In the morning he was in wild spirits again. However, just before he started, he asked with an anxious expression, "Ought I to tell her at once—about—about my mother?"

"I didn't say that. We'll think it over. When you go downstairs you'll see a carriage at the door waiting for you. Give the coachman any orders you like. He's your servant as long as you're in London. Commit your way to the Lord, my boy.''

He returned in high spirits still. He had been graciously received both by Miss Hamilton and her hostess—a kindhearted old lady who spoke Scotch with the pure tone of a gentlewoman. She had asked him to come to dinner in the evening and to bring his friend with him. Robert, however, begged Shargar to excuse him as he had an engagement—in a very different sort of place.

When Shargar returned, Robert had not come in. He was too excited to go to bed and waited for him. It was two o'clock before he came home. Shargar told him there was to be a large party at Lady Patterdale's in two days and Lady Janet had promised to procure an invitation for Shargar.

The next morning Robert went to see Mary and asked if she knew anything of Lady Patterdale, and whether she could get him an invitation. She did not know her, but thought she could manage it for him. He told her all about Shargar, for whose sake he wished to see Miss Hamilton before consenting to be introduced to her. Miss St. John set out at once and Falconer received a card the next day. When the evening of the party came, he allowed Shargar to set out alone in his carriage and followed an hour later.

When he reached the house the rooms were tolerably filled and, as several parties had arrived just before him, he managed to enter without being announced. After a little while he caught sight of Shargar. He stood alone, almost in a corner, with a strange look in his eyes. Falconer could not see the object to which they were directed. Certainly their look was not that of love. He made his way up to him and laid his hand on his arm. Shargar betrayed his astonishment when he saw him.

"You here, Robert?" he asked.

"Yes, I'm here. Have you seen her yet? Is she here?"

"Who do you think is speaking to her this very minute? Look there!" Shargar said in a low voice, suppressed yet more to hide his emotions. "How he could follow me all this way I don't know."

Following his directions, Robert saw a handsome man amidst a little group of gentlemen surrounding a seated lady, of whose face he could not get a peep. The man looked more fashionable than his years justified. He thought he had seen him before, but Shargar gave him no time to come to a conclusion on his own.

"It's my brother Emerich, as sure as death!" he said, "and he's been hanging about her ever since she came in. Ow, what will I do! He's always had a way with ladies; always had *his* way with them, I should say.''

"Why don't you go up to her yourself, man? I wouldn't just stand there if it were me."

"I'm afraid he'll know me. He has eyes like a hawk, that marquis brother of mine."

"What does it matter? You've done nothing to be ashamed of."

"Ay. But I wouldn't have her hear the truth about me from that boar's mouth of his. I would have her hear it from my own, and then she won't think that I meant to deceive her."

At that moment there was a movement in the group. Looking round at Robert, it was now Shargar's turn to be surprised at his expression.

"Are you seeing a ghost, Robert?" he said. "What makes you look like that, man?"

"Oh," answered Robert, recovering himself. "I thought I knew your Miss Hamilton. She looks remarkably like someone whose acquaintance I made in Aberdeen. But it couldn't be her," he added. "But we've been talking too earnestly," he went on, seeking to change the subject, "people are beginning to look at us." What Robert did not tell Shargar was the face he thought he recognized was one that had been associated with none other than Lord Emerich, Baron of Rothie, now lately the marquis of Boarshead.

The two separated, and before another half an hour had passed, Shargar had found his opportunity to be alone with Miss Hamilton without compromising his presence to his brother. Falconer left alone and walked home, trying to resolve in his mind what he should do.

He was at Lady Janet's door by ten o'clock the next morning and sent in his card to Miss Hamilton. He was shown into the drawing room, where she came to him.

"May I presume on an old acquaintance?" he asked, holding out his hand.

She looked in his face quietly, took his hand, pressed it warmly, and said, "No one has so good a right, Mr. Falconer. I have never forgotten what you did for me. You helped me out of that evil man's clutches, you and your friend Dr. Anderson. Do sit down."

He placed a chair for her and obeyed.

After a moment's silence on both sides, "Are you aware, Miss—? he said, and hesitated.

"Miss Hamilton," she said with a smile. "I was Miss Lindsay when you knew me so many years ago. I will explain presently."

Then with an air of expectation she awaited the finish of his sentence.

"Are you aware, Miss Hamilton, that I am Major Moray's oldest friend?"

"I am quite aware of it, and delighted to know it. He told me so last night."

"Did Major Moray likewise communicate with you concerning his own history?"

"He did. He told me all."

"*All?*"

"Everything!"

Falconer was again silent for some moments.

"Shall I presume that my friend will thus be concluding his visits?"

"On the contrary," she answered, with a delicate blush, "I expect him within half an hour."

Falconer's somewhat bewildered look was his only response.

"Do not suppose, Mr. Falconer, that I could not meet Major Moray's honesty with equal openness on my side. We each have our pasts, which are part of us. And in our case the social barriers between him and myself quickly become insignificant. But I owe you equal frankness, Mr. Falconer. There is no barrier between Major Moray and myself but the foolish indiscretion of an innocent and ignorant girl. I thought Lord Rothie was going to marry me. Make what excuse for my folly you can. I was lost in a mist of vain imaginations. I was naïve, had scarcely been out of Aberdeen before, and thought I loved him. After it was over, I felt such a fool. I sought some situation away from Aberdeen, met Lady Janet, who took care of me and brought me to London. She made me acquainted with Sir John Hamilton, a kindhearted old man who had lost his only son and had no daughter. He took to me, as they say, and made me change my name to his, leaving me his property on the condition that whoever I married should take the same name. I don't think your friend will mind making the exchange," she said in conclusion, as the door opened and Shargar came in.

"Robert, you're everywhere!" he exclaimed, as he entered. Then, stopping to ask no questions, "I'm to have a name of my own after all. What think ye of that?" he asked, with a face which looked even handsome in the light of his gladness.

Robert shook hands with him and wished him joy heartily.

Just then the butler announced the Marquis of Boarshead. Miss Hamilton's eyes flashed. She rose from her seat and advanced to meet the marquis, who entered behind the servant. She then retreated one step and stood.

"Your lordship has no right to force yourself upon me. You must have seen that I had no wish to renew the acquaintance I was unhappy enough to form—now, thank God, many years ago."

"Forgive me, Miss Hamilton. One word in private," said the marquis.

"Not a word," she returned.

"Before these gentlemen, then, whom I have not had the honor of knowing, I offer you my hand."

"To accept that offer would be to wrong myself even more than your lordship has done."

She went back to where Shargar was standing and stood beside him. The evil spirit in the marquis looked out through the windows.

"You are aware," he said, "that your reputation is in the hand I offer you. If I so much as tell a single person—"

"The worse for my reputation then, my lord," she returned with a scornful smile. "But your lordship's brother will protect it."

"My brother!" exclaimed the marquis. "What do you mean? I have no brother!"

"Ye have mair brithers than ye know, Lord Emerich," said Shargar, his tongue lapsing into Scotch from the excitement, 'an' I'm one o' them."

"You are either a liar or a bastard, then," said the marquis, who had not been brought up in a school of which either self-restraint or respect for women were prominent characteristics.

Falconer forgot himself for a moment and made a stride forward.

"Don't hit him, Bob!" cried Shargar. "He once gave me a shillin', an' it helpt, as ye know, to haud me alive to face him this day.—No liar, my lord, but a bastard, thank heaven." Then, with a laugh, he instantly added, "If I had been a brither to you, my lord, God only knows what a rascal I might hae been."

"By heaven, you shall answer for your insolence," said the marquis, and lifting his riding whip from the table where he had laid it, he approached his brother.

Miss Hamilton rang the bell for help.

"Keep back yer han', Emerich!" cried Shargar, "I hae faced more fearsome foes than ye. But I have some family feelin', though ye have none, and I wouldn't willin'ly strike me brither."

As he spoke, Shargar retreated a little. The marquis came on with raised whip. But Falconer stepped between, laid one of his great hands on the marquis' chest, and flung him to the other end of the room, where he fell over an ottoman. The same moment a servant entered.

"Ask your mistress to oblige me by coming to the drawing room," said Miss Hamilton to him.

The marquis had risen, but had not recovered his presence of mind when Lady Janet entered.

"Please, Lady Janet, will you ask the Marquis of Boarshead to leave the house?"

Without heeding anyone, the marquis went up to Falconer.

"Your card, sir," he said with a threatening tone.

"Indeed, you'll get no cards here," said Lady Janet, walking up to him. Falconer remained motionless.

"Now leave my house this instant, or I shall have no choice but to resort to force. Go away and consider your gray hairs!"

This was the severest blow he had yet received. He left the room swearing loudly.

Falconer followed him, but what came of it nobody ever heard.

Major and Miss Hamilton were married within three months, and went out to India together, taking Nancy Kennedy, Shargar's half sister, with them.

Falconer lived and labored on in London. Wherever he found a man fit for the work, he placed him in such office as De Fleuri already occupied. At the same time he went more into society and gained the friendship of many influential people. He considered suitable dwellings for the poor one of the most pressing of necessary reforms to which he could give himself. His own fortune was not sufficient for doing much in this way, but he set about doing what he could by purchasing houses in which the poor lived and putting them into the hands of persons whom he could trust. They were immediately responsible to him for their proceedings.

De Fleuri was one of his chief supports. The whole nature of the man mellowed under the sun of Falconer and over the work that Falconer gave him to do. His daughter recovered and devoted herself to the same labor that had rescued her, with Mary St. John as her superior. By degrees, without any laws or regulations, a little company was gathered, not of ladies and gentlemen but of men and women who aided each other. They did not once meet as a whole, but they labored not the less in the work of the Lord, bound in one by bonds that had nothing to do with cobweb committee meetings or public dinners. They worked like the leaven of which the Lord spoke.

De Fleuri had his own private schemes subserving the general good. To those he knew he told the story of Falconer's behavior to him, of Falconer's own need, and of his hungry-hearted search. An enthusiasm of help seized upon those who heard the story, and they in turn told others, so that the story of Falconer's search for his father became known in all that region of London. The man who loved the poor was himself needy, and looked to the poor for their help.

One evening I was returning home from some weak attempts of my own. I had now been a pupil of Falconer's for some time, but, having my own livelihood to make, I could not do so much as I would have liked.

It was late and as I passed through the streets, I could hardly keep from being overcome by the depressing gloom and sadness all about— brutal-looking men, now and then a squalid woman, drunks, vague noises of strife and revelry. I was not very far from Falconer's. My mind was oppressed with sad thoughts and a sense of helplessness. I began to wonder what Falconer might at that moment be about. I had not seen him for nearly two weeks. He might be at home; I would go and see, and if there was light in his windows I would ring his bell.

I went. There was light in his windows. He opened the door himself, and welcomed me. But only as we entered did I first perceive that he was not alone and that I had apparently interrupted a discussion of some kind. As I hesitated, however, he took hold of my arm and led me forward into the room.

"This kind lady and I have just been talking about our work," he explained, then introduced me to his guest, Lady Georgina. "She came to visit me and our talk quite naturally progressed in that direction."

"But, Mr. Falconer," the lady asked, "you still have not given an answer to the question I posed just before your friend arrived. What exactly *is* one's duty? That is the question."

"The thing that lies next you, of course. You can be the sole judge of that."

"Should I go out into the city, as you do, a woman by herself? It might prove very dangerous."

"I simply cannot say what *you* should do, Lady Georgina. But more than anything right now, if you in fact are truly interested, I would have you sit down and count the cost before you do any mischief by beginning what you are unfit for. Last week I was compelled more than once to leave the house where my duty led me, and to sit down upon a stone on the sidewalk, so ill I was in danger of being led away as intoxicated. Twice I had to leave the room I was in, crowded with human animals, and at least one dying."

A mist was gathering over Lady Georgina's eyes.

"And you must spend time preparing yourself. Our Savior himself had to be thirty years in the world before he had footing enough in it to justify him in beginning to teach publicly. He had been laying the necessary foundations all the time. So few that are involved with churches or societies have the knowledge of the poor that I have. Many of them could do something if they would only set about it simply, and not be so anxious to convert them, if they would allow themselves to be their friends."

"So you count societies, then, of no use whatever?"

"I avoid all attempt at organization. What I want is simply to be a friend of the poor. I bide my time. I do not preach or set about to institute a program to remove this or that ill from our society. I go where I am led. In fact, I usually wait till I am asked to offer assistance. And even then I often refuse to give the sort of help they want. The worst thing you can do for them is to attempt to save them from the natural consequences of wrong; although you may sometimes help them out of them. But it is right to do many things for them when you know them, which would not help if you didn't. I am among them; they know me; their children know me. Something is always occurring that makes this or that one come to me. In my labor I am content to do the thing that lies next to me. I await events. In all of life, there is nothing so significant as the next five minutes and whether we use it to do what God lays before us.''

"There is no place for me, then?''

"You have had no training, no blundering, to fit you for such work. Of course there is a place for you, but I could not possibly direct you. I have no way of knowing what the next five minutes, all your life long, will present you with in opportunities for helping others. To get the training you need, you must simply begin where you are, do the thing that lies next to you, help the next person you encounter. I am sorry. I know you thought I would give you more specific direction.''

"Yes. That is why I came to you.''

"Just so. I cannot give you the sort of help you desire. Go and ask it of the One who can.''

"Speak more plainly.''

"Well, then, if God is your Father, he will listen to you his child. He will teach you everything.''

"But I don't know what I want, even what to ask him to teach me.''

"He does. Ask him to tell you what you want. Read the gospels. Read the story of Jesus as if you had never read it before. He was a man who had that secret of life which your heart is longing for.''

Lady Georgina rose. Her eyes were full of tears. Falconer, too, was moved. She held out her hand to him, and without another word left the room.

When we were left alone neither of us spoke for several minutes. At length Falconer sighed and said, "In some ways she reminds me of the rich young ruler who came to our Lord. She came asking me about putting her money to charitable uses through my 'program' with the poor, as she called it. When I told her I could not accept, at first she was surprised, even perhaps offended. But as we talked I felt she truly wanted to do more, even *be* more. But her eyes are still too clouded from all the hogwash she had been taught in the church.''

"Her heart seemed open,'' I ventured to say.

"Yes, I felt that as well,'' Falconer answered, "and I pray she will in the end not turn her back in sorrow as the rich young ruler did. She knows Miss St. John and that will be in her favor."

"Hearing you and her talk puts my doubts and anxieties in their place," I said. "I came to see you tonight out of simple discouragement. There seems so much to be done and my efforts are so minuscule. Yet when I look back, I once stood where Lady Georgina is standing."

"Not exactly," said Falconer with a slight laugh. "You did not have her wealth, which was quite possibly to your benefit. And the openness in her is but a hairline crack in the encrustations of traditional attitudes which surround the life struggling to break free. You possessed an entirely open way of viewing things. That openness almost compelled you to accept the truth the moment you saw it. But in her that encrusted mentality fights against the truth. But we will hope the crack of openness will widen. I trust it shall."

There was another silence.

"But tell me," Falconer went on, "what prompted your discouragement tonight?"

"Nothing in particular," I answered. "The streets just seemed too bleak, the people too beyond hope."

"He that believes shall not make haste," he said. "There is plenty of time. You must not imagine that the result depends on you, or me. The question is, are you having a hand in the work God is doing? It shows no faith in God to make frantic efforts or lamentations. God will do his work in his time in his way. Our responsibility is merely to stand ready and available and to go where he sends and do what comes our way."

"I wish I had your faith and courage," I said.

"You are on the road to having far more of each," he returned. "You are not nearly so old as I am. I will be looking up to you for support ten years from now—but you are out of spirits. Why don't you go out with me tomorrow evening?"

Of course I was only too glad to accept the proposal.

41 / The Attack

The following evening Falconer and I went out together. It was a blowing, moonlit night. The gas lights flickered and wavered in the gusts of wind. It was cold, very cold for the season. Even Falconer buttoned his coat over his chest. He got a few steps ahead of me sometimes and appeared as a towering black shadow in the night. The wind increased in violence. It was a northeaster, laden with dust and a sense of frozen Siberian steppes. Not many people were out, and those who were seemed to be hurrying home.

We came into Whitehall and so to Westminster Bridge. The new bridge was under construction and the old one alongside of it was still in use for pedestrians, rising high above the other. There were boards on the sides, but through gaps we were able to look down on the new portion, which was as yet used by carriages alone.

As we stood on the apex of the bridge, looking at the night, Falconer was staring at the other bridge below. Suddenly he grasped the top of the boarding and his huge frame was over it in an instant. I looked down to see him lying on the bridge some twelve feet below me. He was up the next instant and running with huge paces diagonally toward the Surrey side. He had seen the figure of a woman come flying along from the Westminster side, without a bonnet or shawl. When she came under the spot where we stood, she had turned across it toward the other side. Falconer, convinced that she meant to throw herself into the river, went over as I have related. She had all but scrambled over the edge when he caught her by her garments. He took her in his arms and lifted her down upon the bridge. I had managed to find an easier mode of descent and now came up a little way from them.

"Poor girl," he said, as if to himself, "was this the only way left?"

Then he spoke tenderly to her. What he said I could not hear—I only heard the tone.

"Please let me go!" she cried. "Why should a wretched creature like me be forced to live? It's no good to you. Do let me go."

"Come here," he said, drawing her close to the edge. "Stand up again on the beam. Look down."

She obeyed, in a mechanical way. But as he talked, and she kept looking down on the dark mystery beneath, flowing past with every now and then a dull, vengeful glitter—continuous, forceful, slow—he felt her shudder in his still clasping arm.

"Look," he said, "how it crawls along—black and slimy! how silent and yet how fierce! Is that a nice place to go? Would there be any rest there, do you think, tumbling about among filth and creeping things? Is that the door by which you would like to go out of the world?"

"It's no worse," she faltered; "—not so bad as what I should leave behind."

"If this were the only way out of it, I would not keep you from it. But there is another way."

"There is no other way—if you knew all," she said.

"Tell me, then."

"I cannot. I dare not. Please—I would rather go."

From the mere glimpses I could get of her, she looked about twenty-five. I think she might have been almost beautiful if the waste of her history could have been restored. But now the chief characteristic I noticed were the wild eyes, looking to and fro as she struggled anew to escape from the great arms that held her.

"But the river cannot drown *you*," Falconer said. "It can only stop your breath. It cannot stop your thinking. Drowning people remember in a moment all their past lives and are thus plunged back into the past and all its misery. While their bodies are drowning, their souls are coming more and more awake."

"That is dreadful," she murmured, with her great eyes fixed on his. She had ceased to struggle so he had slackened his hold on her and she was leaning back on the fence.

"But," she went on, "they would not be so cruel there as men are here."

"Surely not. But all men are not cruel. I am not cruel," he said, caressing with his huge hand the wild, pale face that glimmered in the night. She drew herself back, and Falconer instantly removed his hand. "Look in my face, child, and see whether you cannot trust me."

As he uttered the words, he took off his hat and stood bareheaded in the moon, which now broke out clear from the clouds. His hair blew about his face. She looked at him, but then he turned away that she might be undisturbed in her thoughts. What she judged of him I don't know, for the next moment he called out to me in a tone of repressed excitement. "Look, there—above your head, on the other bridge!"

I looked and saw a gray head peering over the same gap through which Falconer and I had looked a few minutes before. I knew of his personal quest by this time, and concluded at once that he thought it might be his father.

"I cannot leave the poor thing—I dare not," he said.

I understood him and darted off at full speed for the Surrey end of the bridge. What made me choose that end, I do not know, but I chanced to be right. Where the bridges met at the other side the tall, gray-haired man passed me with an uncertain step. I did not see his face. I followed him a few yards behind. He seemed to notice me and quickened his pace. I let him increase the distance but continued to follow. He turned up river. I followed. He began to double back. He crossed all the main roads leading to the bridges till he came to the last—at which he turned toward London Street, and continued to walk eastward. It was not difficult to keep up with him, for his stride, though long, was slow. He never looked round, and I never saw his face. But I could not help fancying that his back and his gait, and his whole carriage, were very much like Falconer's.

We were by now in a section of the city I knew nothing about, but it seemed to be one of the worst districts of London, lying to the east of Spital Square. It was late and there were not many people about.

As I passed a court I was accosted.

"Ain't you got a glass o' ale for a poor bloke, gov'nor?"

"I have no coppers," I said hastily. "I am in a hurry besides," I added, as I walked on.

"Come, come," he said, catching up with me in a moment, "that ain't a civil answer to give a chap in need of a drink. Why, I ain't got even a blessed halfpenny."

As he spoke he laid his hand rather heavily on my arm. From the opposite side, at the same moment, another man appeared. He advanced on me at right angles. I shook off the hand of the first and would have taken to my heels, for more reasons than one, but, almost before I was clear of him, the other came against me and shoved me forcefully into one of the low-browed entries which abounded.

I was so eager to follow my chase that I acted foolishly. I should have emptied my pockets at once; but I was unwilling to lose a watch which was an old family piece, and of value besides.

"Come, come! I don't carry a barrel of ale in my pocket," I said, thinking to keep them in good humor. I confess I acted very stupidly throughout the whole affair, but it was my first experience of the sort.

"Now I don't want to hurt you," said the first, coming nearer, "but if you give me any wise-tongue, I'll make cold meat of you and gouge your pockets at my leisure."

Two or three more came sliding up with their hands in their pockets, looking as villainous as ever.

"What have you got there, Slicer?" said one of them.

"We've cotched a pigheaded one here. He wants to fight. But we won't trouble him; we'll just help ourselves. Now shell out, man!"

As he spoke he made a snatch at my watch chain. I forgot myself and hit him. The same moment I received a blow on the head and felt the blood running down my face. I did not quite lose my senses, though, for I remember seeing yet another man—a tall fellow—coming out of the gloom of the court. How it came into my mind I do not know, and what I said I do not remember, but I must have mentioned Falconer's name somehow.

The man they called Slicer said, "Who's he? Don't know the—"

"What! You devil's errand boy!" returned an Irish voice I had not heard before. "You don't know Long Bob, you buffoon?"

"What the devil in a dicebox do you mean?" said Slicer, possessing himself of my watch. "Who is the blasted lout?—not that I care a flash of damnation."

"A man as'll knock you down if he thinks you want it, or give you a half-crown if he thinks you need it."

"What the muck's that to me? But he mustn't lie there all night. Come along you Scotch haddock."

I was aware of a kick in the side as he spoke.

"I tell you what it is to you, Slicer," said one whose voice I had not yet heard, "if this gentleman's a friend of Long Bob, you'd just better let him alone."

I opened my eye now and saw before me a tall, rather slender man, in a big, loose dresscoat, to whom Slicer had turned with the words: "*You* say! Ha, ha! Well *I* say—oh, there's my Scotch haddock coming to himself. Who'll touch him?"

"I'll take him home," said the tall man, advancing toward me. I made an attempt to rise. But I grew deadly ill, fell back, and remembered nothing more.

When I came to myself I was lying on a bed in a miserable place. A middle-aged woman was putting something to my mouth with a teaspoon. I knew it by the smell to be gin; I could not yet move. They began to talk about me, and I lay and listened.

"He's comin' to hisself," said the woman. "I wonder what brings the likes of him into the likes of this place."

"I suppose," said another, "he's come on some of Mr. Falconer's business."

"But who is this Mr. Falconer?—Is Long Bob and he both the same?" asked a third.

234

"Why, Bessy, ain't you no better than cursed Slicer, who ought to have been hung up to dry this many a year? But I forgot, you ain't been long in our quarter. Why, every child hereabouts knows Mr. Falconer. Ask Bobby there."

"Who's Mr. Falconer, Bobby?"

A child's voice made reply: "A man with a long beard that goes about and sometimes grows tired and sits on a doorstep. I seen him once. But he ain't Mr. Falconer—nor Long Bob neither," added Bobby in a mysterious tone. "I know who he is."

"What do you mean, Bobby? Who is he, then?"

The child answered very slowly and solemnly: "He's Jesus Christ." The woman burst into a rude laugh.

"Well," said Bobby in an offended tone, "Slicer's own Tom says so, and Polly too. We all say so. He always pats me on the head and gives me a penny."

"True enough," said the boy's mother. "I seen him once sittin' on a doorstep, lookin' straight afore him and worn-out like, an' a lot o' children standin' all about him an' starin' at him as mum as mice, for fear of disturbin' him. When I came near, he got up with a smile on his face, an' give each one o' 'em a penny all 'round, an' walked away. Some say he's a bit crazed."

I made no attempt to rise. The woman came to my bedside.

"How does the gentleman feel hisself now?" she asked kindly.

"Better, thank you," I said. "I am ashamed of lying here like this, but I feel very strange."

"And it's no wonder, with what that devil Slicer gave you. Nobody knows what he carries in his sleeve that he hits folk with. Only don't you go tryin' to get up now. Don't be in a hurry till your blood comes back."

I lay still again for a little. When I lifted my hand to my head, I found it was bandaged up. I tried again to rise.

"Job, the gentleman's feelin' better."

"I'll go and get a cab," said Job.

I raised myself and by the time the cab arrived I was able to hobble to it. When Job came, I saw the same tall, thin man in the long dresscoat. His head was bound up too.

"I'm sorry to see you have been hurt too—for my sake," I said. "Is it a bad blow?"

"Oh, it ain't much. I got in with a punch in the nose afore he got me with a whack. But as I say, I hope as how you are a friend of Mr. Falconer's, you're not hurt too bad. Anyhow, you'd best stay clear of this quarter. Gentlemen has no business here."

"On the contrary, I mean to come again soon, to thank you all for being so good to me."

"When you comes next, you'd better come with *him*, you know."

As I got into the cab, I said, "Come along with me, Job. I'm going straight to Mr. Falconer's. He will like to see you, especially after your kindness to me."

"Well, maybe I should look after you a little longer."

He climbed in after me and shouted to the cabman to drive to John Street. I can scarcely recall anything more till we reached Falconer's chambers. Job got out and rang the bell. Mrs. Ashton came down. Her master was not yet home.

"Tell Mr. Falconer," I said, "that I'm all right, only I couldn't make anything of it on the errand he sent me on."

"Tell him," growled Job, "that he's got his head broken and won't be out of bed for two days!"

We then drove to my quarters. As I got out and was opening the door, leaning on Job's arm, I said I was very glad they hadn't taken my keys.

"Slicer nor Savory Sam, neither's none the better on account o' you, guv'nor, and I hopes ye're not much the worse for them," said Job, as he put into my hands my wallet and my watch. "Take my advice, sir, an' keep yer sovereigns an' yer half-crowns someplace else, an' keep yer pence in yer breeches. You won't lose much nohow then. Good night, sir, an' I wish you better."

"But you must take something for your trouble," I said. "You'll take a sovereign at least?"

"We'll talk about that another day," said Job; and with a second heartier good night he left me. I managed to crawl up to my room and fall on my bed. I remained feverish all night and the next day, but toward evening began to recover.

I kept expecting Falconer to come and inquire about me, but he never came. Nor did he appear the next day or the next, and I began to be uneasy about him. The fourth day I sent for a cab, and drove to John Street. He was at home. The instant I saw him I understood all. I read it in his face.

He had found his father.

42 / Andrew at Last _____

Having at length persuaded the woman to go with him, Falconer made her take his arm and led her off the bridge. In Parliament Street he found a cab and drove the poor thing to Miss St. John's. Happily, she was at home and no more explanation than a few words was necessary. He jumped again into the cab and hastened back to the bridge where he once more set out on foot, hoping to recover my trail. However, after two hours of wandering he returned home, disappointed and growing weary.

Greeted with the news from Mrs. Ashton that I had been there in questionable condition, accompanied by another man, Falconer grew attentive at once. He questioned her carefully and the moment she remembered that the man's name was Job, he sprang from his seat and was out the door in a flash. He ran all the way to De Fleuri's and roused the groggy, but willing, man from a sound sleep. Within moments the two of them were sitting in a cab heading toward London Bridge. That I had apparently followed the man on the bridge all the way to the precincts where he knew Job lived confirmed many suspicions of his own, and as they rode he found himself more hopeful than at any time in recent memory.

When they reached the bridge, he paid the cab driver, went for a quick visit to Job's to learn what he could from that quarter—which was next to nothing, since his wife did not think the young Bobby's remarks sufficiently of note to recount—and then he and De Fleuri split up to cover the area as best they might at that late hour.

Three hours later, even more weary, disheartened, and alone, Falconer turned sadly toward home. He had not seen a trace of De Fleuri since they parted, and he assumed him by this time back in his own bed. There were few people out. Sunk in his own thoughts, he was startled when his good friend Hugh Sutherland came bounding up alongside him. Both figures halted. "Hello there, Falconer! I hoped it was you I was chasing. I would have been terribly embarrassed running up like this on a stranger. But how many other men in this city are your size?"

"Well, good evening, Hugh. I am certainly pleased to see you, but

236

what are you chasing about for at this time of night?''

"I am a bounty hunter and you are my quarry. De Fleuri sent me to bring you home." Hugh smiled and began striding briskly toward Falconer's home, Falconer following. Hugh continued, "One more thing, Falconer, I shall walk with you on one condition only."

"What's that?" returned Falconer, whose curiosity by this time was quite piqued.

"Simply this, dear friend, you may ask me no questions."

"Come, Hugh, what is this all about? Must I remain a stranger to affairs at my own house? Please enlighten me."

"I told you, Robert, no questions. You will understand all shortly and be fully satisfied, I assure you. I suppose I wouldn't break my promise to De Fleuri if I tell you a little of what has transpired this evening. Margaret and I were out for a late stroll and we passed by your house to see if perchance your light was on. We hadn't seen your face, Robert, in some time, you know. Your light was on, so we knocked at the door. De Fleuri opened to us and immediately when he recognized me, he told me a most interesting story and immediately sent me after you. I am here at his behest. But let us hurry, Falconer, my Margaret will be worried about us."

The two broke into a trot and shortly entered John Street. Even before reaching his own door, Falconer observed that a good many people were about. And there was Margaret, waving to them from the top step. Falconer let himself through without pausing to speak to anyone until he reached her.

"Margaret, I am so happy to see you," Falconer greeted her as he clasped her hand. He grasped Hugh's hand also and gazed kindly at the two of them.

"I'm so glad you two chose each other," Falconer continued as his eyes gleamed. "My heart is lighter just seeing the two of you again." The warmth in his eyes echoed his words. "But why should we stand out here? Come up with me to my quarters and let us get to the bottom of this mystery."

Falconer then opened the door and led the way up the stairs to his own chambers. When he got into his sitting room, there stood De Fleuri, who simply waved his hand toward the sofa. On it lay an elderly man with his eyes half open, and a look of emptiness on his pale, puffy face, which was damp and shining. His breathing was labored, but there was no further sign of suffering. He lay perfectly still. Falconer saw at once that he was under the influence of some narcotic, probably opium; the same moment the almost certain conviction darted into his mind that Andrew Falconer, his grandmother's son, lay there before him. The fact that the man was no doubt his own father he had no feeling about yet. He turned to De Fleuri.

"Thank you, friend," he said. "I shall find time to thank you."

"Are we right?" asked De Fleuri.

"I don't know. I think so," answered Falconer slowly, and without another word his friends withdrew.

Robert's mood was very strange. He felt nothing. No tears rose to the brim of their bottomless wells. He sat down in his chair. The man on the horsehair sofa lay breathing heavily. The gray hair about the pale, ill-shaven face glimmered like a cloud before him. What should he do or say when he awaked? How do you approach such a far-estranged soul? Could he ever have climbed on those knees and kissed those lips in the far-off days of childhood?

He fell on his knees and spoke to the God who had made this man. Then he rose, strengthened to meet the honorable, debased soul when it should look forth from those dull eyes. He felt his pulse. There was no danger from the drug. The coma would pass away. Meantime he would get him to bed.

When he began to undress him, a new reverence arose which banished all the disgust at the state he was in. Everything about the worn body and shabby garments of the man smote the heart of his son, and through his very poverty he was sacred in his eyes. And at the sight of a small lapel pin, the poverty-stricken attempt of a man to preserve the shadow of decency, Robert burst into tears and wept like a child.

He soon had him safe in bed. But while he thus ministered, a new question arose in his mind; what if this should not be the man after all? He would have to somehow determine if he was indeed his father. The man might be fearful and cunning, might have reasons for being so, and for concealing the truth. But this was the first thing he had to make sure of, because, if it was he, the only hold he could hope to have upon him lay in his knowing it for certain. But he could not think clearly; he had had precious little sleep for two nights. Therefore he took a cold bath to refresh his faculties, then went on thinking.

All at once he saw how he might begin. He went again into the room where the man lay and could tell that a waking of some sort was nigh. Then he went to a corner of his sitting room and from beneath the table drew out a long box, lifted Dooble Sanny's auld wife from it, tuned the somewhat neglected strings, and laid the instrument on the table.

Keeping constant watch over the sleeping man, he judged at length that his soul had come near enough to the surface to communicate with the outside world. He put his chair just outside the chamber door and began to play gently, softly, far away. For a while he extemporized, thinking of Rothieden, his grandmother, the bleach-green, the hills, the wasted old factory, and his mother's portrait and letters. As he dreamed on, his dream got louder and, he hoped, was waking a more vivid dream in the mind of the sleeper. For music wakes its own feeling, and feeling wakes thought. He played more and more forcefully, growing in hope.

Falconer heard him toss on the bed. Then he broke into a growl and cursed the music which, he said, the strings could never have learned anywhere but in a cat's belly. Robert was used to bad language, though it gave him a pang of disappointment to hear such an echo to his music. But not even now did he lose his presence of mind. He instantly moderated the tone of the instrument and gradually drew the sound away once more until it was low and distant. But he did not let it die. Through various changes it floated in the thin ether of the soul, till at length it drew nearer and louder once more, bearing on its wings the sounds of "Flowers of the Forest."

Listening through the melody, Robert was aware that the growlings and turnings had ceased. He stopped his playing and listened intently. For a few moments there was no sound. Then he heard a half-articulate murmuring, sounding as if he had almost fallen asleep again: "Play't again, Father. It's bonny, that! I, aye like the 'Flooers o' the Forest.' Play away. I had a frichtsome dream. I thought I was i' the ill place. I doobt I'm no well. But yer fiddle aye did me good. Play away, Father."

All the remainder of the night, till the dawn of the gray morning, Falconer watched the sleeping man, all but certain that he was indeed his father. Eternities of thought passed through his mind as he watched, hoping for a new birth. He was about to see what could be done by one man, strengthened by all the aids that love and devotion could give, for the redemption of his fellow. Deeper and deeper grew his compassion and his sympathy, realizing the tortures the man would have to go through to redeem his will from its lethargy, brought on by the opium, in order to behold the light of a new spiritual morning. All that he could do he was prepared to do, regardless of how he might beg, regardless of the necessary torture, regardless of anger and hate; his was the inexorable justice of love, the law that will not, must not, dares not yield— strong with awful tenderness. And he strengthened himself for the conflict by saying that if he would do this for his father, what would not God do for his child? Had he not proved already that God's devotion was complete and that he would leave nothing undone that could be done to lift such a sheep out of the pit into whose darkness it had fallen?

He called his housekeeper. She did not know whom her master supposed his guest to be and regarded him only as one of the many objects of his kindness. He told her to get some tea ready, as the patient would most likely wake with a headache. He instructed her to wait upon him as a matter of course, and explain nothing. He had resolved to pass for a doctor, as indeed he was; and he told her that if the patient should be at all troublesome, he would be with her at once. She must keep the room dark. He would have his own breakfast now, and, if the patient remained quiet, would sleep on the sofa.

The man woke murmuring, and evidently suffered from headache and nausea. Mrs. Ashton took him some tea. He refused it with an oath, and was too unwell to show any curiosity about the person who had offered it. Probably he was accustomed to so many changes of abode and to so many bewilderments of the brain that he did not care to inquire where he was or who waited upon him. Not only was the opium having its effect on him, he had caught a cold before De Fleuri had found him. He was now ill—feverish and oppressed. Through the whole of the following week they nursed and waited upon him without his asking a single question as to where he was or who they were. Falconer never left the house, but watched by the bedside or waited in the next room. Often the patient would get out of bed, driven by the longing for drink or opium, gnawing him through all the hallucinations of delirium; but he was weak and therefore manageable. If in any lucid moments he thought where he was, he no doubt supposed that he was in a hospital and probably had enough sense to understand that it was of no use to attempt to get his own way. He was much worn, and his limbs trembled regularly.

But there was an infinite work to be done even beyond curing him of his evil habits. To keep him from strong drink and opium would be but the capturing of the merest outwork of the enemy's castle. He must be made such that he would not touch them, even if the longing should return and the means for its gratification should lie within reach of his hand. God only would be able to do that for him. Falconer would do all that he knew how to do, and God would not fail in his part. For this God had raised him up; to this he had called him. For this work he had educated him, made him a physician, given him money, time, the love of his fellows, and, beyond all, a rich energy of hope and faith in his heart.

43 / Andrew Rebels

As Andrew Falconer grew better the longings of his mind roused, until his thoughts dwelt upon nothing but his diseased cravings. His whole imaginations came to be concentrated on the delights in store for him as soon as he was well enough to be his "own master," as he phrased it, once more. He began to see that, if he was in a hospital, it must be a private one, and at last he made up his mind to demand his liberty. He sat by his bedroom fire one afternoon. The shades of evening were thickening the air. He had just had one of his frequent meals and was gazing, as he often did, into the glowing coals. Robert had come in, and after a little talk was sitting silent at the opposite corner of the chimneypiece.

"Doctor," said Andrew, seizing the opportunity, "ye've been very kind t' me, and I don't know how t' thank ye, but it is time I was a'goin'. I'm quite well now. Would ye kindly order the nurse to bring me my clothes tomorrow morning, and I will go." This he said with the quavering voice of one who speaks because he has made up his mind to speak. But as he did, he wriggled and shifted uneasily on his chair.

"No, no," said Robert, "you are not fit to go. Make yourself comfortable, my dear sir. There is no reason why you should go."

"There—there's somethin' I don't understand about it. I want t' go."

"It would ruin my character as a professional man to let a patient in your condition leave the house. The weather is unfavorable. I cannot—I must not consent."

"Where am I? I don't understand it. I want t' understand it."

"Your friends wish you to remain where you are for the present."

"I have no friends."

"You have one, at least, who puts his house here at your service."

"There's somethin' about it all I don't like. Do ye suppose I am incapable of taking care o' myself?"

"I do indeed," answered his son with firmness.

"Then ye are quite mistaken," said Andrew, angrily. "I am quite well enough t' go, and I have a right t' judge for myself. It is no doubt very kind o' ye, but I am in a free country, I do believe."

241

"No doubt. All honest men are free in this country. But—"

He saw that his father winced, and said no more. Andrew resumed, after a pause in which he had been rousing his feeble, drink-craving anger.

"I tell ye I will not be treated like a child! I demand my clothes and my liberty."

"Do you know where you were found that night you were brought here?"

"No. What has that t' do with it? I was ill. Ye knew that as well as I."

"You are ill now, because you were lying then on the wet ground under a railway arch—utterly incapable from the effects of opium, or drink, or both. You would have been taken to the police station, and would probably have been dead long before now if you had not been brought here."

The man was silent for some time. Then he broke out: "I tell ye I *will* go! I do not choose t' live on charity. I will *not*. I demand my clothes."

"I tell you it is of no use. When you are well enough to go out, you shall go out, but not now."

"Where am I? Who are ye?"

He looked at Robert with a keen, furtive glance, in which were mingled bewilderment and suspicion.

"I am your best friend at present."

He started up—fiercely and yet feebly, for a thought of terror had crossed him.

"Ye do not mean I am in a madhouse!"

Robert made no reply. He left him to suppose what he pleased. Andrew took it for granted that he was in a private asylum, sank back in his chair, and from that moment was quiet as a lamb. But it was easy to see that he was constantly contriving how to escape. This mental occupation, however, was excellent for his recovery, and Robert dropped no hint of his suspicion. He never left the house without De Fleuri there, who was a man of determination, nerve, and now that he ate properly, of considerable strength.

Robert did all he could to provide his father with healthy amusement—played backgammon and cribbage with him, brought him novels to read, and often played on his violin, to which he listened with great delight. At times of depression, which of course were frequent, the "Flowers of the Forest" made the old man weep. Falconer put yet more soul into the sounds than he had ever put into them before. He tried to make the old man talk of his childhood, asking him about the place of his birth, the kind of country, how he had been brought up, his family, and many questions of the sort. His answers were vague, and often contradictory. Indeed, the moment the subject was approached he looked suspicious and cunning. He said his name was John Mackinnon; and Robert, although his belief was strengthened by a hundred little circumstances, had as yet received no absolute proof that he was Andrew Falconer. At length Robert brought a tailor and had him dressed like a gentleman—a change which pleased him much. The next step was to take him out every day for a drive, which marked a rapid improvement in his health. He ate better, grew more lively, and began to tell tales of his adventures, the truth of which Robert was not always certain, but never showed any doubt. Finally he took him out walking and he behaved himself with perfect propriety.

One day as they were going along a quiet street, Robert met an acquaintance and stopped to speak with him. After a few moments' chat he turned and found that his father, whom he had supposed to be standing beside him, had vanished. A glance at the other side of the street showed the probable refuge—a public house. Filled with dismay, knowing that months might be lost in this one moment, Robert darted in.

There he was, with a glass of whiskey in his hand, trembling now more from eagerness than weakness. Robert struck it from his hold. But he had already swallowed one glass, and he turned in a rage. He was a tall and naturally powerful man—almost as strongly built as his son, with long arms like his. Robert would not so much as lift his arm, even to defend himself from his father. He received his father's blow on the cheek. For one moment it made him dizzy, for it was well delivered. But when the barkeeper jumped across the counter and approached his father with fists doubled, that was another matter. Robert measured his length on the floor, then seized his father—who was making for the street—and, notwithstanding his struggles and fierce efforts to strike again, held him secure and bore him out of the house.

A crowd gathers in a moment in London, speeding to a fray as vultures to carrion. On the heels of the population of the neighborhood came two policemen. But Falconer was well known to the police.

"Call a cab," he said to one of them. "I'm all right."

The man turned to find one at once. Falconer turned to the other.

"Tell that man in the apron," he said, for the barman had run out after him, "that I'll make him all due reparation. But he oughtn't to be in such a hurry to meddle. He gave me no time so I had to strike him hard."

"Do you want to put this man in our charge, sir?" the policeman asked.

"No. It's a little private affair of my own."

"Hadn't you better let him go, sir, and we'll find him for you when you want him?"

"No. I think he'll agree to be put in my charge. And if you should want him, you will find him at my house."

Then pinioning his prisoner still more tightly in his arms, he leaned forward and whispered in his ear: "Will you go home quietly? There is no other way, Andrew Falconer."

He ceased struggling. Through all the flush of the exertion, his face grew pale. His arms dropped by his side. Robert let him go, and he stood there without offering to move. The cab came up; Andrew stepped in of his own accord, and Robert followed.

His father did not speak a word, or ask a question all the way home. Evidently he thought it safer to be silent. But the drink he had taken, though not enough to intoxicate him, was more than enough to bring back the old longing with redoubled force. He paced about the room the rest of the day, like a wild beast in a cage, and in the middle of the night got up and dressed, and would have crept through the room in which Robert lay, in the hope of getting out. But Robert slept too carefully for that. The captive did not make the slightest noise, but his very presence was enough to wake his son. He started at a bound from his couch, and his father retreated in dismay to his chamber.

At length the time arrived when Robert determined to make a further attempt, although with fear and trembling. His father had again grown gentler and more thoughtful and would sit once more for an hour at a time gazing into the fire. From the expression of his countenance upon such occasions, Robert hoped that his visions were not of the evil days, but of those of its innocence.

One evening when he was in one of these moods, Robert began to play in the next room, hoping that the music would sink into his heart and do something to prepare the way for what was to follow. Just as he had played over the ''Flowers of the Forest'' for the third time, the housekeeper entered the room, and, receiving permission from her master, went through into Andrew's chamber and presented him with a packet which she said—and said truly, for she was not in on the secret— had been left for him. He received it with evident surprise, mingled with some consternation. He looked at the address, looked at the seal, laid it on the table, and gazed again with troubled looks into the fire. He had had no correspondence for many years. Falconer had peeped in when the woman entered, but the moment she retired he could watch him no longer. He went on playing a slow, lingering tune such as the wind plays on an autumn evening through a pine wood. He played so gently that he would be able to hear if his father should speak.

For what seemed hours, though it was but half an hour, he went on playing. At length he heard a stifled sob. He rose, and looked again into the room. The gray head was bowed between the hands and the gaunt frame was shaken with sobs. On the table lay the portraits of himself and his wife, and the faded brown letter, so many years folded in silence and darkness, lay beside him. He had known the seal, with the bush of rushes and the Gaelic motto. He had gently torn the paper from around it, and had read the letter from the grave—no, from the land beyond, the land of light where human love is glorified.

My beloved Andrew,

I can hardly write, for I am at the point of death. I love you still—love you as dearly as before you left me. Will you ever see this? I will try to send it to you. I will leave it behind me that it may come into your hands when and how it pleases God. You may be an old man before you read these words. Oh! if I could take your head on my bosom where it used to lie and just think all the love I have into your heart. O my love, my love! will you have had enough of the world and its ways by the time this reaches you? Or will you be dead, like me, and will only your son, my darling little Robert, someday read these words?

O Andrew, my heart is bleeding for both you and for me. Shall I never see you again? That is the terrible thought—the only thought that almost makes me shrink from dying. But now I must tell you of the dream I had last night, which makes me write this letter. I was standing in a great crowd of people and I saw empty graves about us on every side. We were waiting for the great white throne to appear in the clouds. And I cried, "Andrew, Andrew!" and ran about everywhere looking for you. At last I came to a great gulf. When I looked down into it I could see nothing but a deep blue, like the blue of the sky, under my feet. It was not so wide, but it was, oh! so terribly deep. All at once, as I stood trembling on the edge, I saw you on the other side, looking toward me and stretching out your arms as if you wanted me. You were old and much changed, but I knew you at once and I gave a cry that I thought all the universe must have heard. I was in terrible agony to get to you. But there was no way, for if I fell into the gulf I should go down forever, it was so deep. Something made me look away, and I saw a man coming quietly toward me. He was dressed in a gown down to his feet and his feet were bare and had a hole in each of them. I fell down and kissed his feet, and lifted up my hands, and looked into his face—oh, such a face! And I tried to pray. But all I could say was, "O Lord ... Andrew, Andrew!" Then he smiled and said, "Daughter, be of good cheer. Do you want to go to him?" And I said, "Yes, Lord." Then he said, "And so do I. Come." And he took my hand and led me over the edge, and I was not afraid, and I did not sink, but walked upon the air toward you. But when I got to you it was too much to bear; and when I thought I had you in my arms at last, I awoke crying as I never cried before, not even when I found that you had left me to die without you.

O Andrew, what if the dream should come true! But if it should *not* come true! I dare not think of that, Andrew. I *couldn't* be happy in heaven without you. Dear husband, come to me again. Come back, like the prodigal in the New Testament. God will forgive you everything. I know it was the drink that made you do as you did. You didn't know what you were doing. And then you were ashamed and thought I would be angry and could not bear to come back to me. But I would have been proud to have my Andrew back again.

But I would not be nice for you to look at now. You used to think me pretty—you said beautiful—long ago. But I am so thin now, and my face so white, that I almost frighten myself when I look in the mirror. And before you get this I shall be all gone to dust. I am afraid I love you too much to be fit to go to heaven. Perhaps God will send me to the other place, all for love of you, Andrew. And I do believe I should like that better. But I don't think he will, if he is anything like the man I saw in my dream.

But I am growing so faint that I can hardly write. I never felt like this before. But that dream has given me strength to die, because I hope you will come too. O my dear Andrew, do, do repent and turn to God and he will forgive you! Believe in Jesus, and he will save you and bring me to you across the deep place. But I must make haste. I can hardly see. And I must not leave this letter open for anybody but you to read after I am dead. Good-bye, Andrew. I love you. I am, my dearest husband,

Your affectionate wife,
H. Falconer

Then followed the date. It was within a week of her death. The letter was feebly written, every stroke seeming more feeble than the last. When Robert read it afterward, in the midst of the emotions it roused—the strange bond between himself and a beautiful ghost, far away somewhere in God's universe, who had carried him in her lost body, and nursed him at her breasts—in the midst of it all, the words themselves seemed as alive as if written yesterday. It seemed so long ago when that faded, discolored paper, with the gilt edges and the pale brown ink, and folded in the large sheet, and sealed with the curious wax, must have been written; and here were its words so fresh, so new!—not withered like the rose leaves that scented the paper from the workbox where he had found it, but as fresh as if just shaken from the rose trees of the heart's garden. It was no wonder that Andrew Falconer should be sitting with his head in his hands when Robert looked in on him.

When Robert saw how he sat, he withdrew and took his violin again and played all the tunes of the old country he could think of, recalling Dooble Sanny's workshop, that he might recall the music he had learned there.

For an hour he did not venture to go near him. When he finally entered the room, he found him sitting in the same place, no longer weeping, but gazing into the fire with a sad countenance, the expression of which showed Falconer at once that the soul had come out of its cave and drawn nearer to the surface of life. He looked up at Robert as he entered and then dropped his eyes again. He regarded him as a presence, but doubtful whether of angel or devil. Bewildered he must have been to find himself, toward the close of a long life of debauchery, wickedness, and the growing pains of hell, caught in a net of old times, old feelings, old truths.

Now Robert had carefully avoided every indication that might disclose himself to be a Scotchman even, nor was there the least sign of suspicion in Andrew's manner. The only solution of the mystery that could have presented itself to the old man was that his friends were at the root of it—probably his son, of whom he knew absolutely nothing. His mother could not be alive still. Of his wife's relatives there had never been one who would have taken any trouble about him after her death, hardly even before it. John Lammie was the only person, except Dr. Anderson, whose friendship he could suppose capable of this development. The latter was the more likely person. But he would be too much for him yet; he was not going to be treated like a child, he said to himself, as often as the devil got the upper hand.

Andrew had never been a man of resolution. He had been willful and headstrong; and those qualities, in children especially, are often mistaken for resolution, and generally go under the name of strength of will. There never was a greater mistake. He never resisted his own impulses or the enticements of evil companions. Kept within certain bounds at home, after he had begun to go wrong he had rushed into all sorts of excesses when abroad on business, till at length the vessel of his fortune went to pieces and he was a waif on the waters of the world. But his feelings had never been as vulgar as his actions. There was a feeble good in him. For many years he had fits of shame and of grief without repentance; for repentance is the active, the divine part—the turning away from sin. Instead, he took more and more steadily both to strong drink and opium, and at the time when De Fleuri found him he was only the dull ghost of Andrew Falconer walking in a dream of its lost carcass.

45 / Father and Son

Once more Robert retired, but not to take his violin. He could play no more. Hope and love were swelling within him. He could not rest. Was it a sign from heaven that the hour had arrived? He paced up and down the room. He kneeled and prayed for guidance and help. Something within urged him to try the rusted lock of his father's heart. He slowly walked into his room. There the old man still sat, with his back to the door, and his gaze fixed on the fire which had sunk low in the grate.

Robert went round in front of him, kneeled on the rug before him, and said the one word: "Father!"

Andrew started violently, raised his trembling hand to his head, and stared wildly at Robert. But he did not speak. Robert repeated the one great word. Then Andrew spoke, and said in a trembling, hardly audible voice: "Are you my son?—my boy, Robert, sir?"

"I am. I have longed for you by day and dreamed about you by night. Years and years of my life—I hardly know how many—have been spent in searching for you. And now I have found you!"

The great, tall man, in the prime of life and strength, laid his big head down on the old man's knee, as if he had been a little child. His father said nothing but laid his hand on his head. For some moments the two remained thus, motionless and silent. Andrew was the first to speak. And his words were the voice of the Spirit that striveth with man.

"What am I to do, Robert?"

No other words, not even those of passionate sorrow, could have been half so precious in the ears of Robert. When a man asks what he is to do, there is hope for him.

Robert answered instantly: "You must come home to your mother."

"My mother!" Andrew exclaimed. "You don't mean to say she's alive?"

"I heard from her yesterday—in her own hand too," said Robert.

"I dare not," murmured Andrew.

"You must, Father," returned Robert. "It is a long way, but I will make the journey easy for you. She knows I have found you. She is waiting and longing for you. She has hardly thought of anything but you ever since she lost you. She is only waiting to see you, and then she will go home, she says. I wrote to her and said, 'Grannie, I have found your Andrew.' And she wrote back to me and said, 'God be praised! I shall die in peace.' ''

A silence followed.

"Will she forgive me?" said Andrew.

"She loves you more than her own soul," answered Robert. "She loves you like I do. She loves you like God loves you."

"God can't love me," said Andrew feebly. "He would never have left me if he had loved me."

"He has never left you from the very first. You would not take his way, Father, and he just let you try your own. But long before that, he had begun to get me ready to go after you. He put such love to you in my heart, and gave me such teaching and such training, that I have found you at last. And now that I have found you, I will hold you. You cannot escape—you will not want to escape anymore, will you, Father?"

Andrew made no reply to this appeal. It may have sounded like imprisonment for life, I suppose. But thought was moving in him. After a long pause the old man spoke again, muttering as if he were only speaking his thoughts unconsciously.

"What's the use? There's no forgiveness for me. My mother is going to heaven. I must go to hell. No. It's no good. Better leave it as it is. I dare not see her. It would kill me to see her."

"It will kill her not to see you, and that will be one sin more on your conscience, Father."

Andrew got up and walked about the room.

"And there's *my* mother," Robert said.

Andrew did not reply, but Robert saw when he turned toward the light that the sweat was standing in beads on his forehead.

"Father," he said, going up to him.

The old man stopped in his walk, turned, and faced his son.

"Father," repeated Robert, "you've got to repent, and God won't let you off, and you needn't think he will. You'll have to repent someday."

"In hell, Robert," said Andrew, looking him full in the eyes, as he had never looked at him before. It seemed as if even so much acknowledgment of the truth had already made him bolder and more honest.

"Yes. Either on earth or in hell. Would it not be better on earth?"

"But it will be no use in hell," he murmured.

In those few words lay the germ of the preference for hell of poor souls, enfeebled by wickedness. They will not have to *do* anything there, only to moan and cry and suffer forever, they think. It is not so much the sorrow or remorse of repentance they dread; it is the action it involves; it is the having to be different, behave differently, that they shrink from. And they have been taught to believe that this will not be required of them there; that their wills will not be called into action. But tell them that the fire of God, both around them and within them, *will* compel them; that the torturing spirit of God in them *will* keep their consciences awake—and hell will lose its unnatural fascination for them. Tell them that there is *no* refuge from the compelling love of God, except that love itself, that if they make their bed in hell, they shall not escape him; and then, perhaps, they will have some true perception of the fire that is not quenched.

"Father, it *will* be of use in hell," said Robert. "God will give you no rest even there. You will have to repent someday, I do believe—if not now under the sunshine of heaven, then in the torture of the awful world where there is no light but that of the conscience. Would it not be better and easier to repent now, with your wife waiting for you in heaven, and your mother waiting for you on earth?

"And I tell you, Father, that you *shall* go to my grandmother."

46 / In the Country

But various reasons combined to induce Falconer to postpone their journey to the North. Not merely did his father still require unremitting watchfulness, which it would be all the more difficult to keep up in his native place, but his health was more broken than he had at first supposed. And he was anxious that the change his mother must see in him should be as little as possible attributable to other causes than those that years bring with them. He wrote to his grandmother and explained the matter. She told him to do as he thought best, for she was so happy that she did not care if she should *never* see Andrew in this world; it was enough to die in the hope of meeting him in the other. But she had no reason to fear that death was at hand. Although she was much more frail, she felt as well as ever.

By this time Falconer had introduced me to his father. I found him in some things very like his son; in others, very different. His manners were more polished; his pleasure in pleasing was much greater; his humanity had blossomed too easily, and then gone to seed. But, alas, to seed that could bear no fruit. He had a sly, sidelong glance at times, whether of doubt or cunning I could not always determine. His hands were long-fingered and tremulous. He gave your hand a sharp squeeze, and the same instant abandoned it with indifference. But under all outward appearances it seemed to me that there was a change going on.

One evening when I called to see them, Falconer said, "We are going out of town for a few weeks on a little holiday; will you go with us?"

"I'm afraid I can't."

"Why? You have no teaching at present, and your writing you can do as well in the country as in the town."

"That is true, but I still don't see how I can. I am too poor, for one thing."

"Between you and me that is nonsense."

"Well, I withdraw that," I said. "But there is so much to be done."

"That is all very true, but you need a change. It is our best work that he wants, not the dregs of our exhaustion. So many seem ambitious to kill themselves in the service of the Master—and as quickly as possible. Come with us to God's infirmary in the country and rest for a while. Bring back health from the country to those that cannot go to it.''

"When are you going?"

"Tomorrow."

"I shall be ready, if you really mean it."

"Be at the Paddington Station at noon. To tell you the whole truth, I want you to help me with my father.''

This last was said at the door, as he showed me out.

That night he went to see Mary St. John; De Fleuri sat with Andrew at a game of cribbage. It had been some time since they had had the time for a visit that was not to do with the business of their mutual concerns. When telling me of it several days hence, it was clear from his voice that the memory contained much emotion. What they talked about Falconer never divulged, but it was a conversation he never forgot. His only allusion to it later was the comment that Paul's words toward the end of 1 Corinthians 7 were difficult to bear where love was pure. Leaving her house that evening, she took his large, strong hand and held it between both of hers. Their eyes met, both feeling the duty-bound passion of the words neither could speak but each could hear: "The time will come."

He stooped down and kissed her lightly, then turned and walked out into the night. Mary watched him for a moment, then closed the door slowly and wiped the gathering tears from her eyes. On the street Falconer's sleeve performed a similar function.

By mid-afternoon on the next day we were nearing Bristol. It was a lovely day in October. Andrew had been enjoying himself; but his pleasure was traveling in a first-class carriage like a gentleman rather than any delight in the beauty of heaven and earth. The country was in the rich somber dress of decay.

"Is it not remarkable," said my friend to me, "that the older I grow, I find autumn affecting me the more like spring?"

At Bristol we went on board a small steamer and at night were landed at a little village on the coast of North Devon. The hotel to which we went was on the steep bank of a tumultuous little river. The elder Falconer retired almost as soon as we had had supper. My friend and I sat by the open window, for although the autumn was so far advanced, the air here was very mild. For some time we only listened to the sound of the water.

We did not talk much that night, but went soon to bed. As soon as we had breakfasted in the morning, we set out to climb some nearby craggy hills. It was soon evident that Andrew could not ascend the steep road. We returned and got a carriage. When we reached the top it was like a resurrection, like a dawning of hope out of despair. The cool, friendly wind blew on our faces and breathed strength into our frames. Before us lay the ocean, and the vessels with their white sails moved about over it like the thoughts of men feebly searching the unknown. Even Andrew Falconer spread out his arms to the wind, and breathed deeply, filling his great chest full.

"I feel like a boy again," he said.

His son strode to his side and laid his arm over his shoulders.

"So do I, Father," he said, "but it is because I have got you."

The old man turned and looked at him with a tenderness I had never seen on his face before. As soon as I saw that, I no longer doubted that he could be saved.

We found rooms in a farmhouse on the topmost part of the hill. After an early dinner we went out for a walk. But we did not go far before we sat down upon the grass. Robert laid himself at full length and gazed upward.

"When I look like this into the blue sky," he said after a moment's silence, "it seems so deep and so peaceful that I could lie for centuries and wait for the dawning of the face of God in his awful lovingkindness."

I had never heard Falconer talk of his own feelings like this, but glancing at the face of his father I saw at once that it was for his sake that he had said it. The old man had thrown himself back too, and was gazing into the sky, puzzling himself to comprehend what his son could mean. I fear he concluded that Robert was lacking in common sense and that too much religion had made him a dreamer and a mystic. A mystic Falconer certainly was, but not as his father thought. Still, I thought I could see a kind of awe pass like a spiritual shadow across his face. No one can detect the first beginnings of any life.

The next morning Falconer, who knew the country, took us out for a drive. We passed through lanes and gates out upon an open moor, where he stopped the carriage and led us a few yards on one side. Suddenly, hundreds of feet below us, down what seemed an almost cliff-like descent, we saw the wood-embosomed, stream-filled valley we had left the day before. By the streams and in the woods nestled pretty houses, and away at the mouth of the valley and the stream lay the village. All around, on our level, stretched farm and moorland.

When Andrew Falconer stood so unexpectedly on the verge of the precipitous edge, he trembled and started back with a fright. His son made him sit down a little way off, where he yet could see into the valley, green with grass, and robed in the autumnal foliage of thick woods. The sun was hot, the air clear and mild, and the sea broke its blue floor into innumerable sparkles of radiance. We sat for a while in silence, then talked for a while, then got back into the carriage. By Falconer's orders it was turned and driven in the opposite direction, still very close to the lofty edge of the heights that rose above the shore.

We came at length to a lane bounded with stone walls, every stone of which had its moss and every chink its fern. The lane grew more and more grassy; the walls vanished; and the track faded away into a narrow winding valley, formed by the many meeting curves of opposing hills. They were green to the top with sheepgrass, and spotted here and there with patches of fern, great stones, and tall, withered foxgloves. The air was sweet and healthful, and Andrew evidently enjoyed it because it reminded him again of his boyhood. The only sound we heard was the tinkle of a few tender sheep bells, and now and then the tremulous bleating of a sheep. With a gentle winding, the valley led us into a more open area, where the old man paused with a look of great pleasure.

We stopped, descended, and seated ourselves on the short, springy grass of a little mound. After a little talk, I said, "I have never yet heard how you managed with that poor girl that wanted to drown herself—on Westminster Bridge."

"She is in Mary's house at present," Falconer answered. "Mary has given her those two children we picked up at the door of the public house to take care of. Poor little darlings! they are bringing back the life in her heart already. That is Miss St. John's way. As often as she gets hold of a poor, hopeless woman, she gives her a motherless child. It is wonderful what the childless woman and the motherless child do for each other."

The eyes of the old man were fixed on his son as he spoke. He did seem to be thinking. But it was now time to return to our rooms, and we were nearly silent all the way.

The next morning was so wet that we could not go out and had to amuse ourselves as best we could indoors. The afternoon was still rainy and misty. In the evening I sought to lead the conversation toward the gospel story, and then Falconer talked as I never heard him talk before. No little circumstance in the narratives of Jesus appeared to have escaped him. He had looked under the surface everywhere, and found truth under all the upper soil of the story. The deeper he dug, the richer seemed the ore. The whole thing came alive in his words and thoughts.

"When anything looks strange, you must look deeper," he would say.

In the morning the rain had ceased, but the clouds remained, high in the heavens. The sky partially cleared in the afternoon, but clouds hid the sun as it sank toward the west. We walked out. A cold autumnal wind blew, not only from the twilight of the dying day, but from the twilight of the dying season. A sorrowful, hopeless wind it seemed, full of the odors of dead leaves—those memories of green woods and of damp earth—the bare graves of the flowers.

We were pacing in silence and I fell to brooding over the cloudy mass through which the sinking sun seemed determined to break. It had been a quiet, peaceful day. The two Falconers were at some distance ahead of me, walking arm in arm, climbing a small hill. I could see that Falconer was earnestly speaking in his father's ear. The old man's head was bent toward the earth. I kept away.

They made a turn still farther from home. I still followed at a distance. The evening began to grow dark. The autumn wind met us again, colder, stronger, yet more laden with the odors of death and the frosts of the coming winter.

The next week I went back to work, leaving the father and son alone together. Before I left I could see plainly that the bonds were being drawn closer between them. A whole month passed before they returned to London.

47 / Three Generations

The winter set in with unusual severity. But it seemed to bring only health to Falconer and his father. When I saw Andrew next there was a marked change on him. Light had banished the haziness from his eye and his step was a good deal firmer. I can hardly speak of more than the physical improvement, for I did not see so much of him as before. Still I did think I could perceive more of judgment in his face, as if he sometimes weighed things in his mind. But it was plain Robert continued very careful about him. He busied him with the various sights of London, for Andrew, although he knew all its miseries well, had never yet been inside Westminster Abbey.

It was almost the end of the year when a letter arrived from John Lammie, informing Robert that his grandmother had caught a violent cold, and that, although the special symptoms had disappeared, it was evident her strength was sinking fast, and that she would not recover.

He read the letter to his father.

"We must go and see her, Robert, my boy," said Andrew.

It was the first time he had shown the smallest desire to visit her. Falconer rose with glad heart, and proceeded at once to make arrangements for their journey.

It was a cold, powdery afternoon in January, with the snow thick on the ground, except where the little winds had blown the crown of the street bare before Mrs. Falconer's house. A carriage with four horses swept wearily round the corner and pulled up at her door. Betty opened it, and revealed an old, withered face, very sorrowful, and yet expectant. Falconer's feelings I dare not, Andrew's I cannot, attempt to describe. Betty led the way without a word into the little parlor. Robert went next, with long, quiet strides, and Andrew followed with gray, bowed head.

Grannie was not in her chair. The doors which during the day concealed the bed in which she slept, were open, and there lay the aged woman with her eyes closed. The room was as it had always been, only there seemed a filmy shadow in it that had not been there before.

"She's dying, sir," whispered Betty. "Ay she is. Och hone!"

Robert took his father's hand and led him toward the bed. They drew softly near and bent over the withered, but not even yet terribly wrinkled face. The smooth, white, soft hands lay on the sheet, which was folded back over her chest. She was asleep, or rather, she slumbered.

The soul of the child began to grow in the withered heart of the old man as he regarded his older mother, and as it grew it forced the tears to his eyes and the word to his lips.

"Mother!" he said, and her eyelids rose at once. He stooped to kiss her, with the tears rolling down his face. The light of heaven broke and flashed from her aged countenance. She lifted her weak hands, took his head, and held it to her bosom.

"Eh! the bonny gray head!" she said, and burst into a passion of weeping. She had kept some tears for the last. Now she would spend all that her griefs had left her. But there came a pause in her sobs, though not in her weeping, and then she spoke. "I knew it all the time, O Lord. I knew it all the time. He's come home. My Andrew, my Andrew! I'm as happy's a bairn. O Lord! O Lord!"

And she burst again into sobs, and entered Paradise in radiant weeping.

Her hands sank away from his head, and when her son gazed in her face he saw that she was dead. She had never looked at Robert.

The two men turned toward each other. Robert put out his arms. His father laid his head on the great chest of his son, and went on weeping. Robert held him to his heart.

When shall a man dare to say that God has done all he can?

48 / The Final Chapter

The men laid their mother's body, with those of the generations that had gone before her, beneath the long grass in their country churchyard near Rothieden. They returned to the dreary house, and after a simple meal such as both had used to partake of in their boyhood, they sat by the fire, Andrew in his mother's chair, Robert in the same chair in which he had learned his lessons.

"It was there, Father, that Grannie used to sit, every day, sometimes looking in the fire for hours, thinking about you," Robert said at length.

Andrew stirred uneasily in his chair.

"How do you know that?" he asked.

"If there was one thing I could be sure of, it was when Grannie was thinking about you, Father. She lived only to think about God and you. God and you came very close together in her mind."

Then Robert began at the beginning of his memory and told his father all that he could remember. When he came to speak about his solitary musings in the garret, he said, "Come and look at the place. I want to see it again myself."

He rose. His father yielded and followed him. Robert got a candle in the kitchen and the two big men climbed the little, narrow stair and stood in the little skylight of the house, with their heads almost touching the ceiling.

"I sat on the floor there," said Robert, "and thought and thought about what I would do to get you, Father. And I would cry sometimes, because other laddies had fathers and I had none. And there's where I used to kneel down and pray to God. And he's heard my prayers, and Grannie's prayers, and here you are with me at last."

They returned to the little parlor and resumed their seats by the fire. Robert began again and went on with his story, not omitting the parts about Shargar and Mary St. John. He came to tell how he had encountered him in the deserted factory. "Look here, Father, here'e the mark of the cut," he said, parting thick hair on the top of his head.

His father hid his face in his hands.

"It wasn't much of a blow that you gave me," he went on, "but I fell against the grate. And I never told anybody, even Mary, how I had

260

gotten it. And I didn't mean to say anything about it, but I wanted to tell you a strange dream it made me dream the other night.''

As he told the dream, his father suddenly grew attentive, and before he had finished looked almost scared, but he said nothing. When he came to relate his grandmother's behavior after having discovered that the papers relating to the factory were gone, he hid his face in his hands once more. He told him how Grannie had mourned and wept over him. He told him about Dr. Anderson and how good he had been to him, and at last of Dr. Anderson's request that he would do something for him in India.

"Will you go with me, Father?" he asked.

"I'll never leave you again, Robert, my boy," he answered. "I've been a bad man and a bad father, and now I give myself up to you to make the best of me you can. I dare not leave you, Robert.''

"Pray to God to take care of you, Father. He'll do all things for you, if you'll only let him.''

"I will, Robert.''

"I was dreadfully miserable myself for a while," Robert resumed, "for I couldn't see or hear God at all. But God heard me. It was just like when a little bairnie wakes up and cries out, thinking it's alone, and through the dark come the words of its mother, saying, 'I'm near you, darling, don't cry.' That's how it was for me. And now you must pray to God, Father. You will pray to him, to hold tight onto you— won't you?''

"I will, I will, Robert. But I've been an awful sinner. I believe I was the death of your mother, laddie.''

Some fount of memory was opened; some tide of old tenderness gushed up in his heart; at some window of the past the face of his dead wife looked in; the old man broke into a great cry and sobbed and wept bitterly. Robert said no more, but wept with him.

From that time on the father clung to his son like a child. The heart of Falconer turned to his Father in heaven with thanksgiving. The ideal of his dream had dawned and his life was newborn.

It did not take Robert long to arrange his grandmother's few affairs. He had already made up his mind about her house and furniture. He rang the bell one morning for Betty.

"Have you any money put away, Betty?''

"Ay. I have fifteen pounds in the bank.''

"And what are you thinking of doing?''

"I'll get a little room and take in washin'.''

"Well, I'll tell you what I would like you to do. You know Mistress Elshender?''

"Ay. An' a very decent body she is."

"Well, if you like you can keep this house and all that's in it, just as it is, till the day of your death. And you'll keep it in order and the gable room ready for me at any time I may happen to come in upon you and want a night's quarters. But I would like you, if you have no objections, to take Mistress Elshender to stay with you. She's turning frail now and I'm under great obligation to her Sandy, you know."

"Ay, I know that. He learnt ye t' fiddle, Robert—I beg yer pardon, Mister Robert."

"No offense, Betty, I assure you. You have been good to me and I thank you heartily."

Betty could not stand this. Her apron went up to her eyes.

"Eh, sir," she sobbed, "ye was always a good lad."

"Except when I spoke of Muckledrum, Betty."

She laughed and sobbed together.

"Well, you'll take Sandy's wife in, won't you?"

"I'll do that. An' I'll try t' do my best wi' her."

"She can help you, you know, with your washing and cleaning."

"She's a hard-working woman."

"And when you're in any want of money, just write to me. And if anything should happen to me, write to my friend in London. Here's his address."

"Eh, sir, but ye are kind. God bless ye for everything!"

She could bear no more, and left the room crying.

Everything settled at Rothieden, he returned to Bodyfauld, where his father had been staying. The most welcome greeting he had ever received in his life lay in the shine of his father's eyes when he entered the room where he sat with Miss Lammie. The next day they left for London.

49 / A New Chapter

They came to see me the very evening of their arrival. As to Andrew's progress there could no longer be any doubt. The very grasp of his hand was changed. But Robert would not yet leave him alone.

For some time I had to give Falconer what aid I could in being with his father while he arranged matters for their voyage to India. Sometimes he took him with him when he went among his people, as he called the poor he visited. Sometimes, when he wanted to go alone, I took him to Miss St. John's who would play and sing as I had never heard anyone play or sing before. How she did lay herself out to please the old man! And pleased he was. I think her kindness did more than anything else to make him feel like a gentleman again.

One evening when I went to see Falconer, I found him alone. He had taken his father to Miss St. John's and left him alone in her care.

"I am very glad you have come," he said. "I wanted to see you. I have got things nearly ready now. Next month, I think we shall sail, and I have some business with you which had better be arranged at once. No one knows what is going to happen. Anyway, my will is in the hands of the lawyer, Dobson. I have left everything to you."

I was speechless.

"Have you any objection?" he said, a little anxiously.

"Am I able to fulfill the conditions?" I faltered.

"I have burdened you with no conditions," he returned. "I don't believe in conditions. I know your heart and mind now. I trust you perfectly."

"I am unworthy of it."

"That is for me to judge."

"Will you have no trustees to oversee your affairs?"

"Not one."

"What do you want me to do with your property?"

"You know well enough. Keep it going the right way."

"I will always try to think of what you would do."

"No. Think what is right. And if there is no right or wrong plain in the matter, then think of what is best. You may see good reason to change some of my plans."

"But there is no need to talk so seriously about it," I said. "You will manage it yourself for many more years yet. Make me your steward, if you like, during your absence; I will not object to that."

"You do not object to the other I hope?"

"No."

"Then so let it be."

"But when the time does come—you have compelled me to make the supposition—"

"Of course. Go on," said Falconer.

"What am I to do with the money when my own time comes to follow you, when death should loom over the horizon for me? I am not that many years younger than you, you know."

"Ah! that is one point on which I do want to give you a word of instruction. I want to specify how the property and money are to be bequeathed after you."

"How?"

"By word of mouth," he answered, laughing. "You must look out for a right man, as I have done. Get him to know your ways and ideas, and if you find him *worthy*—that is a grand, wide word; our Lord gave it to his disciples—leave it all to him in the same way I have left it to you, trusting to the Spirit of truth that is in him, the Spirit of God. You can copy my will if you like—as far as it will apply, for you may have, one way or another, lost the half of the money by that time. But, by word of mouth you must make the same condition with him as I have made with you—that is, with regard to his leaving it, and the conditions on which he leaves it, adding the words, 'that it may descend thus in perpetuum.' And he must do the same." He broke into a quiet laugh. "That means, of course," he added, "for as long as there is any."

"Are you quite sure you are doing right, Falconer?" I said.

"Quite. It is better to endow one man, who will work as the Father works, than a hundred charities. But it is time I went to fetch my father. Will you go with me?"

This was all that passed between us on the subject, except that, on our way, he told me to move to his rooms and occupy them until he returned.

"My papers," he added, "I commit to your discretion."

On our way back from Queen Square, he joked and talked merrily. Andrew joined in. Robert showed himself delighted with every attempt at gaiety or wit that Andrew made. When we reached the house, something that had occurred on the way made him turn to a passage in Dickens, and he read to the two of us, to our great enjoyment.

I went down with the two to Southampton to see them on board the steamer. I stayed with them there until she sailed. It was a lovely morning in the end of April when at last I bade them farewell on the quarterdeck. My heart was full. I took his hand. He put his arms around me, and laid his cheek to mine. It took all the strength I had to bear the parting.

The great iron steamer sailed out of the harbor, and I have not yet seen my friend again.